MW01070288

RIKER'S APOCALYPSE: THE PLAN

(Book 2)

SHAWN CHESSER

.

Copyright © 2019
Shawn Chesser * Morbid Press LLC
All rights reserved.
ISBN: 978-1-7325695-3-9

CONTENTS

ACKNOWLEDGEMENTS

For Steve P. You are missed, friend. Maureen, Raven, and Caden ... I couldn't have done this without your support. Thanks to our military, LE and first responders for all you do. To the people in the U.K. and elsewhere around the world who have been in touch, thanks for reading! Lieutenant Colonel Michael Offe, thanks for your service as well as your friendship. Larry Eckels, thank you for helping me with some of the military technical stuff. Any missing facts or errors are solely my fault. Beta readers, you rock, and you know who you are. Special shout out to the master of continuity: Giles Batchelor. You helped make this novel a better read. Thanks, George Romero, for introducing me to zombies. To my friends and fellows at S@N and Monday Steps On Steele, thanks as well. Lastly, thanks to Bill W. and Dr. Bob ... you helped make this possible. I am going to sign up for another 24.

Special thanks to John O'Brien, Mark Tufo, Joe McKinney, Craig DiLouie, Armand Rosamilia, Heath Stallcup, Saul Tanpepper, Eric A. Shelman, and David P. Forsyth. I truly appreciate your continued friendship and always invaluable advice. Thanks to Jason Swarr and Straight 8 Custom Photography for another awesome cover. I'm grateful to Marine veteran Buck Doyle of Follow Through Consulting for portraying Lee Riker on the cover. Once again, extra special thanks to Monique Happy for her work editing "The Plan." Mo, as always, you kicked butt and took names in getting this MS polished up! Working with you over the years has been nothing but a pleasure. I truly appreciate having a confidante I can trust. If I have accidentally left anyone out ... I am truly sorry.

***

Edited by Monique Happy Editorial Services
www.moniquehappy.com

Prologue

Sunday, October 16th, 2016 - Miami Beach, Florida

Lee Riker, or *Leland*, the name given him by his late parents, shut off the Shelby Baja's 6.2-liter V8 and clicked out of his seatbelt. Elbowing his door open, he was assaulted by eighty-five-degree air heavy with humidity and the sweet smell of freshly watered flowers growing around palm trees fronting the Best Buy store.

Without a second glance at his new, shiny metallic-blue Ford, Riker set the pickup's alarm and pocketed the keyless fob.

As Riker strode across the half-full parking lot, he took in his surroundings. A steady flow of vehicles filed by on a nearby six-lane. The one-level building closest to the busy boulevard was occupied by a pizza place and liquor store. Only a handful of people roamed the sidewalks bordering the parking lot.

The Best Buy dead ahead of him was basically a rectangle of mirrored glass framed by faux stacked-stone the color of coffee ruined with creamer. Perched high on the corner of the building was the easily identifiable blue and yellow sign.

The set of mirrored double doors reflected Riker's likeness back at him as he stepped to the low curb fronting the store. As the automatic doors parted, sunlight caught the titanium and carbon fiber prosthesis fitted to the distal nub of scar tissue roughly six inches below Riker's left knee. Designed and fitted for him by a prosthetics specialty store outside the Beltway in D.C., the high-tech item shod in a black Salomon hiker was *not* the only thing he had earned driving high-level brass around in armored SUVs during his short deployment to Iraq. He also lived daily with a low-grade headache—the byproduct of the closed head injury brought on by the same IED that stole his leg and killed everyone aboard his Land Cruiser that awful day, many years ago.

Stepping inside the Best Buy, Riker removed his wraparound Oakleys. Slipping his sunglasses into the breast pocket of his black and gray Tommy Bahama shirt, he performed a quick visual recon of the store's interior.

The air inside the high-ceilinged building was cool and still. Riker smelled the faint odor of electronic components discharging heat. Which didn't surprise him. Much like every Best Buy store he'd ever set foot in, this place featured the ubiquitous rear wall plastered with enough flat-panel televisions to give the Jumbotrons ringing the Times Square pedestrian plaza a run for their money.

Close in was a maze-like area dedicated to smart phones and every must-have accessory made for them.

Swinging his gaze right, Riker saw an assemblage of waist-high desks on which dozens of laptops and tower computers sat. The former were hinged open, while the latter were tethered to flat-panel monitors much larger than anything he had ever seen connected to a computer. Trying hard to compete with their big brothers on the back wall, all of the computers' displays in the section were lit up and beckoned with brightly hued landscapes or 4K video clips meant to show off their high-resolution capabilities.

Riker shook his head. *So much visual bait in one place.*

The store was busy with shoppers. Young men and women in cobalt blue shirts stalked them about the aisles. Other employees stood before glass counters full of shiny new electronic gadgets that, until recently, orbited well outside of Riker's price range.

Only explanation he could think of for the brisk pace of business the place was enjoying at eleven o'clock on a Sunday was that maybe people in this city weren't the church-going type. Or, more likely, there was some kind of a can't-miss sale happening.

Whatever the case, the majority of shoppers in the store were all of a sudden making their way to the phalanx of

2

televisions on the back wall, where a dozen or so were already congregated.

Ignoring the low murmur of voices and the urge to go see what was so important on the televisions that it was dragging people from all around like bugs to the zapper, Riker took two long strides toward the smart phone department, entered the warren of display cases, and cleared his throat to get a nearby clerk's attention.

At six-foot-four, Riker towered over the average-sized twenty-something. In fact, he stood head and shoulders above most everyone.

The kid was seated on a stool behind the counter. Seeing Riker, he straightened up and tilted his head back to make eye contact. As he did so, one hand shot up to push the wire frame glasses back to their perch on the bridge of his nose.

"How can I help you?" asked the kid whose nametag read CHAD.

"I'm looking to finally ditch my old phone and get something new," Riker said.

Flashing a nervous half-smile, Chad said, "You looking to surf the web mainly? You text a lot? You want to watch Netflix on it?"

Riker tilted his head and shot the clerk a questioning look.

"Oh ... drilled it down too deep for you." Chad swallowed hard. "Did you have an iPhone or Android before? Or are you a... *Samsung* guy?"

He said *Samsung* as if the word tasted bad crossing his tongue.

Riker simply stared at the kid.

Rising from the stool, Chad asked, "What are you moving up from?"

"Flip phone to something new," Riker answered, no emotion in his tone.

"Well, I'm an Apple guy," declared Chad. "An early adopter, at that." He smiled at Riker as if he was expecting the obviously tech-challenged customer to bow at the altar of Jobs.

"Sure," Riker said, sounding bored. "I'm easy like a Sunday morning."

Riker's quip drew a funny look, which quickly dissipated as Chad leaned over and worked a key in the lock securing the sliding doors in back of the case.

While Chad was moving things around in the case, Riker studied the crowd gathered along Television Row. He watched the press of bodies until his attention was dragged back to the transaction at hand by Chad placing an overly packaged white box bearing the Apple logo on the glass before him.

"This is the new iPhone 7. It dropped in September. It's your lucky day, because we just got more in. It'll do everything but your dishes," promised Chad. "And I'm sure someone's already developing an app for that."

Geek humor flying way over his head, Riker asked, "How much?"

"Six to nine hundred. All depends on how much memory you want."

"This one?" said Riker, stabbing his finger at the box. "How much is *this* one?"

"It's the one-twenty-eight gigabyte model. You're looking at eight hundred and sixty-nine dollars."

"For a phone?"

"It's like a computer in your palm. Unlocks with your fingerprint." He paused and watched as Riker studied the box. "It's the *Ferrari* of smartphones," he pressed, the hard sell in full effect. "Makes your old phone look like a Model T."

Sounding skeptical, Riker asked, "How's the setup? Pretty easy?"

"You hook it to your computer and follow the directions. Or you can do it over Wi-Fi. That takes a lot longer, though."

"Can I do it without hooking up to a computer?"

Chad shook his head. "You're going to want to sync your contacts and your music."

"Can't I just type them in?"

Chad made a face. "I'm only twenty-two and have a couple of hundred contacts. You're like what...?"

"Thirty-eight," answered Riker.

"So you've got waaaaay more contacts than I do. How many do you figure you have in your old device?"

Riker shrugged. "Five or six."

"Hundred?! Damn, man. That'll take you half a day to input manually."

Riker shook his head. "I have less than ten contacts. Is it doable without connecting to my computer?"

Voice taking on a conspiratorial tone, Chad said, "I guess you could. Where there's a will, there's always a way. You could jailbreak it."

Jailbreaking a phone piqued Riker's interest. He wanted to ask Chad to elaborate, but the throbbing behind his eyes was getting worse with each passing minute. Instead, he produced his debit card.

"I'll take it," Riker said. "And give me whatever cords I'll be needing to charge it."

While Chad made the sale, he offered the requisite extended warranty, which Riker declined. As Chad bagged the white brick, Riker said, "What's everyone watching back there?"

"That's that hijacked British Airways jet. It's been sitting on the tarmac at Heathrow going on four days now. Someone said the British equivalent of our FBI is preparing to storm the plane."

Riker accepted the plastic bag with the phone in the bottom weighing it down. Staring toward the television section, he said, "Four days?"

"Logan to Heathrow, flight seven-sixty-two. Something like three hundred people aboard. The second it came to a stop there the flight crew broke out a cockpit window and they all slithered out. It's been all over the news." He glanced up at Riker. "Where have *you* been?"

"On the beach," Riker answered.

Pocketing the receipt, he set off walking toward the wall of televisions.

Riker stopped a dozen feet away, a shelf of DVD players between him and the nearest person. He had no problem seeing over even the tallest fella in the crowd. Seuss's Cat in the Hat on stilts could have been in front of Riker and he still would have had an unimpeded view. There were *that* many televisions. And most were tuned to BBC. The ones that weren't broadcasting BBC were showing either CNN or MSNBC. And neither one of the American channels were covering the drama at Heathrow. Instead, they were reporting on the ongoing multi-state military training operation everyone was calling Romeo Victor.

Regarding the sixty-five-inch Samsung at his one o'clock, Riker saw that things were indeed getting underway on the Heathrow tarmac. The jumbo jet looked to have been moved some distance from the airport terminals. It was surrounded by a mix of military and emergency vehicles. A tall fence stood between the vehicles, totally encircling the airplane so that only the red and white tail and top third of the white fuselage could be seen. The great distance between where the camera was set up and the tarmac rendered the image a bit grainy. Strangely, the blinds on many of the jet's windows, thirty or forty, from the looks of it, were in the up position.

Riker saw snatches of movement inside the plane's gloomy interior.

Leaning over the top shelf of DVDs, Riker got a middle-aged woman's attention. "Excuse me, ma'am," he whispered. "How many hijackers are there?"

Shooting Riker a sour look, the woman shrugged and went back to watching.

On the screen a dozen men in black uniforms rushed from behind a boxy armored vehicle to the perimeter fence. They moved with precision, barely a foot separating one from the other.

A couple of seconds later the fence parted. Then, with no hesitation, the team, some toting body-length ballistic shields, all brandishing a stubby carbine or pistol, poured through the man-sized seam. Moving as one, the soldiers formed up beside the airstairs pre-positioned below the door just aft of the cockpit.

As two men split from the team and charged up the stairs in single file, Riker heard a voice say, "ISIS is claiming responsibility."

Turning toward the voice, Riker found himself staring Chad full on in the face. Looking at the floor, Riker saw that the young man who'd sold him the phone was standing on a metal folding chair.

"Why would terrorists want to *leave* the United States?" Riker asked. "Their sole aim is to *enter* our country and spread fear by taking as many innocent lives as possible and make martyrs of themselves in the process. Pulse Nightclub ring a bell?"

"Maybe they're just homesick."

"Chad," said Riker. "If you believe what you just said, I fear for the future of this country."

Chad said nothing. He stepped from the chair, folded it real slow, and skulked off.

Riker turned back to the bank of televisions just as one of the soldiers who'd mounted the stairs was placing what could only be breaching charges around the perimeter of the door. Finished, the pair rejoined the others at the base of the airstairs.

A tick later there was a puff of smoke and the door bowed inward. Even before the smoke cleared, bodies were surging through the breach.

Exposed skin a grayish white, the handful of disheveled first-class passengers transited the short landing and poured down the stairs. Some fell at once, sliding face first down the steep run of stairs. Others, pushed from behind, cartwheeled out of control, missing everything but the unforgiving tarmac.

One way or another, all of the bodies in that initial surge ended up in a tangled heap around the base of the airstairs.

The second the first person off the plane stood up from the tarmac and sprinted headlong for the nearest soldier, knocking the shield aside and going for his exposed neck, Riker was certain it was a Bolt—one of the fast-moving zombies he'd first seen kill the elderly couple in Indiana.

When the remaining *passengers*, especially those that shouldn't have survived the long fall to hard concrete, picked themselves up and rushed the soldiers, there was no doubt in Riker's mind that the sickness had jumped shores.

With the cold finger of dread tickling his spine, Riker slung his sack over a shoulder and hustled toward the exit.

Chapter 1

Riker was two strides from the sidewalk fronting the Best Buy and donning his Oakleys when he saw a shadow fall across the oil-stained asphalt to his left. Next came the sensation of being watched. Just a feathery tingle at the base of his spine as senses honed during prehistoric times picked up, subconsciously, something out of balance in his environment.

For ten long seconds, as he walked past parked cars and light standards, angling toward his truck sitting on the lot's periphery, he ignored the strong impulse to turn and search out the source of his unease. Only when he was fifteen feet from his truck did he see in the tinted windows what he was up against.

Two men.

One African American. One Caucasian.

First sight of the pair had Riker hearing Stevie and Paul harmonizing in his head. So he had to tag the duo *Ebony* and *Ivory*. Which made him want to burst out laughing.

Instead, he remained calm and learned what he could from their reflections.

Both pursuers were wiry and wore board shorts and patterned shirts over matching wife-beater tanks. Dead giveaway that at least one of them had on flip flops was the sudden squelch against pavement he heard when Ivory picked up his pace to flank him to the right.

The moment Riker punched the button on the fob, simultaneously unlocking his door and disarming the alarm, he learned that Ivory had drawn a boxy black pistol as he slinked over to the rear of the truck.

In his left side vision, Riker saw a red and black Air Jordan enter the picture and come to rest atop the Shelby's front tire. He saw Ebony's coal-black ankle and muscled calf, but nothing else. The man's sun-darkened skin was in dire need of some moisturizer. "Ashy" is the word Tara would have used to describe the man's skin.

Ebony said, "Whatcha got in the bag, brother?"

A cold chill ran up Riker's ribcage.

No longer able to see the pair reflected back at him due to the shallow angle, he turned slowly away from the truck, toward Ivory. A smooth clockwise maneuver that had him bringing the bag in his right hand to eye level and the other dropping the fob into his shorts' pocket.

"I got a new cell phone in the bag," Riker said, the gooseflesh suddenly displaced by the unstoppable creep of anger that had his trapezius muscles knotting and twin stabs of pain manifesting behind his eyes.

Keeping the gun mostly shielded from view behind one scrawny leg, Ivory took two steps toward Riker. A slight tremor rattling his drug-addled frame, he said, "Nobody but geezers and foreigners call 'em *cell* phones these days. It's *smart* phone, motherfucker. But I won't hold your own ignorance against you if you just hand the bag to *me* and toss your keys and wallet to my pawdna there."

Stalling, Riker said, "Take the phone. Hell, take my wallet, too." He squared up to the shiny blue Ford. "But don't take my baby. She's not even out of her break-in period yet."

"We *need* that whip," Ebony said, his deep voice rising an octave. "Ain't you been watching the news?"

Riker shook his head side to side. A slow wag that let him see that Ebony was unarmed.

"I don't watch the news. Don't read the newspaper, either," he added. "Please fill me in." As he spoke, he was setting his feet a shoulder width apart and gauging distances in his side vision.

"The New York sickness is on the move," said Ivory. "And it ain't bad junk or flakka or some new designer drug causing muthafuckas to eat people."

"Crazy cannibal attacks been happening up in Jacksonville, Orlando, and Daytona," said Ebony. "My cousin saw it with his own eyes. Barely escaped before the *po po* rolled up hard and started cappin' the things."

"Let me guess. The men in black came next," quipped Riker. "And they cleaned things up and took all the evidence and any witnesses with them."

Ebony was slack-jawed and staring dumbly at Riker.

Going light on the balls of his feet, Riker said, "Am I right?"

Ivory said, "Were you there or something?"

Riker thought, *Not exactly the sharpest tools in the shed.*

But out loud he said, "I was *joking*, fellas."

"Well we ain't," Ivory shouted, waving the gun at Riker. "Do like I told ya. Give us all your shit."

When you feel the burn, Riker's last therapist would say, *turn the other cheek. Then turn the anger into humor.*

Riker was in no mood to tell another joke. Not with a man five feet to his right aiming a pistol in the general direction of a lot of irreplaceable body parts. He glared at Ivory. Said, "Come and take it."

A flicker of fear ghosted across Ivory's face.

The other man took his foot off the tire and moved to within an arm's length of Riker.

One hand palm up, the other slowly kneading the pistol's grip, Ivory repeated his demand.

"All right," Riker said. "You fellas can have it all." He feigned like he was reaching into his pocket for the fob. While the gunman was distracted watching him go for his keys, Riker swung the bag in the man's direction and released his grip on the twine handle.

Leaving Riker's hand, the bottom-heavy bag traced a perfect parabola through the airspace between him and Ivory.

Bag in mid-flight, Riker turned toward Ebony, opened his right hand wide, and brought it up lightning quick.

Before the bag struck the ground, Riker had caught the punch coming his way, crushed phalanges and metacarpals in his mitt-sized hand, then spun Ebony around and flung him hard at his partner in crime.

Forgetting all about the pistol, Ivory backpedaled, turned and ran, leaving his buddy to continue on a collision course with hot pavement.

A solid *thunk* sounded as the back of Ebony's clean-shaven head struck the ground with force sufficient to shock his body rigid and loosen his bowels.

Leaning over the prostrate, twitching body, Riker reached out with one arm and snatched his bag off the ground.

As Riker stood straight, in his right peripheral he saw Ivory stumble over a curb, lose one flip flop, and then brace his fall with the hand holding the gun. From the corner of his other eye, he detected movement, maybe twenty feet distant. Glancing over, he made eye contact with an elderly couple just arriving beside their compact Cadillac.

"Call the cops," he mouthed. "This a-hole just tried to rob me."

Face a mask of confusion, the woman reached into her purse.

Knowing Florida to be a stand-your-ground state, and fully aware the lady might just as well drag a .38 Special from her purse before going for her phone, Riker flung open his door to use as a makeshift shield between him and the couple.

For good measure, before Riker climbed into the Ford, he gave a swift kick to Ebony's exposed temple.

Riker didn't wait to see if the elderly couple honored his request.

And no bullets crackled the air nearby—a plus in his book.

Ivory was already lost from sight when Riker wheeled into traffic and started retracing the route that would take him back to his temporary home.

Chapter 2

Riker nosed the Shelby onto West 29th, crossed the bridge to Sunset Island, then pulsed his window down. Rig coming to a full stop in the shadow of towering palms, he removed his glasses, leaned partway out the window, and handed his pass card to the uniformed man in the tiny guard shack.

The guard scrutinized the laminated card for a beat, started the iron gate rolling open, then handed the card back and waved the Shelby through.

Until three days ago, the nicest place Riker had stayed the night was the three-thousand-square-foot home belonging to the parents of a high school friend. And that had been to attend a keg party—the spending the night part was not planned.

Partying came early and fast to the rapidly growing sophomore. Due to his size and abundance of facial hair, Riker quickly became the person enlisted to make liquor store runs, procure kegs from the brewery, or pop in to the local grocer to pick up forty-ounce bottles of Olde English or St. Ides for his neighborhood upperclassmen.

The mansion he'd been calling home for the last four days only made him nervous. It was on the western tip of the island and faced the east side of Biscayne Bay. Tara had said earlier that she thought it had to be worth something in the twenty-million-dollar range. From soup to nuts, everything inside was high-dollar. Seemingly every interior wall held pieces of art that his sister, Tara—the accredited interior decorator—insisted were real and each worth six-figures or more. Just setting foot on the highly polished Cordoba marble entry made him want to shuck off his shoes, which was no easy task due to the prosthesis; nor effective, considering that the fine white sand used to landscape the property grounds found its way inside no matter the measures taken to keep it at bay.

Keying in the code on a lighted pad beside the mansion's entry started yet another gate rolling into a narrow pocket in the twelve-foot wall fronting the property. Painted a muted shade of yellow, the perimeter wall was mostly obscured by tropical flora pressing in on it from inside and out. Though he hadn't taken the time to scrutinize the top of the wall, he guessed there was some kind of deterrent there. Maybe metal louvers with sharpened ridges or crushed glass embedded into the cement.

Wheeling through the gate, Riker was greeted with the sight of the majestic royal palms planted at twenty-foot intervals on either side of the long brick drive. As the mansion materialized from the clutter of drooping palm fronds, he admired the Moroccan/India-inspired architecture.

Owned by a recently traded Miami Dolphin linebacker, the two-story digs rambled off left and right, with the separate guest home's prominent observation tower stabbing into the clear blue sky.

The exterior featured arched windows with copper hurricane shutters and was painted a yellow several shades darker than the perimeter wall. At sunset, the villa's west-facing walls glowed like polished gold.

A star-shaped fountain, home to a marble cherub, bubbled away in the center of the expansive circular motor court.

"Villa Jasmine," Riker said, "I'm going to miss you."

Truth was, save for a couple instances in the Sandbox, he had never witnessed sunsets so stunning. The nighttime views of a brightly lit downtown skyline were also sights to behold for the lifelong Midwesterner.

He parked the out-of-place pickup before one of the doors to the massive six-car garage. Then grabbed the bag with the iPhone inside and closed the door behind him, setting the Shelby's alarm with the fob as he strode toward the covered front entry.

The timber and iron door to the villa opened with yet another code punched into a keypad whose rubber buttons glowed a soft shade of orange.

The foyer, with its marble floors and soaring ceiling, was bigger square-footage-wise than Tara's old apartment back in Middletown, Indiana. A pair of opposing staircases angled left and right, hugging the honey-colored stucco walls as they curled gently to an open landing twenty feet overhead.

Emerging from the shadows under the stairs to Riker's left, Steve-O said, "Boo," and broke out in laughter. Planting his hands on his knees, he added, "Got you real good, Lee. You jumped a country mile."

"Maybe a country inch," conceded Riker. "And that was only my real foot leaving the floor. What've you been up to, Lobster Man?"

Steve-O rose up and fixed Riker with liquid blue eyes fronted by prescription lenses. He was wearing a straw hat in place of his usual white Stetson. Instead of the ubiquitous Western shirt and Levi's starched and ironed to near bulletproof stiffness, the forty-five-year-old man wore swim trunks in a Hawaiian-style floral pattern and a white tank soiled with what to Riker looked like extra-chunky salsa. And sure enough, the reason for the new nickname—save for a patch of white in the shape of wraparound sunglasses he'd been wearing religiously when out and about in the Florida sun—he was sunburned from head to toe.

"Tara can call me Rocket Raccoon all she likes," replied Steve-O. "But you, Mr. Riker, may *not* call me Lobster Man. Lobsters are orange. I am not orange."

"Sometimes lobsters are purple," Riker noted.

Steve-O said nothing. He seemed to be chewing on the validity of the statement.

Breaking the uncomfortable silence, Riker said, "Are you using sunscreen today?"

"None of your business," Steve-O shot. "I'm a grown ass man, remember?"

"Suit yourself," Riker said, suppressing a smile. "What brings you to the back forty of Villa Jasmine?"

"Just looking to make some lunch when I heard your monster truck outside," Steve-O replied. "Why, are you writing a book?"

Riker could no longer contain the smile. As the dam broke, he snorted. "No book in the works, Steve-O. I was just curious."

As the much shorter Steve-O turned toward the wide hallway leading to the front of the house which overlooked the dock where a forty-five-foot Fountain offshore racer was cradled in a boat lift, Riker spotted a large bandage on his friend's right shoulder. Gauze filaments peeked out from under a heavy tape job. An inch or so of the angry red skin around the edges of the bandage glistened with some kind of yellow salve.

Touching Steve-O's arm—an action that made the man wince and pull away—Riker said, "What happened to you? That is *not* covering a bite … is it?"

Shaking his head, Steve-O vehemently denied he'd been bitten.

"Lay it on me," Riker insisted. "What happened? Leave nothing out."

"Last night, while me and Tara were out *shopping*"—he made air quotes as he said shopping—"we both got tattoos. At first the man didn't want to ink me because I have Down Syndrome." He smiled wide. "Tara straightened him out real quick."

"A *real* tattoo?" blurted Riker. Shaking his head, he added, "Explains why you all were gone so long."

"I'm a big boy," Steve-O said as he began to pick at one edge of the bandage.

Riker removed his Oakleys and stuffed them in a pocket. As he ranged around to get a better viewing angle, he asked, "What did you get?"

"Patience," implored Steve-O as he peeled away the bandage, revealing the dark, saucer-sized piece of work glistening with salve.

Chapter 3

Riker couldn't believe his eyes as he squinted and leaned closer. Expertly tattooed on Steve-O's arm was a grouping of faces inset into what appeared to be a craggy mountain full of shadows. The result of the fine line work and shading truly made the work of art *pop*. The thicker lines were raised and red. As if the skin knew it would never again be pasty white, the whole right side of the man's upper arm seemed to be weeping.

"Why Mount Rushmore?"

Steve-O shook his head. "Look closer."

Leaning in so that his face was maybe six inches from the tat, Riker said, "Oh, my," and then chuckled to himself.

Smiling now, Steve-O said, "Can you name them?"

Working left to right, his finger hovering over each face for a beat, Riker said, "Hank Williams, Johnny Cash ... and I think this is a woman—"

"Dolly Parton," interrupted Steve-O, his voice betraying an elevated affection for the buxom blonde.

Finger poised over the final likeness, face screwed up, incredulous, Riker said, "Is this a black guy?"

Steve-O nodded. "It's Darius Rucker. Looks just like him, right?"

Riker reared back. "Whoa ... illegal right turn there, buddy. What the heck does the lead singer of *Hootie and the Blowfish* have to do with the legends of country music?"

Shaking his head, Steve-O muttered, "Rookies," and started off down the hallway, smoothing the bandage back in place as he went.

Riker said nothing. He shrugged once, slung the bag with the phone over one shoulder, and followed the shorter man through the mansion.

They walked the length of the house, stopping in the massive kitchen long enough for Steve-O to make himself a peanut butter and jelly sandwich.

The bank of floor-to-ceiling storm windows facing the bay were open, the panels pushed all the way to the walls left and right of the great room they fronted. A gentle breeze carrying with it the briny aroma of salt water ruffled the sheer linen curtains.

They walked around the pool, through the exquisitely manicured backyard, past more palms than Riker could count, and stepped up onto a wide deck supported by hidden pilings. The shore-hugging deck stretched seventy-five feet in both directions, the wide wooden planks bleached white by the sun and worn smooth by Mother Nature.

On the bay side of the dock was a rail of brushed metal posts strung through with heavy gauge cables.

Tara was in a skimpy yellow two-piece bikini, lounging on a teak recliner. A bucket by her side bristled with the clear, long necks of bottles full of golden liquid. The plush red and white striped pad on the lounge chair shifted under her as she sat up and grabbed a Corona by the neck. Seeing the pair arrive, she gestured toward them with the bottle. "Steve-O? Tilt one back with me?"

"Told you yesterday that I never touch the stuff," said Steve-O before popping the last bite of sandwich into his mouth.

"Pass," said Riker as he sat and stretched his long frame out on the recliner next to Tara's.

"No duh," Tara said. "Last thing I need is to lose track of you for another three months while you chase your demons."

Grimacing, Riker said, "Chasing? I was usually running from them."

"Demons?" said Steve-O. He was squinting against the sun now and making a show of not paying Tara any attention.

"Figure of speech, Steve-O." Riker turned toward the man, took the drug store sunglasses off the low table between chairs, and handed them over. "Grown ass man or not, you better wear these. You're starting to get a bad case of crow's feet."

Steve-O harrumphed and acquiesced, trading out the thick-framed prescription items for the knock-off Ray Bans. "Better?" he asked, smiling.

"Much better," Riker said. "Now take a load off. Looks like you need to work on that *tan* of yours."

"Leave him alone, Lee," Tara said, shooting him a harsh look. She passed an aerosol can of SPF 50 sunscreen over to Steve-O. "He's from Indiana," she added. "That's pretty damn far from the Sunbelt."

Riker batted a hand at the overspray as Steve-O shot the stuff on his arms and chest.

"Get your face," Tara ordered.

Steve-O removed his glasses and did as he was told.

"Sure, sure ... you listen to her," said Riker.

"It's the approach," she said.

"And she's pretty," Steve-O said, fake Ray Bans now riding over a sly smile.

Ignoring the quip, Riker said, "What's *your* new ink?"

"On my back," said Tara. "I got a pair of angel's wings."

"How big?"

She smiled. "Just messing with you."

Incredulous, he said, "Did you know Hootie sings country?"

She looked at him like one would a newly arrived space alien. Said, "What rock have you been living underneath, Lee?"

Riker said nothing. She was right. He wasn't big on caring what the rich and famous were up to at any given moment.

She took a long pull off the Corona, then slipped the half-full bottle into the ice bucket. On the tail end of a loud burp, she said, "I couldn't let Steve-O get inked all by himself."

He looked at her over his sunglasses.

"I had the artist continue the roses across my shoulders and make them meet up near my spine. Wanna see?"

He waved her off. Started to tell her what he'd seen on the televisions in the Best Buy.

"I saw it all," she replied. "I'm amazed they let it play out as long as they did."

"Tells me it's not contained here. No way. I heard some guys talking about some strange stuff happening up north. Apparently the *joint operation*"—now he made air quotes as he said the words—"is expanding south and west."

Craning, she said, "You think the thumb drives I mailed to the newspapers and television stations will get any play once they arrive?"

"Doubtful," Riker conceded. "And they should have arrived by now."

Changing the subject, she said, "You know, there's more boat traffic out there today than the last few days combined."

"And it's Sunday," Riker said. "The Best Buy was hopping, too." For a split-second he considered telling them about coming up against the most inept carjackers in Florida, but was distracted by something out on the water. He sat up straight in the lounge chair, swung his right leg over, and scooted to the edge.

Seeing the sudden change in her brother's demeanor, Tara said, "What is it, Lee?"

Pointing, arm angled to about his ten o'clock, he said, "What do you make of *that*?"

Tara swung her gaze to where he was pointing. Scrutinized the patch of water a half-mile or so out, where a dozen or more sailboats rested at anchor. As she stared, the *that* her brother was alluding to—a white and black motor yacht that dwarfed the other vessels—scythed through the small flotilla, barely missing a large sloop-like three-master.

Waving madly at the people topside on the wildly bobbing sailboats, a man and woman leaped from the deck of the speeding motor yacht.

"*That* is one big ass boat."

"And it's hauling *ass* straight for us," noted Steve-O. "Better finish your beer, Pretty Lady."

20

Chapter 4

Riker cupped his hands around his Oakleys and stared hard at the yacht bearing down on the island. At first blush, he guessed the vessel to be about seventy feet from stern to bow. It was charging hard, twin ribbons of white froth curling away from its prow.

The longer Riker observed its approach, the stronger the feeling grew that it wasn't heading straight for them. Thankfully, the gleaming-white vessel was tracking a few degrees right of Villa Jasmine. If there was no deviation from its present course, it was going to crash head on into the dock fronting the mansion next door.

When the yacht was maybe a quarter mile out, they could hear a low growl reverberating over open water. As the bass-heavy sound rose in volume, it was clear to them all that the pair of laboring engines were not throttling down.

Steve-O said, "That's no *S.S. Minnow.*"

Tara said, "It's not going to stop, is it?"

Riker said nothing. He was again on the edge of his seat, one hand gripping the cushion so hard his fingers were leaving marks. As he pushed off and rose to signal the yacht captain—assuming there was one behind the smoked cockpit glass—the owner of the mansion next door beat him to it.

The *pop-crackle* of the flare leaving the gun in the neighbor's hand caused Steve-O to start, and Tara to blurt, "What the eff?" and spring up off her lounge chair.

Sun warm on his back, Riker watched the flare trace a bright, left-to-right arc across the afternoon sky. It was smoking and sputtering and seemed to be drowning out the noise coming from the yacht's engines. Which baffled Riker, because he was sure the approaching vessel possessed some serious horsepower below deck, thus, the closer it got, the louder the rumble should have been.

Catching on before Riker could process why he was hearing the flare so clearly over the engine noise, Steve-O said, "The engine just died."

"It's still coming, though," Tara said, her voice rising in pitch.

Sure enough, the yacht was still on a collision course with the shared dock fronting the neighbor's mansion. From the looks of it, the point of impact was going to be about a hundred feet to their left. However, without power going to the screws, the yacht's prow had already dipped, and its forward momentum was slowly bleeding off.

"Reminds me of that vampire movie Dad let us watch with him," whispered Tara.

"The scene with the death ship coming into port," replied Riker, raising a hand to shield against the sun glancing off the sharply angled cockpit windows. "I remember it well. Mom was sooo pissed he let us stay up that late."

"*Nosferatu*," Tara said, as people surged from below deck. They were mostly middle-aged, their faces full of confusion and fear and worry.

A woman emerged from a doorway Riker guessed led to the wheelhouse, her back to him. She was screaming and kicking at something he couldn't see.

"That's no death ship," noted Steve-O. He was still sitting and seemed oblivious to the coming impact. "It's a *monster* ship."

Riker tugged on the older man's tank. "Get up," he said and set off jogging toward the neighbor, who had stepped onto the dock and was waving his arms over his head.

The yacht's stern quickly filled up with people. At least a dozen passengers who had been out of sight below deck. Some of them were bandaged. Others had visible wounds to their hands and arms. One man, who wore a white hat and seemed to be in charge, herded them around the starboard-side deck. He was brandishing a flare gun of his own and periodically glancing over his shoulder.

The passengers filed along the narrow starboard-side passageway, leaving behind bloody handprints trailing streaks of crimson on the stark white walls and chrome railings.

Seeing the yacht lose a great deal of speed and go low in the water emboldened the neighbor. He was a sixty-something with a George Hamilton tan and a full head of sun-bleached hair. His white shorts rode up his backside as he went to his tiptoes, cupped a hand by his mouth, and shouted at the yacht, now only fifty yards out and closing.

"Heave to," he hollered, hands shaking as he tried to load another flare into the stubby orange gun.

"Better move out the way," bellowed Riker. "She's not about to *heave* to anything or anyone." He was standing now and reaching out for his sister.

The yacht was twenty feet from the dock when a man emerged from the shadow cast by the gracefully sloping fantail roof. As the sun washed over the man, Riker noted the blank stare directed at the other passengers. He also became aware of the blood coating the man's chin and neck. And then when the man's chin went to his chest and he charged the passengers, Riker had no doubt what he had mistaken for a man, was actually a Bolt.

Riker experienced an overwhelming feeling of helplessness as he watched the creature carom off the starboard-side handrail, smack its head on the opposing bulkhead wall, then pitch forward to the wooden deck, its forward momentum taking it to within a couple yards of the screaming passengers.

The neighbor was raising the gun to fire another warning shot when the yacht slammed into the dock just a few yards to his fore. Course altered by the collision, the yacht finally heaved to. As it did, two things happened at once. First, the narrow walkway protruding from the bow scythed the air inches above the neighbor's head. Next, still sprawled face down and struggling to stand on the pitching deck, the Bolt was sent rocketing head-first to the dock below.

Next came a terrific crash and the vessel groaned and shuddered and straightened parallel to the breakwater. A wave of energy rippled through the wooden planks, leaving some of them splintered and even more twisted and bowed upward.

A half-dozen two-foot-long metal cleats on the dock sheared off at their bases. A resonant ping sounded as each of the anvil-shaped items lost their battle with the massive tonnage still under motion. As the cleats bounced and skittered across the cement walkway, jagged pieces of wood rained down on the neighbor and his lawn.

The passengers not braced for impact didn't fare so well. Two women and a child were catapulted fifteen feet from deck to dock. The thuds their bodies made as they hit the wood planking would stay with Riker forever.

Dodging flying debris, Riker pushed Tara away from him and ordered her and Steve-O into Villa Jasmine.

As the pair turned and ran, he shouted after them. "We're leaving *now*! Grab only what you need!"

Chapter 5

Riker saw Tara and Steve-O reach the border to Villa Jasmine's wide backyard, then turned around just in time to see the badly damaged motor yacht passing left-to-right in front of him. As the dock was slowly chewed up before his eyes, he felt the vibrations coursing up his prosthesis.

By now, people not thrown forcibly from the yacht were jumping over the rail rising up from the starboard-side gunwale. One man lost his footing and was sucked into the narrow chasm between the yacht and breakwater. His screams rose above the cacophony until he was swallowed up by the bay.

The man in the white hat Riker assumed to be the yacht's captain was now gripping the rail one-handed and aiming the flare gun at a downward angle. It was all happening so fast, Riker didn't pay it much mind.

The creature pitched from the yacht upon impact was now up on two feet and hungrily eyeing the neighbor. Three fingers were missing from one hand. Peppering the forearm just inches away were several purple-ridged bite marks. And likely incurred during the fall to the dock, its misshapen head bore a tremendous, bloodless crater.

While Steve-O had stopped to gape at the spectacle unfolding just yards south of Villa Jasmine, Tara had turned back and was inexplicably rescuing Coronas from the ice bucket.

"Forget those!" bellowed Riker. "Get your asses inside!"

Steve-O was rooted and couldn't tear his eyes off Crater Head.

"That's not a man, Steve-O," Riker said in his best authoritarian voice. "It's something you don't want to tangle with. Now go!"

As Steve-O turned and loped off toward Villa Jasmine, Riker shifted his attention to the Bolt on the grass in front of the neighbor's mansion. It wore the uniform of a deckhand: white polo-style shirt, above-the-knee khaki shorts, and thick-soled navy deck shoes.

Prone in the debris-field, it clawed and kicked at the grass as it tried to stand. In addition to the closed head wound, it looked as if its back was wrenched or maybe a leg had been injured in the spill. Obviously feeling no pain, its features remaining slack, it finally overcame whatever had been hindering it and rose up slowly from the grass.

There was a clatter of breaking glass behind Riker. Then Tara was cursing and he heard footfalls retreating toward Villa Jasmine.

Praying the Bolt was slowed severely by its many injuries, Riker risked a quick glance over his shoulder. Saw that Steve-O was already past the pool and threading his way through a clutch of stately palms, with Tara rapidly gaining on him. Still, the pair were far from reaching the mansion, and its west-facing hurricane windows were all wide open.

A lot could go wrong if more Bolts were below deck.

A guttural growling drew Riker's attention back to the neighboring yard, where he saw the owner brandishing the flare gun in a two-handed grip and the bloodied Bolt on the move, head down, arms extended.

Riker's prayer hadn't been answered. The Bolt wasn't hamstrung. It was, in fact, gaining speed and ground, its reaching fingers closing rapidly with the flesh the abomination coveted.

Do it, thought Riker. Then, against his better judgement, lest he draw the Bolt's attention to him, he screamed, "Shoot it!"

There was a *pop* and the gun jerked in the neighbor's grip. The same sizzling sound filled the air as the flaming projectile rocketed from the muzzle. By the time this all registered to Riker, the recoil had hinged the neighbor's forearms back and the Bolt was launching off of one foot.

The neighbor's aim was off.

The Bolt's was not.

Trailing white smoke and winking red and orange, the flare passed harmlessly over the zombie's head, quickly cleared the dock, and then soundlessly pierced Biscayne Bay's blue-green waters.

Even across the distance and over the noise of the motor yacht crashing into Villa Jasmine's dry-docked speedboat, Riker heard the solid *thud* of the airborne Bolt delivering a devastating cross-body tackle, and the sharp *whoosh* of the air leaving the neighbor's lungs.

No sooner had the Bolt tackled the neighbor, driving him into the grass with enough force to make the man's shorts ride down to his knees, did a young, bikini-clad bleached blonde emerge from behind the low hedge fronting the man's mansion.

Riker didn't need to keep watching to know what would become of the doomed neighbor's trophy wife. Before he could warn her to keep quiet, she was screaming and gesticulating at the one-sided attack happening mere feet from her.

Everything the blonde was doing screamed: *All you can eat. Come and get it.*

In fact, Riker had witnessed a similar attack roughly a week ago when he and Tara stopped to offer aid to an elderly couple trying to save their home from burning.

With the anemic spray of water from a garden hose, the elderly man tried to stop a Bolt from killing his wife.

The Lawrence-Taylor-like tackle leveled on him by that Bolt was as vicious as they came.

Riker was reliving that day right here and now. And the attack on the trophy wife's much-older husband was just as deadly.

As the young woman's screams rose to the level of the yacht passenger who'd been thrown and crushed against the breakwater, the Bolt tore into the supine neighbor's exposed neck.

While the attack commenced, three passengers who'd either been thrown or had jumped from the yacht were busy picking themselves up off the ground.

A forty-something man with an obvious compound fracture of the fibula pushed off the grass. He was on his feet for a half-second before the pain sent him crashing to the ground, screaming in agony and punching the lush grass in obvious frustration.

A second man got to his feet and staggered drunkenly toward the commotion.

Riker wasn't a hundred-percent certain, but if he had to put money on whether the passenger was still among the living, or a slow-moving zombie, he would bet the house on the latter.

The third passenger, a severely overweight twenty-something sporting a sunburn several shades redder than Steve-O's, got to his feet and instantly struck a course for the trophy wife. He was challenging the Bolt to *fight someone your own age* when the growling monster rent a fist-sized hunk of meat from the now-silenced neighbor, went to its knees, and rose up off the blood-soaked patch of lawn.

Torn between helping and saving his own ass, Riker watched the Bolt chew the meat once, then twice, then finally fix its shark-eyed gaze on the screaming woman.

Choosing the former, Riker set his sights on the sunburned man. He took two long strides, bellowed, "Don't get in its way," and launched his two-hundred-and-forty-pound frame at the lumbering man.

Mid-flight, Riker watched two things happen. First, the Bolt, seemingly mimicking him, took two quick steps toward the screaming woman and launched itself at her. Then, with the ground rushing up at him, Riker witnessed a projectile ripping through the air a yard to his fore. It came from above and behind and was trailing white smoke, sputtering noisily, and winking red and orange. He caught a whiff of acrid-smelling rocket propellant and watched the flare find its mark. Albeit the wrong mark.

The captain's aim had been off. Way off. Because the flare missed the Bolt and struck the blonde square in the breastbone, knocking the wind from her, which immediately silenced the screams. She was punched backward, her bikini top afire, with the Bolt's bloodied, claw-like hands already knuckle-deep into her taut midriff.

The man trying to intervene went down hard, landing a few feet short of being any kind of help to the dying woman.

"You need to realize that chivalry is dead, buddy," Riker said as he rolled over into a sitting position. "Or *you* will be."

"Fuck you, *buddy*," spat the man. "She *needs* me." He was wearing a determined look and got to his feet surprisingly fast for someone his size.

Riker was shaking his head as he got to his knees. As he pushed up off the grass, the woman drew a breath and picked up where she had left off. Soon her wails were accompanied by the animalistic squeals of her knight in shining armor being killed.

With normalcy bias holding court right here and now on the lawn fronting thirty-some-odd million dollars' worth of high-end real estate, Riker didn't need to steal a final look to know that the man with the useless leg was about to become victim number four to the Bolt.

No amount of money could have saved the neighbor and his wife.

No amount of explaining or pleading by Riker could have stopped the woman's would-be savior from rushing in.

And, sadly, there was nothing Riker could do to keep the rest of the yacht's passengers from suffering the same fate as those who'd already fallen.

With no clue as to how much time remained before the stricken passengers succumbed to their injuries and came back as slow-moving Slogs, or, God forbid, fast-moving Bolts, Riker tried his best to block out the sounds of people dying and set off running toward Villa Jasmine.

Chapter 6

Steve-O was straddling the line between indoors and out of doors. The pool and outdoor living area lay before him. At his back was the luxuriously appointed family room featuring a huge wraparound leather sofa, a billiard-table-sized flat-panel television, and a live-edge oak table large enough to accommodate the Dolphins' entire offensive line.

He was framed by the massive sliding glass panels which, at the moment, were still partially retracted into the west-facing walls.

Emerging from around the infinity edge pool, his gait dropping from a sprint to a slow jog, Riker regarded Steve-O. The older man had shed the tank top, shorts, and flip-flops. He was now wearing dark blue jean shorts. Riding partway over the huge silver and turquoise belt buckle affixed to the wide leather belt holding the shorts up was a button-up Tommy Bahama shirt. The short-sleeved number was cream-colored and emblazoned with hot pink flamingos and multi-colored toucans.

How he had pulled off changing clothes in under two minutes was the sixty-four-thousand-dollar question.

"Give the man a straw hat and ship him to Casablanca," retorted Riker as he slowed to a brisk walk and planted both hands on his hips.

Steve-O didn't respond verbally. His eyes met Riker's for a tick, then quickly panned back to what they'd been fixated on.

Riker stopped short of the threshold to catch his breath. Saw arranged in a semi-circle near Steve-O's cowboy-boot-clad feet a number of black gym bags. Nike, Adidas, Reebok, and Under Armour were all represented.

After a couple of seconds spent hands-on-knees, his back arched and rising and falling subtly, Riker rose up and waved a hand in front of Steve-O's staring eyes. Voice adopting a serious tone, he asked, "Where's Tara?"

Steve-O said nothing. His eyes didn't waver, either.

More screams came from the left, beyond the palms. Someone else was in the middle of dying somewhere on the dock just beyond Villa Jasmine's south wall.

Again with the hand wave. "Steve-O. Earth to Steve-O. Where's Tara?" Riker repeated.

"The boat is sinking," answered Steve-O matter-of-factly.

Riker didn't need to turn to see what the other man was watching. Reflected in the floor-to-ceiling window to his right, he saw the angular white bow jutting a good fifteen feet or so above the dock. And though the image was wavering slightly, he could still tell that it was slowly slipping from view.

"That it is," Riker noted glumly. "Where's Tara?"

"I think Pretty Lady is still packing."

"Did she call the police?"

"I think so," responded Steve-O.

Riker let his gaze roam the open room and finally settle on the television. It was tuned to a cable news channel. A reporter was standing roadside. A long line of stopped traffic could be seen past his right shoulder. The cars and trucks and SUVs were surrounded by water. Everything glittered in the afternoon sun. Nearby, palms grew up beside the beginning of the four-lane causeway. As Riker watched, the fronds were lifted up by a lazy offshore breeze. Ripples coursed their length, making the green-brown tips of the leaves waggle at the reporter, like a sort of half-hearted wave.

"I'm right here," Tara said. "Been here all along." She was slumped on the couch, just the tight braids atop her head visible. "Are you seeing this shit?"

"I see it. Hope that's not the only way out of here. If so—"

"Then you won our bet," finished Tara. "Mister *I Told You So,* victorious yet again. Things never change with you, Lee."

31

Steve-O's voice carried in from outside. "Houston," he said, "we have a problem."

Tearing his eyes from the television, where people were starting to emerge from their vehicles and surround a trio of just-arrived Humvees, Riker looked out at the bay. The yacht was gone from sight. Where it had been was the captain and a middle-aged woman. Clothes thoroughly soaked through, she was in the process of dragging him onto the destroyed dock. Fingers scrabbling for purchase, eyes gone wide, the captain shouted a warning to his rescuer.

Finally getting the captain onto the dock, the woman rose and beckoned toward a much younger woman coming in from the left. Riker put her in her twenties. From ankle to shoulder her entire right side was marred by angry red abrasions weeping blood. As she hobbled toward the older woman, her black bikini top struggled to remain on her gymnast's body. Revealing snatches of bright white skin bracketed by tan lines, the skimpy bottoms hung on by a single hip-hugging string. Casting harried glances over her shoulder, she was quickly coming to the realization she was losing her slow-speed race with the newly-turned and equally tanned neighbor.

"Are you going to help them?" asked Steve-O.

Riker was about to answer when the undead deckhand suddenly appeared. Presenting as just a flash of white and crimson at first, the Bolt bowled over the neighbor, stretched both arms toward the younger woman, and went horizontal to the dock.

It was over in seconds.

Riker's mind was made up in half the time it took the Bolt to rip a mouthful of flesh from the young woman's neck and then move on to the others.

Nearly a dozen victims, just like that, thought Riker. *If they all come back as Bolts, we're doomed.* No sooner had he thought it, than the trophy wife—fake boobs exposed and gyrating wildly in two different directions—came sprinting into the picture from the left. She was wearing a sheen of blood from the neck down, and not much else. The white bottoms she'd been wearing when the flare hit her in the chest were now in tatters, the remaining fabric dotted crimson and stained with mud and grass.

Answering Steve-O, Riker said, "They're beyond help. All of them. Get inside here!" Turning toward Tara, he added, "I need your help to get these things closed."

As Riker pulled the first of the storm windows into place between the outdoor living area and great room, he instructed Steve-O to start moving bags to the front foyer. Locking the first pane into place, Riker witnessed the neighbor rise to his feet, pan his head in their direction, and set off across the grass toward the pool.

Closing the massive hurricane-proof windows went faster with Tara's help. When the last two panes snapped into place, the noises made by the dead and dying were silenced.

Ignoring the chaos on the television to his left, Riker cast his gaze toward the couch where a half-dozen tan Luis Vuitton bags, bulging with who knew what, were arranged like soldiers, in a neat line, atop the couch cushions.

"You grab the atlas and laptop?" Riker asked.

Tara nodded.

"You call the cops?"

Again with the nod.

Grimacing, he said, "I hope we get off the island before they have a chance to seal it off."

"I did what I thought was right." She paused. "I did it for those poor people."

Riker said, "You did more than me."

She moved toward the couch.

He said, "I'm guessing the rest of the stuff on our shopping list is in those ugly-ass bags, am I right?"

Hands on hips, slight sideways tilt to the head, Tara shot her brother an *I'm not an idiot* look.

Steve-O donned his white Stetson and then looked to Riker, who had just put his hands up in mock surrender. "Did you pack the *boomstick*?"

Lowering his hands, Riker regarded the man. "You know I did," he answered just as the thing that used to be the next-door

33

neighbor hit the hurricane windows with force sufficient to rattle them in their channels.

"So we're enacting the *plan*?" asked Tara, hefting a pair of designer bags and shooting a sour look side-eyed at the fake-tan-wearing dead thing tonguing the glass.

Riker glanced at the Fountain offshore racer. It was nearly inverted after the collision and hanging off the lift. The bow looked to be under water. Sighing, he said, "Plan *B*, though. All the things we talked about are starting to happen *here*. And with our ride out of commission, if we don't get going now, we're gonna find ourselves trapped on Zombie Island."

To punctuate Riker's statement, the deckhand Bolt slammed at full speed into the same glass panel the neighbor zombie was licking. Only this time the window didn't just flex and bang around noisily. Cracks appeared and near instantly runners shot off at crazy angles from the initial point of impact.

Riker said, "Let's get before those things bash their way inside." Then he snugged his Atlanta Braves hat low on his head and fixed Tara with a hard stare. "Is any damage to the villa going to be billed to us?"

Shrugging, Tara brushed past him and strode off toward the front door. Along the way she passed a similarly weighted-down Steve-O and continued on without saying a word.

Riker thumbed the FORD fob, disengaging the Shelby's locks. He depressed a second button to remotely start the big 6.2-liter V8. "Use the peephole first," he called ahead. "One of those things may have found its way alongside the villa."

There was no response. Only the echo of footsteps coming from the long hall leading to the multicar garages fronting the circular motor court.

After spending a few moments on his feet in the great room, his attention torn between the drama playing out on the television and the dead things pressing their bodies against the storm windows, Riker followed after the others.

Walking down the hall that would eventually spill him into the grand entry, he took a sudden detour toward the main kitchen. Stopping at a narrow door just outside the kitchen, he eyed the commercial-looking lock just above the handle. It was the push-button type where a code was needed to actuate the bolt. It was also the only thing standing between him and what he guessed to be a fully stocked pantry. Hell, he'd watched a couple episodes of the HBO show Hard Knocks in which the cameras followed a certain team during training camp. And given all the stuff the NFL players on the show stocked in their oversized subzero refrigerators, he figured there would be more than enough behind the door to keep them from having to stop for little more than gas and bathroom breaks. If push came to shove, the former could be achieved through siphoning, and the latter by putting aside modesty in favor of survival.

Once on the road, keeping contact with people to a minimum during the journey was a high priority on his list.

"I've got your code right here," Riker said, rearing back and delivering a sharp kick to the door just below the ring of numbered buttons.

The fancy lock proved to be the lipstick on the pig. The door was thin, and the lock's bolt was seated rather shallow into the jamb.

There was a crash and puff of fine white dust as the jamb failed and the doorknob punched a hole in the drywall. There was no equal and opposite reaction; the knob remained embedded in the wall, trapping the door open.

As Riker had suspected, the Dolphins linebacker had utilized his Costco card. The shelves were fully stocked with food and all manner of drinks.

Riker began taking items off the shelves and sliding them across the floor at the doorway. He hollered, "A little help here," and turned back toward the cases of bottled water stacked chest-high to him.

Chapter 7

The guard shack was empty when Riker nosed the Shelby up to the gate.

"He was here when I drove in earlier."

"He ain't here now," stated Tara. "That little golf cart of his is gone, too."

"Maybe he had to go take a pee," proffered Steve-O.

Meeting the older man's gaze in the rearview, Riker said, "I've never seen it unmanned. I'm sure he'd have called a replacement in to spell him for a piss break."

Flashing a wide smile, Steve-O said, "Swear jar. Pay up."

Eyes roaming the mirrors, Riker said, "We're playing that game again? I thought you hopping aboard the Pretty Lady Gravy Train made it unnecessary."

"I'll save it for a rainy day."

Tara said, "I've a feeling money is going to lose its luster when those 'rainy days' do arrive."

"If," said Riker. "Glass half full. Always." He reached under his seat and came out with the stubby Shockwave shotgun.

Voice a near whisper, Tara said, "Where do you think you're going with *that?*"

The wail of a siren interrupted them momentarily. Once it had trailed off, Riker said, "Not the time to play *Mom ... Sis.*"

Steve-O said, "My mom always said it is better to be safe than sorry," then started belting lyrics from the Brenda Lee song *I'm Sorry*.

Elbowing open his door, Riker peered over his shoulder. "What are you sorry about, Steve-O?"

"Nothing, really," he said. "Just that my mom played Miss Brenda's record *all the time.*"

Riker stepped to the hot blacktop. Shotgun pressed tight against his right thigh, he looked all around. Seeing nothing, he closed his door.

Moving to the front of her seat, Tara said, "Be careful, Bro."

Nodding, Riker stalked off toward the guard shack.

The shack was fairly small for the amount of money spent on the gate. In fact, Villa Jasmine's main pantry had a larger footprint.

Spread out on the counter was a copy of the *Miami Herald* newspaper. That it was left behind told him the guard split in a hurry. The headline on the paper read: **What Is Operation Romeo Victor Prepping Us For?** Below that was another question Riker had only heard roll off the tongues of conspiracy theorists on late-night radio: **Does Martial Law Loom? Will 2016 Presidential Elections Be Suspended?**

Next to the paper was a charging stand designed to hold a half-dozen radios. Five slots were empty. He heard voices emanating from the remaining radio, the words unintelligible. Curious as to what was being said, he tried the door.

Locked.

Pressing one ear to the wire-embedded safety glass allowed him to make out snippets of the harried conversation. Things on the southwest end of Sunset Island were not rosy. The shit was hitting the fan, to be exact. Having heard enough, Riker decided to take things into his own hands—literally.

He set the Shockwave on the ground beside the shack. Then he bent down and grabbed the L-shaped doorknob in a firm two-handed grip. He planted his Salomons close together, toes against the metal jamb. Bending his knees slightly, he drew a deep breath.

Rearing up and yanking back on the handle produced the result he was looking for.

The door here fared no better than the one inside Villa Jasmine.

There was a squeal and a pop, and the sliding door left the bottom track. He put all his weight against the door and with his right fist delivered a trio of blows near the header.

Another couple of loud pops preceded the wheels atop the door leaving their tracks completely. The cumbersome slab of glass and metal appeared to be light as a feather as Riker easily tossed it aside.

He entered the shack to the sound of a male voice coming from one of the radios. As he listened in, he learned orders had been given for everyone on the net to disengage and wait for reinforcements.

Unable to handle the problem on their own—thus keeping it "in house"—Riker figured the rent-a-cops had no other choice than to wait for the Miami-Dade PD. And if the boys in blue happened to arrive and he was still here, at the least, considering the damage to the guard shack, he would be leaving in a pair of chrome bracelets, facing hours of questioning.

Working as fast as possible in the cramped confines, Riker scooped up the lone radio and newspaper. After folding the paper and sticking it under one arm, he punched the red button labeled EXIT - OPEN/CLOSE.

He hinged up in time to see the gate shimmy and begin its slow left-to-right roll.

He scooped up the shotgun and was back inside the Shelby and putting it into gear before the gate was a third of the way into the full-open position.

Steve-O was on the edge of his seat, both arms draped over the seatback. He said, "What is Plan B, Lee Riker?"

"Sticking to the Gulf Coast side, we drive north to the Panhandle. From there we go west, hugging the coastline for as long as we can. I figure that will keep us as far from the epicenter of infection as possible."

"*Epicenters*. Plural. more than one," Tara said.

The gate had reached the halfway point when Riker said, "I'm not talking Middletown. I think that was small potatoes compared to what we all saw in New York. I did the math. In only a dozen or so hours Manhattan was entirely overrun, and Tower 4 was completely compromised."

"The day the world changed again," Steve-O said. Then, hooking a thumb over his shoulder, he added, "And now the golf police are coming."

"Shit," Riker exclaimed. Releasing the brake and letting the oversized pickup roll forward, he stole a glance in his wing mirror. Sure enough, there *were* two golf carts full of guards speeding toward him from the west.

Craning to see past Steve-O, Tara asked, "Are they armed?"

Riker said, "Yep. And there looks to be a whole lot of them."

"Then get us the *eff* out of here," she ordered. "Because where there's smoke, there's fire."

"And lots of *Johnnys*," Steve-O added as the exit gate hit the stops. He let out a yelp and was propelled back into the bench seat as Riker applied a generous amount of throttle. Too much, it seemed, because the Shelby reared up on its suspension, the rear tires chirped, and, in the truck's wake a puff of blue-gray smoke lifted off the hot pavement.

Johnny was the moniker Steve-O had assigned to the mysterious black-clad, gun-wielding mercenaries who'd tried and ultimately failed to seal off Middletown. After witnessing a squad of the totally anonymous soldiers gun down unarmed civilians at a roadblock north of Middletown, Riker dubbed them MIBs— short for "men in black." Oblivious of the movie of the same name, however, Steve-O thought the reference was to Johnny Cash (the original Man in Black) and instantly shortened it to Johnny.

Recalling the black helicopter that had pursued them from that roadblock to a nearby cornfield, Riker said, "Tangling with more Johnnys is the absolute *last* thing we need. I want to get us as far as possible from here. Because we all know that ... that *zombie* attack back there won't be reported as such." He shook his head. "It'll be spun in a way so that we become the bad guys."

The *thunk-thunk* of the Shelby's off-road tires rolling over strategically placed speedbumps sounded inside the cab.

Riker went on. "I can see the headlines now: **Armed Desperados On The Run**. We'll be branded as the squatters who robbed Villa Jasmine and murdered the next-door neighbors."

"Don't forget sinking the big speedboat," interjected Steve-O. "That baby probably cost a fortune."

Riker said nothing. And he didn't let up on the gas after the Ford cleared the gate. It was times like these when skills honed in the United States Army came in handy. That three-day driving course in the desert had been a high point of his deployment.

And he got to put those skills to use almost daily, driving high-level military brass and foreign dignitaries to and from the Green Zone in Baghdad, Iraq. He threw many an up-armored luxury SUV into turns usually unrecoverable in a stock vehicle being driven under similar circumstances.

The course instructors over there taught him how to recognize bad guys looking to pin in his vehicle. He also learned how to blow a hastily set roadblock while keeping alive the principal on board. And it was over there that he perfected his favorite, the bootlegger's reverse—or moonshiner's turn—a maneuver used to escape a lethal situation by reversing quickly and then whipping the vehicle around in a controlled high-speed one-eighty.

And it just so happened that Riker's highly modified Shelby Baja pickup, though not armored, was closer in pedigree to those up-armored Land Cruisers and Range Rovers he used to drive than the civilian F-150 it was based on. This rig was full of power and much more nimble than its outward appearance and ride height would suggest.

Riker kept on the pedal, powering through the shallow right turn onto the 29th Street bridge. He reeled the rear end in by counter-steering against the slide.

The bridge across the channel was a narrow two-lane affair. It didn't lend to high speed travel by a vehicle with as wide a stance as the Shelby. So Riker let off the pedal and employed the brakes. He did so just in time, because as soon as the speedometer needle dropped down to the speed limit, three emergency vehicles, their red and blue lights ablaze, careened around the far corner at a high rate of speed.

Riker kept a death grip on the wheel as the pair of Miami-Dade PD Tahoes and the armored SWAT vehicle trailing them whizzed by in the opposing lane with just inches to spare.

Exhaling, Riker said, "Almost lost my mirror there." He flicked his eyes to the rearview. Saw first the very top of Steve-O's Stetson. The man had slouched down in his seat and gone quiet. Beyond the crease in the hat, he saw the retreating vehicles, still moving fast, and, thankfully, the sight of the Shelby leaving the scene didn't have their brake lights flaring red.

Tara said, "Looks like lightning-fast response times are part of the package if you live on good ol' Sunset Island."

"I don't think they came with enough resources to make a difference. I couldn't be sure, but it looked as if the security guards had taken some licks before retreating."

The blue-green waters of the bay inlet flashing below the Shelby gave way to land dotted with palm trees and green lawns fronting homes much smaller than the ones on the island.

Relaxing a bit, Riker slowed and stopped for a red at Alton Road, where traffic was much heavier than when he'd returned from the electronics store.

Across the four-lane, beyond a copse of trees, a trio of golfers stood in a knot on a massive green.

Riker went left when the light changed.

Tara said, "The navigation unit has us going right."

"Change of plans," said Riker as he nosed the Shelby into the lane feeding onto I-195 West.

By the time they started moving again, Steve-O was back at his perch between the seats. Hat brim cutting the air, he looked to Tara first, then fixed Riker with an inquisitive gaze. "So we're going to Plan *C* now?"

"Not exactly," Riker said. "While you two were *shopping*"—he had wanted to do air quotes as Steve-O had earlier, but couldn't on account he was driving—"I was doing the same ... and a bit more. Buckle up, Steve-O. You'll both see soon enough."

Tara made no reply. She was turned in her seat, face nearly touching the window, jaw hinged open.

"What is it?" Riker asked, keeping his eyes on merging traffic.

"The hospital," she replied. "It's a full-on shit show."

Riding the momentum of the turn, Steve-O slid to the passenger side, belted in, and turned his attention to the cluster of buildings that made up Mount Sinai Medical Center's sprawling campus. "Lots of pretty lights," he noted.

Tara said, "Those pretty lights are ambulances and police cars. Dozens of them."

Slipping to the right lane, Riker stole a glance past Tara and could hardly believe what he was seeing.

Chapter 8

Riker wanted nothing more than to crane to see with his own eyes the embattled Mount Sinai Medical Center and all that was happening there. Instead, keeping his eyes on his lane, he asked Tara to explain what she was seeing and take a video with her phone if possible.

"Already one step ahead of you, Bro. I'm *waaay* zoomed in, so it's bound to be grainy."

"What do you *see?*"

"Monsters," Steve-O interjected. "I saw mostly slow ones."

Twisted around in her seat with one arm entangled in her shoulder belt and the iPhone aimed at the passing hospital, Tara said, "I'm afraid he's right. Dozens of them."

Focused solely on the gathering traffic, Riker asked, "Inside? Outside? What are they doing?"

Tara drew in a deep breath and exhaled. Voice wavering, she said, "There are lots of them. They're mostly clustered around a bunch of ambulances queued up on the side street. A smaller group is congregated in front of what looks to be the main entry."

Riker slipped over into the far-right lane as the interstate began a gradual dip prior to the long level stretch that shot off straight across the bay. "Where are the patrol cars in relation to the zombies?" he asked.

"They're set up near Alton Road. A long line of them. But they're out of sight now." She paused and turned to face front. Fiddling with her iPhone, she went on, "Let me get the video going. I can zoom in on that specific area of the footage and get a better read for you."

Riker glanced at the display in the center of the dash. The navigation program was already pulled up. On the right, in a separate pane, was a list of the upcoming exits. After saying the names of the next three softly under his breath, he sped up and checked his mirrors.

"I saw the Law," Steve-O said. "They were drawing down on the monsters with shotguns and pistols. Saw it all clear as day from back here."

Riker asked, "Were they shooting? Did you see flame coming from their muzzles?

"No, sir," Steve-O said. "But it was coming. I'm sure of it. Looked like Custer's Last Stand."

Tara said, "The zombies are the natives, I'm guessing."

Riker said, "And the police would be the 7th Cavalry. We all know how *that* ended."

"Not good for the soldiers," Steve-O said. "Not good at all."

Crossing over Biscayne Bay, the four-and-a-half-mile stretch of I-195 called The Julia Tuttle Causeway consisted of six lanes, three eastbound to Miami Beach, and three heading west to midtown Miami. At about the middle of its run, the causeway bisected a small island bristling with towering palms.

Nearing the island, at a point in the span where the roadway bumped up to allow passage for boats traversing Biscayne Bay's sparkling waters, Tara caused Riker and Steve-O to jump by blurting, "Holy hell!"

Pushing his glasses back on his nose, Steve-O said, "What do you see, Pretty Lady?"

"The EMTs are *still* bringing infected people to the hospital. If they haven't yet, I think they're real close to losing the whole place to the dead."

"Hippocratic oath," muttered Riker as the Shelby geared down to compensate for the beginning of a gradual incline that seemed to go on forever.

"Hungry Hungry Hippos," said Steve-O. "I *loved* that game."

"It's the sacred oath all doctors take after completing medical school. It says they are bound to help anyone in need of medical attention. No... matter... what," explained Riker. "And it looks like their adhering to it is the root of all that madness down there."

"Here you go," Tara said, tilting the iPhone screen toward Riker. "I only captured twenty seconds of footage, but in there I found a few frames where you can see those same black body bags like we saw at the high school."

He glanced sidelong at the device. "Anything moving in them?"

Tara shook her head. "They're all lying flat and staying that way. Looks like someone is learning from past mistakes."

As Riker mulled over this troubling new development, the dull throb behind his eyes returned. Taking the Biscayne Boulevard exit off the 195, they found traffic beginning to back up. The speedometer needle dipping below twenty was the straw that broke the proverbial camel's back. The usual slow creep of tension up his back and neck muscles didn't happen. Instead, all of the stress accumulated during the day's events was back at once. It manifested in the form of a tsunami of pain that surged from the base of his spine to the nerves behind his eyes.

Traffic was backed up due to an F-DOT work crew running a pair of jackhammers at a section of Biscayne Boulevard. Both lanes had come to a full stop at the red light, with cars in the left lane beginning to edge over. Good thing, because Riker was nearly incapacitated. Tracers danced before his eyes and the dull throb had become a full-on migraine. It was as if the pair of guys in orange vests had fitted their jackhammers with needles and turned them on the inside of his skull.

As Riker bowed his head and rubbed his temples, waiting for the light to change, a hand gripped his shoulder.

"CTE back?" Tara asked, concern evident in her tone.

Riker nodded, the simple act amplifying the pain.

"Want me to drive?"

"No," he answered, "it's ebbing."

A lie.

In fact, the pain was spiking and his tinnitus was jangling away at rock-band volume as he continued to pray for a few more seconds of red from the traffic control light over Biscayne.

"Let me know when you do." She went quiet as the light cycled to green and the half-dozen cars in the lane ahead slow-rolled forward.

When the Shelby slipped through the light and they all had a clear view down Biscayne, Tara broke her silence.

"*Crap*," she said, pointing to the red and yellow sign rising over a Shell gas station a block distant. "That's not cool."

Though Riker's vision was a bit fuzzy around the edges, he could still read the large illuminated digital numbers dominating the Shell sign.

"Seven ninety-nine a gallon? For regular!? Hell," he noted, "it was hovering somewhere south of four dollars a gallon yesterday."

"Bend me the eff over," said Tara, incredulous. "It doubled in price overnight. Means the populace is beginning to see through the government's bullcrap."

From somewhere out of sight came Steve-O's voice. "That's not lady talk, Tara."

She turned and said, "Remember, dude ... you're a grown ass man. So why don't you build a bridge and get over it."

Steve-O made a sound like a balloon deflating.

"That was harsh," scolded Riker.

"Tough love," she said.

Accelerating and jumping over to the right lane afforded a better view of the station coming up on their left. Though the prices were exorbitant, there was no shortage of customers willing to pay it.

The pumps were all in use. A double line of vehicles waiting their turn to drink from the well snaked out onto Biscayne and continued on around the block to the east. Some drivers were out and leaning against their static vehicles. Others remained at the wheel, engines stilled and windows cracked.

One particular compact bearing Tennessee plates had drawn a small crowd of gawkers. They stood on the street in a rough semi-circle a few feet from the driver's side door. One man was tapping on the windshield. Another was waving a finger near the open driver's side window.

Face a mask of animalistic rage, jaw pistoning nonstop up and down, the female driver lunged at her antagonists.

As the Shelby came even with the scene, it was clear to Riker that the driver was infected. And with the zombie straining against the taut shoulder belt keeping it from worming through the window, the circle of onlookers tightened, some with phones in hand and getting near to the snapping teeth just to get a selfie with the thing.

It was natural to be curious. Riker got it. He had seen it before. Years ago while visiting Yellowstone with a friend, he had watched a grown woman get too close to a bison. It didn't end well for her. She messed with the bull and got the horns.

He had a feeling the encounter he had just witnessed in the fuel line was going to end badly for one or more of the idiots.

Steve-O said, "Kids used to do that to me at school. Once I got older, it stopped."

Tara turned to face him. "I'm so sorry you had to go through that. Kids can be such assholes."

Steve-O looked overtop his glasses.

"I know, language. I'm sorry, Steve-O."

Riker felt for the man. He'd been there. Except his experience was a little different. Kind of inverse. Kids had been assholes to him at first. But once he fought back, it all stopped. Until he became an adult, that is. Then his size made him the target of every wanna-be tough guy with a chip on his shoulder or one too many drinks in his system. And he had the scars on his knuckles as proof.

Glancing at Tara, he said, "If this sickness continues to spread, prices are going nowhere but up. That is if the gas even makes it from refinery to station. Not only do the truckers have to make random stops at weigh stations and keep their eyes peeled for state troopers, now they have to skirt National Guard roadblocks. No getting around it, Sis. Things are going to keep getting worse until this all gets sorted out."

"*If* it gets sorted out." She flipped the passing Shell station the bird as Riker hung a right turn. "Fuck if I'm *ever* going to pay eight bucks for a gallon of gas."

Again Riker shot her a sidelong glance. "Bet you wished you still had that SMART car of yours."

"Thumbelina," she said, one brow arched. "It's not the money, Lee. I've got plenty of that."

"What's the problem then?"

Voice full of conviction, she said, "It's the *principle*, man. Eff the opportunists."

"OK, then," challenged Riker, "go ahead and see how many miles per gallon that righteous indignation is gonna get you,"

"It just pisses me off. That's all." Tara looked out her window as Riker slowed, moved to the middle turn lane, and signaled a left turn. Through gritted teeth, she went on, "There's gotta be a law on the books against that kind of price gouging, right?"

Riker said nothing. He figured there was a whole slew of laws against the practice—especially in Hurricane Country—but didn't know enough about the subject to add his two cents.

Chapter 9

Miami, Florida

Jonny's Shooter's Supply, a four-thousand-square-foot, one-level structure encompassing the majority of a city block, was mostly windowless and constructed from cement block painted battleship-gray. To say the place resembled a bunker would be a vast understatement. The only landscaping to speak of were four palms standing sentinel on each corner of the parking lot. Mostly empty, the lot fronted a single set of double doors mirrored against the sun and protected by a pair of waist-high cement posts painted safety orange.

If not for the red awning displaying the store's name in white lettering, the business could easily be mistaken for an automotive parts warehouse or maybe an import/export concern.

Riker steered the Shelby onto the lot and reversed into a corner spot in the shadow of one of the towering palms. He left the engine idle and kicked up the air a notch. Rolling the transmission into Park, he said, "We're here. Your question is answered, Sis."

"A gun store?" Tara said. "That's where you've been during your frequent shore excursions? I figured something was up seeing as how you only have this old-man shirt of yours"—she flicked the sleeve—"Tommy Obama ... or whatever it's called, to show for all the *shopping* you said you were doing."

Recalling the ire directed his way by Tara after he disassembled and discarded the Beretta he'd taken from the soldier at the high school in Middletown, he nodded and said, "I confess. Just in case my background check didn't pan out, I kept

49

this place to myself." Hands up in mock surrender, he went on, "I did make a few purchases here. I think you'll forgive me when you see what I picked up for us." He unbuckled and shifted in his seat. "Florida has a three-day waiting period on handgun purchases. That's why I kept coming home empty-handed."

Clicking out of her belt, she asked, "What were you doing with the rest of your time?"

Following the others' lead, Steve-O clicked out of his seatbelt. Filling up the space between the front seat headrests and wearing a wide smile, he said, "Lee's been a busy little beaver."

Riker nodded at Steve-O. Responding to Tara's question, he said, "I ran a few hundred rounds through the same type of firearms I ordered from Jonny. I also learned how to break them all down and give them a thorough cleaning. The people who work here are real helpful."

Steve-O looked to Riker. Voice taking on an inquisitive tone, he said, "I thought you were in the Army, Lee. Shouldn't you already know how to shoot and clean your guns?"

"I was a *driver* in the Army, Steve-O. I did very little shooting over there. And when I did get to put a few rounds through a Beretta or M4, it was at the outdoor range and under strict supervision."

Tara said, "You served your country honorably, Lee. You left a piece of yourself over there, too. And you have the Purple Heart to show for it. You should *never, ever* diminish your contribution."

Flashing Tara a pretend scowl, he said, "Coming or staying? I'll leave the engine running and the A/C on if you don't want to come with."

Tara craned to see the instrument cluster. "Tank's full, I see. Let's keep it that way." She reached over and shut the engine down. "I say we all go in."

"I'm going," said Steve-O. "I like looking at the antique guns."

"Not many of those in here," Riker said. "It's a retail store and indoor range. All the good antiques usually end up in museums."

Steve-O said nothing. Holding his hat with one hand, he elbowed open his door and exited the truck.

As the door thunked shut, Tara said in a low voice, "You did get everything done on our list, right?"

"Most of it. Which is pretty good seeing as how we're bugging out two days early."

Again with the brow lift. "Did you fill the gas cans?"

Riker flashed a sheepish grin.

"Lee."

"I made the daily bank withdrawals. Stopped at the gold and silver place afterward. Every day, like *we* agreed. Did *you*?"

Now Tara was the one flashing the guilty smile.

"Well?"

"Only twice," she conceded.

"Better than none. I'll let it slide if you let the gas can thing go."

She nodded and winked, then pushed open her door.

Riker and Tara caught up with their new friend a few paces from the front doors. The parking lot was half-full, with three more vehicles rolling in as they trooped across the lot.

"Allow me," said Riker as he reached past the shorter man and opened the door for him. As Tara slipped past him, Riker set the Shelby's alarm and pocketed the fob.

Riker watched Tara make a beeline for the waist-high glass display cases lining the left wall. Arranged neatly on glass shelves within the cases were all manner of handguns. Neon-green price tags affixed to white packaging string dangled from the trigger guards of revolvers, semiautomatics, and single-shot derringers. The weapons came in every finish imaginable. Most were black or blued. A few were flat dark earth—a fairly dark shade of brown. Others were desert tan—a brown lighter in tone than the ones done in FDE. Sitting on one shelf next to a number of chromed items—mostly revolvers—was a boxy semiautomatic finished in Cerakote nearly the same hue of hot pink as the flamingos on Steve-O's tropical shirt.

Remaining tight-lipped, Steve-O walked straight toward the rear of the store, where the entire wall was adorned with all manner of taxidermy: waterfowl posed in flight. A raccoon standing on its hind legs. A weasel of some sort slinking through artificial foliage.

Centerpiece of the taxidermy was a Florida panther, its tan fur and yellow eyes lifelike. The way it had been posed on the faux rock base, coiled and ready to pounce, made it seem as if the pair of patrons handling long rifles below were about to come under attack.

A number of forked antlers mounted to display plaques flanked the panther. Riding above it all was the rack from a bull moose. Riker guessed if the beast it once belonged to was at his level and charging, even with his wide wingspan he'd have a hard time touching both edges of the rack at the same time.

A wiry Asian man wearing a camouflage ball cap on which *Desert Storm Veteran* was stitched in gold approached Riker from the right. He looked to be late forties. He wore some kind of tactical pants tailored from a sturdy tan fabric. They were held up by a leather belt on which rode a holster containing a boxy black semiautomatic pistol. Worn over a tucked-in white tee shirt was a red vest bearing the words *Range Officer* front and back.

Smiling and extending a hand, the man said, "Mister Riker. Good to see you again so soon. Shooting today?"

"Not today, Jon," answered Riker as he and the man shook hands.

"That grip," said Riker, pretending to massage his right hand.

The man smiled wide as he removed yellow-lensed shooter's glasses and tucked them into a vest pocket.

Riker said, "Did you get the Ithaca out to Indiana?"

Nodding, Jon said, "It shipped this morning." With a slight tilt of the head, he asked, "What kind of a favor does a guy have to do for you to earn a twelve-thousand-dollar over/under?"

"Too long of a story to go into right now," answered Riker.

"Understood," replied Jon.

Hopeful tone to his voice, Riker asked, "Did my paperwork clear?"

"As someone, somewhere once said," said Jon. "Timing is everything. Your 4473 came back yesterday. You're good to go, Lee."

"William Shakespeare," interjected Tara as she materialized from a nearby aisle. "That's who you're quoting."

"I'll take your word for it," said Jon. "You must be Lee's better half?"

"Ewwww," exclaimed Tara. "He's my booger-eatin' brother half. At least he was still eating them in middle school. Can't speak on it now."

"Ahhh ... siblings." Jon nodded. "My apologies for assuming. You're both close in age."

"Quit diggin," Tara said. "Lee is four years *older* than me."

"Again, please forgive me. I'm youngest of four. Two brothers and a sister. They all still live in Texas."

"That would explain the accent within the accent," Riker said. Shooting his sister a sour look, he changed the subject. "Is there a rear door I can back up to so we can load up?"

Jon shook his head. "No need. I'll have Hector and Shane carry your purchases out for you." He whistled to get the attention of a pair of men fixated on whatever was playing out on the small flat-panel TV on the wall behind the counter. It was flanked by a neon GLOCK sign and what looked to be an 8x10 headshot of Uncle Phil from Duck Dynasty. On the screen, a FOX News reporter was watching some kind of large-scale melee taking place. On the left side was a phalanx of riot-gear-clad police officers, or soldiers, no way of telling across the distance. One thing was clear—the civilians screen-right were having their way with the thinning ranks, splitting them here and there and taking a few to the ground. If the scene at Mt. Sinai Hospital was a "shit show" as Tara put it, this was a shit storm. Or, better yet, a shitnado.

Simultaneously Riker's attention was commandeered by Tara and Steve-O.

She was saying, "I want that pink pistol," and Steve-O was coming at him brandishing the largest Nerf gun he'd ever seen. It was orange and blue and fitted with a huge drum magazine and some kind of optics. "Can I get it?" he asked.

Holding Steve-O off with an upturned palm, Riker answered Tara first. "We don't have three days to wait." Then, addressing Steve-O, he said, "Only if I get one too. And grab us a couple of hundred of those foam bullets and some batteries for the guns."

As Steve-O stalked off, Nerf rifle at port arms, Hector and Shane arrived. Both men wore overstuffed black Arc'teryx backpacks. Hector was pushing a four-wheeled cart loaded down with a pair of black Pelican trunk lockers containing the weapons, ammo, and gear Riker had ordered. Shane followed after, a Pelican Storm rifle case in each hand.

Steve-O returned shortly after, armed for bear.

Jon ranged around the counter and rang up Steve-O's *guns* and *ammo*. Addressing Riker, he said, "Who's your friend?"

"I'm right here, dude," Steve-O said as he went to work freeing the guns from their packaging.

"Half cousin," Riker lied. "And he likes to speak for himself. Gets pretty pissy when folks talk past him or for him."

Jon apologized for a third time. Making small talk as he ran Riker's debit card, he asked, "Where you going with all these goodies? You have a redoubt to stock or something?"

"Or something," replied Riker. Picking up his Nerf gun and batteries, he followed Steve-O and Tara to the front door and out into the harsh light of high noon.

While the store employees lugged the gear across the lot to the Shelby, Riker disarmed the alarm, unlocked the rigid tonneau cover, and dropped the tailgate.

As the men shrugged off the packs and stacked the Pelican cases on the blacktop beside the truck, Tara went to work manhandling the packs onto the tailgate and shoving them all the way to the front of the load bed.

With Hector and Shane helping, Riker loaded the cases, arranging them beside the backpacks and assorted camping gear he had picked up at a Dick's Sporting Goods store two days prior.

Riker closed the tailgate and squared up to the men. Extending a hand, he said, "Thank you, fellas."

The taller of the two men, Hector, shook Riker's hand first. He stood a couple inches north of six-foot and came close to being able to look Riker in the eye. He ran his fingers through his long, black beard a couple of times and said, "What do *you* think of the Romeo Victor operation?"

The question took Riker by surprise. Playing it cool, he shrugged and looked to Shane. "What do you think?"

Shane said, "I think Jade Helm was a dry run for all of this."

Hands on hips, Hector nodded.

Shane went on. "Me and Hector been talking. We both think Romeo is the precursor to a nationwide gun confiscation."

Hector nodded in agreement and worried his yellow ball cap. On the cap was a replica of the Gadsden flag, complete with coiled snake and, stitched in red, the admonition *Don't Tread On Me*.

"Only advice I have to give you," Riker said, "is that you *must* believe *everything* you see. Don't let normalcy bias dull your edge."

"What do you mean?" asked Hector. "Elaborate."

Riker shook his head. "It's still very confusing to me, gentlemen. If I had the time to spare, I'd stay and tell you my story. Let you be the judge. But I don't." He paused long enough to start the Ford's motor with the fob. "Just know that this place and who you're with, you're ahead of the curve if things do go sideways. Just trust your gut, fellas."

The men stood there contemplating the advice as Riker climbed behind the wheel. They were still rooted in place as he pulled forward and exited the lot.

Riker pulled into traffic and didn't look back.

He retraced their route back to the 195, along the way passing the Shell station, where out front of the pumps two men were swinging wildly on each other.

Next to the compact with Tennessee plates, two obese men and a tall, rail-thin woman worked together to hold the thrashing driver face-down on the blacktop.

Looking to Tara, Riker said, "It's starting, alright. And you, little Sis, win the award for Understatement of the Year."

Chapter 10

At the juncture to I-195, things had gone from bad to worse. Motorists honked and jockeyed lanes to get past the flagger the F-DOT work crew had recently deployed. While the man in the orange vest held a hand out to calm the drivers he was detaining with a handheld STOP sign, the other workers were packing up tools and policing up traffic cones.

The onramp to 195 West was blocked with unmoving vehicles.

The rising tempest of shouts and blaring horns was reacquainting Riker with the unease that the successful stop at Jonny's had helped to quell.

Leaning forward and swiping the touchscreen, Tara said, "I'm pulling up the nav unit so I can reroute us to the second option that'll swing us west to Naples."

Knowing where west was in relation to his direction of travel, Riker let his gaze roam his mirrors.

Clear.

Seeing a break in the approaching traffic, he hauled the wheel over and stomped the gas pedal.

There was a whine under the hood as the Whipple turbocharger spooled up. Then the horsepower surge was transferred to the rear tires, which grabbed for half a heartbeat, sending the truck into a sharp turn to the left. In the back half of the beat, the tires broke free and the Shelby snapped into the adjacent lane facing west and partially obscured by a drifting veil of blue-white smoke.

The sudden maneuver resulted in a flurry of honking from the cars in the lane previously occupied by the Shelby. One-fingered salutes accompanied the racket as Riker sped through midtown Miami, where traffic was getting worse.

Two blocks west of the interchange, the reason became evident. Like the Shell station, a long line of vehicles waiting to get into a grocery store's already full parking lot wound out into the street, causing traffic ahead to slow down as drivers began to pass in the center turn lane.

Across the street, a convenience store was equally busy.

As if a Cat-5 hurricane was bearing down on the city, Miamians were finally making a run on the stores.

Tara tapped the touchscreen and cycled from the navigation screen to one that detailed fuel consumption. She put her finger on the available range listed there. Sounding rather encouraged, she said, "This says we can go a little over four hundred miles on the gas currently in the tank. That's pretty good, right?"

Taking the wind from her sails, Riker said, "Dolly's tank holds thirty-six gallons."

Tara's brows rose an inch. She said, "What's that … a whopping eleven gallons per mile?"

"Twelve or so. It'll go up by a mile per gallon as soon as we get out of this stop and go traffic."

"Well, well," Tara said. "That almost gives us a whole *forty* extra miles."

"Thirty-six," corrected Steve-O.

"I'll take your word for it," Riker said. Slowing considerably, he slipped the Shelby over to the right lane.

A second later a pair of matte-black Cougar Mine-Resistant Ambush Protected vehicles rolling on six massive tires came barreling around a corner. Bumpers nearly touching, a column of six blacked-out Suburbans following the MRAPs blew the red light to make the turn.

"Looks like Johnnys," Steve-O said. Adding his own gunfire sound effects, he leveled the Nerf rifle at the passing vehicles and pretended to engage them.

Riker said, "Keep it low, man. We don't need that kind of attention."

Coming to Steve-O's defense, Tara said, "These windows are tinted darker than you, Lee. Cut the man some slack."

Riker bristled at the quip. If spending time with people he cared about was teaching him one thing, it was how to pick and choose his battles. And this was one he didn't want to wage. Not now. Not ever. Because Tara's temper belied her stature. If you asked anyone who knew her, they'd declare her a worthy opponent in most arenas—verbal jousting, notwithstanding.

So he bit his tongue and drove on.

***

In less than an hour they were beyond the Miami city limits and pushing west on Interstate 75.

On the outskirts of Miami, the Florida Highway Patrol had been having a field day. Just before the county line they saw three different motorists pulled over. The first two they came upon had been caught by helmeted troopers riding futuristic-looking motorcycles. The third unlucky driver was behind the wheel of a topless, canary-yellow hypercar of Italian heritage. The patrol vehicle parked at an angle behind the million-dollar sports car was a blacked-out Dodge Challenger Hellcat. Only giveaway that the seventy-thousand-dollar American muscle car was a police cruiser was the red and blue lights secreted behind the slatted grille. Flashing rhythmically, the lights seemed to be taunting the bigger fish currently on its hook.

The heightened law enforcement presence kept Riker honest in the speed department until they were forty miles outside of Miami. Here the interstate went laser-straight as it cut into Big Cypress National Preserve, where places to hide a cruiser were few and far between—especially during the day.

Feeling confident, Riker let the Shelby Baja stretch its legs. With passing mangroves and cypress trees becoming a green blur outside the windows, he said, "Keep your eyes open for a gas station or a sign pointing to one."

"I bet stations are hard to come by out here in the sticks," Tara replied as she leaned over to consult the navigation unit. After cycling through the different screens, she made a face, then looked over at Riker, who had the speedometer needle holding steady at ninety miles per hour. "The faster you drive," she added, "the more gas it burns per mile, right?"

"*She* burns gas," said Riker. "It's proper to refer to ships, aircraft, and vehicles as 'She.'"

"OK, smartass. Why are you riding Dolly so hard?"

He smiled. "That sounds kind of nasty."

As the Shelby roared past a pair of SUVs loaded down with camping gear and bristling with bike racks and rooftop gear boxes, Tara stole a glance into the backseat area.

"His ears are no longer virgin," Riker said.

"Doesn't matter," she shot back. "He's fast asleep."

"That pisses me off."

Tara said, "What pisses you off?"

"That he can just switch off like that. That *anyone* can just fall asleep at the drop of a hat."

Tara didn't respond to that. She craned and leaned forward. Then, belt tight on her shoulder, she said, "We've got company."

Riker's eyes flicked to the rearview mirror. "What kind of company?"

"More patrol cars. Up ahead on the right," she said. "They may be setting up a roadblock. They've already got a couple of cars pulled over. You better be ready to stop."

"Seeing as how they're not in my lane, I think I'll play it by ear." Still, Riker braked hard and craned to see what was going on. As their speed dropped below the limit, the nearest patrol car, which had the squat profile of a Dodge Charger, moved to close off the fast lane.

As the Shelby drew to within a couple of hundred feet of the cruiser, Riker got a better look at the stopped vehicles and realized he had let himself get caught up in a hastily constructed checkpoint.

Stopping just shy of the last civilian car in line, Riker saw a trooper approach a car near the front of the line. The trooper stopped beside the passenger window and peered inside. After a beat or two, he leaned over the windshield. Throughout the inspection he moved slowly and methodically, one hand never leaving the butt of his holstered pistol. Everything about the trooper's body language screamed *danger.*

The trooper in the Charger started the light bar strobing, popped open the trunk, and stepped out of the car. Riker saw that the trooper was a woman nearly his height. She covered her trussed brunette locks with the white, wide-brimmed Smokey the Bear Hat and walked around to the open trunk.

Riker said nothing until the female trooper walked to the length of highway in front of her cruiser and started deploying road flares.

"Timing is *not* on our side here. Looks like we missed getting through this by a minute or two, tops." He killed the motor then moved his hand to the back of his neck. Setting the e-brake, he dipped his head and massaged his spasming neck muscles.

Tara said, "Relax, Lee. It'll be all right."

Riker drew in a deep breath and said, "Those Pelican boxes are full of firearms and ammunition."

"They're all legal, right?"

Riker exhaled and nodded as he answered. "They're all legal. However, there's enough of them in there to raise eyebrows. Make someone think we're starting some kind of uprising."

Steve-O stirred in the backseat. A tick later he cut a long, drawn-out fart.

Ignoring Tara's smirk, Riker said, "Plus, there's a loaded shotgun under my seat."

The lady trooper returned to her cruiser, went into the trunk, and came out with more flares.

Tara watched the lady trooper pass on the right, then tracked her in the wing mirror as she lit the flares and set them out at ten-foot intervals.

Meanwhile, Riker was watching the slow approach of the pair of gear-laden SUVs he had passed a couple of miles back. As the lead vehicle came to a halt near the Shelby's rear bumper, the lady trooper materialized outside of Riker's window. She wore a stoic expression and was stabbing a finger toward the road— universal semaphore for *run your window down.*

Chapter 11

Keeping his right hand on the steering wheel, Riker showed his left to the lady trooper, extended his pointer finger, and with it made a show of depressing the button to start his window motoring down.

The trooper said nothing. Her nametag read *Sharpe*.

The window seated and the motor went silent. Steve-O's fart won the battle with the humid, pine-scented air rushing in. If the stench wafting by registered to Trooper Sharpe, she didn't let on.

All business, thought Riker as the trooper remained rigid, staring at him from behind mirrored aviator's glasses. He imagined the eyes roving the interior. Taking inventory of him and the others.

Could she sense the unease he was experiencing due to the presence of the loaded Mossberg 590 Shockwave secreted underneath his seat and mini-arsenal of weapons in the load bed?

Nonsense, he told himself.

Adjusting the brim of her hat, Trooper Sharpe said, "Just the three of you traveling today?"

He nodded. Hoped his Braves cap was absorbing the sheen of sweat he felt developing on his forehead.

Tara leaned forward and shot the trooper a questioning look.

Ignoring Tara, the trooper asked, "Where are you all headed?"

Both hands strangling the steering wheel, Riker said, "We're going camping somewhere on the Handle." A lie, but not exactly. He truly didn't know when or if the gear in the bed would come into play.

The trooper nodded and put a cupped hand against the rear window. "Who's sleepy head back there?"

"Our half-cousin," declared Tara. "We're showing him the great outdoors."

"Well, you all be careful," said the trooper. "Lots of gators. Even more two-legged predators. Might want to stay on the gulf side for a spell. Steer clear of Jacksonville and Orlando. Best if you stay west of I-75."

Riker said, "Why the roadblock?"

The trooper hesitated and spent the time eyeing the SUVs and pair of newly arrived cars sliding in behind them.

Up ahead, the other trooper had concluded his inspection of the first two vehicles and was ushering them through.

Finally, the lady trooper said, "We've got a BOLO for a cop killer last seen in West Miami." No sooner had she said "cop killer" than the handset riding on her shoulder epaulet emitted a burst of squelch, followed by a voice issuing a stand down order.

As the trooper processed the update, her stoic demeanor cracked. Smiling, she looked to Riker. "They got the scumbag."

The smile on the trooper's face was enough to release some of the tension having taken hold in Riker's shoulders and neck.

"Alive?" he asked.

Smile fading, she said, "Unfortunately, yes."

"So we're clear to proceed?"

"In a bit."

"Care to elaborate on what's going on in Jacksonville and Orlando?"

At first Trooper Sharpe said nothing. She cast a furtive glance forward, then covertly checked behind her. Finally, she said, "People are getting sick. They say it's as contagious as Ebola... but—"

"But? But what?" Riker probed.

"But it's transferred like rabies."

Tara crowded Riker. Meeting Trooper Sharpe's gaze, she said, "Through a bite ... right?"

The trooper nodded.

"Are they locking down Orlando and Jacksonville?"

Another brief nod followed by, "And Miami. You know, I really shouldn't be telling you this."

The driver of the SUV behind the Shelby leaned on his horn.

Riker said, "It says to protect and serve on your car. I think what you're doing falls under the former. Do the quarantines have to do with the military op?"

Again the horn blared.

Trooper Sharpe raised a hand at the 4Runner. One finger was extended, telling the driver to wait.

"Get as far away from Florida as possible."

Tara asked, "Is Georgia safe?"

Interrupting the trooper's response, Steve-O said, "California?"

Simultaneously, the siblings shook their heads and blurted a resounding "No!"

"One infected," said the trooper, swallowing hard. "Well, one of the *fast* infected, can infect a dozen others"—she snapped her fingers—"just like that."

Playing dumb, Riker asked, "So there are fast *and* slow infected?"

Now the horn of a vehicle at the back of the line was blaring.

Eyes still hidden behind the mirrored glasses, Trooper Sharpe said, "Stay away from crowds. Don't get bitten." She turned to go to her Charger, then paused to add, "They're dead. So destroying their brain is the only way to stop them. Cut out their legs, they'll keep crawling until they get you. They're relentless. One bite is all it takes."

"She's talking about Bolts," stated Steve-O. Hefting the Nerf gun, he made the sound of a machine gun and pretended to strafe the woods on Tara's side of the truck. "I'll stop those Bolts in their tracks."

Trooper Sharpe held Riker's gaze for a three-count, then turned and strode back to her cruiser.

They had to wait while the troopers policed up their spike strips. Within five minutes the cruisers were on the shoulder and Trooper Sharpe was waving the long line of vehicles on their way west.

**

Immediately after leaving the roadblock behind, Riker matted the pedal and passed the trio of vehicles that had been in the line ahead of him.

With the location of three of Florida's State Patrol cruisers known to him, he wasn't too worried about coming across another until they got closer to Naples, a city on the gulf side where I-75 made a sharp jog to the north.

Thirty minutes into the thunder run through the preserve, some eighty miles from the gun store, Riker slowed to the speed limit and began to pay attention to the right side of the road.

Shifting in her seat and stretching her arms above her head, Tara said, "Looking for a place to pee?"

"A place to stop. Not necessarily to pee."

"That's right," she said. "You were famous for being able to hold yours forever. Always got me in trouble with Dad. Thanks for that, by the way."

A short while later, Riker spotted a rectangular brown sign announcing one of the Cypress Preserve's many wildlife viewing areas.

Riker said, "You gotta go?"

"Ever since the roadblock."

Riker called over his shoulder. "Steve-O ... do you need a bathroom break?"

"I thought you'd never ask. I have to pee like a racehorse."

On the verge of laughter, Riker looked to Tara.

Mouthing, "No you don't," Tara stabbed a finger at the rapidly approaching secondary road. "Here, here ... slow the eff down, Lee."

And he did. But there was nothing graceful about how he went about it. Obviously forgetting all about the cargo in the bed, not to mention his passengers, he applied the brakes as if a brick wall loomed. Next, he slalomed over to the narrow secondary road paralleling the interstate. Then, at the last moment, with Tara holding the grab bar by her head in a two-handed death grip, and Steve-O clutching Tara's headrest in a desperate act of self-preservation, he drifted the truck off of the secondary road and onto the feeder road. Not quite a right-angle maneuver, but damn close.

There was a loud bang in the bed from the shifting contents coming to an abrupt stop against the driver's side wheel well.

The squeal of the tires failed to override Tara's screamed epithets.

"A little warning next time," said Steve-O as he fought to retain his hold on the front seatback.

Bringing the truck back under control, Riker said, "Hold on," and let out a wild war whoop.

Smoothing out the front of her shirt, Tara said, "Feeling alive, Lee?"

"Just seeing what Dolly's capable of. How she handles transitioning from pavement to gravel. That's all." With rocks pinging off the undercarriage, he drove on a couple of hundred yards, then, still smiling, pulled hard to the side of the narrow road and put the transmission into Park.

"You couldn't have done that somewhere between New Jersey and Miami? Maybe pulled that *juvenile* bullshit while you were out running errands by yourself?"

Riker killed the engine. Facing Tara, he said, "I thought we were in big trouble back there at the roadblock. I would've been winging it … driving blind if you will, had I been forced to rabbit and try to outrun the cruisers and their radios."

Face screwed up in a scowl, Tara simply shook her head and stared daggers across the cab.

Steve-O said, "*Everybody* knows you can't outrun a radio."

Tara said, "The man has a valid point."

Changing the subject, Riker elbowed open his door, saying, "We have, at most, a five-minute lead on the rest of the pack. Let's get this done." He looked into the backseat. "Steve-O ... want to be our eyes and ears?"

Hefting the Nerf gun, Steve-O said, "After I pee, I'll be on the lookout for black trucks and Johnnys."

Swinging her gaze to Steve-O, Tara said, "And Bolts. Don't forget about them."

Throwing a mock salute, Steve-O piled out on the driver's side. Nerf in hand and wearing a wide grin, he traipsed to the shallow ditch full of brackish water and ran his zipper down.

Popping the tonneau and dropping the tailgate, Riker got his first look at the unintended consequences of his high-speed turn. The Pelican cases were mashed against the tailgate when it hinged down. The backpacks and sports bags were wedged against the Pelican cases.

The camping gear had fared no better. No longer in a tidy bunch in the corner near the cab, it had been distributed to all points of the compass. And speaking to the violence of the high-g turn, one of the plastic-wrapped cases of bottled water had split open, scattering roughly twenty of the twenty-four bottles about the bed. Amazingly, the case of sports drinks Riker had grabbed from Villa Jasmine's pantry was still intact.

Returning from her quick squat in the nearby woods, Tara said, "Amazing it's not all out on the interstate after that dumbass maneuver, Lee."

"Just good ol' boys," sang Steve-O, smiling ear-to-ear.

"Never meanin' no harm," finished Riker, his gaze settling on Tara.

Shaking her head, she said, "You better have a pink pistol in one of those boxes, Lee Riker, or I'm going to be pissed."

Riker said nothing as he popped the press-and-pull latches on one of larger Pelican cases.

On her toes as Riker lifted the lid, Tara grabbed the bed rail and stared down into the box. "You bought yourself enough guns to start a war, Lee. And not one of them is *pink*."

"We'll get you a can of spray paint at the next hardware store we come across." He reached in and came out with a black plastic case not much larger than a hardcover novel. Embossed on the top was the word Glock, the "G" large and stylized.

He popped the pair of latches and opened the lid. Not going so far as to perform a game-show-model arm-sweep, he spun the box around and made a show of presenting its contents to Tara.

Standing a yard away, Nerf at port arms, Steve-O was taking it all in.

Reaching for the compact black pistol, she said, "For me? What is it?"

Riker waved her off. "First I want to say a couple of things."

Crossing her arms, Tara said, "Go ahead and hit me with your public service announcement."

Hefting the Glock from the padded case, Riker said, "When Jon found out how long it's been since I transitioned, he made me listen to the same spiel."

Tara sot a furtive glance at the distant interstate, then leaned against the truck bed. Eyes on her brother, she crossed her arms over the bed rail and said, "I'm all ears."

Holding the semiautomatic pistol at eye level to Tara, muzzle aimed away from all three of them, Riker said, "Glock 19. Magazine holds seventeen rounds of nine-millimeter. Safety is on the trigger ... *here*. You're a righty so the magazine release you'll use is on the left side ... *here*. And the slide stop lever you'll use is this little metal tab on the left ... *here*." He set the pistol on the foam and, beginning with, "Always assume a firearm is loaded," then, from memory, went down the basic list of firearm safety, at times lifting the Glock from the case to illustrate how to properly handle it. Finished, he set the pistol down and instructed Tara to show him what she had learned.

In the end, after having Tara muzzle-sweep his midsection twice, and rack the slide with her finger inside the trigger guard, he put the pistol away and handed her the Glock's owner's manual and a small brochure listing everything he'd recited to her during his roadside presentation.

"I got it," Steve-O bragged.

Riker stopped unloading the box long enough to cast a glance at his friend. Sure enough, the man had his trigger finger outside of the Nerf gun's trigger guard and was holding the rifle with its non-lethal muzzle aimed in a safe direction.

"You're the man, Steve-O," said Riker, flashing a thumbs-up. "Now help me transfer this ammunition and the rifle cases to the cab."

As Steve-O and Tara began shuttling stuff to the cab, Riker loaded a pair of magazines with 9mm, slammed one home into the well of one of his identical pair of Sig Sauer P226 Legion semiautomatic pistols, and dropped the spare magazine into his pocket.

The black handgun was the new RX Full-Size model and fit his large hand nicely. It was fitted with a ROMEO1 Reflex Sight that had a nifty auto on/off feature. Activated by movement—or lack thereof—the red holographic pip in the reticle was always there when needed.

Riker snugged the weapon into the Fobus paddle holster Jon had so expertly upsold him, climbed behind the wheel, and stowed the holstered pistol in the center console.

Steve-O jumped in back and arranged the rifle cases on the floorboard.

Hearing the tailgate slam shut, Riker watched Tara close and lock the tonneau, then make her way around the passenger side.

Once Tara was back in her seat, Riker started the motor and rolled forward, first and foremost on his mind finding a place to get the wide-body rig turned back toward the interstate.

Chapter 12

Getting the Shelby turned around was easier said than done.

Riker drove about a hundred yards north, to where the road took a shallow bend to the left and the ground-hugging brush fell away from the shoulder on both sides.

Seeing this, he jinked the wheel left, buried the Shelby's beefy bumper into the foliage, and ground to a halt. With the discordant jangle of twigs marring the virgin paint, he spun the steering wheel hard right until it reached its limit. Power steering pump squealing in protest, he ran the transmission lever to Reverse and fed the V8 some gas.

There was a crackling of branches breaking as the truck lurched backward. More of the same entered the cab as he ran the tailgate into the bushes. Silence in the cab as Riker stopped the Shelby perpendicular to the road and eased up off the throttle.

Riker was cranking the wheel in the opposite direction to finish the last leg of the three-point-turn when Tara rapped her knuckles on her window. "Bro," she said, "there's a car blocking the road just past the bend." She paused for a beat, craning to see more.

"Doesn't matter, we're turning around."

"Does it matter if there's a woman waving at me?"

Steering wheel hitting the stops, Riker said, "It's not our business." As he added power, the front end gouged away a good chunk of the intruding forest.

"What if she's having car trouble?"

"What if?" he answered, finally getting the truck pointed back the way they had come.

"What if she has a kid with her? Would that change your mind?"

Steve-O said, "Yeah, Lee. Since when did you start leaving ladies and kids behind?"

Sighing, Riker glanced in the rearview. Sure enough, partially hidden behind the woman's leg was a little boy. Blond hair. Big brown eyes. Healthy tan.

Tara stared at Riker with puppy dog eyes.

Shaking his head, Riker threw the transmission into Park and shut off the engine. Retrieving the Sig from the console, he slipped the paddle over his waistband and adjusted the holster so that it rode comfortably on his right hip. Elbowing open his door, he said, "Steve-O, I want you to hold down the fort while me and Tara go and see what's up."

Steve-O rolled his window on the driver's side halfway down. Poking the Nerf gun's muzzle through the space, he said, "Aye, aye, Rikers."

By the time Riker and Tara had covered half the distance to the woman and kid, a lot more was revealed. The car was a Subaru Forester wagon with Florida plates. It was in the shadows, so its dark green paint made it blend in perfectly with the trees beside the road. Which was why he had missed seeing it in the first place. It also sat a little higher than most cars, which led him to conclude that it wasn't high-centered or stuck in a roadside ditch.

The woman had stopped here willingly.

And as if the wagon had seen a lot of off-road driving, the side and rear windows were coated with road grime. Out back, the rear window wiper had scoured a shape in the dirt that resembled an Oriental fan. The clean patch of window glass was mostly obscured from within by tiny crimson handprints.

Riker said, "Hello."

The woman held her child's head against her hip.

Tara said, "We mean you no harm. We just stopped to pee."

The lady was dividing her attention between her car and the slow-walking siblings.

Riker asked, "Is your car broken down?"

The woman shook her head. Calling across the distance, she said, "It's my oldest boy. He's real sick. He won't talk to me, either. He just growls and bangs his head against the pet partition."

While the woman was speaking, more handprints appeared where the wiper had left its mark.

Knowing the answer to the question before he posed it, Riker asked, "Your oldest, he's in the car now?"

She took a step away from the car.

That was all the confirmation he needed. Now that a bar of sun was hitting both the woman and her kid, Riker got a better look at her face. It was unlined and smooth. So he put her in her early to mid-twenties. And since the top of her head came even with the Subaru's roof rack, he guessed she stood a tick under five foot tall. On her head was a navy-blue ball cap. Poking through the back of the cap was a dishwater blonde ponytail.

As the boy stepped out from behind the young mother, Riker saw that he was still in diapers.

Holding both hands up to show the pair he meant them no harm, he said, "Why'd you stop here?"

With no hesitation, she said, "To separate the boys. It was a real struggle to get my oldest into the back and close the hatch."

Riker said, "You got gas?"

"Half a tank."

He said, "Then I recommend you get in that car of yours and drive straight to a hospital." And though he knew the likely reason for the boy's animalistic behavior, he added, "Better get *both* your boys checked out by a kid doctor."

"Pediatrician," whispered Tara.

Eyes widening, the young mother said, "I don't want to go back into the city. I *won't* go back into the city. The people are all going crazy."

"Where're you coming from?" Tara asked.

"Pine Hills ... just outside Orlando."

"What's your name?" Riker probed.

The woman brought the boy out from behind her leg. Put her hands on his shoulders and said, "Susan. I go by Sue, mostly."

Lowering his hands, Riker said, "Alright, Sue ... what's your boy's name?"

She rubbed sudden tears from her eyes. "That's Samuel in the car. He likes us to call him Sammy."

The toddler smiled and said, "Smell is being mean."

Forcing a smile, Susan said, "Shawn can't say Samuel yet. And he refuses to call him Sam or Sammy. This one's a little hard-headed."

As if on cue, the little boy banged his head into Mom's hip and buried his face in her knee-length skirt.

Riker stole a glance at the Shelby. Saw Steve-O hanging out the window, Nerf gun trained at something down the feeder road. Panning back to Susan, he asked, "Tell me again why you put Sammy in the back?"

"Because the seatbelt wasn't keeping him from getting to Shawn." She paused and regarded her car. Without regaining eye contact, she went on, "Sammy bit Shawn. Barely broke the skin, though. I'm sure he didn't mean it."

Riker didn't like where this was going. "How'd Sammy get whatever he's come down with?"

"A little shit at Sunday school bit him on his back." She made a face. "It's infected. I'm sure of it. It's giving off that smell. Sweet and kind of sour at the same time. Like spoiled ground beef. Here, you take a look." One hand holding the toddler at bay, she reached back and grabbed the handle on the wagon's hatch.

Right hand going for the Sig on his hip, Riker chanted, "No, no, no. Don't open—"

Too late.

Chapter 13

Since when did you start leaving ladies and kids behind?

Riker heard Steve-O's fateful words in his head as the Subaru's rear hatch was on its upward journey. As he saw a pair of small hands slap the glass from within, his Sig Legion was clearing leather and he had come to accept full responsibility for what he was about to do.

Aware of her close proximity to what—with her luck of late—*had* to be a Bolt, Tara turned away from the wagon, dipped her head, and made a break for the Shelby.

All of this came at Riker in slow motion.

Leveling the pistol in the direction of the car, he saw a stick-thin leg kick through the widening gap between the bumper and the rear hatch's lower edge.

Backing away from the slow-to-open hatch, the woman said, "Stop your kicking, Sammy." Looking back to Riker and the rapidly retreating Tara, she added in a low voice, "He's on the *spectrum* and can be a handful sometimes."

Back arched and growling like a cornered badger, the woman's "handful" hit the ground on all fours.

Complete with muddy hands and knees, the boy snapped up and stood erect underneath the open hatch. Sammy was a foot or so taller than Shawn. Head panning slowly right to left, from Tara to Riker to Susan, the boy suddenly went silent. Only when his wild-eyed gaze fell on the toddler did the low growl that had emanated from deep within his gut return.

Hair on his arms and neck snapping to attention, Riker motioned toward the road in front of his feet with the gun. "Susan," he barked. "You have to get away from Sammy."

Run or you're fucked, is what he was thinking as the sound of a palm slapping metal told him that his sister had made it back to the Shelby.

"You behave," Susan bawled. Body shielding Shawn, she put an open hand on Sammy's forehead to keep him at bay.

The move didn't end well for the woman, or Shawn. On the first lunge she lost the tips of two fingers to Sammy's snapping teeth. She shrieked and instinctively brought her hands close to her face for inspection, the unconscious reaction leaving Shawn open to attack.

Riker was already backpedaling to the truck when Sammy pounced on his brother. Blood spritzed from the toddler's neck, the fine mist painting a ragged arc across the mother and the Subaru's side glass.

"Get inside the truck," Riker bellowed, his eyes never leaving the scrum taking place beside the Subaru. He was nearly to the tailgate and still watching his back when he heard what had to be Tara's door slamming shut. As he turned his head to get his bearings, out of the corner of his eye he saw the thing that used to be a young boy named Sammy sprinting straight for him.

With the screams of the hysterical mother rising over everything, Riker reached the truck and looped around the tailgate. No sooner had he come up even with the rear tire on the driver's side than his legs were swept out from underneath him.

Hooking one arm over the bed rail saved Riker from falling flat on his back.

Nearly out of breath, and with the beginning of one hell of a migraine churning in his skull, he pulled himself to standing. Sweeping his gaze groundward, he saw the boy's pale hands wrap around the stainless-steel pylon connecting the ankle joint to the carbon fiber socket snugged onto his stump. Fingers kneading the prosthesis, the thing bit down hard on the steel rod.

The sound of teeth clinking on metal brought Riker instant relief.

Unwilling to use the Sig on a child—monster or not—Riker resorted to kicking at the fifty-some-odd pounds of writhing muscle and sinew chewing on his fake leg.

Riker's first kick to the Bolt's ribs produced a sickening crunch. The follow-on blow saw the tip of his Salomon sink inches deep into the thing's torso without drawing blood—or its attention. Kick number four caught it square on the temple, causing it to blink repeatedly and loosen its grip on the pylon. The fifth, and final blow from Riker's shoe sent the beast rolling away in a cloud of dust. Dislodged by the follow-on sweep of his size 12 Salomon, a shotgun-like blast of gravel rattled the roadside brush at ground level.

By now Tara had been screaming for him to get inside the truck for what seemed like an hour. In reality, the entire event from the clink of teeth hitting metal to the sound of gravel pelting the dry brush had lasted no more than ten seconds.

When Riker turned toward the truck, he found himself looking down the muzzle of a gun. Then there came a whirring noise and Steve-O saying, "Better duck, Lee."

Riker complied, dipping his head under the orange rifle and shooting a hand for the Shelby's door handle. As the flurry of zombie-green Nerf bullets scythed the air where his head used to be, he hauled the door open and stole a look at the scene behind him.

Rising off the gravel, the Bolt was peppered about the head and neck by a flurry of foam projectiles. Behind the unfazed creature, where the shallow bend in the road began, Susan was kneeling, the bloodied and limp form of her youngest cradled in her arms. As the young woman's jaw hinged open and shut, the wound on her neck—nearly identical to the one that stilled Shawn—fed the air in spurts with a fine crimson mist.

"They're all as good as dead," Riker conceded. Slamming the door and firing the motor, he added, "Nothing at all I could have done to stop it."

"*We*," noted Tara. "Nothing *we* could have done to stop it. It's not all on you, Lee."

In the backseat, Steve-O started his window running up and tossed the gun aside. Emitting a trademark *harrumph*, he clicked his seatbelt home and slapped his hands together, brushing imaginary dust from them.

"Good shootin', Tex," Riker said, tromping the pedal.

The truck lurched and fishtailed and twin brown rooster tails erupted from under the rear tires.

Flashing a quick glance at the rearview, Riker witnessed the tiny Bolt running headlong into the barrage of kicked-up rock and dirt. Mouth agape, shark-like eyes affixed to the retreating vehicle, it continued the pursuit for a dozen feet before stopping in its tracks, arms hanging limply at its sides, head beginning a slow pan in the opposite direction.

Knowing what was to come, and not wanting to add the image to his burgeoning vault of nightmare fodder, Riker tried focusing on the white fog-line paralleling the gray stripe of interstate a hundred feet distant.

However, like a passerby at a fatal wreck, he quickly folded and lifted his gaze to the rearview. And he found it playing out just as he had imagined. The Bolt, drawn back to Susan by her wailing, was already atop her prostrate form. Kicked up by flailing arms and legs, a dust cloud hung low over the road.

Just as Riker braked and was dropping his gaze back to the interstate ahead, he saw the toddler rising from the road on shaky legs. As the truck ground to a halt, its wide front end crowding the secondary road, his imagination filled in the blank spots, adding splashes of color and sounds and smells to the feeding frenzy happening on the road behind him.

Tara buried her face in her hands. "We tried," she said. "Lord knows we tried."

Riker said nothing. He was already running the scenario over in his head. War gaming it, so to speak.

The truck was buffeted by the slipstream of a passing eighteen-wheeler.

Wiping away the tears, Tara said, "That's strike two, Lee. You had a gun this time. Why didn't you use it?"

"Because *I* had his back," declared Steve-O. "I took the shot."

Turning right onto I-75, Riker said, "I saw the kid, not the Bolt. I froze. Simple as that."

"Can't say I wouldn't do the same," conceded Tara.

Changing the subject, Riker said, "Who's hungry."

Tara turned in her seat to face Riker. Incredulous, she said, "After all that?"

"I'm famished," said Steve-O.

Sitting back hard in her seat, Tara said, "Place better have toast and saltine crackers."

"And plenty of Tums," added Riker. "Check the computer thingy to see what's coming up."

Chapter 14

A few miles west of the secondary road, they came upon a sign advertising a state-run campground. A shingle hanging off the bottom of the sign read CAMPGROUND FULL.

"If push comes to shove," said Tara, "and we have to sleep in the outdoors, I *will not* want to do so around a whole bunch of other folks."

"That may be the smartest thing I've heard out of you all day," Riker said. Considering what had just happened to Susan at the hands and teeth of her offspring, the last thing he wanted to do was rub elbows with people who might be infected or were harboring loved ones that were.

Ignoring the quip, Tara said, "I may just trump that." She tapped the SYNC display which was already showing the navigation screen. "Naples is right here. It's a big enough city. But not so big that people are starting to act a fool. I'm guessing we'll find a station there where we can top off Dolly's tank."

"Even if it's ten bucks a gallon?"

She said, "I won't like it. But after what happened back there, I just want to get as far away from *people* as possible."

"That's the plan," interjected Steve-O.

"What do you know about the *plan?*"

"I heard you talking with Lee."

"Genie's out of the bottle, then. We're still going to see about finding your cousin, right?"

Brim of the Stetson again cutting the air between the Riker siblings, Steve-O said, "I want to go wherever you two are going."

"You don't want to see if Beverly is still living in Knoxville?"

"No way, Jose. I have fun when I'm with you and Lee."

Riker met the man's gaze in the rearview. "If this is your idea of fun, Steve-O—I'm afraid to experience your idea of a bad day."

Steering the conversation to food and gas, Tara said, "Once we come out of the preserve, look for Exit 101 to Naples. I'm sure we'll have our pick of places to grab a bite and maybe there's an out-of-the-way gas station where we can fill up the tank."

***

The roadblock was some eighty miles behind them on I-75 when they encountered yet another sign of the Romero Virus's rapid spread.

Riker spotted the roadside sign first. It read **NAPLES Pop. 22,272**. Below the first line were the words **8 Miles - Exit 101**. Scrawled with red spray-paint below the F-DOT-supplied information, the cursive letters slightly jumbled, was one word: *Closed!*

"Like, the whole town?" questioned Tara.

"Remember how Middletown rolled up their sidewalks the day we fled?"

A silence descended on the cab as Tara processed that for a moment. During the handful of seconds she was quiet, Riker saw her contemplative expression disappear and the rising and falling of her chest accelerate. He guessed his words had just taken her back to that point in time, and as a result she was reliving their flight from Middletown.

Nodding, she said, "I remember how all the bars were closed. And there was very little police presence."

Riker said, "There was *zero* police presence, if I remember correctly."

"Those guys looting the furniture store sure weren't worried about getting caught."

Steve-O said, "Marcy called the police on some people acting strange out in front of the group home."

Tara turned to face him "What were they doing?"

"They were fighting." He drew in a deep breath. Clearly the memory was troubling to him. As if he was the one fighting the monsters, he balled his hands into fists and brought them before his face. "Marcy was really scared."

Riker asked, "Where was the rest of the staff?"

"Darren was busy putting our bags in the van."

"Did he break up the fight?"

Steve-O shook his head. "He came inside and we all kept quiet until the monsters went away."

Though he was sure of the answer, Riker asked, "The police never came?"

Again with the head wag. "Nope. So we waited until the fight was over."

Eyes scanning the road ahead, Riker said, "They just stopped fighting and left?"

"Yep," said Steve-O matter-of-factly.

"Together?"

"Uh huh. Like they were best buds."

Tara turned in her seat to face him. "Then you all piled in the van?"

"Yeppers."

"And that's how you got to the high school where we were, right?"

Steve-O didn't have a chance to answer. Because Riker spotted movement beside the road, on the right, roughly a quarter-mile ahead.

He pointed as a flaxen-haired woman tumbled from the low scrub fronting a cluster of cypress trees. Crisscrossing pale skin already reddened in places by a horrible sunburn was a road map's worth of angry purple welts.

Likely alerted by the noise of the V8 engine, the woman whipped around to face the approaching vehicle.

At first glance, Riker put the woman in her mid-twenties prior to dying the first time. The tight-fitting khaki shorts she wore that fateful day were muddied and bore dark-red vertical streaks. Barely clinging to her slight frame was a tattered yellow tank. It, too, was stained a shade of crimson that matched the blood dried on her chin and neck.

"Look out," Tara warned.

A quick glance to the mirror told Riker the nearest vehicle was a good distance back. He braked hard, rapidly halving their speed.

He brought the truck to a dead stop perpendicular to the cypress grove from which the figure had just emerged.

Craning to see past Tara, he said, "I already saw *it*." Not *her* or *the woman*—just *it*. And it hadn't been some kind of slip on his part. One look at those dead eyes roving in his direction—even viewed from a great distance and at speed—had cemented his initial assessment.

The abomination was just as far from deserving the title "human" as was the zombie deckhand that had torn into the neighbor and his trophy wife on Sunset Island.

The zombie took a few stilted steps through knee-high grass bordering a rectangular pond of brackish, standing water. Then, oblivious to the obvious outcome, the creature trudged headlong into the pond. Immediately it was waist-deep in the inky morass and continuing onward at a much slower pace.

The surface frothed white for a tick, then the water all around the zombie turned the color of milk chocolate as sediment was kicked up.

Powering her window down, Tara said, "She looks pretty young."

"Younger than you, Pretty Lady."

Shooting Steve-O a look that only a woman whose age had just been questioned could conjure, Tara said, "What I was getting to, Steve-O. Is that she isn't moving very fast. She doesn't seem to have the same dexterity as the other Bolts I've seen."

Watching the zombie struggle to reach the dirt berm on which the nearby guardrail had been planted, Riker said, "Unlike you, Sis ... this one's kind of worn out. Check out those scratches and abrasions. Looks like she died during a bender weekend at Burning Man."

Tara said nothing. She was mesmerized by the tenacity shown by the thing. Its eyes never left the idling truck as it got to the near side of the pond, where the water was knee-high to it.

"Don't you think we ought to put it out of its misery, Lee?"

"What, do you have a mouse in your pocket? Because I'm not part of that *we* alliance you're talking about. That ... *it*, whatever, used to be someone's daughter. Hell, that's even old enough to have been someone's mother." He regarded his wing mirror. Saw the red speck bearing down on them in the right lane become distinguishable as an SUV. Then he recognized the roof-mounted gear boxes.

It was the same rig that had been on their bumper and honking at Trooper Sharpe back at the roadblock.

The zombie was now face down on the pond's muddy shore and struggling to stand. But every time one bare foot would find purchase, the other would shoot out from under it.

Riker stole another quick glance at the SUV. Saw that its right blinker was now strobing.

Clued in to the vehicle rapidly approaching from behind, Tara said, "You can't let them walk into this situation. They're probably going to stop, see it as a bloodied young woman needing help. And then ... they're going to be compelled to help." She dragged the Sig from the console. Handed it butt-first to her brother. "You have to kill it, Lee."

Without warning, the sensation of a vice squeezing his head was back. He could almost feel his shoulders being drawn together due to the instant rigor manifesting in his neck and back muscles.

Wishing he'd remembered to grab his bottle of ibuprofen before leaving Villa Jasmine, Riker shook his head. He said, "Not my job. They're going to have to choose their own fate. If they're stupid enough to let it get close, it's on them." Without signaling his intention, he slipped his foot off the brake and again opened the throttle up, making the truck fishtail and dirt and gravel belch from under the right rear tire.

As the Shelby straightened out and both rear tires found traction on the interstate, Steve-O jumped right back into Waylon Jennings's Dukes of Hazard theme.

Riker watched the red SUV come to a slow-rolling stop on the exact spot on the shoulder the Shelby had just vacated. "Don't let the mud fool you," he muttered to himself as he witnessed all heads in the SUV turn toward the wallowing zombie.

Under her breath, Tara said, "I think you just signed their death warrants, Lee."

"It's not my responsibility, Tara. I'm no cop."

"You've always been the sheepdog. It wasn't just Dad who was always telling me not to be a follower. You had a part in that. In words *and* deeds."

"I joined the Army for a job, Sis."

"And to help get back at the kind of zealots who dropped the Twin Towers. You used to care, Lee."

"I still care. I care more right now than you know." He paused as he regarded the rearview mirror. Seeing three people on the shoulder by the red SUV, and another crawling over the guardrail, he added, "I just want us to survive long enough to get to where we're going. We do that, maybe you can convince me how becoming a big black Mother Teresa is a good strategy going forward."

Face screwed up in thought, Tara said, "How many zombies do you think we've seen since this all started?"

"Not counting the ones on the footage you found on the deep, dark web, or the thousands we saw crowding Battery Park, maybe forty or fifty."

"Deep Web," she corrected. "And how many of those, let's say, fifty have we seen just today in Florida?"

They passed a roadside sign promising all manner of services at the next exit.

Riker said, "Five or six from the yacht—"

Interrupting, Tara stuck out a thumb and motioned toward the headliner. "Higher."

Reluctantly, Riker revised the count. "*Ten* from the yacht. Villa Jasmine's neighbors. Susan and her kids. And now we have Swamp Girl and however many from the SUV she infects."

"Let's assume Swamp Girl gets to all four of them." Tara had been ticking the victims off on her fingers. "That's twenty right there. Then you have the pair of security guards who tangled with the yacht zombies. The responding Dade County PD and SWAT team we passed on the bridge. Are they going to gun down the yacht zombies and rich bitch neighbors? Or are they going to try and subdue them and render aid?"

Brows lifting, Riker said, "I just doomed whoever happens to come across Susan and her kids."

"Add all those up, throw in *their* potential victims, and I think we're looking at another Manhattan scenario, but on a much larger scale."

Steve-O planted both elbows on the front seatbacks. Jabbed a thumb over his shoulder. "You forgot about all the monsters back at the hospital."

Nodding, Tara looked to Steve-O. "I somehow blotted that out." Staring out her window, she added, "And Mount Sinai, I'm sure, is just one of many besieged medical facilities."

Suddenly Riker was dragged back to the night the 4WTC building fell. He was in the helicopter and looking down as they overflew the southern tip of Manhattan en route to the golf course landing in New Jersey. In his mind's eye he saw the group of terrified people trapped between the seawall and stalled-out ambulance. They were huddled down, bloodied, and surrounded by hundreds of zombies. He saw one survivor dragged under the ambulance and into the throng of dead, only to be ripped apart before he could avert his eyes.

As the helicopter passed over the survivors, every one of them had looked expectantly skyward. The sight had chilled him to the bone. In that moment—though every face wore a hope-filled expression—he had shared in the helplessness of their situation.

Throwing a visible shudder, Riker said, "It's scary to hear you put it into words, Sis. But I think you're *hammer on the head* right."

Chapter 15

Coming out of Big Cypress National Preserve, groves of its namesake trees thinned considerably. Shortly thereafter, all at once, the landscape opened up and the interstate cut through parcels of land dotted with old farmhouses, swaybacked outbuildings, and monstrous barns.

The narrow slough of brackish water that had been a common fixture beside the interstate for most of its run through the preserve dried up within sight of the first Naples exit.

Maybe fifty feet from the interstate were a pair of Ford Crown Vic police cruisers, parked across the exit ramp, red and blue lights strobing rhythmically.

A lone officer stood before the nearest cruiser. He was thick around the waist and wore a wide gun belt containing a holstered pistol and all manner of gear. Clutched in one gloved hand was a black AR-style rifle. In the other was a lighted baton which he waved lazily as Riker signaled his intention to exit at the ramp.

Though a powder-blue surgical mask covered the officer's mouth, his message was clear: *Exit closed. Move along.*

So Riker drove on.

A bit further down the interstate, between Exit 101 and 105, positioned within sight of each other, were a number of police motorcycles. Each beefy Harley had an officer astride it. And like the rotund officer manning the first exit, the motor officers were armed with carbines and wearing blue surgical masks.

So Riker drove on.

Nearing Exit 105, where Riker first saw a long line of vehicles being turned away by more of Naples' finest, it became clear to him their plan needed adjusting.

Craning to see the gun-metal gray writing on the sides of the white Ford Explorer SUVs parked sideways across the exit, Tara said, "These are Naples PD, too. The bastards are sealing off the city."

Nodding, Riker said, "Naples is under quarantine."

Steve-O said, "I'm hungry enough to eat a horse."

Sliding into the fast lane, Riker said jokingly, "Civilized people don't eat horse meat, Steve-O."

Steve-O sat back and buckled in. "No duh," he said. "It's just a saying, Lee."

Tara dove a hand into the center console and came out with a pair of Clif Bars. She handed them over the seat. "These will have to do until we find something else."

"Thank you," said Steve-O as he tore into the packaging.

"Steve-O approves," quipped Riker, passing another closed exit ramp. Looking to Tara, he said, "What's our navigation computer showing as the next city?"

"There's a bunch of smaller ones all bunched up between here and Fort Myers."

As Tara manipulated the screen's zoom function, Riker steered the Shelby through a long sweeping right-hander. Soon the interstate straightened out, the twin gray stripes running due north for as far as they all could see.

"Kick on the radio," ordered Riker as another closed ramp blipped by. Only this time, instead of the armed police presence, it was manned by men and women in civilian attire and armed with a smattering of weapons. Blocking the end of the ramp was a lifted late-model Chevy pickup and some kind of foreign compact car.

Tara started the radio scanning through the FM band. It scrolled past the dead areas and skipped the weak signals before acquiring the strong signal of a station broadcasting out of Miami. The female announcer was going on breathlessly about the area hospitals filling to capacity with people who had all of a sudden snapped. "Seen it," said Tara as she pressed a button to continue the scan. "And with my own eyes, too. But, *hon*, those weren't people off their meds." She went quiet and watched the digital numbers climb the dial. Remained attuned to the static coming from the speakers between stations filled mostly with music. On a station based in Cape Coral the deejay was reporting on widescale unrest happening in some of the bigger cities in the central and northern parts of the state. Areas Riker knew they'd have to skirt if they wanted to get out of Florida alive.

Continuing the scan on the AM band, Tara again buried her face in her hands. "I don't know if I have it in me."

Coming upon yet another exit closed off by what looked to be members of an armed militia, Riker said, "You navigate and leave the rest to me. I promise you I won't freeze up next time."

When Tara regarded her brother, the low-hanging sun made her skin glow with a radiance that belied her expression. "I'm not wired for this, Lee."

"And you think I am?"

She said nothing.

Filling the silence, Steve-O issued a plea for more cereal bars.

"You got a tapeworm or something?" she asked as she again dipped her hand into the voluminous center console.

"Or something," Steve-O replied as he thunked his hand palm-up onto the seatback.

After fulfilling the backseat order, Tara cycled back to the navigation screen, scaled it down, then recited the names of the cities in their path.

"Coming up we have Bonita Springs, Estero, and then San Carlos Park, which is real close to Southwest Florida International Airport."

Riker signaled and moved over to let a trio of fast-moving European imports pass. "I hate those bright blue lights kids are putting on their cars these days."

"You sound like Dad, Lee."

"Wish he were here about now. I'd love to pick his brain." He stared off at the westering sun for a beat. Finally, he said,

"The fact they have an international hub here tells me we're going to be passing by some heavily populated cities. What'd that sign back there say the population of Naples is?"

"Twenty-two thousand, two hundred and seventy-two," answered Steve-O.

Looking to Tara, Riker asked, "And how big are those cities coming up?"

By the time they were nearly upon the exit to Bonita Springs, his question was answered by the sign announcing the city and listing its population at 45,659.

Tara said, "That answers that question. Hard to gauge the others because Naples is really affluent, and the homes are mostly spread out. If I had to guess, which is what you're asking me to do, I'd put Estero and San Carlos Park at around the same population as Naples."

"I don't like it," Riker stated. "If those places are not already quarantined, we can't let ourselves get trapped with twenty thousand other desperate people when they do make the call."

"Nothing about Martial Law on the radio," Tara said. "Don't they have to declare it before they go and start denying people the right to travel freely?"

"I have a feeling this is all still localized," answered Riker.

The northbound exit to Bonita Springs loomed, and it, too, was blocked. However, instead of police or civilians and their respective vehicles denying entrance to the city, a dump truck carrying a load of what appeared to be sand sat across both lanes. Speaking to the seriousness of the powers that be in Bonita Springs, the dump truck was backstopped by a Florida National Guard Humvee and a squad of soldiers outfitted in camouflage fatigues and wielding carbines. And like all of the previous exits along I-75, the scene was mirrored a stone's throw away at the opposing southbound ramp.

"I think you're right, Lee." Tara flipped the guardsmen the bird as they passed them by.

"Not cool, Pretty Lady," declared Steve-O. "Those soldiers are just doing their jobs."

Riker edged Dolly back into the fast lane. Cutting the blinker off, he said, "I think Tara was flipping off the situation, not the messengers."

"Since when did you start talking for me, Lee? You channeling Dad now?"

Wisely, Riker said nothing.

Voice adopting a hard edge, Steve-O said, "You're better than that, Tara Riker. Those soldiers would probably rather be at home with their families than standing out in the sun."

"You have a valid point," she conceded. Then, changing the subject, she proposed they drive for as long and far as possible before stopping.

"I'm hungry," said Steve-O."

Tara offered up her share of the Clif Bars.

"You can eat mine too," said Riker. "And when we see a place similar to the Iron Pan, we'll stop and get chicken fried steak and all the fixings."

Steve-O's hand appeared in the airspace between Riker and Tara. Flashing a peace sign, he said, "Two orders and a milkshake and we have a deal."

Speaking nearly in unison, the Riker siblings agreed to the compromise.

Chapter 16

A hundred yards south of the cloverleaf, where arterials branched west to Fort Myers and east to Southwest Florida International Airport, multiple Florida Army National Guard Humvees and what looked to be a couple of squads of soldiers were busy locking down travel on I-75.

With a long run of cement noise-abatement barriers rising from the earthen berm paralleling the southbound lanes to Riker's left, and the narrow slough bordering the northbound lanes to his right, he couldn't fathom a better place to control access to the rest of Florida and all points beyond.

Looking left, Riker saw a number of multi-story apartment buildings, their red-tiled roofs rising a dozen feet over the noise barriers. To his right, beyond the narrow strip of standing water, was a large shopping mall. The acres of gray asphalt ringing the sprawling affair were mostly devoid of cars. He saw nothing moving over there. Not a single person on foot. No vehicles sliding into a lined parking spot. Nothing.

Dead ahead, though, a pair of armed soldiers stood before a barricade decked out with reflectors and flashing amber lights. A third soldier stood a safe distance from the driver's door of the first vehicle in a short line of three. As Riker braked and slid Dolly into the right lane, he saw the driver of the silver-gray minivan at the head of the line step out onto the freeway lane and form up in front of the soldier.

Setting the brake and leaving the motor running, Riker craned and watched the minivan driver remove his shirt and turn a slow pirouette before the African American soldier.

After inspecting the man's arms and torso, the soldier crouched to give his bare legs a once over. Rising, the soldier held a short conversation with the man, then sent him back to his vehicle and waved him through.

The scene was repeated two more times, and both times the drivers and passengers were subjected to the same inspection and then allowed passage.

"Our turn," Riker said, slow-rolling the pickup forward. While the African American guardsman had been busy inspecting the driver and passenger of the second car, Riker had slipped the Sig underneath his seat with the shotgun and, with his heel, shoved them both as far back as possible.

As the guardsmen put the driver and pair of passengers of the third vehicle through the same inspection—the two women being scrutinized by a female soldier, off to the side where the Humvees provided a modicum of cover—Riker, Tara, and Steve-O had huddled together to get their stories straight.

While one guardsman moved the barrier aside to let a cleared vehicle pass, the African American who seemed to be running the show waved the Shelby forward.

Speaking out of the side of his mouth, Riker said, "Be cool," and let his foot off the brake.

"Like the Fonz," Steve-O remarked, flashing a thumbs-up between the front seat headrests.

"Exactly," said Riker. "Like the Fonz."

Perplexed, Tara looked to Riker. "Who?"

Rather dismissively, Steve-O said, "Never mind. He's before your time."

The soldier in charge watched the Shelby's approach, finally putting a hand up when the bumper was nearly to his knees. Unlike the other guardsmen, he wasn't wearing a pair of Gargoyles or Oakleys. He fixed a no-nonsense gaze on the Ford and walked confidently to Riker's door.

Chin level with the road and the brim of a soft top cover shielding his eyes, the soldier asked, "What's your business?"

Smiling, Riker sized the man up. The tape on his MultiCam uniform read: *Wilcox*. The black triple chevrons on the patch on his sternum told Riker he was a sergeant. And if he were forced to guess the cleanshaven kid's age, he'd put him anywhere between twenty-five and thirty.

"We're going camping on the Panhandle. But first, we need to stop for gas and supplies. Is Fort Myers open for business?"

As Riker spoke, the sergeant was surreptitiously sizing him and the others up.

Eyes now roaming the tonneau cover, the sergeant motioned another soldier to the passenger side and asked everyone to exit the truck. "This will just take a minute or two, then you'll be on your way."

Famous last words, thought Riker as he stepped from the truck. Turning toward the sergeant, he found they stood nearly eye-to-eye. However, the younger man had at least thirty pounds on him, all of it muscle. As he ordered Riker to remove his shirt, he backpedaled away from the open door and moved to one side. Even at six-foot-three and two hundred and sixty some-odd pounds, the kid moved like a predatory big cat.

Riker complied, unbuttoning and removing his shirt. Draping it on the mirror, he stuck his arms out and performed the pirouette before being ordered to do so.

"How do you explain these recent scratch marks on your back?"

"Rough sex," Riker said, offering up the same lie he'd told the female soldier at the high school in Middletown, a week ago, when all this madness began.

"You'll have to drop your shorts."

Riker hesitated a tick before complying. He wanted to say: *Is this all necessary?* but knew deep down that it was. He also had a suspicion it all fell in the "too little, too late" category.

As Riker conducted another clockwise rotation, the sergeant scrutinized his legs, front and back.

Finishing his second clockwise rotation, Riker met the sergeant's steely gaze.

Voice softening a bit, the sergeant asked, "Where'd you get the scars on your legs and torso?"

"Iraq," said Riker. "Roadside IED. Same one that left me with the bionic south of my knee." He lifted up his Braves cap. Showed the sergeant the pink scarring running from one ear, over his forehead, and down the opposite temple. "The burns were the icing on the cake."

From across the bed, the younger of the two guard soldiers shouted, "Sarge ... you've *gotta* see this dude's tattoo."

Shooting a glare suitable to quiet the subordinate, Wilcox handed Riker his shirt and scooped his shorts off the ground for him. Leaning in, he said, "You can go west or north from here. Fort Myers's businesses have raised their prices through the roof. But it's pretty much the same everywhere."

Tara called out, "Can we get going, Lee?"

Riker saw her in his side vision. Just her head and shoulders over the nearby Humvee. She was pulling her tee shirt on. Spotting a snatch of her lacy bra, he averted his eyes and raised his palm to let her know he'd heard her. Staring past the sergeant at a spit of grass under cover of a distant overpass, where a couple of dozen civilian vehicles sat amongst a number of colorful airport shuttles, he asked, "What's the interstate look like from here to the Florida/Georgia line?"

"Same as south of here—hit and miss. Some towns are shutting down. Some are open for *gouging*."

"Is this about the sickness?"

Sergeant Wilcox nodded.

Both doors on the other side of the truck opened, then quickly slammed shut. The rig was rocking slightly as Riker said, "How bad is it?"

"Romero owns the Atlantic Seaboard from Maine to Miami. We're on the verge of losing the entire eastern half of my state."

Incredulous, Riker said, "Romero? You've got to be kidding me. That's what the no imagination crowd inside the Beltway are calling this bug?"

The sergeant said nothing. However, he *was* shaking his head.

During the entire time spent stopped on the interstate—ten minutes, max—Riker had noticed the total absence of air traffic landing or taking off from the nearby airport.

Nodding toward the airport shuttles, Riker said, "The airport is *real* quiet. What are the shuttles for? You taking anyone with a fresh scratch or who you suspect was bitten to the airport? Stow them in a hangar or something?"

The sound of a racing motor broke the still. A sidelong glance told Riker he was hearing the same red SUV that seemed impossible to shake. It was still quite a ways out and coming at the roadblock with a full head of steam.

Motioning for one of the guard soldiers to open the makeshift gate, brows furrowed, the sergeant said, "I'm going to say this and then you have to be on your way. The supposed training exercise they're now calling Romeo Victor started out as Vigilant Sweep. Something happened early on and its designation was changed. Call it what you will, but it was all about early containment of the Romero bug. As we speak, CDC and USAMRIID are setting up shop at the airport. MacDill is the operational hub of the southern containment efforts. USSOCOM is tasked with creating a north/south firewall to allow time for assets to be relocated along the Ohio River Valley." He stopped long enough to get another soldier's attention and order him to tend to the injured people spilling out of the red SUV. Turning back to Riker, speaking in a near whisper, he added, "One soldier to another ... if I was in your shoes, I would get to somewhere real light in population and bivouac there until we get a handle on things."

The Shelby's horn blared, causing both men to start.

Shaking the sergeant's hand, Riker offered a sincere and heartfelt thanks.

Shooting Tara a sour look, he climbed into the Shelby, started the motor, and got them moving north, toward the exit to Fort Myers, where he hoped to find food, fuel, and a bathroom—but not necessarily in that order.

Chapter 17

Washington, D.C.

White House Situation Room

President Henry Tillman tore his slate-gray eyes from the flat-panel monitor dominating the wall at his end of the five-thousand-square-foot rectangular space officially known as the John F. Kennedy Conference Room.

Situated a dozen feet beneath the West Wing, its rebar-reinforced concrete ceiling and walls able to withstand a near direct hit from an ICBM-delivered nuke, the White House Situation Room was abuzz with activity.

On the President's right sat the Secretary of Defense, retired United States Marine Corps General Thomas "Tank" Marigold. A highly decorated former Commander of the 1st Marine Division in Iraq, Marigold had seen combat on multiple continents during his thirty-year stint in the Corps. The fireplug of a man twirled one end of his handlebar mustache and continued to watch what the President would not.

On the monitor was live footage shot by an MQ-9 Reaper unmanned aerial vehicle flying a racetrack orbit half a mile east of the White House. Parked in an inverted V, behind two rows of two-thousand-pound cement Jersey barriers, some of the SecDef's Marines were in the fight of their lives.

In ones and twos, fast-movers would appear from the shadows of buildings or burst from within a large pack of slow-moving zombies spread out across Pennsylvania Avenue. The skirmish line was very near to the National Archives building, inside of which was housed the Declaration of Independence, Bill of Rights, and many more of America's most treasured documents.

Highly mobile, newly turned specimens the soldiers were calling "Zips" met the Marines' fierce barrage of fire head on. Speeding bullets tore limbs from bodies and fresh blood painted the street and sidewalks as the infected sprinters' bodies spasmed and fell here and there.

Many of the felled creatures would stand again, waver for a beat, and then renew their attack as if hurtling hunks of lead hadn't just cleaved meat from their bones or blown holes clean through their torsos. Shredded muscle and tendon or severed spinal cords stole from large numbers of Zips and slow-movers the ability to rise again. Undeterred, the multitudes of fallen zombies simply dragged themselves off of curbs, along sidewalks, or across oil-stained thoroughfares to get to the meat manning the cupola-mounted machine guns atop a pair of up-armored Humvees.

The SecDef turned to President Tillman, who was leaning forward, eyes closed and massaging his temples with his thumbs.

"As confident as I am in the training those men out there have had, not to mention the combat experience the vast majority of them have accrued from multiple deployments in the Sandbox, I cannot, in good conscience, let them continue on this fool's errand."

Meeting Marigold's gaze, the President said, "Quit beating around the bush, General. What's your assessment?"

Without pause, the SecDef said, "Containment has failed. The District is lost. Which means the White House is also lost."

The President steepled his fingers and looked a question at Department of Homeland Security Head Maria Salazar.

The petite Hispanic met Marigold's steely gaze. Held it for a beat, then said, "I concur." She broke eye contact and aimed a remote control at the wall-mounted monitor across from the President.

The display snapped on. Front and center on a field of blue was the Presidential Seal. The seal faded quickly, giving way to a full-sized map of the Continental United States. Alaska and Hawaii were not represented.

The highly detailed map was awash with red dots from the Carolinas north. Small clusters of green dots were interspersed with the red outside the more populated cities.

Washington D.C. was an island of red amongst a spreading sea of the same.

West of the Carolinas, green dots vastly outnumbered the red, with the latter beginning to appear in real-time in and around the larger cities with stunning regularity.

The states surrounding Lake Michigan were mostly red. From the amount of color on the eastern edges of Iowa, Missouri, Arkansas, and Louisiana, it looked as if Romero was making a steady push west.

Evidence of the outbreak was nearly nonexistent from Texas on up to North Dakota, and as far west as Colorado.

A few blips of red marred the map between the Rocky Mountains and the West Coast, where the virus had established a firm foothold in California.

"What about Hawaii and Alaska?" asked the president.

"So far Alaska is sterile and should remain so. Hawaii and Oahu, on the other hand, are not. They are both sealed off to sea and air. Have been since Tuesday last when the first jets carrying infected landed."

"The other islands?"

Salazar grimaced. "So far, so good," she said.

Tillman exhaled. Fearing the answer he was about to receive, he reluctantly proceeded with his next line of questioning. "How are our borders? And foreign aid ... is it coming?"

"Mexico has beefed up its Northern and Southern borders. Coyotes are still moving bodies into CONUS, but apprehensions are way down. Canada was working with us on containment. However, in the last twenty-four hours they've closed all border checkpoints. They're going hermetic on us." She paused and locked eyes with the SecDef. After detecting his subtle nod, she went on with the bad news. "Thanks to the Logan incident, the genie is not only out of the bottle, he's on a worldwide tour."

As she paused again, the SecDef said, "For the moment, while our allies and enemies alike work on containing the virus on their own soil, we, Mr. President, are on our own."

Tillman downed the remainder of the Scotch in his glass and slammed the crystal item down hard on the desk. "And now Mother Nature is adding insult to injury. What's the latest on Owen? Glancing blow or is he going to kick us in the balls?"

"These are the latest developments," said Salazar, indicating the monitor across from the President.

As President Tillman and the others assembled around the table looked on, she enlarged the image on the monitor until the South Atlantic states and Hurricane Owen—still a Cat-2 spinning lazily over open water—dominated the monitor.

"This time a week ago," bellowed the President, "we had *three* flashpoints … Middletown, Manhattan, and Logan International?" He paused to pour himself more Scotch. Looking his SecDef in the face, in a voice devoid of emotion, he asked, "Tank, tell me how in the hell this thing got away from us."

For the first time in his sixty-six years on the planet, Thomas Marigold was struck speechless.

On the monitor the image finally scaled to reveal dozens of new red dots erupting in Georgia and Florida. Simultaneously, in Atlanta, Orlando, and Miami, multiple clusters of green dots winked out, only to be replaced by more red.

"This is still real time?" asked President Tillman.

Salazar nodded. "We are losing hospitals to the sickness faster than we can dispatch teams to combat the outbreaks."

Indicating the small pockets of green remaining on the Eastern Seaboard, President Tillman said, "We throw two brigades of the 82nd, nearly half of the 75th Ranger battalion, and every last man of the third Special Forces group at this problem, and that's *all* we're holding to the east?"

Having processed what he was witnessing on the multiple monitors spread about the rectangular room, the SecDef said, "This is no ordinary enemy. These things aren't affected by wounds that would stop a normal combatant. They don't halt their advance to check on their fallen. They can't be demoralized. They show no remorse. And they *never* tire. Which means they don't stop to rest or sleep. Furthermore, they *are not* predictable in their movements. Especially the Zips. One second a sniper has one of them in his sights, the next, the sniper is trying to shoot something that's moving like a chicken that just had its head lopped off."

Salazar asked, "How's the bombing campaign panning out?"

"It's not," admitted Marigold. "Oh, a thousand-pound bomb thins them out a bit, but nothing—and I mean *nothing* we have tried so far slows their advance. The virus not only brings them back after death, it also awakens a dormant prehistoric instinct to hunt and feed. And it's us they *must* hunt and consume. And they're beginning to form packs to do it." He took a sip of water. "With all their degrees and infinite wisdom," he went on, "even the pointy heads at USAMRIID say there's nothing we can do to rewire those responses."

As the SecDef paused and drew a breath, President Tillman asked, "How long does it take for them to fully degrade?"

Like the infection on the map, red had creeped up from under Marigold's collar and spread to his cheeks. He loosened his tie, then said, "Still undetermined. The scientists think the virus is continuing to mutate. The tweaks Zen Pharma made to Romero during trials that prolonged life in the original test subjects, the same tweak that allowed them to stay in the fight even after a mortal wound that had the test subjects bleeding out"—he shook his head, a look of incredulity on his face—"may be doing the same to the flesh of the infected *after* death."

The President threw his hands up, then snatched the crystal tumbler off the table. Downing the Scotch, he asked, "Why didn't we have our own people inside Zen?" He didn't wait for an answer. He knew that just as lobbyists' money greased the skids in the Capitol Building just up the street, plausible deniability was the grease that kept blowback of dark projects gone awry from sticking to those in power who tacitly endorsed said endeavors.

"Don't answer that," muttered the President as he looked around the room. Finished scrutinizing the faces of those assembled for what was likely the last meeting in the White House for the foreseeable future—if not ever—he pounded a fist on the table. "Damn it all to hell. We were there for the rest of the world when they needed us. Where in the *hell* are they now?"

"They're battling this, too," noted Salazar. "That debacle at Logan International saw to that. Sent thousands of infected travelers winging blissfully away to all points of the compass. I have to be frank with you, sir. You dragged your heels on grounding all air travel."

"Can't dwell on the past. We have to think about what's in front of us right now. And right now, it's clear that we're on our own," said the President to no one in particular. Regarding Marigold, he asked, "So where *do* we go from here?"

The SecDef opened a briefcase and removed a stack of sealed envelopes marked EYES ONLY. He placed one on the table before the President. Passing the rest around the table to the essential players, he said, "I recommend you enact Protocol Delaware."

A heavy silence descended on the room as manila envelopes were unsealed and documents scrutinized.

Chapter 18

Just as the National Guard sergeant had promised, Fort Myers was indeed open for business.

And business was booming.

Sparing no detail, as he continuously scanned the two-lane ahead for a suitable gas station, Riker filled Tara and Steve-O in on all that the sergeant had divulged to him.

"Romero? Really?" Tara said, throwing her hands up. "Naming the flippin' virus after the *King* of the zombie genre?"

Riker said, "At least that explains why the soldiers the reporter overheard were calling it Romeo Victor." He shook his head. "Romero Virus. No imagination, is right."

Speaking in a near whisper, Tara said, "Lee, there were people in the Hertz van back at the cloverleaf." She swallowed hard. "And I could have sworn I saw a few body bags on the grass between the Budget and Enterprise vans. Only these bags were white, not black."

Having been focused on slaloming past debris left on the interstate by a multicar pileup, Riker hadn't been able to get a good look at the assemblage of airport shuttles, let alone the grass infield where they were parked. So he asked the obvious question. "Did you see any movement in the bags?"

She shook her head. "Nope. But it was clear to me they were all full."

In the backseat Steve-O was singing a song likely inspired by something Riker had said during his recounting of the conversation with the tall sergeant.

Tara turned in her seat. "'Cleansed from the demons who were stealing my freedom.' Damn prescient lyrics you were belting there, Steve-O. Whose are they?"

"Florida Georgia Line. From a really, really good song called H.O.L.Y."

Together, the siblings nodded in understanding. Lord knew each had faced their share of demons. Albeit nothing like the creatures created by the aptly named Romero Virus.

The exit Riker took curled off the interstate and eventually fed onto Alico Road, which was lightly traveled in both directions. The Shelby was in the pole position at the light and all alone on the two-lane. Once the light cycled to green, Riker turned left and stayed in the far lane.

More options should evasive driving become a necessity.

The stress knot that had developed between his shoulders during the strip search was now just a dull ache. And, thankfully, the beginnings of a migraine had ebbed to that familiar throb behind his eyes.

"Should have gone right," Tara said. "Lots of food choices that way."

"For one, I didn't like the vibe the mall was giving off. My gut is still telling me to stay the hell away," Riker answered. "Besides, fuel is our first priority."

Steve-O said, "Maybe your gut's trying to tell you it's hungry. Because *my* gut is telling me to find a cow and eat it. I am *that* hungry."

"So hungry you could eat a *whole* cow, eh, Steve-O? I'm with you on the beef. Maybe just a ribeye or porterhouse, though. Not the whole damn bovine."

Tara laughed for the first time in a long while.

After a few blocks, they came upon the first opportunity for gas. Seeing the long line of cars beginning at the pumps and snaking around back of the 7-Eleven, Riker shook his head.

"Eight ninety-nine a gallon for regular unleaded?" crowed Tara. "Bend us over, why don't you."

"You forgot the nine-tenths," joked Riker.

"Eff their sneaky extra nine-tenths of a penny," declared Tara as she zoomed in the map on the navigation screen a couple of stops. "Lookie here. There's a RaceTrac station two blocks up, on our right."

"I see it," said Steve-O.

Riker slowed and threw on his blinker.

The pumps at the RaceTrac were all occupied. However, unlike the nearby 7-Eleven, there was no line worming out onto the street.

Where the 7-Eleven was happy to display evidence of their price-gouging on their reader board, RaceTrac's was blank.

As Riker slalomed the Shelby onto the station's white cement pad and parked behind the Toyota Tundra pickup currently connected to the pump, he noticed a sandwich board on the sidewalk. It faced Alico Road. NO EBT - DELI CLOSED was written in neat block letters on a sheet of paper taped to the top of the sign. NO DIESEL - REGULAR AND SUPREME ONLY - INQUIRE INSIDE FOR PRICE had been scrawled directly on the sign.

The last piece of *information* gave Riker pause. For it was likely the reason the lines at the pumps were nonexistent. In his experience, word usually traveled fast when it came to both good *and* bad deals.

Stabbing a finger at her window, Tara said, "Look at that. There's no price per gallon on the pumps, either. Last time I checked, a bunch of zeros all in a row was still zero."

Steve-O said, "Woo hoo! Looks like gas is *free* today."

Talking over his shoulder, Riker said, "Nothing in life is free, Steve-O." He regarded Tara. "I'm going to leave the keys. Make sure you lock up right away. And keep a close eye on our stuff in back."

"On it," said Steve-O. Nerf gun in hand, he unbuckled and went to his knees on the seat.

"Good job, bud," said Riker. Then he took orders for snacks and drinks.

The glass in the door to the RaceTrac minimart was streaked with who knew what. So Riker barged through, elbow leading the way. A bell dinged and the door closed behind him.

Off to Riker's right, two men stood before a counter cluttered with all manner of small items for sale. Shoehorned in among the clutter was a cash register and lottery machine. Behind the counter was a man with a deep tan. He was average-sized and wore a blue tunic with *RaceTrac* across the front. The cashier's short hair was coal black, parted down the middle, and glistened under the overhead fluorescent lights.

When the bell dinged, the customers turned their attention from the transaction at hand to cast identical glares at Riker.

Ignoring the men, Riker grabbed a plastic basket from the floor by the door, wove his way between the aisles, and filled it up with items from the list he'd just committed to memory. After cruising the back of the store and adding cold beverages atop the snack items, he spotted, lined up side-by-side on a low shelf, a half-dozen five-gallon gasoline cans. Seeing no price tags, he slipped the basket handles over one arm, grabbed two cans per hand, then got in the checkout line.

Standing before the counter, an empty newspaper rack crowding him on the left, and two middle-aged wheeler-dealer types on his right, Riker passed the time by listening to the men haggling over prices and watching the television above the stoic cashier's left shoulder.

The young guard sergeant's insider info was confirmed when on the Chyron below a scene showing a roadblock somewhere in Middle America, Riker read the words **Operation Vigilant Sweep**. As the ticker scrolled on, he learned that a high-level official turned whistleblower had mailed to a number of news outlets proof of a cover-up that went all the way to the top. A cover-up that was confirmed when a number of thumb drives containing footage shot in various places in the Central and Eastern parts of the United States showed up in the mailrooms of many of the same news outlets.

Clearly the cat was out of the bag nationwide. And Tara was partly responsible. Though Riker couldn't be sure, it was highly probable the thumb drives alluded to were the ones his sister had mailed out to news outlets days ago. This new revelation made Riker wonder just how long the President would let the charade continue before he was forced to declare Martial Law.

As the men at the counter continued to bitch at the cashier about his pricing, Riker kept one eye on the lookout for anything that might indicate he was about to be in the middle of a holdup, and the other on the television. Just as the smaller of the two men gave in to whatever his issue was, and slapped cash and coins on the counter, a balding man wearing a white dress shirt and red power tie filled up the television screen.

The man loosened his tie and popped the top two buttons on his shirt. He donned a pair of readers and began to slowly unfold a sheet of paper. During all of this he didn't speak or look directly at the camera filming him. When the man finally lifted his gaze and looked into the camera, it dawned on Riker exactly who he was staring at.

"*Aleksei Volkov*," Riker muttered. "What does that *dick* want?"

No sooner had Riker voiced it than a graphic popped up on the screen with the Russian President's name and a tag indicating the feed was live and being shot in an undisclosed location somewhere in Russia. Then the graphic was replaced by the words: *Russian President Aleksei Volkov accuses U.S. of releasing bio-warfare agent on Russia soil.*

Not caring who was listening, Riker said aloud the words he was reading on the crawl. "Volkov officially declares he has put his military and nuclear forces on Elevated Combat Readiness—third highest level."

"I would bet that putting the Motherland on a true war footing is next on his list," said one of the men ahead of Riker as the shorter of the two grabbed their bags and headed for the door.

"Next," said the cashier.

As he moved forward and looked down on the cashier, Riker saw that *Enrique* was embroidered in red on the left breast of his RaceTrac work shirt. And the name made perfect sense, because it went with the cashier's thick Cuban accent.

Riker placed the gas cans on the floor, then set the overflowing basket on the counter. Meeting Enrique's hard stare, he said, "This stuff in the basket, the four gas cans on the floor ... and I'll need to gas up the truck at pump four."

Enrique didn't say a word. He went to work, taking the items from the basket and placing them one at a time in a pair of large paper sacks.

Riker watched for a moment, noted the man wasn't using the register to his left to add up the items, then returned his attention to the television.

Seeing Riker staring past him, the cashier glanced at the television. At once, words dripping with venom, he said, "*Aleksei Volkov* ... the *defender wolf*. He is *nothing* of the sort his name would suggest. *Wolf?* For sure. *Defender?* Of only his own interests."

Snapping back to the moment, Riker said, "Regarding your sign out front. I'm guessing the answer is along the lines of *If you have to ask. You probably can't—*"

"Afford it," interrupted Enrique. "That's your problem, not mine. Twenty bucks a gallon. Unleaded, supreme—same price."

Good thing for you Tara's not here, Riker thought.

But out loud, he said, "I'm coming from Miami. We have a long slog north. Sure there's no flexibility in price?"

The bell above the door rang and a man and woman entered the store. He was carrying a plastic gas can. She immediately peeled off and fast-walked toward the rear of the store.

Enrique regarded the couple, then his eyes made a quick lap of the security mirrors positioned about the store. Finished, he returned his gaze to Riker. "Last fuel truck came this morning. If there will be another shipment, it won't happen until next week. See where *I'm* coming from?"

Riker shrugged. "I figure my rig needs twenty gallons. It'll take the same to fill these cans."

"A hundred and eighty dollars for the groceries."

Six-hundred-percent markup, Riker thought. Still, he matched the cashier's stoic demeanor and went on staring at the television as the Russian President blamed every one of the Motherland's woes over the last twenty years on the United States and her allies. Volkov had just gotten around to blasting President Tillman personally for the Romero virus reaching Russian shores when Enrique said, "Your total is one thousand, one hundred and eighty dollars."

As Riker dragged out his wallet—a new hand-tooled leather item he'd picked up at a truck stop outside of Fayetteville—the bell rang again and two African American teenagers entered the store.

Riker slapped his debit card on the counter. "Answer me this, Enrique. What's the extra two hundred bucks for? Your kid's college fund?"

"Cash only," Enrique demanded. He stood on his toes, head craned toward the rear of the store, and watched the teens' every move.

Finding himself being totally ignored, Riker cleared his throat.

Enrique looked sidelong at Riker. "The two hundred is for the gas cans," he sneered. "Nothing is free in this world, *my man.*"

My man?

Fifty bucks apiece for a fifteen-dollar item?

Riker didn't like the man's attitude and was beginning to feel the slow burn of anger he knew all too well.

Looking up at Riker, Enrique said, "Pay my prices or go shop somewhere else."

Violating Riker's personal space, the teens reached past him and slammed down a pair of forty-ounce bottles of Budweiser. Rattling the glass counter, the artillery-shell-shaped bottles ended up just inches from his hand.

No apologies followed.

Riker closed his eyes and looked toward the ceiling. When he opened them a moment later, he happened to be looking at the television and couldn't help but read on the bottom crawl that the Russian president was considering the release of the Romero virus as "tantamount to an act of war."

This asshole to my fore.

These assholes to my left.

And that asshole on the television.

Out of the blue, something Riker had heard in a song long ago came to him. So he hummed a few bars, then sang, "Stuck in the middle with you."

"Better keep your day job, brother," said one of the teens. The top of his head came up to Riker's shoulder, with the expertly picked-out afro extending a few inches beyond.

"Focus on you paying the man," said the other teen. "I wanna get my drink on."

The couple that had entered before the teens got into line. She was loaded down with two baskets overflowing with junk food. He was still carrying the gas can and had picked up a case of beer and a big bag of ice.

Riker met the man's gaze. Saw that the man was scared of something, and it wasn't him. Because the man said, "You need to hurry the *fuck* up. Things are happening out there as you idiots dilly-dally in here."

Crack jokes, not bones, was what one of Riker's anger management counselors urged him to remember during encounters such as these. And bolstering that sage advice, in just about every self-help book Riker had ever read on the subject, rule number one to getting the most dangerous of emotions in check called for diffusing the situation with humor.

Demanding payment, Enrique waggled his fingers at Riker.

As Riker dragged a thick wad of hundreds from a pocket, maybe five thousand dollars' worth, Volkov's likeness was replaced on the television by a graphic showing a colorful storm tracking north by west across the Caribbean. Superimposed over the graphic was a local weatherman. Reading the crawl, Riker learned that a developing tropical storm named Owen was being upgraded to hurricane status. As the rotund Hispanic reporter went on to describe the actions Floridians were taking to prepare, Riker slowly peeled off twelve crisp hundred-dollar bills and gently deposited them on the counter next to the fiery Cuban's upturned hand.

Turning the other cheek is better than going to jail, Riker reminded himself as he looked the impatient group over, one by one. Settling his gaze back on the proprietor, who was waving a limp twenty-dollar bill in his face, Riker said, "What did the leper say to the prostitute when he was finished?"

Still holding the twenty, Enrique said, "Spit it out."

"You're real close, Enrique." After a brief pause, during which Riker grabbed his bags and corralled the empty gas cans, he said, "Keep the tip."

Leaving Enrique holding the Andrew Jackson, the teens staring slack-jawed at each other, and the middle-aged man and woman laughing hysterically, Riker strolled out of the store all the richer for it.

Chapter 19

White House Situation Room

The six men and two women assembled around the rectangular table had remained silent for several minutes as they pored over the top-secret documents.

Sixty-year-old Speaker of the House, Carter Ashe, spoke first. Looking over the top of his bifocals, he said, "Splitting the government up and relocating it to the Greenbrier, Mountain Weather, and … *Site R*, makes sense for continuity. However, I have two questions. One, why aren't we utilizing NORAD headquarters in Colorado? It's arguably our most secure site." He pointed to the map. "And there's more green than red in Wyoming and the surrounding states. The sites mentioned in the brief are all near major population centers whose hospitals have already fallen, or are on the verge of doing so." He paused to sip from a bottled water. Resuming, he said, "The hospitals in Colorado Springs are all still operational. Plus, you have Fort Kit Carson, and a couple of Air Force Bases just a short helicopter ride from the Cheyenne Mountain Complex."

Marigold raised a hand, silencing Ashe. "With all due respect, Mister Speaker. Your points are valid. However, Colorado Springs is too far removed from D.C. We relocate there and the majority of the population will think we're abandoning them. That we're leaving them to fend for themselves."

"Isn't that essentially what we're doing by leaving the White House?" said Ashe. "Hell, moving the Joint Chiefs from the Pentagon to this Site R all but screams *we surrender*."

The President said quietly but emphatically, "That's all settled." Regarding the Speaker, he asked, "Did you have anything else to add?"

Leaning forward in his chair, Ashe said, "Refresh my memory. What is this *Site R*?"

"Site locations and assignments are on page three," said Marigold testily. "But to save you the trouble of looking for yourself, it's short for Raven Rock Mountain Complex. It's in Pennsylvania. Near Blue Ridge Summit."

Ashe made a dismissive gesture at the SecDef. "I've toured it before," he admitted. "All the military speak and designators are lost on me. At any rate, I don't like it at all. First time POTUS broadcasts from Raven Rock, the jig is up."

Marigold shook his head. "We have a mock-up of this very room at Site R. Even if you've set foot in here, you'd never be able to tell the difference between the two."

"It's already been decided," repeated President Tillman. "Let's get a move on."

The President's three-man security detail stood at attention with their backs facing the Situation Room's main entry. They sprang into action as the President rose from his leather chair. Two of the detail, armed with compact Heckler & Koch MP7 personal defense weapons, flanked the President as he approached the door. The third man, a former member of SEAL Team 6, carried the *football*—a leather briefcase containing various items necessary to react to a national emergency, including the 3x5 card containing the President's nuclear launch codes.

The agent pressed the football to his leg and brought up the rear, effectively sealing President Tillman inside the "bubble"—the designation given by the Secret Service to the immediate area around the President when he was on the ground and on the move. In fact, the moment the decision to leave was made by the most powerful man in the free world, the agent with the briefcase cuffed to his left wrist lifted a radio to his lips and said, "Wolverine is on the move."

President Tillman was hustled from the situation room, up the stairs to the South Portico entry, and then out onto the

South Lawn where three identical MV-22 Ospreys sat, nose to tail, their massive rotors a blur of motion atop upturned engine nacelles.

The air outside smelled of the kerosene-tinged exhaust produced by the three pairs of Rolls Royce AE 1107C engines whining away on the trio of hulking aircraft. Colorful leaves swirled in the tempest produced by the down blast created by Marine One, but a short sprint from the White House and already going light on its tricycle landing gear.

And sprint was exactly what the President and his security detail did. Head down and surrounded by armed agents, President Tillman, once a track and field standout at the University of Michigan, ran the entire distance from the White House to Marine One—the nearest of the three dark-green Ospreys.

Drawn by the mechanical contraptions loitering noisily on the South Lawn, dead things—Zips and slow-movers alike— found their forward advance stalled by the chest-high perimeter fencing. Now and then a Zip would hit the crush of undead from behind at full speed and make its way up and over and onto the lawn.

At first, Secret Service Uniformed Division officers wearing windbreakers over body armor and brandishing M4 carbines eliminated the random Zips as soon as a breach occurred.

Now, after having been wheels down for nearly five minutes, the effect the Ospreys were having on the dead was noticeable. And dangerous. Because the number of Zips making their way over the fencing and onto the White House grounds easily outnumbered the men and women assembled to protect the awaiting Ospreys.

Just as President Tillman set foot on Marine One's rear ramp, a pair of Zips came loping in from the west. As fast as the threats had appeared, the former SEAL with the football reacted.

Letting go of the suitcase, he gripped his MP7's stunted forestock with his newly freed hand and shouldered the weapon. Going to a knee, the agent engaged the first Zip, dropping it well beyond Marine One's rear ramp with a trio of 4.6 mm x 30 bullets fired single shot. Zip number two was just receiving a face full of congealed blood and brain tissue from Zip number one when the agent's second volley tore into its neck and chin. Lower jaw bouncing around on a tether of shiny muscle, the female Zip continued to advance.

Disregarding his own safety, the agent rose and, tethered football carving a furrow in the lush lawn, launched himself at the Zip's legs.

President Tillman was ducking his head and mounting the ramp when, out of the corner of his eye, he saw the agent's takedown of the second Zip. What he didn't see as he was pushed forcibly into a nearby seat by an agent and a Marine crew chief descended to loop safety belts over his shoulders, was the agent who had been to his left delivering a lethal double-tap to the already face-shot Zip.

The ramp was just motoring up and the Marine crew chief was cinching Tillman's belt when the pair of trailing agents tumbled inside, football safe and sound, and both men unscathed.

As Marine One launched vertically into the gray October sky, President Tillman was peering out the hip window and watching the Osprey carrying key cabinet members as it went wheels up.

He saw agents on the ground engaging dead pouring through a failed section of perimeter fence. Licks of flame lanced from their weapons and brass tumbled to the grass as they fought valiantly to the last man.

By the time the third Osprey lifted into the air and cleared the skeletal branches on the trees bordering the South Lawn, it looked to President Tillman as if a soccer match had just ended and hundreds of jubilant fans had spilled onto the pitch.

Donning a pair of headphones offered to him by the Marine crew chief, the President heard one of the Marine aviators up front say, "The White House has fallen."

Chapter 20

Fort Myers, Florida

Riker shuttled his haul from the RaceTrac to the Shelby. He set the cans by the pump and handed the bags to Tara through her open window.

Nodding toward the backseat, he said, "Steve-O's throwing off more BTUs than a space heater. That burn can't feel good. There's some aloe vera lotion in one of the bags."

As Tara fished the lotion from the bag, she said, "Let me guess, twenty bucks a gallon?"

Riker nodded reluctantly.

Lips pursed, Tara examined the colorful bottle. "Tropical scented aloe vera?"

"All they had."

Without another word on the matter, Tara pulsed her window up.

***

Ten minutes later, Riker had topped off the Ford's tank with supreme and was working on filling the third spare gas can when he felt something being jabbed into his ribs. Down on one knee, with his prosthesis supporting most of his weight, put him at a severe disadvantage. And to add insult to injury, the person holding to his ribs what he assumed to be a gun, either through dumb luck or calculated strategy, was doing so on his left side.

Glancing at the Shelby's passenger wing mirror, Riker saw his sister in the reflection. She was staring down at her phone and totally oblivious to his current predicament.

If Steve-O was watching his back, Riker couldn't tell due to the heavy tint on the crew cab windows.

The muzzle moved up to his left armpit as the person wielding it shifted their weight and leaned in real close.

"Don't move, motherfucker."

The male voice sounded familiar to Riker. The beer breath convinced him it was one of the teens from the store.

Head down, Riker saw only the oil-stained cement, the toes of a pair of spotless, leather Nike high-tops, and the gas can he had been in the midst of filling.

Though he knew the answer to the question, he asked anyway. "What do you want?"

"That wad of Benjamins in yo' pocket, for starters. And then you can give me that big ass watch on yo' wrist. And when you're done with that, dig out yo' wallet."

Two attempted robberies in the same day, thought Riker. Wondering about the odds of it happening, he craned to see the store, but his view was blocked by the gas pump. Working to comply with the first order, he said, "Where's your buddy? He not into robbing people of their hard-earned money? I bet he's into earning his keep? Am I right?"

"Just do what I asked," growled the robber.

The muzzle slipped lower on Riker's side. Feeling it being pushed hard against where he guessed his liver to be, he handed over the money. As he did, he heard the tell-tale sound of one of the two windows above his head being run down.

Then three things happened near simultaneously.

First, Riker heard Tara tell the person holding him up that she was going to "blow the afro off your head."

Then he felt the muzzle shift away as, presumably, Afro looked to see what kind of danger he had gotten himself into.

Finally, just as Riker was about to make a go for Afro's gun, the kid cried, "Don't shoot. Please, ma'am ... do not shoot me. It's just a—"

Taking advantage of the lapse in Afro's vigilance, Riker dipped his right shoulder and fired his left elbow at where he suspected Afro's head to be.

117

Propelled by fast-twitch muscles toned from a combination of genetics and daily pushups, the lightning-quick move swept Afro's gun hand away, then kept tracking on a counterclockwise upward arc.

The impact was jarring for both Riker and his would-be assailant.

With the equal and opposite component of Newton's Law kicking in, Riker lost his balance and fell forward.

The robber's plea for mercy was cut short by the breath-robbing blow to his ribs.

The distinct sound of bones breaking was not lost on Riker as his right shoulder, keeping pace with the left's rotation, brought his upper body around full circle. Breath exiting his lungs, he landed flat on his back, staring into Afro's scrunched-up mug and seeing in the kid's hand not a gun, but a rusty Phillips-head screwdriver.

In the next beat, mouth working like a fish out of water, Afro dropped the tool, clutched his ribs, and fell backward, ending up tangled in a dangling hose and wedged tightly between the pair of opposing gas pumps.

Riker came to rest stretched out beside the truck and trying to find his own wind. An arm's reach in front of his upturned face was Tara. She was hanging out the window with his Sig Sauer clutched in a two-handed grip. It looked ridiculous in her small hands. To her credit, the weapon was not wavering. Riker was also pleased to see the safety thrown and her trigger finger braced alongside the pistol's frame.

As Riker worked to right himself, he saw the kid's hand snake out and palm the wad of cash. When he looked up at Tara, she was gesturing toward the street with the Sig's muzzle.

Voice full of menace, she said, "Drop the cash and get the *fuck* out of here."

Without a word, Afro flipped the folded-up money at Riker, scrambled to his feet, and sprinted across the parking lot toward where his buddy was loitering and drinking from a bottle in a brown bag.

Ignoring the cash scattered on the ground, Riker reached up and tapped Tara's elbow. "Thanks, Sis. But you better put that away before someone calls the police on us."

There was a soft click as she engaged the safety. As she drew the pistol into the cab, she said, "*I* tried to call the police on *him*."

"And?"

"I got the stock 'all circuits are busy' message." Her brows lifted as she said, "That kid was empowered. Makes me think Fort Myers' PD has a lot on their plate."

"You may have a point," said Riker as he policed up the scattered bills. "Nonetheless, we don't need to draw that kind of attention to us. Gas. Food. Then we're on the move north." He made a face when it occurred to him he still had to pee.

"All that Florida/Georgia line talk worrying you?"

He nodded, then resumed filling the remaining gas cans. After capping the third can and starting in on the fourth, he told Tara what was really bothering him.

She listened without interruption, then said, "This Volkov may be on to something. I don't think our government let Romero go on purpose. Still, their actions after the fact really suck. Men in black. All those black Suburbans. The MRAPs and unmarked helicopters." Now she was the one shaking her head. "And you know what they say about the cover-up."

Capping the final can, Riker rose and placed it in the bed with the others. Turning back to Tara, he said, "The cover-up is almost always worse than the crime." He made a quick recon of their surroundings. Seeing only a man and woman fueling their respective vehicles at the far pumps, and a smattering of vehicles headed toward the interstate, he turned back to Tara. "I'm not so sure about that in this instance. Anything as deadly as Romero needed to be kept under lock and key. If you ask me, they should have never engineered something like it in the first place."

After lifting the tailgate and locking the tonneau, Riker took his seat in the Shelby. Sniffing the air in the cab, he said, "All of a sudden I crave a piña colada."

"That's funny," Steve-O said. "I have a craving for coconut cream pie."

"Maybe we can find a sit-down and sate both of our cravings."

Shooting Riker the look, Tara said, "*Virgin* piña colada."

Voice taking a serious tone, Riker said, "Back to the subject at hand. There was that jet on the tarmac at Heathrow, and now Volkov and all his sword rattling. I have a bad feeling that Romero is not only in the U.K. and Russia, I'm afraid it could have spread all over the globe."

"How?" shot Tara. "It's only been a week since those dead things started showing up."

Riker fired up the motor and eased Dolly into traffic, heading east toward the interstate to, hopefully, a rendezvous with a symbol recognizable the world over.

Stopping at the series of traffic lights metering the flow to the freeway ramps, he said, "A week is an eternity, Sis. How many international flights does JFK service in a week? How about Logan? Reagan? *Atlanta?*"

Unable to fathom the number of people going through Atlanta on a busy travel day, let alone all of them combined, Tara merely shook her head.

The familiar *symbol* Riker had spotted from the freeway was on the far side of the shopping mall. It was yellow and decorated one of the last signs in a long row of them rising up above various fast food joints. As they passed a Taco Bell, PDQ, and Zaxby's Chicken Fingers and Buffalo Wings—all darkened and surrounded by empty parking lots—Steve-O said, "Closed. Closed. Closed."

Riker pointed across the dash. He said, "But lookie right there. Your favorite is all lit up and open for business."

Steve-O put his elbows on the seatbacks. "You said no more McDonalds."

"I worked Mickey Dees in high school," Riker said. "Let's just say I had my fill of the Golden Arches."

"And then some," added Tara, smiling. "You always hooked us up at home. I couldn't wait for the McRib to come back every year."

Riker met Steve-O's gaze in the rearview. "We can find somewhere else."

"I doubt if we're going to find a place like the Iron Pan around here," Tara said.

Turning into the drive-thru lane, Riker said, "I can already smell the fries cooking. Something that once you've been part of the team, you will *never* forget."

Tara and Steve-O ordered Big Macs, fries, and Cokes. Riker opted for just coffee. The largest they'd sell him. It came in a thirty-two-ounce cup that brought a smile to his face.

Before driving away, Riker dug into the bag and passed out the food.

Steve-O presented the box of fries to Riker. "Want one?"

Leaning away from the offering, Riker said, "I've eaten enough of those to last two lifetimes. Thank you, though."

While Tara and Steve-O made quick work of the fast food, Riker did his best to breathe through his mouth and backtracked to the ramp to I-75 northbound, where he turned right. Halfway down the onramp, where turning to go back wasn't an option, he conceded that once again he'd forgotten he needed to pee.

"You gotta be kidding me," said Tara, jamming a half-dozen fries into her open mouth. "How'd you manage that?"

The grass infield with the airport shuttles and body bags was coming up on the left. Answering Tara's question, Riker said, "I was too preoccupied with what was on television to ask Enrique for a key."

"Then having that screwdriver jabbed into your ribs," Tara said, "You thinking it was a gun and all ... it's a wonder you didn't piss yourself right then and there. No sense in dying with a full bladder."

"Depends," said Riker, expecting at least one of the others to get the joke.

Crickets.

121

Tara was busy staring at a red SUV negotiating a narrow lane left between the lined-up shuttle vans and abandoned civilian vehicles. She thought it was the same Toyota 4Runner that had followed them across the preserve, only now it wasn't loaded down with people. There was a single soldier at the wheel, and it was being driven slow and deliberate, not like it was stolen and the driver was running from the law.

The grassy area north of the parked vehicles was mostly mud and marred by tire tracks. Only explanation Tara could think of was that maybe the infield had been used as a staging area for the military vehicles stationed on the exit ramps south of here.

As the 4Runner came to a halt on the periphery of the civilian vehicles, her attention was drawn to a pair of guardsmen escorting a blonde woman through the warren of civilian vehicles. Noting the torn and soiled yellow top hanging off the woman, Tara realized who she was looking at.

Faster on the draw, Steve-O said, "That's the Pretty Lady who was wading in the swamp."

Craning to see what Steve-O was alluding to, Riker got a good look at both the woman and the soldiers. Instead of noting what she was wearing, he keyed in on the device spanning the distance between her neck and the soldier guiding her ahead of him.

"Damn," he said. "They're using one of those dog catcher's thingies to keep her from getting to them."

"Damn smart," Tara said. "She looked hungry coming out of the pond back there. I bet the folks in the 4Runner had no idea what they were getting themselves into."

As the ramp widened and Riker steered the Shelby back onto the interstate, he said, "I tried warning them."

Tara shifted in her seat to pick up the action through the rear window. "The other soldier has a gun aimed at it."

Riker nodded. "I saw that, too."

Sighing, Tara said, "This shit's a mirror image of what they did to us at the high school. I'm thinking we slipped out of Fort Myers just ahead of it being put under quarantine."

Watching the scene recede in his wing mirror, Riker agreed with Tara's assessment. Turning his attention to the road ahead, he added, "And we all know how well that turned out for Middletown."

"And New York," Steve-O added.

Tara said, "Which means we need to get as far away from here as possible."

Noting the range indicated on the trip computer, Riker ran a quick calculation in his head. "With the tank full and extra fuel in the cans in back, we should be well into Georgia before we need to think about stopping again to top off."

Tapping on the SYNC display, Tara pulled up the navigation screen. "I don't think we should wait until we're running on reserves. Fill up when we can seems like the best strategy."

"War game it," Riker said. "Find all the stations from here to Tampa and flag the ones that look the most promising. Preferably mom and pop outfits first. Then single out the ones that are set farthest back from the interstate."

As Tara went to work on the touchscreen, zooming and scrolling and changing the views between *Road* and *Aerial*, fat drops of rain smacked the hood and windshield and roof.

Riker shot a sour look at the darkening sky. Flicking on the wipers, he said, "And now Mother Nature is entering the fray."

Chapter 21

Raven Rock Mountain Complex
Blue Ridge Summit, Pennsylvania

President Tillman sat in a forward-facing seat in the MV-22 Osprey designated *Marine One*. During the twenty-minute flight from the White House, the Marine aviator flew the big twin engine tilt rotor like he had stolen it. Flying *nap of the earth* and so low that Tillman could see license plates on vehicles transiting the Pennsylvania backroads, the constant adjustments in altitude had the President's safety harness working overtime.

After thundering over a white farmhouse complete with the requisite red barn and grain silo, the pilot dipped into one last narrow valley prior to final approach to Site R—the United States' "underground Pentagon" and vital component of the three-piece puzzle designed to ensure continuity of government in the event of a national emergency.

Looking a little green around the gills, President Tillman regarded his Secretary of Defense.

"Almost there," Marigold said. "One final pop up and a smooth transition to horizontal flight."

Tillman grimaced. He knew "smooth" wasn't an appropriate adjective to use when describing anything this behemoth did while airborne. In fact, a spin on the Hulk rollercoaster at Universal Studios was like riding in a Bentley compared to the Osprey's flight characteristics.

The "smooth transition" had Tillman's stomach crowding his tonsils when the twin-engine nacelles began their steady pivot to vertical. There was a groan and a shudder raced through the airframe as forward speed bled and the massive rotors took big bites of air to keep the ship aloft. Save for the takeoff from the White House's South Lawn, the descent and landing at Raven Rock was about the smoothest part of the journey.

On approach, Tillman had looked out his window and surveyed the facility.

The entrances and support buildings serving the deep underground communications facility sat perched on a crescent-shaped tract of cleared land running along a fifteen-hundred-foot-high, mile-long hill located near the Mason-Dixon line.

The installation's two-lane service road ran between two pair of buttressed tunnel entrances fitted with enormous thirty-ton blast doors. Set back from the road were a number of buildings: a firehouse, a remote receiving building, guard houses, and assorted structures arranged around the entry portals feeding to the underground tunnels.

The entire site was ringed by redundant twelve-foot-high fences topped with coiled concertina. The gates at the east and south ends of the road were manned with armed personnel.

Save for the buttressed entrances below, and array of dishes, antennas, and other communication gear bristling from the peak, Site R looked as if it could be owned and maintained by any number of mundane governmental agencies. However, the small convoy of military vehicles entering the east tunnel quickly dispelled that illusion.

Marine One jounced once as it landed on the alternate helipad deep in the woods and concealed from prying eyes by mature trees. The rear ramp was already open, and the President's three-man Secret Service detail were hustling Wolverine toward the rectangle of light even before Marine One's wheels had ceased all forward movement.

On the way out of the Osprey, Tillman dipped his hips and cast a weary glance at the hurricane fencing paralleled by a dense thicket of trees.

Seeing his protectee duck and scan the woods, Special Agent Dan Kite said, "There are no infected in the woods, sir. Site R is sterile. Entrance is this way."

Stubby HK MP7 aimed at the ground, Kite hustled Wolverine through the open gate, nodding at the similarly armed agent manning it.

At his back, Tillman heard the turbine whine rise exponentially. The sound was reassuring. It meant the bird was heading to Virginia to collect his family from the Mount Weather Emergency Operations Center. Clamping a hand down on his ball cap, he threaded through the gate and followed the lead agent through a sort of tunnel carved from dense foliage surrounding the landing pad.

After a dozen yards or so they passed over a gravel road awash in sun. Squinting against the harsh light, Tillman drew a deep breath of fresh air and followed Agent Kite into a poured-cement tunnel large enough to admit a bull elephant. At the end of the tunnel, maybe fifty feet from the entrance, was a miniature version of the site's main blast doors. Thick with several inches of hardened steel and skinned with titanium, it stood open and was flanked by a pair of Marines in MultiCam camos and brandishing some kind of exotic weaponry.

The President of the United States was led to an elevator door. As he stood there running the events of the last week through his head, the door to outside was dogged down, and he finally exhaled the breath trapped in his lungs.

Lake City, Florida

With Riker driving the Shelby at speeds well over the posted limits, they quickly outpaced the first effects of the outer bands of Hurricane Owen. Save for a brief pit stop at a rest area thirty miles north of Sergeant Wilcox's checkpoint, during which Riker swapped his Tommy Bahama shirt and shorts for a plain gray tee shirt and khaki 5.11 Tactical pants, he had been driving nonstop for nearly five hours.

Having come to the conclusion during her brother's pee break that charting a course close to the shore on the gulf side would likely double their travel time, Tara convinced him they should stick to I-75 until its merger with I-10—roughly three hundred miles to the north.

For most of the trip north, traffic moving with them had been sparse. Most was civilian in nature, the majority of the vehicles loaded down with camping gear, generators, and various supplies. Now and again they would come upon and overtake small military convoys consisting mostly of multi-wheeled troop carriers and Humvee ambulances.

Riker chalked up the dearth of civilian vehicles fleeing north to the fact that the early reporting on Owen had it making landfall near the Carolinas as a medium-strength hurricane registering a 2 or 3 on the Saffir-Simpson wind scale.

Hot on the heels of Nicole comes another tropical storm seemingly cut from the same cloth. And so far, it would seem, Floridians are content with staying put and guarding their castles, was what Riker remembered the reporter on the television in the RaceTrac as saying. Which would explain the abundance of flatbed trucks heading south with full loads of sheet plywood. People staying to ride out a hurricane needed supplies to fortify their "castles." And if Riker hadn't seen evidence of Romero pop up in Miami with his own eyes, he would be prone to believe the southbound National Guard convoys consisting of troop carriers, MRAPs, and Humvees bristling with gun turrets were merely the leading element of a proactive response to the fifteenth-named hurricane of the season.

Coming up fast on Lake City, also known as "The Gateway to Florida" due to its close proximity to the intersection of Interstate 75 and Interstate 10, Riker felt his eyelids growing heavy.

The sky had been blue for most of their trip; however, over the last hour, as dusk drew near, the sky to the west seemed to catch fire.

Backlit by a burnt-orange sky dominated by the rapidly setting sun, roadside palms and their swaying fronds added a hypnotic effect that had Riker wishing for coffee, or, better yet, one of those five-hour energy drinks.

Suddenly an alarm chimed as the driver's side tires crossed over the fog line and rode over the grooved rumble strips for a couple of hundred feet. As Riker was shocked alert, he played it off, making a minute course correction to get the Shelby back to tracking straight in the fast lane.

Going rigid in her seat, Tara asked, "You want me to drive?"

"I'm fine," replied Riker, watching a Prius a lane over speed up. He checked his surroundings in the mirrors. Saw the station wagon that had been pacing him fall back a couple of car lengths.

From the backseat came a long, drawn-out fart.

Holding her nose, Tara said, "If that doesn't wake you up, nothing will." She chuckled, the noise coming out of her mouth funny-sounding in her own ears.

"More likely it'll knock me out cold." He made a show of swerving within his lane. Just a subtle left to right to left to right jiggle of the wheel that had the Shelby carving long graceful arcs, each spanning several hundred feet of blacktop.

"Stop swerving," ordered Tara. "Last thing we need is to be pulled over because you're goofing around." She rummaged in her bag and came up with a tall aluminum can. Squiggly neon-green letters on a black background spelled out *Monster*.

Riker said, "I wasn't goofing around. I was *trying* to rouse our friend back there. He farts a lot less when he's awake."

Tara popped the top on the energy drink. "Not cool," she said, handing it to Riker.

Taking the can in hand, Riker said, "It's warm. I can't even stomach one of these if it's ice cold."

"Just do it, you big baby. You want to risk the alternative? Run us off the road into a palm tree?"

Far off in the distance, brake lights flared red.

Holding the steering wheel steady, Riker tipped the can and took a couple of long pulls of the tepid, semi-sweet, lemon-lime-flavored pick-me-up. Face screwed up in disgust, he belched loudly and went to stuff the empty can into his door's side pocket.

"It'll kick in," she promised. "Soon your hair will be on fire and everything that moves will be a squirrel to you."

"Very funny," said Riker. He was having trouble getting the can to seat in the map pocket, so he resorted to using brute force.

There were a couple of metallic pops as the aluminum was reshaped.

When Riker returned his attention to the road, he saw that vehicles ahead in the right two lanes were stopping. The Prius had pulled over to the passing lane and wasn't slowing down.

With maybe a half-mile to make up his mind, Riker said, "What do you think, Sis? We coming up on another checkpoint?"

"Looks like a couple of big rigs stopped for something. Better slow down, Ricky Bobby."

Tara's Talladega Nights reference was lost on Riker. He wasn't into Nascar, let alone movies with motorsports a central theme.

With less than a quarter-mile to go to the tail end of the backup, Riker steered the Shelby to the left lane, bled speed to put several car lengths between him and the Prius, and then regarded Tara. "You put the Sig away, didn't you?"

"I did. But not under your seat. I put it back in the console where I got it."

Spotted only by Tara, a person standing on the grassy median activated a road flare and tossed it to the ground in the break-down lane.

Still regarding his sister, Riker said, "Great. That means it's sitting on the paperwork from the dealership I'll need to dig out to prove this truck is mine and not stolen."

Instinctively planting both feet on the floor and reaching for the grab bar above her right ear, Tara pointed over the dash and shouted, "Look out, Lee!"

As Riker swung his gaze forward, he saw that his following distance had gone from six truck lengths to two, and the Prius in his lane, its trio of brake lights blazing solid red, was fishtailing like mad.

Long dormant training kicked in. Riker braked hard and jinked the wheel left. The risky maneuver sent the wheels on his side into the grassy median, and the ones on Tara's tracking down the center of the breakdown lane.

From the new vantage, Riker saw the jam—both figuratively and literally—that his brief lapse of situational awareness had gotten them into.

A pair of eighteen-wheelers had stopped in the right lanes. In the middle distance, maybe two hundred feet beyond the pair of big rigs, a third semi hitched to a tandem was jackknifed and blocking the entire interstate. Having come to rest at a right angle to the first of its two linked trailers, the multi-wheeled Freightliner tractor, all by itself, took up two-thirds of the left breakdown lane.

As blue-gray smoke from the Prius' tires poured from the tiny hybrid car's wheel wells, Riker drifted Dolly all the way onto the median and felt through his boot sole the antilock braking system kick on. Brake calipers grabbed massive discs, causing the Shelby's nose to dip. As Riker fought to control the slewing rig, twin rooster-tails of dirt and grass erupted from her back tires, and he saw that things weren't going to end well for the Prius driver.

Chapter 22

A tick after the Shelby's right-side tires rolled back onto the asphalt shoulder, the Prius driver's fate was sealed. Instead of countering the slide by steering left to the median, he or she must have panicked, because the brake lights went dark and the slow clockwise spin accelerated dramatically.

With maybe thirty feet to go before the person who'd dropped the first flare became a permanent fixture on Dolly's grille, Riker muscled the steering wheel straight and put his trust in the ABS system.

In the process of igniting a second flare, the woman, who looked to be in her mid-thirties, looked up and saw the two vehicles converging on her.

Though the Prius driver never recovered from the slide, somehow the car missed the woman entirely.

Maybe the person at the wheel decided to sacrifice their life for the woman's, thought Riker. He would never know, because half a beat later the Prius slammed into the Freightliner still travelling at what looked to be about forty miles per hour.

Instantaneously kinetic energy was absorbed and there was a tremendous bang and explosion of glass as the hybrid seemed to fold in on itself.

Still holding the grab bar, Tara saw the woman go wide-eyed and bring her arms up to her face. In the next beat, likely still processing the near miss, the woman dropped her arms to her sides and unleashed a primal scream.

Still moving north of thirty miles per hour, the Shelby passed by the woman on her right side. And though she *was* spared from becoming a permanent fixture on Dolly's grille,

Tara's wing mirror clipped her head, silencing the scream and sending her crashing vertically to the ground as if a trapdoor had opened beneath her.

Having slept through the jackhammer-like pounding of the ABS rapidly slowing the Shelby from seventy to thirty, Steve-O was spilled off the rear seat when, near instantaneously, all forward momentum went from thirty to zero.

The Shelby ended up stopped on the shoulder with just a few feet separating Tara's door and the tractor's grille guard. So close that Riker saw what looked to him like blood and human detritus clinging to the wrist-thick bars.

Jerked out of a deep sleep, Steve-O rose from the floor and poked his head between the front seats. "Holy shit," he exclaimed in a sleepy voice.

"Well I'll be," Tara said. "I'm reinstating the swear cup. Pay up."

"No time for jokes, Sis." Riker had already decided the Prius driver was dead and was reversing the Shelby to get a better look at the stretch of I-75 sandwiched between the jackknifed tandem and pair of static eighteen-wheelers.

The scene was utter carnage. Apparently, the tandem had run over two, maybe three people prior to sideswiping a minivan, which looked as if it had gone airborne and rolled a couple of times before coming to rest thirty feet past the tandem and on the other side of the far guardrail.

On the shoulder this side of the guardrail, nearly equidistant to the three semis boxing in the large debris-strewn swathe of interstate, stood a man and a woman. Both wore trucker's hats, blue jeans, and boots. And both were fussing with cell phones as they paced separate courses along the breakdown lane.

Closer in, body parts lay scattered over three lanes. Scraps of flesh, clumped hair, a glistening pool of blood, articles of tattered clothing, a mismatched pair of shoes, and one mangled leg all marked what appeared to be the initial point of impact. Multiple blood trails paralleled a hundred or so feet of intertwined skid marks put down on the blacktop by the tandem as it jackknifed.

A dozen feet behind the second of the tandem's two trailers, near where the skid marks and one of the blood trails came to an abrupt end, was all that was left of a rather portly man. It amounted to basically a shirtless torso sprouting one pulverized arm and a badly misshapen head.

What should have been a cooling corpse was twitching and bucking in a sad attempt to get itself rolled over.

Riker had missed all of this as he fought to avoid two separate collisions.

Because Tara had been focused solely on the woman she feared was about to lose her life, she, too, had been spared seeing all the gory details now on full display a few yards off her right shoulder.

Tara regarded the dark black skid marks left by the Shelby on I-75. Then she walked her gaze to the median, where its big off-road tires had carved twin snaking furrows deep into the mud, then gaped at the single twenty-foot-long streak of still-smoking tire rubber. Finally, fixing her brother with a look of incredulity, she said, "That was so effin close on so many levels. I am sooo grateful I gave you my last Monster."

"I was acting on muscle memory," he said. "Energy drink or not, the outcome would have been the same."

As Tara opened her mouth to ask the obvious, the woman who had been setting out flares knocked on her window.

"You going to open it?" asked Steve-O. "Because I think she needs our help."

Tara looked a question at her brother.

Riker consulted his side mirror. The vehicles that had come upon the scene and had stopped behind the Shelby were now on the move, using the grass median to bypass the accident scene.

When Riker looked back to Tara, she was still staring at him with the "what should we do?" look on her face. And behind her, the thirty-something woman, face white as driven snow, was still rapping lightly on the glass.

"Run it down," Riker said. "Let's see what she needs."

Chapter 23

What the mousy woman tapping on Tara's window needed more than anything was a sedative and to have her bleeding head bandaged. However, all Riker had to offer her was a sincere "Sorry" for hitting her with his mirror.

Hands shaking wildly, the woman ignored the apology and asked Tara to call 911.

Thumbing her phone to life, Tara quickly tapped out the emergency number and put the phone to her ear.

"Hope yours works," said the woman. "None of us could get through on ours."

Shaking her head, Tara said, "No love. Circuits are all busy. I'm guessing you already tried calling for help on your CB."

The woman nodded. "Same as the phones. Nobody answers on Channel 19. All I get up and down the rest of the dial is white noise. I'm guessing it's because of the coming storm."

Coming storm is right, Tara thought. She reached out the window and placed her hand on the woman's trembling shoulder. Trying to calm her, in a soft voice she asked, "What's your name?"

Matching Tara's gaze, the woman said, "Nicole."

"What happened here, Nicole?"

Eyes roving the macabre scene, Nicole bit her lip and tugged at a loose strand of her long, auburn hair.

Shock is *setting in*, thought Riker as he craned to see past Tara to get a better look at the woman.

Gesturing at the tandem with the inert road flare, Nicole finally said, "I need help getting *it* unstuck from my back wheels."

135

Though she *thought* she knew what the woman was getting at, Tara said, "*It?*"

Nicole nodded. "It's the same as that one." She pointed with the flare at the mass of road rash twenty yards distant. "It should be dead, but it ain't."

"You try backing up to free the one from your truck?" was all Tara could come up with.

Nicole stared slack-jawed as a single tear broke from the corner of her eye and rocketed down her pale cheek. "There's no helping either one of them. Better to just let them die."

Good luck with that, thought Riker. He said, "Is that what you told the others? Is that why they're keeping their distance?"

Nicole drew a hand to her face. Biting her knuckles, she met Riker's gaze and said, "What am I going to tell them? Somehow the woman flattened between my rear tires is still moving her fingers? Try to convince them that a guy with no legs whose heart and lungs are *totally* missing from his chest ... is still alive? Is still moving? How do you explain that without looking like a goddamn crazy person?"

"So ... you didn't tell them?"

Shaking her head, she said, "I left her right where I found her, then covered him up real quick with my parka. Told the others they were both dead. They took my word for it. Shit"—she gestured at the interstate—"it's all there for them to see. Fucker knocked my coat off with that torn-up arm. I just don't understand. Am I seeing things?"

Though he knew the truth, Riker told her what he thought she wanted to hear. "It's going to be OK, Nicole. The paramedics will be here in no time and get things under control."

The trucker grimaced. Her modest makeup application was beginning to smear. Upon further examination, Riker concluded she was closer in age to him than Tara. Though blanched from the shock of nearly dying, her face wasn't marred by the stresses he guessed an over-the-road trucker likely endured on a daily basis. *Hell*, he thought, *ten minutes driving in city traffic have me wanting to wring necks and go all demolition derby on fools who should have never been issued a license to drive.*

136

Steve-O ran down his window and thrust a stack of napkins taken from the McDonalds bag in the woman's direction.

As Nicole dabbed at the tears, Riker asked, "So what went down here? Walk me through what you saw."

Composing herself, Nicole said, "The man and woman were fighting … I guess. She was trying to get away from him. Just jerked her arm from his grasp. She ran from the van. She got a ways away and turned back to see he was after her. When she did that, she ran into my lane. I don't think it was on purpose, though." She paused and drew a deep breath. Continuing, she said, "I swerved to miss her, and then *he*"—she pointed again with the flare at the half-man—"just bolted out after her."

Bolt is right, thought Riker.

"The van?" asked Tara. "How'd it get over there?"

The drivers of the pair of parked eighteen-wheelers had approached and were standing near the Shelby. They had both pocketed their phones and were waving traffic by and chatting intermittently with a couple of motorists who had witnessed it all and then stopped to help.

"After I ran the two over," said Nicole. "I swerved back into my lane and one of my trailers whipped into their van. I felt it … just a big bang, but didn't see much." She shook her head. "I was too busy trying to ride my rig to a full stop and worrying about the couple I just hit to be concerned about the van or who might still be inside it." She went quiet for a beat. Wiping fresh tears, she added in a choked voice, "I didn't know. I swear to God I didn't see them in there."

"Who?" asked Tara.

"The kids in the van."

Tara asked, "Are they *its,* too? Or do they need medical help?"

The woman's mouth moved, but no words came. After a second or two, she began to sob uncontrollably.

"I'll go check on them," Riker said to Tara. "You hold the fort down." He opened the console and came out with the Sig. After rummaging around at the bottom of the compartment, he located the ultra-compact Scorpion tactical flashlight and Gerber multi-tool he'd picked up during their run from New Jersey.

Pocketing the multi-tool, he stuck the paddle holster in his waistband. Pulling his shirt over the pistol, he stepped to the road.

Drivers and passengers in passing cars reluctantly tore their eyes from the scene of vehicular mayhem to regard Riker as he made his way around the Shelby to the crumpled Prius.

One look inside the hybrid car told him all he needed to know. The front seats were tilted in toward one another. The airbags had deployed and now hung limply from their housings. White powder dusted the interior and driver who was unmoving and compressed into an impossibly small space. All Riker could see of the corpse was the right arm. The masculine-looking hand once attached to that arm had been severed at the wrist. It sat upright on the twisted transmission hump, palm toward Riker, almost as if it was waving "goodbye" to him. Urging him to take care of more pressing matters.

Finished with the grim task, he surveyed the interstate for any sign of the paramedics he had promised Nicole.

He saw nothing. No strobing red and blue lights of responding state patrol units. No flashing red and yellow lights or screaming sirens to indicate emergency services were closing in. He saw only the headlights on approaching cars flicking on as first twilight began to give way to dusk.

Leaving the Shelby behind, Riker walked diagonally down the interstate. As he threaded through the debris field, he kept one eye on the passing traffic, and the other on the half-man. Nearing the mound of bloody flesh, he saw that Nicole was right: her navy-blue parka had indeed slipped off to one side.

He slowed his gait long enough to get a good look at what was left of the man. And it wasn't much. Most of the subtly twitching torso's dermis and flesh and hair was now a long trail of sludge bisecting two lanes of interstate. Only one milky eye remained in the skull. Riker caught a case of the chills watching it rove in wide circles within the fractured orbital socket.

His salivary glands kicked into overdrive when his gaze reached the thing's chest. As if an alien spawn had just made an unwelcome appearance, a number of ribs had been ripped from the sternum. Like arthritic fingers, they jutted forth at crazy angles. Marrow was seeping from the ribs that had been sheared off during the violent event. Save for ropy strands of sinew and a spinal column reduced to a fraction of its normal length, the cavity where a heart and other internal organs should have been was now a dark and bloody cavern.

Riker felt a burning in his esophagus, the rising bile bitter on his tongue. Just as he passed by the thing that used to be a living, breathing human, it lifted its head off the road and made a mewling sound.

That stopped Riker in his tracks. The hair on his neck and arms snapped to attention. Unable to stop the process the sights and smells assailing him had started, he put his hands on his knees and emptied his stomach on the center lane of I-75. The *Monster* tasted worse coming up.

Wiping the spittle on the back of one hand, Riker noticed the one working eye in the thing's skull stop moving and fix solidly on him.

I covered him up with my parka. Told the others they were both dead. They took my word for it. Shit, it's all there for them to see.

Riker cast a covert glance at the truckers and witnesses. They were standing in a rough semi-circle, their backs to him. He went to one knee next to the living corpse. With an economy of movement, he slipped the Gerber from his pocket, flicked out the knife blade, and positioned his body to shield against prying eyes.

"It's for the best," he said in a funereal voice as he hovered the blade above the thing's eyeball.

The living corpse tried mightily to lift its flattened arm off the road, groaned one last time, then went completely still. Cadaver still. As a corpse should be. As if it knew sweet release was imminent.

When Riker leaned against the Gerber, he heard a soft pop and crunch as tempered steel met resistance with brain tissue and cranial bone.

The half-man's final act consisted of the appendage passing for its arm quivering once and then a subtle settling of the torso as the remaining muscles went slack.

This death was nothing like the handful Riker had witnessed up close in Iraq. There was no pleading. No fighting its finality. No final breath was exhaled. Which meant he was spared the ubiquitous death rattle of trapped air leaving the deceased's body.

Riker drew in a ragged breath, closed his eyes, and vomited again beside the corpse. Stomach still roiling, he closed the Gerber and glanced over one shoulder.

Nicole, the truckers, and the motorists were still near the Shelby and talking amongst themselves. Riker was confident they hadn't noticed the corpse moving, nor the questionable deed he had just performed.

If they had, nobody was letting on.

Riker repositioned the jacket over the twice-dead corpse, then rose and bowed his head. He said a silent prayer for the man, then whispered, "I'm going to see to the lady and kids, now. Rest easy, sir."

Chapter 24

Riker thumbed on the tactical light and kept its bright beam trained on the ground as he backtracked to the jackknifed Freightliner. He stayed right of the sputtering flare and skirted another wide swath of human detritus soiling the fast lane.

Crossing in front of the Freightliner's grille guard, his beam picked up clumps of organic matter clinging to the blood-spattered grille.

Coming around to the passenger side, he saw that the truck's fender and right headlight had taken a beating. The former was cracked and streaked with silver paint, the latter had been knocked askew of its housing and was hanging on by a jumble of twisted wires.

He also surprised a younger man who was crouched beside the tractor's rear wheels and snapping photos of himself. Startled by Riker's sudden appearance, the twenty-something lowered the arm holding the smartphone, rose, and started off toward a tiny red Mini Cooper parked on the shoulder a dozen yards away. His pace was slow, gait nonchalant.

Nothing to see here. I'll be on my way.

"Hey Red! Stop right there," Riker ordered.

As if used to being called "Red," the guy halted mid-stride and started a slow pirouette in Riker's direction.

Maybe five-ten and a buck-fifty soaking wet, the man had the posture of someone much smaller. A shock of red hair peeked out from under an olive-green Castro hat. He wore oversized black cargo shorts and a black tee shirt bearing Marilyn Manson's likeness. On his feet were thin-soled flip-flops—also black.

When Red finished the rotation, the smartphone had mysteriously disappeared. As if saying *what's your problem*, he raised both arms horizontal to the road, palms out.

Now away from the chemical odor produced by the burning flare, Riker caught a whiff of a stench he knew all too well.

Crushed bowels and freshly spilled blood each had their own distinct odor. Mix those two together, throw in fumes from trash and shit being burned with diesel, and you have what he had been exposed to on a near daily basis while serving in Iraq.

The reek now hitting Riker's nose was very similar. However, he wasn't back in-country. He was here, on an interstate in Florida, downwind from the woman the lady trucker had accidentally turned into street pizza.

Ignoring Red's blank stare, Riker covered his nose with one hand, faced the truck, and crouched down in roughly the same spot where Red had been crouched and snapping his selfie.

Riker craned and illuminated the shadowy recesses where the first of the two connected trailers hitched to the tractor. There, partially hidden behind the inside set of tires, was what used to be a woman.

Being sucked underneath the semi had reduced her to a bloody, near-featureless slab of meat. Somehow, she had traveled the length of the chassis and became wedged inexorably between the tractor's second and third axles.

Riker inched closer and played the beam on the body from another angle. Saw that the entire left side of her face was ground down to bone. Prolonged contact with the tread on the massive rear tires had also turned the left side of her chest into hamburger. From being dragged along the road as the driver fought the swerving truck to get it to where it sat now, the woman's left hip and upper leg on that side had been ground down to half its normal size.

Every stitch of clothing had either been blown off from the force of the truck's grille guard hitting her or had been ripped from her frame during time spent underneath the rig.

Though Riker couldn't see much detail due to the gore deposited on and around the suspension and braking components, it appeared that her left arm had gotten wrapped all the way around the axle. Which, he guessed, had spared her from being churned under the two trailers and then spit out on the interstate to die alongside the half corpse.

Rising, Riker looked to the redhead.

"Come here," he growled.

The younger man took a few tentative steps toward Riker, then halted just out of arm's reach.

Riker held a hand out. "Give me the phone and the keys to your go-kart."

Red stared blankly at Riker for a beat. When he finally blinked, his upper lip rose on one side. "Fuck I will," he sneered. "You have no right to my belongings." Eyes flicking to his ride, he took a half-step backward, in the direction of the guardrail, which was across two lanes and a wide, debris-strewn shoulder.

"Prosthetic leg or not," Riker said, framing the kid's face with the flashlight beam, "you will *not* outrun me." He waggled his fingers. "Hand them over, asshole."

A soft phlegm-addled moan emanated from the gloomy space between axles.

The kid's eyes went wide and his body snapped to attention. *Even if he wanted to rabbit*, thought Riker, *it's clear his legs won't be obeying the impulse.*

"Now!" Riker barked.

Slowly, Red reached into a pocket and came out with a set of keys and the thin silver smartphone.

Riker held his palm out. Glaring at Red, he said, "Power it on, tap in your password, and then hand it all over."

Thumbing the screen to life, Red stated, "My thumbprint unlocks it." With no further hesitation, he dropped the phone and keys into Riker's palm.

"Right," Riker said, a touch of skepticism showing in the tone. Pocketing the keys, he looked at the screen, then tapped the camera icon.

After Riker scrolled through the most recent photos, he cued up the first of a pair of short videos taken minutes ago.

The first video was of the woman wrapped up in the axle. It lasted about a minute and was shot from less than a foot away.

The light from the phone illuminating her face and neck revealed what was clearly a series of bite marks. Two were superficial, barely breaking the skin. The one below her jawbone, where a sizeable hunk of flesh was missing, was to the bone and still oozing blood.

As the woman's body twitched, the person doing the filming—Red, no doubt—recoiled and took the Lord's name in vain. A second later the clip ended.

Red had been shifting his weight from foot to foot as he watched Riker watching the video.

Video number two had a nearly three-minute running time. The footage began outside the crumpled van and quickly moved to the interior. Like a low-budget horror flick, it was a bit jittery. Red had started shooting at the front end where the driver's side door was sheared off, then continued on to the rear seats where three girls remained strapped into their seatbelts. Two were grade-school-aged, at best. The third, seated nearest the blown-out picture window on the driver's side, was more developed upstairs than the others.

All three were dead. That much was clear. Necks bent at impossible angles, they all wore surprised looks, eyes wide open and already beginning to lose their natural gloss as prolonged exposure to air dried them out.

Inexplicably, a thin, ceiling-mounted monitor was still deployed and showing the end credits of one of the Twilight movies. Red's phone had even picked up the audio: a pop ditty sung by some squeaky-clean female recording artist Riker couldn't quite place.

Riker winced when Red zoomed in on the teenager's torn shirt and partially exposed right breast. He had a feeling as he continued to watch that he knew what was next. And sure enough, the image went wild for short while before steadying somewhat as a disembodied freckle-dotted hand entered the frame and dove under the torn fabric. The groping went on for a few seconds but didn't stop there. There was some grunting going on off-screen and Red's hand continued south, the camera angle changing to record the despicable acts he was doing to the lifeless teen.

As Riker averted his gaze, he realized he was on the way to blowing his stack. Muscles in his neck and shoulders and back tight as steel cables, he silenced the video and pocketed the phone. Wanting nothing more than to tear the guy's pasty arms off, stick one, hand-first where the sun doesn't shine, and then beat him within an inch of his life with the other, Riker instead drew in a deep, cleansing breath.

Chapter 25

Thank God for anger management and Alcoholics Anonymous,
thought Riker. That short pause when agitated had saved Red's
life, and likely spared Riker his first look at the inside of a prison
cell.

When Riker finally swung his gaze back to Red, the
younger man wouldn't make eye contact. So Riker ordered him
closer to the Freightliner, saying, "You want to cop a feel?" He
grabbed the back of Red's head, knocking his hat off in the
process. Shoving hard so that Red's face hovered just inches
above the flesh-choked tread on the outside tire, Riker growled,
"She's closer in age to you than that girl in the van. Go ahead …
get yourself some of that. Gives a whole new meaning to *stinky
finger*, don't you think?"

As if she'd understood some of what Riker had said, the
three remaining fingers on the undead woman's right arm
waggled.

"Look, she's game." Riker grabbed the belt on the guy's
shorts and maneuvered his face closer to the fingers.

Red was beginning to shake and whimper, begging to be
let go.

"Alright," Riker said, hauling Red back and spinning him
around like a top. "While I decide what to do with your perverted
ass, I have a task for you to complete."

"What is it?" Red stammered.

Looking down on the smaller man, Riker half-expected to
see a puddle of piss pooling on the ground around his flip-flops.
Instead, he saw a frightened child with his hand caught in the

cookie jar. Still, that shit didn't fly. The guy was going to have to pay.

"Climb into the cab," ordered Riker, gesturing at the Freightliner while telling Red what he wanted him to look for while inside.

Red climbed up and disappeared into the sleeper. In less than a minute he was back in the passenger seat with a long-sleeved shirt in hand and a worried look on his face. "No tire iron," he said.

Riker watched the man step to the road, then relieved him of the shirt. Dropping the shirt to the road, he said, "There's a panel on the back side of the cab. I'd be willing to wager the driver keeps her tools in there. If there's not a tire iron, a long-handled screwdriver will do."

Indicating the blood-and-guts sullied tires, Red said, "You expect me to climb up on one of *those*?"

"Now," ordered Riker. He thought about brandishing the Sig to get his point across, but quickly discarded that as a foolish move.

Red did as he was told, bitching and moaning as he mounted the tire. He reached his arm in and popped the panel. Rummaging around in the cubby, he came out with a screwdriver nearly as long as his forearm.

"Will this do?"

Riker nodded and stabbed a finger at the interstate.

"Get down!"

Standing on the freeway, Red shot a questioning look at Riker, then tried handing him the tool.

Riker said, "You're going to need that."

"For what?"

"Patience," Riker said, a knowing look ghosting across his face. "First, I want you to reach in there and cop a feel. Make it good, it might be your last contact with the opposite sex for a real long time."

Far off in the distance, a siren wailed.

Red balked.

"Too old for you, eh? You only like the *young* ones. The ones you can fool into liking you. Or force booze or pills on until they can't fight you off. Isn't that how guys like you do it?"

Red swallowed hard. It was becoming clear to him there was no talking his way out of this one.

"Do it!" Riker bellowed, the veins on his neck bulging.

Red threaded a hand between the tires. Keeping clear of the corpse's pistoning jaw, he palmed the lump of skinless blubber that most resembled a breast.

"Hold that pose," Riker said as he angled closer and brought the phone up. Seeing that the screen had gone dark due to inactivity, he looked a question at Red.

"I told you," Red exclaimed. "It reads my thumbprint. Let me out of here and I'll unlock it for you."

In a no-nonsense tone, Riker said, "You can give me the code, or I can cut your thumb off and unlock it that way." To drive the threat home, he dragged the multi-tool from a pocket and deployed the serrated saw blade. "It's your call."

"Six, nine, six, nine."

"Isn't that *cute.*"

Riker tried the code. Seeing the phone light up and the lock screen disappear, he located the flashlight utility and thumbed it on.

"Is this necessary?"

"Totally," said Riker, the memory of Tara calling him with news she'd been raped after clubbing in Fort Wayne fresh as it had been the night she'd entrusted him with it.

At the time their mom had been waging her losing battle to cancer. No way Tara could burden her with that. So she called the second most important person in her life. And a helluva burden it was. A weight Riker had been carrying on his wide shoulders for nearly a year now.

Not being there for Tara when she needed him most was the worst feeling in the world and had nearly driven him back to the bottle.

As if his only sibling knew he was thinking of her, the Shelby's familiar-sounding horn blared two times—a preordained code to let him know who the sirens belonged to.

Riker tapped the camera icon, swiped to *Video* and started filming. With his free hand, he pantomimed what he wanted Red to do. First, he mimicked what he'd seen the pervert do to the teen's breast.

Once he had captured Red copping a feel on the living dead thing, he made a stabbing motion to his own eye.

Shaking visibly, Red withdrew his hand. It too was trembling and slick with blood. As he regarded Riker, a single tear welled up, then traced his cheek.

Riker pointed at the screwdriver in Red's hand. Then, with a tilt of the head, gestured toward the twitching corpse and repeated the stabbing motion to his own right eye.

Red's eyes widened.

Message received.

"Do it," Riker mouthed.

The pool of piss Riker had expected earlier became a reality as Red followed through with the task.

Riker videoed Red shoving the screwdriver into the dead thing's eye, then thumbed the phone off and slipped it into the pocket containing the keys to the Mini Cooper.

He said, "Drop the screwdriver."

Red complied.

Without another word, Riker scooped up the shirt and used it to truss Red's arms behind his back. Remaining tight-lipped, he steered the man around the Freightliner and back to the Shelby. Along the way, he picked up strobing lights in the distance. They were red and blue and growing nearer.

Two honks.

Police.

Riker looked to the Shelby. Tara was at the wheel and flashed him with its brilliant high beams.

Riker walked Red to the truckers and pushed him to the ground at their feet. "This is one sick individual," he said. "And a murderer, to boot." He handed the phone and keys to Nicole.

"Evidence is on the phone. Look at your own risk." He told her the code and gave her the keys to Red's car.

The horn blared again as the Shelby started rolling in reverse.

Riker stood in the breakdown lane with the sputtering flare at his feet and his back facing the procession of slow-moving vehicles getting by on the grass median. He was staring down at his own shadow when the Shelby ground to a halt a foot off his right shoulder.

The tinted window on the driver's side rear door pulsed down. Steve-O's face appeared in the void. He beckoned to Riker with one hand, the other clamped firmly atop his white Stetson. "We have to go right now," he said. "The Johnnys are coming."

Satisfied Red would get what he was due, Riker hauled open the driver's door and traded places with Tara.

He dropped the transmission into drive as he waited for her to loop around the truck. Eyes going to the mirror, he saw that the flashing lights were almost upon them. And sure enough, they belonged to a fleet of black Suburbans.

Once Tara was seated and belted in, Riker entered the steady flow of northbound traffic, the story of what he'd just done spilling forth, and the tension between his shoulders beginning to melt away.

Chapter 26

The only detail Riker had left out during his retelling of the story was him putting down the undead half-man.

Steve-O was staring at the jackknifed Freightliner when they transitioned from breakdown lane to interstate. "My money is on monsters," he declared. "Am I right?"

"More like *victims*," Riker answered.

"I saw what you did back there," said Tara, softly. "It was the right thing to do, Lee. He would have wanted it."

"Still felt like murder. Which is why I didn't mention it," Riker conceded. "It wasn't like the one coming at us in the tunnel. With that one ... I just acted. If you break it down, he, *it* ... the *Bolt*—whatever name you choose, impaled itself on the push bar."

"I get it. And I agree wholeheartedly," said Tara. "That time in the tunnel was all about survival. What you did back there on the road was an act of compassion."

Riker said nothing as he watched the speedometer creep north of seventy. Settling into a nice cruising speed of seventy-five, he glanced at Tara. Voice taking on the same soft tone as hers, he said, "'*Who was he?'* is all I was thinking when I did it. Was he a dad? Someone's brother? Was he some little ol' lady's son and on his way to help her survive this thing?"

Tara said nothing. She was busy dabbing at her eyes with a napkin.

Voice adopting a hard edge, Riker went on. "It's so fuckin' messed up what this Romero thing is doing to us. What it's making us do to people just like us."

Following Riker's thoughtful observation, Steve-O said, "Then we have to think of something better to call them than *monsters.*" He went quiet for a few seconds. Finally, voice trailing off as he sank back into the crew cab, he added, "I'll think on it."

After skirting south of Lake City on the 75, Riker took the Shelby through a sweeping right-hand interchange that spit them out on westbound Interstate 10—the southernmost cross-country Interstate Highway in the American Interstate Highway System. Exiting the interchange, they found all westbound lanes of I-10 choked with fast-moving vehicles. After merging with the flow of traffic and settling into the center lane, Riker stole a look at the SYNC screen and concluded they were witnessing the beginning of a mass exodus from Jacksonville, some sixty miles to the east.

Bordered by mangroves and palm trees, I-10 seemed to go on forever, splitting a flat, desolate landscape dotted with swamps, open fields, and the occasional homestead.

On the distant horizon, the bottom half of the sun was just beginning to merge with the ground clutter. Bisected horizontally by a thin black cloud band—no doubt dumping rain somewhere in their path—in just a few seconds the yellow-orange orb seemed to swell to twice its normal size as the millennia-long battle against night's approach began anew.

Ten minutes after leaving the accident site, the Shelby's automatic headlights flared on, illuminating both northbound lanes with twin cones of blue-white light.

They rode in silence for more than an hour, keeping pace with thinning traffic, and not once seeing evidence of Romero's touch, the Florida National Guard, or Johnny and his fleet of black vehicles.

But that all changed southwest of Madison, in the midst of Hixtown Swamp, when Riker saw blue and red lights far off in the distance.

"Better slow down," urged Tara.

Riker thought, *Aye, aye, Mom.*

But out loud, he said, "And give off a guilty vibe?"

"You're going ten over."

Steve-O said, "Dolly goes ten over when she's parked."

"The man has a point."

Riker kept the same pace. Thirty seconds after spotting the red and blues, the Shelby's headlights washed over a Dodge Charger with Florida Highway Patrol on its door. It was parked at an angle behind a silver Tesla.

In passing, they all got a quick snapshot of the scene.

The lone trooper was on the shoulder behind his vehicle and busy cuffing a wild-eyed man baring a mouthful of bloody teeth.

Sitting on the shoulder, back to the Tesla's rear bumper, was a middle-aged woman. She wore a pained expression as she pressed a blood-soaked compress to her abdomen.

The Shelby was moving just south of eighty miles per hour, and maybe three truck lengths beyond the Tesla's sloped front end, when Tara said, "Shouldn't we stop?"

Wanting nothing to do with what he'd just seen, Riker said, "Looked to me like the trooper had the situation under control."

Though he didn't voice it, it was clear to him that the trooper was going to have a full back seat. And that meant the likelihood of the trooper getting into his loaded-down Charger and giving chase was right up there with the Cubs winning the World Series.

It wasn't until an hour later, when Tallahassee showed up on the navigation pane as a mess of red, traffic-choked roads, that, once again, they began to see strange happenings—clear evidence of the infection's rapid westward surge.

About midway through the gentle east/west parabola I-10 took as it skirted north of Tallahassee, they came across another multicar pileup. Though there were no emergency vehicles on scene, the static brake lights gave Riker enough advance warning to slow down and get an eyeful of what was happening.

Unlike the previous incident back on I-75, there were no flares being deployed and no good Samaritans looking to help.

Six vehicles were tangled and blocking the right lane and shoulder. The Shelby's headlights picked up multiple pools of what looked to be automotive fluids.

On the shoulder beyond the wreck, a dozen adults were engaged in a wild and bloody melee.

As the Camry Riker had been keeping pace with for some time signaled and began to drift to the left breakdown lane, he said, "That right there makes driving in Atlanta look like a trip down Sesame Street."

Which prompted Steve-O to ask, "Who's your favorite puppet?" The man was back to hanging on the seatback and holding a half-eaten Twinkie in one hand. Having shed the Stetson, his wispy graying hair was plastered helmet-like to his head.

Without missing a beat, Tara said, "I know who Lee's *least* favorite puppet is."

Face intruding into Riker's personal space, Steve-O chanted, "Who? Who? Who?"

Riker shook his head.

Steve-O continued to badger Riker as Tara looked on, smiling.

"Big Bird," divulged Riker. "Always was and always will be. I hated his nasally voice. I really, really hated how he stooped over top of everyone he met."

Sounding genuinely inquisitive, Steve-O said, "Why?"

Tara said, "Because Lee was always super self-conscious of his size."

"I'd love to be as tall as you, Lee. Then people wouldn't look down on me."

Lump forming in her throat, Tara said, "Who's your favorite puppet, Steve-O?"

Chin upthrust, he said, "Snuffleupagus."

Eyes going watery, Tara asked, "Why him?"

"Because he's Big Bird's imaginary friend," said Steve-O somberly. Going on, he added, "I was a lot of people's imaginary friend."

"What do you mean by that?" Riker asked.

"At school people would only talk to me when we were alone."

Blinking away tears, Tara said, "And they ignored you in the halls, right?"

Steve-O nodded. "At the dances, nobody talked to me. In gym class, nobody picked me to be on their team. At lunch, nobody sat with me."

Tara exhaled and began to sob. Her chest heaved and she buried her face in her hands.

Shooting Tara a concerned look, Steve-O said, "Did I say something wrong, Pretty Lady?"

Tara looked his way and shook her head. Said, "You did nothing of the sort."

Riker handed his sister a napkin, then regarded Steve-O. "It's not you, big man. Tara has been there. She's been bullied. Looked over for positions and stuff."

Nodding, Tara said, "I'll be on your team, Steve-O."

"We're friends now, Lee and Tara Riker. From now on you can call me Steve." He paused and handed Tara another napkin. "But only if you want."

"No way, Jose. I'm fond of Steve-O," said Riker. "Is it cool with you if I keep calling you that?"

"Sure thing. Just don't call me Jose. That's not even close to Steve or Steve-O."

Riker said, "You got a deal."

Still dabbing away tears, Tara cracked a smile and nodded in agreement.

Chapter 27

With the lights of Tallahassee proper illuminating a distant bank of low clouds, they passed a chain truck stop disgorging eighteen-wheelers, many of them colliding with each other in their wild dash to escape some unseen horror within the sprawling group of squat buildings.

"Look," Tara said. She was pointing at the Mobil station when a semi tanker truck caromed into one of the fuel islands, taking out a bank of pumps and sending the roof overhead sliding from the poles supporting it.

No sooner had Tara opened her mouth than a massive explosion lit up the night sky. It was so bright the glow of nearby Tallahassee was completely washed out.

Tara drew in a sharp breath. As she did, the Shelby was hit broadside by the shockwave and rocked on its suspension. As a result, the steering wheel jerked in Riker's hands.

It felt as if the Shelby had been hit broadside by a hundred-mile-an-hour-plus wind gust.

It took a handful of seconds for Riker's night vision to return. Even longer for him to believe what they had just witnessed.

Driving blind along a hundred yards or so of I-10, arms locked and knuckles going white, was nearly as frightening to Riker as sharing that dark stadium tunnel with the Bolt at the high school back in Indiana.

My money is on monsters, thought Riker, the flames and smoke cloud roiling over the business concern but a jumble of orange and yellow dots thanks to his compromised vision.

Shielding her eyes from the growing conflagration, Tara dragged out her phone and thumbed in 911. Putting the device to her ear, she made a face and drummed her fingers on the dash.

There was a secondary explosion at the station. Due to the distance travelling nearly eighty miles per hour had put between the Shelby and the secondary explosion, they heard nothing and escaped being rocked by its shockwave.

Tara shook her head and scrutinized the iPhone screen. With the winking lights dotting the sprawl of north Tallahassee reflecting as a soft glow off the smartphone's glass, she said, "All circuits are busy, please stay on the line. Lot of good that'll do *right now* for whoever's still inside that truck stop."

"The infection is chasing us west," Riker noted. "I'm pretty confident we're going to find the border to Alabama closed and soldiers screening for signs of sickness."

"Sickos!" blurted Steve-O, "is much nicer than monsters."

Cop-a-feel Red was the real sicko, thought Riker. "They are carrying the sickness," he agreed. "And one little bite spreads it. 'Sickos' works for me, Steve-O."

"I agree," Tara said. "They used to be people just like us. Just because they want to eat us doesn't mean we can't show them a little respect."

Riker kept the Shelby in the right lane as they skirted Tallahassee and pushed west, passing half a dozen blocked off-ramps feeding to beaches to the south and nearby towns and smaller cities flanking the interstate.

Much like the handful of freeway exits between Naples and Fort Myers, access to Midway, Greensboro, DeFuniak Springs, Crestview, Holt, and Milton were all being protected by a mixture of National Guard soldiers, local law enforcement, and armed citizenry—a nearly two-hundred-mile corridor where the only choice they had was to watch the gas needle creep south and continue driving west.

Carry on. You're not welcome here, was how Riker interpreted it all.

***

After travelling two hundred miles in a little over three hours, with the only drama being a tailgating asshole whom Riker wanted to fill with buckshot, traffic ahead on both lanes of Interstate 10 began to slow, then stopped altogether.

Beyond the flaring red lights on braking vehicles were two rows of stopped cars, trucks, and SUVs. Most were darkened inside and out. Some, however, became a beacon in the dark when a person inside tapped a brake pedal or flicked on a dome light.

Tara asked, "What do you make of this?"

"I'll reserve judgement until I can check it out for myself."

"Conduct a little ... what do you Army guys call it? Recon?"

"Exactly." Riker slewed to the left lane and brought the Shelby to a full stop, leaving a yard or so between the rig's grille and the boxy little import that had just conducted the same maneuver.

Riker looked back at the half cloverleaf interchange they'd just bypassed. It was maybe half a mile distant. The silhouette of a darkened SUV could be seen on the overpass looming above the interstate.

Amber marker lights giving their position away, a number of vehicles blocked the onramp to westbound I-10. And to add insult to injury, a back loader, its roof-mounted lights ablaze, was building a dirt berm across the off-ramp feeding the overpass from eastbound I-10.

No turning back now, thought Riker as he started mulling over their next move.

A group of people were congregated around a jacked-up pickup equipped with a cabover camper. On the rear of the camper was a porch light of sorts. It threw off a weak yellow spill that illuminated a graphic featuring a smiling caveman wearing woolly mammoth fur and brandishing a wooden club.

A rack on back of the camper shell held gas cans, an old-style ratchet jack, and a pair of high-dollar mountain bikes.

Tara said, "Doesn't look like trouble."

Riker said, "I don't see flares or anything pointing to another wreck." He leaned over and eyed the navigation pane. It was mostly blue, with I-10 represented as a solid green line that continued on for an inch or so before entering the sea of blue pixels. Tapping the spot where I-10 started out over the digital water, he asked, "How far are we from this bridge?"

Tara said, "Not very."

Riker looked a question at her.

"Less than a mile, I guess,"

He rapped the steering wheel. "*Pisses* me off that we've made it all the way from Miami, keeping one step ahead of Romero, and then we come up against *this*."

Interjecting himself into the conversation, Steve-O said, "I don't like it here. There could be *Sickos* lurking about."

Not sure if he truly liked the newly adopted name for the infected—no matter their stage on the journey to undeath or their ambulatory speed thereafter—Riker started the emergency flashers to blinking, set the e-brake, and shut down the engine.

"Keep your eyes peeled for ... *Sickos*, Steve."

Tara mouthed, "Steve?"

Riker shrugged.

She said, "You're going it alone again, aren't you?"

Nodding, he reached into the center console and snatched up the Sig Sauer.

"If you take that," Tara said, "best you be ready to use it."

Shooting her a look that seemed to say *no duh*, he reached under his seat and came up with the stubby Shockwave.

"Buckshot, slug, buckshot is how I loaded her up. You have six shots. Only point it at something you're willing to destroy. Finger off the trigger until you need to do the destroying." He elbowed the door open, causing the dome light to bathe the interior with its warm yellow glow. He studied her face in the light for a couple of seconds. Saw she was beginning to drift off, her features slowly adopting her patented *you're not my parent* look.

Riker stepped to the road. "Keep it locked," he instructed, then shut the door. As he passed by Steve-O's window, he met the man's gaze through the glass, made a V with the first two fingers on his left hand, and pointed to his own eyes.

Watch my back.

Seeing the man throw a *message received* salute, Riker stalked forward to a cube of a vehicle that, ironically, just so happened to be a Nissan Cube. Through the Cube's wraparound rear window glass, he saw that the entire back of the vehicle, everything behind the two front seats, was occupied by bags of groceries, blankets, and camping gear.

Both front seats were empty. Where the driver went, he hadn't a clue.

Moving on, he heard the hiss of radials on asphalt as more vehicles arrived. Brakes squealed and then doors were opening and closing. Finally, as he came up alongside the minivan ahead of the Cube, he heard harried voices questioning the cause of the jam-up.

About to find out, he thought as he walked nonchalantly past the gaggle of people standing beside the pickup with the cabover.

Tipping his Braves hat at the people as they all craned toward him, Riker raised the flashlight beam waist-high to them and gave them a quick once-over.

There were five total, two men and three women. Judging by their relaxed postures—the men holding long-necked Buds one-handed and facing each other as they talked, the women standing in a tight little circle, knees close to touching—Riker concluded they all knew one another. Maybe they were travelling together in the truck looming over them, or, some of them were riding in a nearby vehicle.

As Riker kept on moving, he studied the scene frozen in his mind's eye. The men were both Caucasian and much older than him. The one he'd made eye contact with was narrow in the face, maybe five-ten, and lean for a man his age. The bushy soul patch under his lower lip was ringed by a neatly trimmed silver goatee. His hair was mostly gray and parted down the middle. A braided ponytail showed itself when he turned his head. Silver earrings inset with some kind of green stone sparkled in the residual light thrown from Riker's Scorpion.

The second man was about six foot and looked to be pushing three hundred pounds. He wore his gray hair cut high and tight and was dressed in nondescript clothing: worn blue jeans, a gray cotton shirt with the sleeves hiked up past his elbows, and a blue kerchief knotted around his neck. On his stockinged feet were a pair of Birkenstock sandals that looked old enough to have seen their fair share of Grateful Dead concerts.

The women were all a bit younger, with the tallest among them deeply tanned. She wore her raven-black hair in a short bob cut. Rimless glasses rested on an aquiline nose centered perfectly between high cheekbones. Artisan-style silver earrings decorated both ears. Intricate necklaces, also sterling silver, encircled her neck. Every one of her fingers, thumbs included, bore at least one silver ring. Most of the woman's jewelry was adorned with the same green stone as Ponytail's earrings. Turquoise, was Riker's best guess.

In that split-second pass, Riker had pegged Ponytail and the tanned woman showing similar interests in jewelry as a couple. How the two unassuming women fit in with the couple and Birkenstock-clad man remained a mystery.

Riker continued on down the seemingly unending line of inert vehicles. After passing about fifteen or so, he veered left, toward the front fender of a low-slung Corvette, and covertly let his fingertips drag the length of the car's swooping hood.

Still warm.

So he walked another hundred yards, head down and watching where he was stepping. Without breaking stride, he reached over and touched the hood of a full-size import pickup.

Cold.

Taking into account the outside temperature, which at the moment was closer to sixty than seventy, he guessed the rig's motor had been shut down for quite some time.

Standing as tall as possible, hand still braced on the cold hood, he peered down the long line of vehicles. Though he couldn't see an end to the queue, where I-10 curved gently left, maybe a mile distant, he did spot some kind of emergency vehicle, its flashing red and blue lights lending an ominous feel to the entire scene.

Taking into account the number of vehicles stretching from his position to the distant flashing lights, he guessed the span must have already been closed for a couple of hours before the pickup arrived.

As Riker contemplated continuing on to the bend, to see what lay beyond, a disembodied voice filtered from the truck's partially open window. "Keep your hands to yourself, a-hole."

Raising his arms in mock surrender, Riker continued on, striding past another ten vehicles before giving wide berth to a small group of people fighting over a half-full can of gasoline.

Finally, after walking what he guessed to be another third of a mile, all the while craning and angling to see more of what was happening near the beginning of the water crossing, he found a spot near the bend with direct line-of-sight to the roadblock.

Packed in tight bumper-to-bumper between him and the bridge were thirty to forty vehicles. Where there were only intermittent strands of barrier cables running parallel to the east and westbound lanes near the Shelby, here I-10 was divided by concrete Jersey barriers.

The flashing blue and reds he'd spotted from a distance were mounted atop the pair of armored vehicles blocking both westbound lanes. One man stood beside the nearest vehicle. He was illuminated by the strobing light spill.

Riker saw that the man was outfitted in dark BDUs. On his head was a tactical helmet sprouting some kind of night vision device. A long gun was held at a low-ready. Hanging off one hip were pre-looped flex-cuffs. A holstered pistol rode low on his right thigh.

Though the man wore a uniform with no insignia to speak of, he carried himself with the disciplined poise of someone with years of military training.

Having learned little more than the rough estimate of how long the bridge had been closed, and that crossing was likely not happening any time soon, Riker commenced the long walk back to the Shelby.

Chapter 28

On the initial leg of Riker's recon trip forward, people barely looked at him, and not one person—save for the owner of the pickup who'd called him an a-hole—had spoken to him.

Now, on the way back, his pace quickened by his desire to turn the Shelby around and find an alternate route, people were poking their heads out of windows and asking him what he had seen.

Bridge is still closed, was his stock answer, until he reached the spot in the road where he'd come across the New Age couple and their three friends.

Ponytail was sitting on a camp chair beside the pickup and strumming a pretty damn good rendition of Neil Young's *Old Man* on an acoustic six-string. His partner was standing before a folding table and heating a pot of something on a Coleman camp stove. She'd donned a woolen shawl with a Navajo design and looked up when Riker diverted the flashlight beam from the road a few feet ahead of him to the ground near the couple.

Before he had shifted the cone of light, he learned the others were no longer there.

He said, "Sorry for encroaching with my light. Didn't want to step on anyone's toes in the dark."

"No worries," said the man, speaking slowly. "We're just passing time until they reopen the bridge."

There was an underlying Southern twang to the man's voice that Riker couldn't quite place.

"I don't think they'll be letting anyone across," Riker proffered. "At least not in the dead of night. My guess is that the inspections and strip searches will be commencing shortly."

Standing and clicking on a flashlight of his own, the man said, "You may have a point." He leaned the guitar against the pickup and extended a hand. "Name's Tobias Harlan." Nodding as Riker clasped his hand, he added, "Maria here is my better half."

"Lee Riker," he said. "Pleased to meet you both." He had already removed his ball cap to shake Harlan's hand, so he merely nodded at the woman. "How long have you all been waiting here?"

Harlan said, "Going on about ninety minutes, give or take."

Riker's previous guesstimate of an hour, when coupled with the time it took for him to make his round trip, added up to nearly ninety minutes. *Not bad for a spitball estimate.*

A low rumbling started way off to the west.

Harlan said, "We been hearing that about every thirty minutes or so."

"There's a big naval air station south of Pensacola," Riker noted. "Means those are probably Hornets."

The rumble rose in pitch and grew louder by the second. In less than a minute, the air was filled with the howl of a flight of four jet aircraft. As they darted left to right, low overhead, Riker spotted twin cones of flame shooting out back of each individual ship.

Riker thought back to when they'd skirted Tampa earlier in the day. With the United States Special Operations Command headquartered at MacDill Air Force Base just a stone's throw south of the city and sitting pretty exposed on a spit of land jutting south into Tampa Bay, he had expected to see lots of military aviation activity transiting the base's restricted airspace.

But he had not.

Not a single F-15 or Osprey. No transports or refueling birds lumbering into the sky.

Not a thing had been airborne over Tampa, either. No news choppers monitoring traffic. No shiny Airbus helicopters shuttling VIPs from place to place.

Nothing. Now that he thought about it, perhaps the airspace over the city had been designated a no-fly zone.

Still focused on the rapidly dimming cones of fire, Riker wondered where the northeasterly heading they were holding would take them. Over Georgia and then the Carolinas? Perhaps points further north or east? Maybe they were going to bank hard to starboard real soon and rocket downstate.

He'd never find out. However, that they were currently flying on afterburner made it clear to him they were needed somewhere in a hurry.

"They were really gettin' it on," observed Harlan.

"Damn straight," agreed Riker.

Taking her hands from her ears, Maria said, "I wonder where they're all going."

Voice betraying a hint of disgust, Harlan said, "Probably in support of that ongoing training exercise been fouling up the roads everywhere we've been."

Changing the subject, Riker said, "Your plates are New Mexico, I see."

Nodding, Harlan said, "Me and Maria are treating my baby brother's boy to a road trip."

"He's not really a *boy* anymore, Tobias," interjected Maria. "He's twenty going on thirty. Wise beyond his years, that one."

Gesturing with the flashlight, Harlan said, "You got that right, honey."

Maria turned on a battery-powered lantern and started pouring steaming water into enamel camp mugs. "Instant coffee, Mr. Riker? Water's real hot."

Sacrilege, thought Riker. Out loud, he said, "No thanks. I better be getting back to my family."

Harlan swung the beam at Riker. Said, "Family? Where you all headed?"

Wondering where the nephew was, Riker was about to give a vague answer to the question when a soft clicking noise preceded the sudden materialization of a wiry form astride a matte-black mountain bike.

Harlan was first to react to the sound, his flashlight beam following as he pivoted to his right.

Maria set aside the pot and lifted the lantern off the table.

Now awash in the light from the lantern and flashlight beam, Riker saw that the person dismounting the bike was a young man.

The nameless nephew.

The rider wore black BDU pants, the pockets bulging. Riker noted the cuffs of the uniform pants were tucked into a pair of coyote-tan desert boots and bloused to perfection.

Long dark hair flowed from underneath a floppy brimmed hat sporting a woodland camouflage pattern. A headlamp, its light extinguished, rode high on his forehead where it was mostly concealed by the hat's drooping front brim.

"I found a workaround," said the nephew, pausing a few beats to catch his breath. "There's an old guy running a ferry." Harlan tilted his head and stared daggers at the young man, who continued on, saying, "He's set up for business at a boat ramp a few miles south of here."

"Jess," said Maria sharply. "Put your bike away and lock it up so it doesn't get stolen." She didn't wait to see if he was complying. She had already turned away and was dumping the water and coffee out on the road.

Looking at Riker, Harlan said, "Jessie is a little restless, so we sent him on a ride."

More like a silent recon, thought Riker. And though he was watching Maria hastily breaking down her stove and table setup instead of looking directly into Harlan's faded blue eyes, he still nodded to show the man he had been listening.

Harlan introduced Jess to Riker, who stood his ground and said, "Pleasure."

"What's going on?" asked Jessie.

Shooing the young man away, Harlan said, "I figure this jam will be breaking soon. Better get things situated for the long drive ahead. Nice meeting you, Lee."

Having heard and seen enough, Riker nodded again and pointed east. Saying "Family awaits," he turned and walked on, the dull ache and incessant throbbing in his stump beginning to wear on him.

Chapter 29

Nearly to the Shelby, Riker was momentarily blinded when its HID headlights flared to life. Though he didn't know it because he had instinctively brought a hand to his face and closed his eyes, the headlights had gone dark a half-beat after they had snapped on.

After caroming off a mirror and banging into the gray SUV now sitting broadside to the Shelby, Riker's night vision was beginning to come around.

There was a whirring sound and Tara's head poked out of the passenger window. "What took you so long?" she whispered.

Giving her a dose of her own medicine, Riker lit her face up with the Scorpion's blue-white beam. *Karma's a mother* was what was crossing his mind when the low moaning riding the onshore breeze reached his ears. Hair on his neck pricking, he looked over the hood, aiming the beam at the tree line just beyond the desolate eastbound lanes. Seeing nothing there, he regarded Tara. "What's up, Sis?"

"While you were away on your *evening* stroll, two dudes showed up."

Riker dragged the Sig from the holster and made a slow pirouette. Finished, he said, "What did they do?"

"One of them looked in my window—"

Interrupting, Riker said, "He didn't see you?"

She shook her head.

"You were always the darker one," he ribbed.

"Screw you, Lee."

Steve's window powered down. In his hands was the Nerf rifle, locked and loaded from the looks of it. "I was ready," he stated. "But Tara told me to lay low. That they'll probably move on."

Again, a drawn-out moan sounded from directly across the interstate. It was followed closely by the sharp cracks of branches breaking.

"But they didn't," said Riker, looking in the direction the sounds were coming from.

Tara shook her head. "Nope. One backtracked and started messing with the lock on the tonneau cover."

Steve said, "We think the other butthole was messing with the gas cap."

Riker looked the length of the interstate. Saw the Harlans' truck jockeying around on the shoulder. The white backup lights bracketing the camper shell were accompanied by intermittent flashes of red as the driver stabbed the brake pedal. Meeting Tara's gaze, he said, "Nobody came to your aid?"

"It's nighttime, Lee. And the teenagers were wearing dark clothes. Doubt if anyone even saw them. Besides," she added, "once I rolled down the window and aimed the shocker at the one on my side—"

"Shockwave," corrected Steve-O.

"Whatever," responded Tara. "They saw the gun and scurried off from wherever they came."

"Which way did they go?"

Tara stabbed a thumb behind her.

"I'm going to top off the tanks," Riker said.

"Then what?"

Riker pointed at the Harlans' camper. Whoever was driving had just gotten it straightened out and was reversing it eastbound in the westbound breakdown lane. Seeing the top-heavy rig creeping along in reverse, shimmying and rocking to and fro, made Riker think of a wooden sailing ship fighting rough seas. Eyes locked on the pickup, he told Tara and Steve-O about meeting the Harlans and then touched on what he'd seen at the roadblock. As he was wrapping up his short retelling of his recon by detailing Jessie's unannounced return on the bike and what was said immediately thereafter, the rear of the Harlans' pickup, camper shell complete with spare gas cans and trio of mountain bikes, motored past the Cube and drew even with the Shelby's front bumper.

Transmission emitting a shrill whine, the rig continued on, slipping by the Shelby with very little room to spare.

Riker tracked the Chevy as it chugged along with Tobias Harlan behind the wheel and Maria in the passenger seat, her face a mask of concern.

As soon as the Chevy was nearing the last of the dozen or so vehicles lined up behind the Shelby, it bounded up onto the road and came to a complete stop, rocking subtly on its springs.

"Topping off the tank can wait," said Tara, indicating the retreating truck. "We need to follow them."

Agreeing with Tara, Riker ordered Steve-O to close his window. As he brought the Scorpion to bear on the tree line, he heard one of the truck's windows being run down.

Bracketed in the wide cone of light was a trio of zombies. The pair to emerge first from the woods were geriatric and appeared to have died and reanimated some time ago. Their ashen skin was marked up with long, angry red gashes. Twigs and leaves clung to the scraps of clothing hanging off their emaciated frames.

The male's stomach was marred by dozens of bite marks. The likely fatal wounds wept black liquid and, with each stilted step, seemed to open and close like the hungry mouths that made them.

The undead woman following the man out of the woods was missing several fingers on each hand. Her pink blouse was in tatters and soiled with something that had turned it black in places. On her exposed ribcage were a half-dozen purple-rimmed craters where dermis and flesh had been violently rent.

Behind the plodding geriatrics was a bikini-clad twenty-something. Cause of first death was clear: a trio of puckered gunshot wounds that made up a bloody triangle north of her navel. Like earthworms emerging after a good rain, shiny intestine bulged from a long tear opening up between two of the golf-ball-sized holes.

Riker was reaching blindly for the Shelby's door when Bikini Girl's lifeless eyes locked with his. Before he could haul open the door and climb in, several things happened in rapid succession.

He heard the tell-tale noise of the Nerf powering up and saw a stream of neon green foam bullets launch from the open crew cab window.

Then, head taking a downward tilt, Bikini Girl's pace quickened exponentially.

From the safe confines of the Shelby, Tara bellowed, "Get inside, Lee!"

Riker heard the admonition but didn't respond. He was chanting "Shit! Shit! Shit!" and throwing the Sig's safety. As he brought the pistol up and tracked the Bolt with the Sig's red holographic reticle, it somehow found a third gear and the fast lope became a head-down sprint.

Gun hand braced on the wrist of the hand with the tac-light, Riker set his feet a shoulder width apart and leaned forward to accept the coming recoil. Big mistake on the latter. Not on account of mechanics, though. That was pretty much the way the Army had trained him to shoot more than a decade ago. The *problem* was the mental acceptance that the recoil was imminent. Because the second he pressed the trigger, the anticipation caused him to overcompensate, which, in turn, made him drag his first three shots down and to the left.

While not striking the Bolt in the face where he had been aiming, the screaming rounds pulverized its right shoulder and humerus to the point that the only things keeping the arm attached and still in motion were a few ribbons of pale dermis and a single glistening strand of muscle.

Incredibly, Bikini Girl had covered both lanes of I-10, the breakdown lane, and had made it halfway across the grass median by the time Riker was aware of the damage caused by his errant shots.

With Bikini Girl still crossing the median a few feet to Riker's fore, he drew a calming breath and aimed for the bridge of her nose. But before he could press the trigger, inexplicably, the nearly naked walking corpse was lost from sight.

Again Tara wailed, "Get in, Lee. They're getting away!"

The ineffective storm of neon bullets ceased at once.

Eager to see what had dropped the Bolt in its tracks, Riker set off across the ankle-high grass. Two long strides and a quick left to right sweep with the tac-light and he had it in his sights. It was on its back just this side of a taut barrier cable meant to guard against head-on collisions.

The damage from the impact with the cable was immediately evident. Horizontal red lines were abraded across both thighs. And speaking to the violence of the rapid deceleration, the shiny intestines that had been playing peek-a-boo with Riker were now just a big greasy pile of guts lying on the grass beside the thrashing creature.

Dipping his finger into the trigger guard, Riker sighted on the undead woman's face and pressed the trigger twice.

Tobias Harlan reversing the wrong way down the I-10 had started people gawking.

Tara's shouts, followed by the ensuing gunplay, brought most of them out of their vehicles.

Unfortunately, with no traffic noise, and the Navy jets long gone, the guards likely heard it all as well.

A woman in the Cube's passenger seat screamed at the top of her voice.

As Riker turned his gun on the geriatric zombies, a heavyset man rushed from the dark.

Shooting Riker a disgust-filled glare, the thirty-something stepped gingerly around the pile of guts, dropped to his knees, and wrapped his arms around Bikini Girl.

"I wouldn't get that on you," Riker said. "She's got the virus."

"You killed her," declared the man. Looking around, he added, "Someone call the cops."

A shouting match erupted somewhere in the dark to Riker's left. Two distinct voices rose exponentially, and it became clear to him that a couple was fighting over whether the woman should or shouldn't cross over the cable barrier to help the geriatrics.

Apparently, the fairer sex won the argument. Because a few seconds after it had started, it was over, and a woman hopped from a nearby minivan and jogged off toward the pair of Slogs.

"They're dead and infected with a deadly virus," Riker bellowed. "Stay away from them."

The woman didn't listen. She vaulted over the barrier and stood facing him, arms above her head.

"Forget about them," Tara called. "Can't fix stupid."

Behind Riker, the Shelby's V8 roared to life.

Ruing the fact he hadn't taken care of business earlier where Susan and her kids were concerned, he waved off Tara's plea and stalked toward the barrier. Aiming the Sig at the Slogs, he ordered the woman to step aside.

She did the exact opposite. She moved in front of the Sig, then abruptly spun away and into the outstretched arms of the undead man.

"Lady, you just won yourself a Darwin Award," muttered Riker as he watched the Slog's gnarled fingers thread into the woman's shoulder-length hair. He was drawing a breath and about to fire some hastily aimed shots when the undead woman arrived, and the combined weight of the pair dragged the good Samaritan off her feet.

Before Riker could do anything to change the woman's fate, all three had crashed to the ground, arms and legs entangled.

Coming to realize the outstretched arms were not a welcoming gesture, the woman screamed and started to plead for someone named *Mike* to help her.

A man sprinted from the minivan. He was wiry and agile and fast. He hurdled the cable with ease, reaching the scrum just as a fan of blood scythed the air a foot in front of his face. The woman abruptly stopped screaming and the man Riker guessed to be *Mike* started to pry the clutching fingers from the woman's hair. The man was focused solely on freeing the woman when the female Slog bit down hard on his forearm.

"Nothing I can do," Riker said as he decocked and holstered the Sig. Hustling back to the truck, he added, "If only you'd listened to me."

Getting behind the wheel, he saw the Shelby's headlight spill cut by a number of people in a rush to help the minivan couple. As he clicked his seatbelt home, he also saw a crowd of angry people glaring at him and angling for the Shelby.

Tara said, "Get us out of here. Now!"

All of a sudden feeling a lot like Frankenstein's Monster, Riker dropped the transmission into gear and began the delicate dance of extricating the pickup.

Chapter 30

Ignoring the people outside the Shelby calling for him to stop and answer for shooting Bikini Girl, Riker focused on getting the Shelby onto the breakdown lane.

Though he had left a couple of yards buffer between the pickup's grille and the tiny Nissan Cube, the SUV crowding the Shelby's rear bumper left him with very little room to maneuver. So he had to resort to a whole bunch of incremental movements front and back, while cutting the wheels left and right, just to get the front end past the Cube.

Having no other option than to move out of the way while the pickup was in motion, as soon as it came to a halt, the crowd moved in again.

"Steve-O," called Riker. "I want you to keep an eye on the Harlans' camper. Let me know if they cross the median or take a ramp."

"Aye, aye," responded Steve-O. "They're a long way off right now."

Flicking his eyes to the rearview, Riker said, "I see them." In reality, all he saw was a pair of dim, red tail lights.

Twisting around in her seat, Tara said, "You're going to have to haul ass to catch them."

Riker grunted. He didn't really have the energy to formulate an answer.

After cranking the steering wheel hard left, Riker had the Shelby back to moving forward with nothing blocking his path but pissed-off bystanders.

A few seconds after beginning the pain in the ass maneuver, the Shelby was parallel to the cable barrier and facing east.

Just as Riker was putting the transmission back into Drive for what seemed like the twentieth time in just a couple of minutes, a man showed up out of the gloom and slammed a closed fist on the driver's window.

Seeing a whole bunch of people standing in the Shelby's path, Riker shook his head and waved the man off.

The guy wasn't having it. He continued to bang as Riker gunned the engine to get people moving out of their way.

Once the Shelby started to roll, the man placed both palms on the window and yelled, "You killed her!"

Ignoring the indictment, Riker laid on the horn.

The man at the window recoiled.

The gawkers assembled on the grass median and asphalt shoulder shielded their eyes against the headlights.

Riker flashed them with his high beams.

Get out of the way.

A few people shuffled back to their cars.

Tara had been hanging on to the grab bar and staring murderously at the man banging on her brother's window when another man appeared at her window and began haranguing her to *get out*.

Mouthing, "Back the fuck off," she brought the stubby shotgun up off her lap and aimed it squarely at the twenty-something.

Taking a cue from Tara's action, Steve-O rolled his window down and jammed the Nerf's orange muzzle to the other man's neck. "Back the—" Steve-O didn't get to finish the order, because the truck was lurching forward, its huge V8 and Borla exhaust joining forces to create a sonic tempest that started a rift opening up in the crowd.

Last thing Steve-O remembered as he was punched into the seatback was the man at the driver window freezing mid-knock and going wide-eyed as he realized a gun was being pressed to his neck.

In the passenger seat, as Riker tromped the gas, Tara was seeing more of the same. It was painfully obvious to her that the man had never stared down the business end of a shotgun. He mouthed "Oh shit" and raised his hands in surrender, then dropped from view.

As the people who had exited their cars and assembled on the shoulder and median dove out of the accelerating Shelby's path, the gathering of people beyond the cable barrier slid by in Riker's side vision. What had started out as a wannabe good Samaritan and pair of Slogs rolling around on the grass was now a waist-high mound of writhing bodies.

Letting go of the bar by her head, Tara dropped her gaze to the wing mirror. Though it was dark and the form kneeling on the ground was diminishing rapidly, she got the impression she had provided the guy who had been at her window his very first *come to Jesus* moment.

She cracked a smile at the notion that she may have also caused him to crap his pants.

"Truck is turning," noted Steve-O.

Riker said, "I see it," and matted the pedal.

The line of stopped vehicles were now behind them. Up ahead, save for the sweeping spill of the pickup's headlights, the westbound stretch of I-10 was clear. Riker had the road all to himself. So he killed the headlights and pushed the speedo needle past seventy.

The path the Harlans' Chevy pickup had cut through the median and between a break in the cable barrier was a short drive from where they had started.

Riker decelerated rapidly and bumped the Shelby onto the grassy median.

Due to the extra weight of the camper, the tire tracks sank deep in the grass and proved easy to follow. Negotiating the chicane left between the run of cable for State Troopers and emergency vehicles to reverse direction on the I-10 without having to go to the distant overpass was not an easy task in the wide body Shelby. It proved especially difficult in the dark. But

Riker had no choice. Last thing he wanted to do was turn on the HID lights and risk spooking the Harlans and having them rabbit.

Slowly and from a distance was how Riker intended to follow his quarry.

Tara was pulling up the navigation window on the SYNC screen when the Shelby rode up onto I-10 eastbound. She was zooming in and moving the image around with her finger when Steve blurted, "They're turning."

Looking up, she estimated the distance to the spot on the stretch of interstate she'd last seen the taillights. Regarding the nav screen, she tried to determine where on the pixelated map the pickup had turned south. Which was not an easy task. She quickly found that gauging distance in the dark and then trying to convert that to the scaled-down digital map was akin to performing Chinese arithmetic while blindfolded.

Squinting at the glowing screen, she said, "I'm not seeing a named road where they just turned."

Riker asked, "Is there a *road*?"

She shook her head. "Not an established thoroughfare. If something is there to turn off on, it's a driveway, feeder road, or something like that."

Nearing the spot on the right where Tara thought she saw the truck turn off, Riker slowed the Shelby to a crawl and flicked on the headlights.

After travelling another hundred feet or so, the headlight beams washed over the entrance to an unmarked access road branching off to the right. Only difference between this road and the one in Big Cypress, where they had encountered the woman and her two kids, was the mangled gate. It was hanging wide open and being supported by just one undamaged hinge. Beyond the gate, the narrow track seemed to get swallowed up by the surrounding foliage.

"This has got to be it," observed Tara. "The gate—"

"And the trees," interrupted Riker as he steered onto the road and stopped beside the steel post to which the one remaining hinge was bolted.

Tara said, "Trees?"

Riker indicated the trees crowding the road on both sides. Some of their branches were bent and broken from ground level to about the height he guessed the Caveman cabover rose above the road. The road itself was littered with leaves and small limbs that had come off the trees.

Riker said, "See how the trees took a beating from the camper?"

Tara eyed the trees, then craned to see the gate. "What color was the guy's pickup?"

"In the dark it looked silver," answered Riker. "Could just as well have been gunmetal gray."

She said, "Well, there *is* gray paint on the gate."

"I saw that," conceded Riker as he pulled the truck into the trees, killed the engine and extinguished the headlights.

"It's real dark here," Steve-O said. "Hope there aren't any *Sickos* lurking around."

It was real quiet, too. Only sound was an owl hooting somewhere far off.

Tara tightened her grip on the Shockwave. Throwing a hard shiver, she said, "Can we go now?"

Riker shook his head. "We're going to have to drive with the lights on. Means we'll need to give them a few more seconds' head start so they don't make us and run for it."

Propping both elbows on the seatback, Steve-O said, "Be like Hansel and Gretel, Lee Riker."

Nearly in unison, the siblings said, "Huh?"

"They followed crumbs. You can follow broken branches."

Riker had already been thinking along the same lines. However, not wanting to steal Steve-O's thunder, he turned to him and said, "I like the way you're thinking. That there is some Grade-A, Sherlock-Holmes power of observation."

While they waited on the dark road, time moving painfully slow, Tara manipulated the satellite image on the navigation screen until the shoreline left of the closed bridge was the focal point. It was irregular and dropped away south by east. She traced a finger along a half-inch-long stretch of shoreline equidistant to the roadblock northwest of them and the small bay to the south.

Due south of the spot on the map where the bridge began its long run out over water was the end of the road they were currently parked on. The road met a T. The left branch snaked off toward the bay, while the right wandered off toward a series of docks on the nearby waterway. Though mostly obscured by trees, the roofs of a house and several outbuildings could be seen through the lush canopy.

"Here," she finally said. "It's a treed cove. Looks to be sheltered from prying eyes on the bridge." Tapping a cracked fingernail on the screen, she added, "And this road we're on will take us to it."

Adopting a passable British accent, Steve-O said, "Elementary, my dear Watson." Then, voice returning to normal and wavering slightly, he asked, "Can we go now?"

Chapter 31

The Shelby had taken a beating as Riker tooled it along the unimproved track of a road leading away from the interstate. Five minutes after leaving the I-10 behind, they were stopped at the T in the road, the big V8 thrumming away under the hood, and the house they had spotted on the navigation screen visible through a copse of mature trees. Someone was definitely home, as nearly every light inside and out were ablaze.

The house was a two-story affair with clapboard siding, sprouting multi-windowed dormers at each point of the compass. Up close, it didn't present as nicely as it had from space. The blue paint was faded and chipped. Its wraparound porch had also seen better days. Many of the white balusters were missing and the planking was buckling in places. Under cover of the porch roof were a number of cheap plastic chairs and a lone love seat, the cushions making a pronounced dip in the middle.

Seeing headlights approaching from the left, Riker turned right onto the two-lane road. After a short run on pavement, he nosed the Shelby left onto the gravel drive leading to the house.

The place was open. That much was clear. At the mouth of the drive was a sandwich board advertising crossing fees. It wasn't a professional-looking item. The old price of $50 per vehicle and $25 per single-axle trailer had been crossed out. The new fares were written on the sign below the old in big block letters.

Incredulous, Tara said, "A thousand bucks a car? And another grand if you have a trailer? Are they fuckin' *crazy*?"

"Nope, these folks are shrewd risk-takers," Riker said. "There's probably some kind of statute on the books says you can't ferry people across when bridges around here are shut down. Supply and demand drives the price."

"That's a lot of Big Macs," declared Steve-O.

"That's highway robbery," sneered Tara. "No different than the dick selling gas at a four-hundred-percent markup."

Riker didn't want to argue with Tara. It was a losing proposition, any way you sliced it. She was a bit of an idealist. Which wasn't necessarily a bad thing. However, when someone had something you and a whole bunch of other people *really, really* needed, maybe even coveted, the people holding the commodity were the ones in the driver's seat.

The drive took them past outbuildings and then curled around back of an enormous glass greenhouse. Coming out into the open, they saw a number of things not visible on the satellite image.

Halide lights mounted high up on wooden posts bathed everything close to the water in soft orange light. On the right, facing the inky black water, was an open-air boathouse twice the size of the greenhouse. On the dock beside the boathouse was a pair of rust-streaked gas pumps. Abutting the boathouse was a general store of sorts. A sign on the store's shingled roof read SHORTY'S BAIT AND TACKLE. On the wall facing the boat ramp, directly below the sign, was a single door with one glass window bearing a CLOSED sign.

On the low porch, left of the door, was a freezer dedicated for block and cubed ice. A handwritten sign on one of the freezer doors indicated Shorty was all out of both. Right of the entry was an old refrigerator emblazoned with the words LIVE BAIT.

Each of the store's four darkened windows hosted a glowing neon beer sign.

Dead ahead, at the end of the drive currently occupied by a number of vehicles was the "ferry landing" Jessie had spoken breathlessly of—Harlan's gunmetal gray Chevy last in the long line.

As far as *ferry landings* went, this slab of concrete disappearing into the dark water was nothing more than a boat ramp lined by orange traffic cones to show where vehicles needed to line up prior to boarding.

Riker set the brake and shut the motor down. Turning to Tara, he said, "I'm going to go check things out. See if I can find *Shorty* or his boss."

"I'm going," declared Steve-O. "I have to pee like a racehorse."

Riker nodded and grabbed the Sig from the console. Looking to Steve-O, he asked, "Do you ever have to pee like any other animal?"

"Don't be a smartass to your elders, Lee."

Riker had no answer for that.

Suppressing a smile, Tara said, "Be careful, Bro."

Riker said, "I will. You be careful too." And though he really wanted to instruct her to gun up and lock the truck behind them, he decided to see what she would do if he didn't.

Like a wild animal freed from a leg trap, Steve-O launched out the door and began walking toward the bait shop.

Riker closed both doors and lifted his gaze to Tara. She was staring at him through the window glass, worry in her eyes.

Just as he was beginning to second-guess leaving her behind, the locks thunked shut, she showed him the little pump gun and then mouthed, "Hurry back."

As Riker rushed to catch Steve-O, he looked the length of the line of cars and saw a man in a black hoody and olive-green hip waders turning away from the Harlans' Chevy.

"Wait up, buddy," called the man, his long shadow seeming to weave and bob with each purposeful step he took in Riker's direction.

Though high in pitch and a bit reedy, the voice definitely belonged to a man.

Riker said, "You work here, *buddy*?"

Nodding as he pulled the hood back, the man said, "I'm collecting fares for Shorty. Cash, gold, silver, like-new stuff in trade … *we* take it all."

Riker sized the man up. Found there wasn't much *size* to him. He looked to be a couple of inches north of five foot and a few years north of fifty. A plug of tobacco puffed out his lower lip, the brown juice dribbling from the corner of his mouth as he talked. The picket of yellowed teeth were crooked and flecked with tiny black tobacco granules. Explaining the nasal tone to his voice was the boxer's nose. Broken multiple times, the nose jagged left then right like a lightning bolt before culminating in a curled-over nub of flesh home to blackheads and broken capillaries.

After a pregnant pause, during which the man looked Riker up and down and Steve-O disappeared around back of the bait shop, Riker shook his head emphatically. "First I need to speak with Shorty," he insisted.

"Suit yourself," said the man. "First come first serve is how we work it here. And Shorty is just about to load two more *paying* customers and shove off."

"You the deckhand or something?"

"Or something," answered the man.

Riker craned to see the corner where he had last spotted Steve-O.

Nothing.

"How long is the round trip?"

The man spat tobacco juice on the ground. Wiping his lips on his sleeve, he replied, "'Bout thirty minutes. Give or take."

The rumbling of jet engines began anew. Riker panned his head and determined the noise was coming from behind the boathouse. Which told him the boat ramp was oriented in roughly the same direction as the bridge. And that meant the ferry was probably going to motor south by west before making landfall somewhere near the naval air station.

Regarding the little man, Riker said, "Where does Shorty make his drop-off?"

"Depends."

Riker stared the man down.

Finally, the man said, "Depends on where a fella wants Shorty to take him."

Trying another tack, Riker asked, "Where does the *thousand-dollar* trip end?"

The man spat again. "A short ways south of here, but on the east side of the air base."

Riker lifted his shirt and dove a hand into his pants pocket, inadvertently revealing the Sig in the process. Displaying the wad of hundreds, he peeled ten from the stack and handed them over.

"Do I get a receipt?"

"Don't worry," said the man. "You know where to find me." With that he was on to the next vehicle in line.

Riker called, "I'm not much of a worrier," and struck off toward the bait shop.

The bait shop's "restroom" was a pair of Honey Bucket port-a-pottys secured side-by-side and locked to the trunk of a nearby fir. Riker was wondering what kind of freak would want to steal several hundred pounds of plastic shithouse when his attention was drawn to the curled corner of a dark-green tarp covering something laid out on the ground behind the fir.

Taking a step around the trunk, Riker leaned over and lifted the tarp. The sight of a pale human hand, its dirty fingers curled tightly into a fist, started his "Spidey sense" tingling.

Uncovering the corpse's naked upper body revealed clues that set him somewhat at ease. The milky eyes were open and stared skyward. Cause of death appeared to be the pencil-eraser-sized hole in the young man's temple. Having seen his share of true crime documentaries, Riker identified the tiny black dots on the pale skin surrounding the hole as powder burns. Clearly someone had put this one down up close and personal.

The cheek facing Riker was ripped away, the bloody flap suspended by a ribbon-thin length of skin. Lifting the flap, he saw that the stark white molars were still locked down on what looked to be the better part of someone's thumb.

Beginning on the corpse's neck, just below the ear facing him, were a number of deep furrows still weeping blood. They were angry red and continued over the shoulder and on down the right arm. Where the meandering scratches ended, the bite marks began. They were puckered and oozing blood. The jagged ridges ringing the half-dozen inch-deep wounds peppering the well-muscled forearm were purple and curling over.

Coming to the conclusion that this was likely the corpse of a Bolt, and that the severed thumb meant it got to someone else before being put down, Riker dropped the tarp and tucked the corner under. No sooner had he hinged up and backed away than the door on the nearest outhouse opened and Steve-O stepped out.

"Hey there, Man-O-War," said a still slightly shaken Riker. "You drain every last drop out of that trouser snake of yours?"

Still cinching his belt, Steve-O smiled and nodded.

"Let's go check out this ferry."

Looking up at Riker, one hand adjusting his Stetson, Steve-O said, "You look pale, Lee Riker. Like you just saw a ghost."

"Maybe it was something I ate," Riker lied. "My stomach *is* a bit queasy." Waving Steve-O along, he struck off toward the distant boat ramp.

Chapter 32

Riker felt Tobias Harlan's eyes tracking him and Steve-O as they walked past the man's high-riding Chevy. The man was leaning against the truck's grille and talking quietly with his wife and nephew.

Ignoring the trio of gazes following him, Riker continued on by with Steve-O in tow and none the wiser to the scrutiny.

To the left of the boat ramp was the long dock Riker had spotted on the satellite image. It was lit up with soft light thrown from frosted globes atop nearby stanchions. Though he'd gotten a feel of the scale of the thing from the brief glance of it on the Shelby's navigation screen, the true scope of the operation didn't hit him until he saw it close up. It looked as if a dozen ski boats or runabouts could tie up here at one time. Presently, a thirty- or forty-foot vintage motor yacht was moored near the ramp. Thick, taut ropes coming from the yacht fore and aft wound around burnished metal dock cleats. White fenders hung at intervals from the yacht's deck rail.

With all the gleaming mahogany and brilliant chrome trim, Riker had the vessel pegged as a Chris-Craft. A super high-dollar item when new decades ago, the waxed and buffed beauty still projected that *if you have to ask how much, you probably can't afford me* attitude. As the motor yacht strained against the lines, the fenders rubbing against the gleaming white hull produced a symphony of squeaks.

Why the owner wasn't already moving her to a safer port was lost on Riker.

Out of the blue, Steve-O stopped walking and pointed at something off to his left. "Jet skis," he called to nobody in particular.

Riker followed his arm and spied, parked underneath the magnolia tree fronting the house, a single-axle trailer carrying two newer-looking Yamaha WaveRunners.

FOR SALE - $1000 EACH - TRAILER FREE IF YOU BUY BOTH was spray-painted in white on a plywood sheet propped against the trailer.

Steve-O asked, "Can we ride one?"

"Not tonight," Riker said. "Maybe when we get to where we're going, we can look into buying a pair of them."

Obviously excited by the prospect, Steve-O said, "There's water where we are going?"

"There's got to be a lake or two nearby."

"Tara won't tell me where we're going. Every time I ask it's just 'West, Steve-O.'" The Stetson brim cut the air as he shook his head in frustration.

"Sorry about that. It's just—" Riker went quiet for a tick. "It's just that we don't want to say it aloud and end up jinxing it."

"I understand," said Steve-O. "But we're going to need three jet skis. One for each of us." And just like that, he was on the move toward the boat ramp.

During the brisk walk, Riker counted eight vehicles waiting their turn to cross. Of the eight, two were passenger cars currently in the process of loading. Behind them was a newer Honda Ridgeline pickup and an import minivan. The pickup's load bed was covered with a blue tarp. Judging by the sharp angles of the items underneath the tarp, Riker guessed it was filled with furniture.

The minivan contained only humanity. The seats in back were all occupied by kids of indeterminate ages. A man and woman—both in their thirties—sat up front. Their faces turned expectantly toward the short man in the hoodie as he barked orders at the driver of the car he was guiding onto the ferry.

Lashed to the minivan's roof was a plethora of camping gear. Riding beside the colorful stuff sacks, Rubbermaid bins, and Coleman cooler was a black Yakima box, its contents a mystery.

Behind the van full of kids was an SUV with a young couple in the front seats. It was crowded from behind by a tiny import car with a lone elderly driver at the wheel.

The Harlans' Chevy and Riker's Shelby were lined up behind the import. Since Riker had pulled in, additional vehicles had arrived, the long line now curling out of sight behind the greenhouse.

Riker caught up with Steve-O at the water's edge. The older man was standing on the algae-slickened ramp, hands on hips, watching a four-door Caprice nosing close to the Ford Taurus wagon already in place on the ferry.

After walking backward a few feet to get a panoramic side-view of the vessel, Riker breathed a sigh of relief. Thankfully, the "ferry" lived up to its name. It was basically a motorized barge able to accommodate two vehicles lined up grille to bumper. And though it sat low in the water, it looked pretty stable.

Riker saw no creature comforts to speak of—just a closet-sized pilothouse sitting port-side amidships that looked to have been designed to accommodate the pilot and one other person.

A plaque on the pilothouse read *Miss Abigail*.

A waist-high railing ringed the vessel on three sides. On the bow was a rectangular steel plate that acted as the ramp when deployed. When retracted, the ramp completed the railing.

All in all, while not a ride worthy of the original fare, let alone many times that amount, *Miss Abigail* appeared seaworthy.

The man in the hoodie was standing near the ramp and working some out of sight controls. As the ramp began to motor into the up position, Riker strode over to the ferry and stopped a yard short of the bow. Placing a hand on the port-side railing, he made eye contact with the man who had taken his money. Though he suspected he already knew the answer, he called out loudly, "Where's Shorty?"

When the ramp clanged against the port and starboard bulkheads, the man hurriedly battened it down. Finished, he regarded Riker and said, "What do you call a fella with a bass drum strapped to his back, cymbals between his knees, and an accordion in his hands?"

With a tilt of the head, Riker said, "A one-man band?"

There was a high-pitched turbofan whine in the sky behind them.

The man said, "Exactly," just as a pair of Hornets inbound to Naval Air Station Pensacola flew low and slow overhead.

Noting the planes were flying "lights out," Riker stared at the orange glow of the retreating engines until their noise diminished. Finally, he stared up at the man on the ferry and said, "That would make you *Shorty*."

The man smiled, showing off tobacco-stained teeth. He said, "The one and only," and spit a stream of juice overboard.

And the shoe fits, thought Riker.

A window on the Caprice whirred down and a man demanded the ferry get underway. "I paid good money," he called ahead of a couple of choice swear words.

Shooting the impatient fare a *keep your pants on* glare, Shorty said, "And you are?"

"Lee Riker."

"What is it that you want in addition to the ferry ride, Lee Riker?"

"I saw that thing under the tarp."

Shorty stared hard for a second, then said, "And I saw that *pistola* tucked into your waistband, so fucking what?" He drew his hand out of his pocket and showed off a compact Glock. Gaze swinging from the rear of the bait shop to the motor yacht, he added, "That *thing* attacked the owner of *Liquid Assets* there. Came running out of the dark and tackled him. Bit his thumb clean off then came at me with a full head of steam. I had no choice. Hell, everyone here saw me do it. And not a single person said a thing. Nobody called the cops. And not one of those pricks helped me drag the body to where I stashed it."

"So you think they don't know about the virus? Just figured you were acting out of self-defense?"

"Oh, they know," conceded Shorty. "It's just that if they acknowledge the virus—acknowledge that the *runners* and *shamblers* exist—then they have to admit that the show on AMC, or that movie at the Cineplex ... *Twenty-Eight Days* whatever ... is not just entertainment. That it's all real as a heart attack." He reached two fingers into his mouth and removed the plug of tobacco.

Knowing exactly what Shorty was talking about, having not only seen it on display in others, but having also experienced his own brand of normalcy bias early on, Riker said nothing.

"You know why I do this?" Shorty said, wiping his fingers on his wet-weather pants. Without allowing Riker time to answer, he pulled out a can of Copenhagen and went on talking. "I have a daughter in college at NYU. You know how much that costs per year? It's a lot of bait and tackle and fuel, *that's* how much."

Riker shook his head. "I have no idea the dollar amount." He paused for a beat and watched Shorty dive his fingers into the packed tobacco and stuff an insane amount between his lip and gum. Suddenly the events of a long day landed on his shoulders. From seeing Shorty reload his pick-me-up of choice, Riker craved something to give him a jolt. A big steaming cup of black coffee. Maybe a Red Bull. Hell, even one of those nasty Rip Its Halliburton had flown in to Iraq sounded kind of refreshing right about now. Finally, he said, "Have you heard from your daughter?"

Eyes wet with tears, Shorty shook his head. "Not since Monday of last week."

"I know something about what happened in New York. And it was far more than the terrorist attack story they're still trying to prop up. I also know what I saw while driving from Miami to here." He fixed his gaze on the vast blackness beyond the light's reach.

Steve-O had been listening in on the conversation, his head panning back and forth as each man spoke.

Meeting Shorty's glassy-eyed stare, Riker said, "I have a proposition for you."

Shorty wiped his eyes and then looked a question at Riker.

"Steve-O," said Riker. "Why don't you go back to the truck and check in on Tara."

Happy to have a job to do, Steve-O threw a salute and trundled up the ramp, the first very prescient words of a well-sung rendition of Cash's *God's Gonna Cut You Down* hanging on the humid night air.

Raven Rock Mountain Complex

Sitting in a black leather chair emblazoned with the Presidential seal, President Tillman leaned forward, planted his elbows on the table whose identical counterpart sat in the White House situation room seventy miles away, and steepled his fingers.

Three fingers of Knob Creek in a crystal highball sat on the table before the President. It had been ignored since DHS Secretary Ashe placed it there ten minutes prior.

After enduring a full ten minutes of deep, brooding silence, sixty-one-year-old Chairman of the Joint Chiefs of Staff, Marine Corps General Gerald F. Dunlap, cleared his throat and said, "Mr. President—"

Interrupting, Tillman said, "Jerry, we're going to be in here together for awhile, so let's stick to first names.

Bowing his head, the general said, "Alright, Hank. First names it is. The bombing campaign is failing. We're seeing little attrition. All we're accomplishing is the destruction of infrastructure while suffering unfortunate instances of collateral damage. With all due respect, I think you need to ground the assets. I also think it's time to call for a National Emergency. While we're going down this road, you need to consider sending out a nationwide Presidential Alert. With Aleksei Volkov rattling his rubber sword, the American people need your assurance that we are able to at once take steps necessary to quell Romero's spread *and* stand up to any aggression the Russians may take."

Tillman had been nodding the entire time. He said, "Recall the bombers. Call the alert. First time using the alert, am I right?"

The Chairman nodded.

"Then bring me the draft. I'll need ten minutes to look it over and make necessary revisions."

Addressing the head of DHS, Dunlap said, "Maria, get up to Communications and have them take Town Crier through a dry run. I want this to get out to as many citizens as possible."

Nodding, the petite brunette said, "You got it, Gerald. On my way."

Regarding his SecDef, Tillman asked, "Any word from Executive Foxtrot Two?"

"They picked up your family from Weather, Hank. Last I heard they were diverting to exfil Maria's husband."

The President said nothing.

Understanding the silence for what it was, a need for more intel, Marigold said, "He's a lobbyist with Higgin and Hart. He made it by car to Arlington Memorial, found some high ground, and is in contact with Executive Foxtrot Two."

Downing the bourbon in his glass, Tillman said, "Alert me when they're on final approach. I want to be there to greet them."

"Will do, Hank."

With that, the room cleared, leaving the President alone with his thoughts and the lion's share of Knob Creek left in the bottle.

Chapter 33

Riker said his piece to Shorty, then untied the ferry from the dock and tossed the line over to the man. He didn't bother to watch as *Miss Abigail* reversed away into the dark.

The throbbing of *Miss Abigail's* engines passing behind *Liquid Assets* confirmed what Shorty had said.

A short ways south of here, but on the east side of the air base.

As he passed the minivan full of kids, an outburst of laughter drifting over from the direction of the house piqued Riker's curiosity. Slowing his gait, he craned and saw a small group of people sitting on camp chairs arranged in a rough circle underneath the magnolia tree. A lantern placed on a cooler doubling as a card table sputtered away as people hoisted beers and consulted some kind of playing cards.

And the Titanic's band played on.

Tobias Harlan and his nephew, Jessie, were waiting for Riker when he neared their Chevy.

Jessie stepped into Riker's path and stared up at him. "Only *dicks* eavesdrop," he sneered.

Riker stopped and stared down at the kid. Planting both hands on his hips, he said, "I'm not a *dick*. However, I'm guilty as charged. Desperate times called for desperate measures."

Harlan put a hand on the teen's shoulder. "Stand down, boy."

Shrugging, Riker said, "Hey, you beat us here. No blood, no foul."

Harlan said, "Jessie's just mad at himself for displaying poor OPSEC."

Playing dumb, Riker asked, "What's OPSEC?"

"Operational security," answered Jessie, his tone softened. "Uncle Tobias just likes to keep his cards close to his vest, that's all."

Riker looked the length of the Caveman camper. He saw Steve-O standing beside the Shelby and refilling its tank with gas from one of the plastic jugs. Tara was out of the truck, too. She was standing with her back to Steve-O, the Shockwave clutched in a two-handed grip.

God job, Sis.

A trio of young men standing next to the SUV behind the Shelby seemed to be staring her down.

Keeping one eye on the guys ogling his sister, Riker said, "I'm with Tobias. I tend to keep my business, *my* business."

"Listen," Tobias said, extending his hand, "I would have done the same damn thing if I were in your shoes. Since we're going to be sharing space on *Miss Abigail* for a spell, no sense on us bringing bad blood aboard."

As Riker agreed and reached out to shake Harlan's hand, the phone in the case on the man's hip emitted a klaxon-like tone. Simultaneously, the same annoying sound belched from every phone within earshot, Jessie's included.

Surprised to hear the foreign tone, Harlan yanked the phone from its holder and stared at the illuminated screen.

"Uncle Tobias, did you just get a Presidential Alert?"

Harlan's mouth was moving, but no words were coming out. Finally, finished reading the lengthy message, he nodded. "Yes, I did. And judging by the sounds of things"—he looked around at the other people staring into their devices—"I think everyone here got the same message we did."

Sidling over to Riker, Jessie said, "What's your phone say?"

Wearing a sheepish look, Riker explained how he'd accidentally left his old phone in Miami and that his new smartphone was still in the box and not activated.

Harlan said, "I've never even heard of a text message that has its own unique ring tone. Because that sound that just came out of my phone is *not* one of the ones that came preloaded." He looked to Jessie.

"Mine neither. Aunt Maria," called Jessie. "Did your phone get a message?"

A window high up on the camper shell slid open. The woman's narrow face appeared between parted curtains. "It's in the cab," she said. "Go ahead and check it."

Jessie located the phone and confirmed it had also received the Presidential Alert.

Cold ball forming in his gut, Riker up and left without saying a word to the Harlan clan.

The thuggish-looking twenty-somethings were still standing by their SUV when Riker made it back to the Shelby. And same as Tara, they were all staring down at their phones.

Seeing Riker, Steve-O smiled and gestured at the cans assembled in a neat line beside the pickup's rear tire. "All gassed up," he said, beaming.

"Thank you, Steve-O. You've been a big help this trip. I'd say you're worth more than your weight in gold."

"Do you have a hundred eighty pounds of gold, Lee Riker?"

Not that much, thought Riker. He said, "Figure of speech, Steve-O."

Still holding the Shockwave one handed, Tara looked up from her phone.

Riker asked, "These guys bugging you?"

Tara lifted her gaze and turned her head. Incidentally, the shotgun's lethal end followed.

Stopping the muzzle sweep with his right hand, Riker took the pump gun from her and concealed it behind his leg.

"To answer your question, Lee. No they did not. One look at the shotgun and things got cordial real quick. Pretty much kept to themselves after that."

Riker patted Steve-O on the back. "You can leave those out," he said, indicating the empty gas cans. He nodded at the phone in Tara's hand. "You got the Presidential Alert thing, too?"

She nodded. "Never seen one of these before. Amber alerts, sure. Those are usually localized. Or sent out to a few adjoining states. This one says it went out *nationwide*."

From the front of the line came the sound of engines starting. Soon, the line was rolling forward, including the Harlans' Chevy.

"What did it say?"

"A whole lot of stuff we already know. Plus, in my opinion, a bunch of bad advice."

"Spill," said Riker.

"President Tillman says the hospitals are filled to capacity. He wants everyone to shelter in place and wait for authorities to come and take them to one of the nearest regional FEMA facilities currently being set up around the country."

Riker held up a hand. "I want to read it for myself." He traded Tara the shotgun and the keys to the Shelby for her iPhone. "Need to watch the deadly end of that thing."

Tara said, "My finger was nowhere near the trigger."

"Good job. Still, watch the muzzle sweep."

Steve-O opened his door, leaned in, and came out with the identical Nerf guns.

Examining the iPhone, Riker said, "What's your code? Or does it just read your fingerprint?"

"Here," she said, leaning over and tapping in the code for him.

"Ah," said Riker. "I recognize those numbers."

"Shhh, Lee. Let's keep it our little secret."

Riker read the lengthy text. Finished, he looked at Tara, one brow raised. "It's getting real."

Nodding, she said, "Real scary."

Looking to Steve-O, Riker said, "Why are you gunnin' up?"

"Sickos," he replied as he tried to hand Riker one of the toy guns.

Shaking his head, Riker lifted his shirt and showed Steve-O the Sig in the paddle holster. "I'm good," he said. Dropping the shirt over the semiauto pistol, he leaned over and scooped three of the gas cans off the ground. "Grab one, Steve-O. I prepaid Shorty for twenty gallons."

Wearing a skeptical look, Tara said, "I don't want to know how much Shorty charges per gallon, do I?"

That's not the half of it, thought Riker. Looking to Tara, he said, "Ignorance is bliss, little Sis. Ignorance. Is. Bliss."

Chapter 34

Steve-O stood between the pumps, Nerf carbine held at a low-ready, and guarded Riker while he worked the key Shorty had given him into the padlock on the pump handle.

"How much did he charge you, Lee?"

"Considering the circumstances," Riker admitted, "not nearly as much as he could have."

By the time Riker had filled all four cans and lugged them, two to a hand, back to the Shelby, he heard the first distant engine sounds signaling *Miss Abigail's* imminent return.

A couple of minutes passed before the empty ferry materialized from the dark, nosed into the boat ramp, and Shorty shut down her dual outboards.

In no time, the next two vehicles in line were loaded and Shorty was backing her away from the ramp.

After watching the inky darkness swallow up the retreating ferry, Riker ushered Steve-O inside the truck and then climbed in after, claiming the passenger seat for himself.

Face washed red from the brake lights on Tobias's pickup, Tara regarded Riker. "You've been up for nearly twenty hours," she said gently. "You should close your eyes and take a nap. You'll feel better."

Grunting, Riker shook his head. "I'm going to wait until we get underway."

"That's what ... fifteen minutes, at most?" said Tara. "By the time you close your eyes, we'll be on the other side. What's *that* going to do for you?" Indicating the pickup just beginning to creep toward the ramp, she went on. "There's still two vehicles ahead of *this* monstrosity. That's a full hour. It's eleven o'clock right now. How about I wake you at the witching hour?"

Popping open an energy drink, he said, "Six eyes are better than four any day. Plus, there's bound to be more—"

"Zombies out there," she interrupted. "That's what I was just thinking. If they come, what good are you to us if you're fatigued?"

"Well, I'm pretty sure I'm worthless to us *asleep*," he stated soberly.

"Good point," said Tara. She started the motor and pulled the Shelby forward, leaving half a truck's length between the two pickups. When she shut the motor down, Steve-O was already snoring loudly in the back seat.

"Just like that we're down to two sets of eyes," Riker said as he tipped back the tiny silver and blue can and emptied it in one long pull. "That settles it. And as I was saying before you so rudely cut me off—which, you know, you've been doing since before you could talk—I do think we'll be seeing more zombies before the night is over."

Beneath the magnolia tree to their left, the card game had grown in size and become a raucous affair. Bottles clinked and folding chairs creaked as the white cards were dealt around for what seemed like the hundredth time.

As far as Riker could tell, no money was changing hands. Which made him wonder how the game was keeping a dozen adults engaged, considering all that was happening in the large cities east and south of the panhandle.

Windows rolled down a couple of inches, Tara and Lee watched the people assemble cards in their hand and throw others down.

"What game is that?" asked Tara.

"I was wondering the same thing," he replied.

As they waited for the ferry to return, short periods of absolute silence were bookended by eruptions of uncontrollable laughter brought on by the dealer reading the players' discards.

Ear cocked toward the action, Tara said, "This game is nasty." She turned to face Riker. "What's *bukkake*?"

"I have no idea," he replied. "Maybe it's Japanese for *Here zombie, zombie … please come and chomp on us.*"

"If they don't shut up," said Tara. "I'm going to go over there, break their lantern, and tell them to."

"That won't derail their game, Sis. Most of them are wearing headlamps."

"Then I'll threaten them with Miss Shockwave."

"That's a bit extreme, don't you think?"

"It's almost *that* time of the month," she shot back, smiling. "On second thought, I won't be needing the shotgun."

"Remember, you show off a gun … you better be willing to use it. It's my experience that bluffing only works in Texas Hold 'em or when threatening to end a relationship."

While they watched and listened to the amusing displays of immaturity the game was bringing out of the players, the ferry returned and then disembarked again with the next two vehicles onboard.

Riker took his eyes off a woman doubled over in laughter and regarded Tara. "Fire her up and wait here until I call you forward. Don't ask questions, just do whatever I say. OK?"

She opened her mouth but didn't say anything. She saw in his eyes an intensity that usually preceded him doing something he wasn't going to enjoy. So she nodded and shooed him out the door.

Riker elbowed open the passenger door, then shut it quietly behind him. Under the Caveman's steady gaze, he looped around front of the Shelby. Seeing Tobias Harlan watching him in the Chevy's wide, driver-side wing mirror, Riker approached the occupied cab, hands in plain sight and calling the older man's name.

Attention again drawn to the card game, Tara missed the short animated conversation between Riker and Harlan. When she looked forward, the Chevy's lights went dark and her brother was motioning for her to crank the wheels right and drive the Shelby around.

Dropping the transmission to Drive, she released the brake and edged around the wide camper shell.

Standing by the Chevy's right front fender, Riker met Tara's gaze as she rolled the truck by. "Pull up to the water's edge," he instructed.

After doing as she was told, Tara shut the truck down and set the emergency brake, giving it an extra hard press of her toe. Something about parking the truck on a decline this close to the water was highly unnerving to her.

Appearing outside Tara's window and staring in at her, Riker said, "Why don't you get out and stretch your legs. Best bring Miss S with you."

Not following, she shot him a quizzical look.

Speaking slowly, he said, "Bring the Shockwave."

Tara powered the windows up, stepped out, and set the locks. Peering in the back window at a sleeping Steve-O, she said, "Think he'll be OK by himself?"

With a tilt to his head, Riker looked down at her.

"I know, I know," she replied. "He's a grown ass man. I'll try to remember that."

Out of the Chevy and sitting on a folding chair, Jessie cast a watchful eye on the pair.

Riker said, "Let's walk and talk," then struck off in the direction of Shorty's house.

Passing the card game, Tara cupped a hand to her mouth. Whispering, she asked, "Why did we pull ahead of the Harlans?"

"I told them Shorty wanted my truck loaded first."

"When did he tell you that?"

"He didn't. I lied."

"And they bought that?"

"When Tobias asked why, I told him that since the engines are set back near the stern, and his rig is so darn big, a little balance was required to keep *Miss Abigail* from riding low in water at the ass end."

Tara stopped to inspect the pair of WaveRunners for sale. Looking up, she said, "Any truth to that?"

Riker shook his head. "I know a lot about cars and how to drive them. But I'm Sergeant Schultz when it comes to stuff that floats."

"Sergeant who?"

"Come on," he said, incredulous. "Miss *I Fall Asleep To Old Television Reruns* doesn't know who Sergeant Schultz from *Hogan's Heroes* is? Does Stalag 13 ring a bell? How 'bout Colonel Klink?" In a terrible German accent, he went on, "I see nothing. I hear nothing. I know nothing," then looked at her, one eyebrow arched.

Crickets.

Nearing the edge of the spill from the porch lights, Riker stopped and stared into the dark.

Tara said, "We better head back."

Riker nodded but said nothing. In his mind he was already on the ferry and wondering what awaited them at the end of the trip.

As they started to turn back toward the house, a lone form launched from the dark a dozen yards to their right. It was snarling and twitching and didn't see them. Arms and legs pumping, the male Bolt, somewhere in its twenties, hit the low hedge bordering the rear of Shorty's home at full speed.

Equal and opposite reactions being what they are, as the runner's legs were arrested by the foot-and-a-half-wide thicket, its upper body whipped forward.

Hitting the ground face-first on the grass beyond the hedge, the zombie went heels over head and continued to tumble, rag-doll-like, until all forward momentum was spent.

After having witnessed the reactions of people who have suffered from similar embarrassing situations, Riker half-expected to see the Bolt sit up, flash a sheepish grin, and then proceed to spit out the dirt and grass that had accumulated in its gaping mouth.

Instead, as if the hedge incident had never occurred, the Bolt rolled onto its stomach, went to all fours, and then shot off for the noisy card game, covering almost a dozen feet before once again going bipedal.

"Oh shit!" Tara blurted even as she was scanning the darkness for more of the dead things—her own self-preservation first and foremost in her mind.

"Where there's one," Riker said, "there's bound to be more." He tugged her shirt sleeve and, after reminding her to not flag him with the Shockwave's muzzle, motioned for her to follow.

Keeping low with the Sig drawn and a round chambered, Riker led them in the direction they had come, past the left side of the house and across the front walkway. Just as they arrived behind the WaveRunners, the card game hit a lull and the laughing and chattering ceased.

The silence lasted for a second, maybe two, before there came a loud thud and crash and the lantern and the cooler it had been sitting atop was sent flying.

From fifty feet away, Riker heard a guttural grunt followed closely by the unmistakable sound of air leaving someone's lungs.

In the next beat people were rocketing from their camp chairs and the noise of bottles breaking filled the air.

The screams came next.

Acting as a sort of lookout, a man on the dock bellowed, "It's one of *them*," and hustled toward the lawn.

A woman, her voice suddenly going shrill, warned, "There's more coming," then turned and ran.

Riker saw two bodies rolling around on the ground beside the overturned cooler. The man on the bottom kicked and threw wild haymakers at the undead assailant.

There was an ear-splitting boom as a gun discharged. The lick of flame accompanying the report lit up the lookout, now brandishing a pistol and running up on the pair on the ground. Wearing a stunned look, the shooter did a little happy dance over the unmoving Bolt. Voice displaying equal measures incredulity and confidence, he cried, "I got it. Hot damn, I got it."

No sooner had the man let his gun hand drop to his side than a second Bolt rushed from the gloom and laid him flat out on the grass amidst a jumble of beer bottles and game cards.

The impact with the ground stole the air from the man's lungs and knocked the revolver from his hand.

Light glinting off its chrome finish, the stubby weapon went tumbling end-over-end through the air until gravity brought it back to earth on a patch of trampled grass a dozen feet away.

Beyond the unfolding mayhem, Riker spotted a trio of dark forms trudging slowly toward him. They were spread out in a ragged line on the dock and nearing the Chris-Craft. As they entered the warm light spilling from the yacht's many above-deck windows, the long shadows trailing them shrank to nothing and Riker learned he was looking at two women and a man.

The women were in their late forties when they died. With defensive wounds on their hands and forearms, it was obvious to Riker they had fought back hard against their attackers. Along with the remains of their bloodied clothing, ribbons of dermis and long strips of partially rendered flesh dangled from their pale extremities.

The man had been fit and young before death. He wore only a tiny yellow swimsuit, which Riker called a *banana hammock* and wouldn't be seen dead in. Cause of death wasn't clear. There were no visible bite marks or gunshot wounds. Judging by the way the gray skin hung slack from the walking corpse, Riker figured it had spent some time submerged in water after succumbing to the virus and reanimating.

Drawing a breath, Tara said, "He's hung."

"Like an elephant," Riker said, at once feeling a tinge of inadequacy and the hot rush of embarrassment for gawking at the baby arm sloshing around within the swimsuit's sheer yellow fabric. That the twenty-something wasn't already head down and sprinting for them made Riker think of Swamp Girl. The two had been roughly the same age and fitness level before joining the ranks of the living dead. And both looked to have been among those ranks for quite some time.

Maybe Bolts do suffer some kind of degradation after time, was what he was thinking as undead Magic Mike was cut down by gunfire from above.

Standing on the Chris-Craft's deck, just a few yards from the siblings, was an elderly gentleman. He wore a captain's hat, its polished black brim gleaming under the dock lights. The pointed ends of the red kerchief knotted around his neck hung over a stark white tunic. In his hands was a scoped long rifle, a wisp of gun smoke curling from its upturned muzzle. Working the bolt to eject the brass casing, the man shouted, "There's more coming. Save yourselves while you still can."

As the man fumbled in his pocket for something, a fresh round, presumably, Riker noted the blood-stippled bandage wrapping the hand. And though he couldn't tell from the angle, he guessed the severed thumb in the mouth of the head-shot corpse behind the porta potty likely belonged to the captain.

Ignoring the warning, Riker swung the Sig toward the pair of plodding women.

Thanks to the motion sensors in the reflex sight, the holographic pip was already activated and glowing red when he threw the safety off and lined up for a shot at the leading zombie. Drawing a breath, he exhaled slowly and pressed the trigger.

Once again, he must have been anticipating the recoil, because the first bullet struck low and left, tearing a substantial chunk of flesh from his target's neck. Riker's eyes were closed when the second round discharged, so he missed seeing where it impacted.

When Riker reopened his eyes, the first undead woman was sprawled on the grass near the dock walkway, a gaping, smoking hole where a nose should have been. In the next beat, there was a sharp crack to Riker's right and again a tongue of flame erupted from the captain's rifle.

Taking a direct hit through the crown of its head, the second slow-mover pitched forward and landed atop the face-shot woman, brains pushing from the rear of its ruptured skull.

A few yards left of the walkway, the man who had shot the first Bolt with the pistol was on the ground, unarmed, and fighting with both hands to push the second Bolt off of him.

Sitting cross-legged on the grass within arm's reach of the ongoing struggle was the man who had been tackled off his camp chair. He was bare from the waist up and pressing his blood-soaked tee shirt to the back of his neck. Clearly in shock and oblivious to the flecked bone and brain tissue sliding down one side of his face, he simply rocked back and forth, a thousand-yard-stare fixed on nothing in particular.

The captain was berating the siblings for sticking around when Tara peeled off to her left.

Over the ringing in his ears, Riker detected the harmonic thrum of *Miss Abigail's* twin outboards. That he could hear them at all told him the ferry was close to docking. When he turned to alert Tara, he saw she was navigating the debris field underneath the magnolia tree and coming up real fast on the Bolt's blind side.

The man on his back was tiring. Though both arms were locked at the elbow, they were beginning to quiver.

Showing zero signs of fatigue, the Bolt continued to claw at the prone man's face, each wild swipe bringing its yawning maw a little bit closer to tasting the flesh it sought.

Bringing the Shockwave level to the ground, Tara encouraged the man to keep his arms locked and his head down.

Hearing her brother in her head saying: *Never aim a gun at something you don't want to destroy,* Tara stopped a yard from the melee, planted her feet a shoulder-width apart, and slipped her finger into the trigger guard.

"Sorry," she said as she pressed the trigger and subconsciously closed her eyes.

Nothing.

No *click.*

No *boom.*

All that reached her ears was the snarling of the dead thing a foot from the shotgun's business end and the steady thrum of boat engines somewhere to the right and behind her.

Yelling to be heard over the ferry, Riker said, "Safety."

When Tara threw the safety, she immediately pressed the trigger.

The ferocity of the ensuing report was wholly unexpected and hit her like a clap of thunder. The violent recoil ripped the stubby shotgun's bird's head grip from her right hand. And since the fingers on her left were threaded through the nylon hand-strap attached to the shotgun's fore-end, when she lost control of the weapon, that arm was taken on a wild counterclockwise ride over her head.

Still rooted in place, Riker saw the second Bolt's face all but disappear in a puff of pink mist. He also noted the effects of the recoil and grimaced as Tara's body followed the travel of the five-pound weapon attached to her arm.

The initial expression of shocked surprise on her face was expected. He was sure he'd worn one similar when he forgot to throw the safety on his Sig back at the swamp.

Her reaction to the shotgun's abbreviated grip hitting her squarely between both butt cheeks caught Riker by surprise. Still wearing that look of intense pain, she covered the distance to him with the Shockwave dangling from one hand and the other beckoning for him to meet her halfway.

With a few feet separating them, and Tara developing a pronounced limp, she bellowed, "Take this evil motherfucker," and thrust it at Riker butt first.

"Tell me how you really feel," he joked as he took the shotgun from her. "I didn't warn you that thing's recoil is like a mule kick?"

"Shoulda, coulda, but didn't," she fired back.

On the deck of the yacht above the two, the captain's rifle discharged.

Behind them, Jessie and Tobias were yelling for them to hurry back and get the Shelby started.

A volley of pistol fire sounded from the lawn near the magnolia tree. When Riker looked, he saw a petite blonde, shiny revolver in hand and firing at the dead things filing out of the dark.

For the first time since they'd been waiting in line, a fog horn on the ferry sounded as it nosed in against the boat ramp. Just a short toot to get Riker's attention. "The ferry is docking," he said, tugging on Tara's hand.

Resisting his pull, Tara said, "Lee," and pointed at a fast-mover coming down the dock, straight for them.

"Go," he said, "I'll catch up."

A shouted warning came from the captain above.

Not wanting to shoot the Shockwave one-handed and suffer the same fate as Tara, Riker raised the Sig, threw off the safety, and superimposed the glowing red dot on the Bolt's neck. Knowing the pistol's recoil would drag his gun hand upward a tiny increment with each shot, he pressed the trigger repeatedly.

The pistol belched orange flame and leapt in his hand as a half-dozen nine-millimeter slugs walked a jagged line from the Bolt's sternum to its left eye.

The pattern the bullet strikes made would be a good thing on a 401k statement.

For the Bolt, the devastation was catastrophic. It jerked and began to lose its feet as the first rounds punched neat holes in its upper chest. It commenced to spin away toward the yacht as the next two bullets ripped hunks of meat from one side of its neck. And as the final two lead missiles struck the cheek and eye, gravity and inertia were already working together to bring it down. But it didn't land face-first on the dock's textured concrete treads. Instead, it struck the yacht's hull headlong at nearly full speed, the sound of misshapen skull striking fiberglass but a hollow thud amongst a cacophony of sounds.

Next came the hair-raising sound of bare skin dragging against the hull as the Bolt's twice-dead body contorted strangely and slithered through the narrow space between the Chris-Craft and dock.

When all was said and done, the only evidence Riker had just killed what was once a college-aged man was a number of shell casings on the ground and the pair of crimson streaks running vertical down the yacht's white hull.

Hearing the familiar whine of *Miss Abigail's* ramp lowering into place, Riker flicked the safety, holstered the Sig, and struck off for the Shelby.

Chapter 35

Steve-O was awake and staring wide-eyed at the siblings as Riker's palms slapped against the driver-side door. Since he had thrown the locks and started the V8 with the fob seconds before reaching the Shelby, the only actions he needed to take to get them moving toward the open ramp was select Drive and disengage the parking brake.

Standing on the ramp, Shorty waved them forward. Backpedaling as the Shelby crept up the ramp and onto *Miss Abigail*, only the man's shoulders and head and hands could be seen over the pickup's hood.

Seeing the tailgate clear the ramp, Riker let the Shelby roll forward another foot or two, then shut her down and set the brake.

Looking sidelong at her brother, Tara said, "You're stopping here?"

"Yep," said Riker, digging out the Glock from the center console. "Take this and follow my lead."

"How is Tobias going to get his truck on if you stop here?"

Speaking slowly, Riker said, "Follow my lead."

"How can *I* help?" asked Steve-O.

Regarding Steve-O over his shoulder, Riker said, "Same as before. Watch our backs from in here."

Steve-O said, "You got it," and threw Riker a crisp salute.

When Riker reacquired Shorty's gaze, the man's head had a slight tilt to it and his graying brows were scrunched together. Taking the Shockwave off the floor, he drew the Sig and stepped from the cab.

The gunfire near the house died out about the same time Riker's boots hit *Miss Abigail's* steel deck.

To get away from the zombies trudging across the lawn toward the bait shop, cars and trucks were turning wide circles on the drive and speeding off.

The headlights on Tobias Harlan's Chevy flashed and the horn blared once.

Hanging his head out his window, Tobias hollered, "What the hell are you doing stopping right there?"

Standing with his back to the Shelby's open door, Riker raised both arms level to the deck, aiming the Sig in his right at Shorty, and the Shockwave in his left at Harlan.

Eyes still locked on Harlan, the tone in his voice all business, Riker said, "We're going it alone."

The passenger door on the Chevy opened and out stepped Jessie with some kind of a rifle in hand.

Riker glanced at the pilothouse, saying, "Shorty, get us underway." Shifting his gaze to Tara, he instructed her to train her Glock on Shorty.

Without waiting to see if Shorty or Tara were going to comply with his calmly delivered orders, Riker edged around back of the Shelby and crouched down near the ramp controls.

Jessie screamed, "You asshole," and stalked toward the dock crowding *Miss Abigail's* port side.

Shockwave following Jessie's every move, Riker pressed the up arrow, starting the motor to whine and the ramp to lift off the wet boat ramp.

"We had a deal," bellowed Jessie. "First you tail us here. Now you're hijacking our bought and paid for ride?"

"Shorty will return for you," promised Riker. Seeing the young man's rifle start that slow swing to horizontal, he warned, "You don't want to do that."

Jessie hesitated for a tick.

Taking advantage of the pause, Riker nodded at the Shockwave. "I just saw what this thing will do to a man's head. It's not pretty."

Just as the ramp hit the stops and the electric motor went silent, Riker felt a surge of energy ripple through the deck underfoot. Next, his upper body was being tugged toward the bow as *Miss Abigail* surged away from the boat ramp in reverse. He holstered the Sig and, keeping a low profile, backpedaled aft, alongside the Shelby, the Shockwave's muzzle never leaving Jessie.

Thirty yards from shore there was a disconcerting *clunk* and a shiver ran through the barge cum ferry. Then the outboards went real quiet for a moment as Shorty put them at idle and allowed accrued momentum to carry *Miss Abigail* into the dark.

As the ferry completed the reverse J turn and slowed to a near standstill broadside to the end of the dock, some sixty feet from where it had started, there was another *clunk* and the engines spooled back up.

The Harlans' pickup was reversing up the boat ramp when Riker dropped the Shockwave's muzzle, told Tara to "stand down," then introduced her and Steve-O to Shorty.

Shorty started to laugh.

"What the fuck are you talking about?" she asked, the Glock still pointed at Shorty.

Just to annoy her, Riker spoke real slowly as he repeated himself. "You can stand down now, Sis. Put the *pistola* away."

Shorty was doubled over and laughing hysterically as Tara stuffed the Glock into her waistband. Then, regarding a still dumbfounded Tara, he stopped laughing long enough to spit a stream of tobacco juice into a paper cup. Wiping his lip, he said, "You should have seen the look on your face when Lee told you to put that heater on me. It went all tight. So tight I figured those braids atop your noggin were going to come undone."

"Your face would be tight, too, if you just about had your arm ripped from its socket by a damn shotgun," shot Tara as she began massaging her left shoulder. "And if that wasn't bad enough, the gun whipped over my shoulder and whacked me right between my ass crack."

Without missing a beat, Shorty said, "Want me to *massage* it for you? I can assess the well-being of your coccyx while I'm down there."

"Oh boy," said Steve-O, his cheeks flushed red.

Flipping Shorty the bird, Tara looked to Riker. "Spill your guts, Bro. And it better be good. Hell, I ought to put this *heater* on your dumb ass. Put a little pressure on *you* while you come clean with me and Steve-O."

Sheepish look on his face, Riker raised his arms in mock surrender. "Sis," he said, with a subtle head wag, "it had to go down like it did."

"Are you effin kidding me, Lee Riker? You just had me point a loaded weapon at a living human being, for, like, ten whole minutes." She put her hands on her hips. "And the most jacked-up part of it all is that I didn't even need to."

"It was two minutes, *max*," Riker said. "But who's counting?"

Shorty said, "I sure as hell was counting. How about *you* try staring down the barrel of a Glock."

"With as much as you're charging me," Riker shot, "I feel like I'm the one staring down the barrel of a gun."

Shorty thrust his hand out of the pilothouse. "That reminds me," he said. "Time for you to pay up the other half you owe me."

"I'll pay you the other half when we get to where we're going," insisted Riker.

Without warning, Shorty steered *Miss Abigail* into a shallow turn to port.

Riker leaned against the Shelby as the ferry's stern bit into the water. Adding the threat of being dropped off back at the boat ramp among the angry mob and hungry dead things to the top of his list of effective bluffs, Riker said, "Give me a second. It's in the truck."

Steering to starboard and once again lining the ferry's bow with a dim bubble of light far off on the horizon, Shorty said, "While you're at it, I need you to center your rig on the deck."

Riker nodded and made his way around front of the truck. As he reached the driver's side door, he paused and stared out into the darkness.

Standing on the ferry tooling along the river with nothing to orient himself to was quite unnerving. Though he knew the tree-lined banks were near, that he couldn't see them and wasn't at all in control of their ultimate destination had started the muscles in his neck and back to tense.

Looking up at the moonless sky with its funeral veil of high clouds only added to the sense of vertigo that had been building within him since leaving Shorty's and the dock lights behind.

Leaning out of the pilothouse, Shorty called out to Tara, asking her to help by hauling in the fenders.

Approaching the pilothouse, a puzzled look on her face, Tara said, "Boats don't have fenders."

Pointing out a two-foot-long pill-looking item lying on the deck atop some coiled ropes, Shorty said, "*That's* a fender. You'll find three of them hanging by ropes from the port-side rail. Pull them out of the water, please." After a short pause, he added, "On a boat, *port* means left."

"And starboard is right," Tara replied. "Why should *I* have to do it? First off, I'm not your deckhand. Secondly, we're paying you way more than I think a fifteen-minute boat ride should cost."

"We underpaid, *big time*," interjected Steve-O. "Lee said so."

Shorty ignored Steve-O's comment. Still meeting Tara's glare, he said, "Your brother didn't tell you where we're going?"

Tara stopped massaging her shoulder and her hands went back to her hips. She craned around and bellowed, "Lee ... what happened to our *plan*?"

Already inside the Shelby with the door closed, Riker detected the sudden shift in his sister's body language. Saw her brows furrow and neck muscles go rigid as she squared up to the Shelby's grille. Just as her mouth started moving, he added fuel to the fire by drowning her out with the Shelby's big V8. Waving her aside, he drove forward a half-dozen feet.

After setting the brake and stilling the engine, Riker climbed out wearing a *What did I do?* expression and carrying two banded straps of uncirculated fifty-dollar bills. Each short stack was wrapped by a brown paper band with $5000 stamped across it.

"No way," shot Tara. "You're paying him *more* money?"

"It'll be worth it, Sis. I promise." Sensing the conversation was about to get heated, he sent Steve-O off with orders to get one of the fuel cans from the bed and take it to the stern.

Riker cast his eyes toward the sky as the man plodded off. It was dark as the inside of a coffin. No moon. No stars. And to add to the inland waterway's claustrophobia-inducing atmosphere, there was no ambient light coming from either shore.

Once the sound of Steve-O's cowboy boots clicking on the metal decking had ceased, Riker swung his gaze back to Tara.

Slapping the tight stacks of cash against his palm, he said, "Doing what I ... I mean, what *we* did, gives Shorty plausible deniability once he goes home."

Sour look on her face, Tara said, "Why didn't you tell me?"

"I had to sell it, Sis."

"It was my idea to keep you in the dark," Shorty conceded as he switched on *Miss Abigail's* running lights. "If I wasn't already on the bottom of your shit list, guess I'm there now."

"You sure as hell are, Shorty." She paused and they all watched Steve-O doddle by with a weighty jug containing five gallons of fuel.

"Put it near the stern rail," said Shorty. He spat into his cup, then looked to Riker. "Thought we agreed the second half was to be paid in the same manner as the first."

Riker shook his head. "That's you acting on assumption. You want more gold, which is shooting up in value by the hour, you're going to have to take us a lot farther than our original agreement."

Obviously mulling over his answer, Shorty stared at Riker for a long ten-count. "OK," he finally said, turning on the pilothouse lights. "I don't like it, but you have a deal."

Riker pocketed the cash and dragged out the blue Crown Royal sack he'd lifted from the Miami mansion. It was heavy in his hand, the velvet soft on his skin as he palmed the bulging sack. Items inside clinked together as he loosened the gold drawstring.

"As of this morning, gold was trading for twelve hundred and fifty dollars an ounce. If my math is correct," said Riker, "I owe you eight ounces."

Tara was massaging her left wrist and fingers on that hand. The same hand that had been trapped in the Shockwave's pump strap when she face-shot the Bolt. "Eight ounces is ten grand. Ten *effin* grand." She shook her head. Being wealthy was new to her. Her upbringing had taught her that money was not easy to come by and should *never* be squandered. *There goes Lee spending like a drunken sailor*, was what she was thinking as she watched him drag a handful of different-shaped pieces of gold from the sack. As he separated the round coins from the square ingots, the assortment in his mitt-sized palm glittered orange under the soft light spilling from the pilothouse.

While Riker was counting out the coins, Shorty had been steering the ferry hard to starboard. Once *Miss Abigail* was again tracking straight on calm water Shorty called Blackwater Bay, the far-off bubble of light Riker assumed to be Pensacola was off the bow to starboard and no longer the sole point of visual navigation.

Ranging out from Pensacola, left to right, were a half-dozen similar patches of light Riker assumed were smaller towns on the larger city's inland periphery. Ambling along left of *Miss Abigail* was a long spit of land dotted with lights too numerous to count.

Ashore on the starboard-side were the flickering orange and red flames of dozens of camp fires.

Now and again they saw the sweep of headlights on vehicles traveling unseen roads on the distant shores.

Finished with his task, Steve-O stopped at the open door to the pilothouse. Pushing the Stetson's brim up with one finger, he fixed Shorty with a blue-eyed stare. "What's next?" he asked. "The Pacific Ocean?"

"East Bay is next," said Shorty. "Then Pensacola Bay." Indicating the twin horizontal rows of halide lights bisecting their path ahead, he added, "First we'll motor under Garcon Point Bridge. Next bridge down the way connects Pensacola and Gulf Breeze. We call it Three-Mile. After we leave the two bridges and a couple of more miles of Pensacola Bay behind, we'll be home free on the Gulf of Mexico."

As they motored underneath the first bridge, Shorty asked Steve-O if he wanted to steer the ferry.

"Heck yeah, I want to steer Miss Abigail."

Shorty made room in the pilothouse. "Stand right here and take the wheel."

Steve-O took a spot next to Shorty. Thanks to his cowboy boots, he stood eye-to-eye with him.

Speaking slowly and repeatedly asking Steve-O if he had any questions, Shorty went over the controls. Next, he pointed out the lights on Three-Mile's cement supports. "Keep the throttle where it is and aim for the *middle* of those lights."

A wide smile on his face, Steve-O said, "Aye, aye, Captain." Eyes fixed forward, he asked, "How fast is she going?"

"We're pushing ten knots."

"Is that her top speed?"

"That's classified, kid." Shorty snickered. "Think you can man the helm while I go shake the dew from my lily?"

"I peed like a racehorse a while ago."

"That's a yes?"

"I got this," said Steve-O with all the confidence of a seasoned bar pilot.

Having been privy to the whole interaction, Riker flashed a thumbs-up to Shorty when he stepped from the pilothouse.

In passing, Shorty said, "Not a lot to see from here on out. You and your sister ought to get some sleep."

Riker looked to Tara for her input.

She said, "Hell if I'm going to fall asleep and let that thing I just killed start haunting me."

Shaking his head, Riker said, "I'll sleep when I'm dead."

"Suit yourselves," Shorty said. "I've got to hang one over the rail." Winking at Tara, he added, "You can watch if you want."

Smiling, Tara said, "I'm afraid I'll be needing binoculars to view that peanut in your pants."

Calling back over his shoulder as he strolled past the Shelby, Shorty said, "That can be arranged."

Chapter 36

As *Miss Abigail* neared the Garcon Point Bridge—a two-lane, three-and-a-half-mile-long span—the flashing blue and red lights atop a number of emergency vehicles sixty feet overhead cast an eerie purple hue on the mostly still surface of East Bay.

Out on the open water, the air temperature fluctuated greatly. As the ferry entered a pocket much cooler than anything on the inland waterway, Riker buttoned his shirt to his neck and rolled his sleeves down.

Standing just outside the pilothouse, Shorty leaned in and said, "You got it, Steve."

"I know I do. But it's still Steve-O to you, sir."

"Understood," Shorty said, tapping himself on the head. "My memory, she ain't so great these days."

Standing just off Shorty's right shoulder, Riker asked, "Worrying about Megan?"

Shorty stuffed his lip full of chewing tobacco, then said, "I'm worried sick. But I feel in my gut she's still alive."

"Which is why you took on our business?"

Shorty nodded. "Meg was staying with a couple of other students in an apartment in Jersey. What you told me earlier gives me hope of finding her. And I'm damn well going to give it my best shot."

"She could be coming to you," proffered Tara. She was sitting on the Shelby's hood and working her fingers into her left shoulder muscle.

Shorty shook his head. "I would have gotten a call from her by now."

Tara stopped what she was doing long enough to take a long pull from a warm energy drink. Climbing down from the hood, she said, "Cell coverage *was* real spotty all across New York and New Jersey. Even as we drove down the Eastern Seaboard, more often than not my phone had zero bars."

Shorty spit into his cup. "Like I told your brother, I haven't heard from her since the day the building fell." Conviction creeping into his voice, he said, "She's holed up in her apartment. Of that I am certain."

"I'd offer you a ride," said Riker, "but we're going in two entirely different directions."

"I figured as much. I'm going to test the waters and see what I can get in trade for this old girl. Worst case scenario, I procure myself a set of wheels."

"How am I doing?" asked Steve-O

Tara leaned toward the pilothouse. "I think you need to trade that Stetson in for a captain's hat."

"No way," he replied, then launched into a spot-on rendition of John Fogerty's *Proud Mary*.

Shorty took a pair of binoculars down from a hook on the pilothouse wall. Thrusting them toward Riker, he said, "You're taller. Take a look and see what's going on up on the bridge."

Helping Steve-O sing the chorus about a "riverboat rollin' on a river," Tara intercepted the binoculars and pressed them to her face. She scrutinized the emergency vehicles on the bridge until *Miss Abigail* was passing beneath them.

Shorty asked, "What do you see?"

Smirking, she said, "Not that itty-bitty thing in your pants."

Shorty was about to respond when Riker said, "Sis ... what'd you see up there?"

"Couple of police cruisers and a bunch of dudes in uniform. One of them is watching us through a way bigger pair of binoculars than Shorty's here."

Grimacing, Shorty asked, "Can you tell how the cruisers are painted?"

"All white with gold and blue stripes down the sides."

"Sounds like Gulf Breeze PD," noted Shorty. He took the binoculars from Tara and trained them on the cruisers. After a short pause, he added, "Sure is. And that's no sobriety checkpoint. Too many patrol cars for that. My guess is they're sealing themselves off from the mainland."

"We saw the same thing all the way up from Miami," Riker said. "Sometimes it was local law enforcement doing the job. Other times it was the National Guard blocking the freeway exits. Even saw a couple of off-ramps guarded by local yokels."

Indicating the arrival of a number of vehicles lit up with red and blues atop the rapidly approaching Pensacola Bay Bridge, Shorty said, "It's really taking a foothold." Then, jaw adopting a granite set, he turned to Riker. "Back there at my place—was that the first one of them you killed?"

"No," admitted Riker matter-of-factly. He pulled a plastic chair from the stack of them behind the pilothouse. Sitting down, he removed his prosthesis and launched into their story, beginning with the first time Tara uttered the word *zombie* back in her apartment in Middletown. He went on to detail their incarceration and subsequent flight from the high school in Middletown. Touched on how Steve-O came to be their *road dawg*, then described how they almost got rolled up in the ever-tightening noose consisting of Johnnys in black SUVs and their unmarked helicopter, the Department of Homeland Security in their white Tahoes, and National Guard units from multiple states. It wasn't until Riker got to the half-man he had stabbed in the eye on I-75 outside of Lake City that he broke down.

"He was the first," Riker said, drawing a deep breath. "Shouldn't have been, though. There were others that I should have put down. Had I not been too afraid to act … or too inept when I finally did, I might have saved some people who didn't deserve to die in the manner they did."

Tara put her arm around her brother's shoulder, causing him to start.

"Don't beat yourself up, Bro."

Riker buried his face in his hands and leaned forward in the chair.

Unable to support the sudden transfer of two hundred and forty pounds, the chair's front legs buckled. As a result, Riker pitched forward and to his left. Instead of planting his bare stump on the deck and further inflaming the already irritated skin there, he tucked his chin to his chest and rolled, letting his left shoulder suffer the brunt of the fall.

Shorty and Tara both dropped to their knees next to Riker.

"I couldn't react quick enough to catch you," explained Tara.

"I didn't even see what happened," said Shorty.

They both took ahold of one of Riker's muscled arms. Standing up straight and straining mightily, they lifted a still sobbing Riker back onto the chair.

Giving the siblings their space, Shorty crowded into the pilothouse with Steve-O and shut the sliding door behind him.

Concern evident in his tone, Steve-O asked, "Is Lee hurt?"

"Not physically," Shorty said. "He's just real sad."

"I'm sad, too," declared Steve-O. "Sad for the Sickos. Sad that Lee had to shoot some of them tonight. Sad that the Sickos can't help what they're doing to healthy people."

"I'll be sad right along with you, Steve-O."

Lighted support columns rose from the water to the arched Pensacola Bay Bridge looming high over *Miss Abigail*.

Focused intently on the narrow strait between the nearest columns, Steve-O made minute course corrections. As *Miss Abigail*'s bow drifted to port, he said, "If you want to, Shorty, you may call me *Steve*."

"Good to know I'm not on your shit list, Steve-O."

"Steve, if you want. Your choice."

"I think I'll follow your friends' lead and stick with Steve-O. It has a certain ring." Turning the volume up on the marine radio to drown out the conversation happening on the other side of the door, he spent a few seconds poring over the gauges.

Declaring *Miss Abigail* "good to go," Shorty trained the binoculars on the distant dog-leg left and glassed it from shore to the entrance to the Gulf of Mexico, where he saw way more surface traffic than should be present at one in the morning.

Beyond the western point of Gulf Breeze, situated on an immense parcel of land dotted with bright runway lights and nearly surrounded by water, Pensacola Naval Air Station was strangely quiet. No Hornets on afterburner leaping into the night sky. No headlights sweeping the tarmacs with yellow cones of light. Not even a single set of flashing lights associated with taxiing aircraft waiting permission to launch.

It was as if all air operations had ceased.

Not knowing what to make of it, Shorty decided to keep his mouth shut until they were well clear of the mouth to the Gulf.

As *Miss Abigail* neared the turn to the Gulf, where the waterway narrowed considerably, Shorty took the helm.

"I have a job for you, Steve-O."

"Whatcha got?"

Indicating a plastic crate on the floor under the console, he said, "Drag that out. See if you can find my spotlight."

"Got it," said Steve-O.

The item Steve-O came up with was yellow plastic and featured a lens nearly large enough to double as a dinner plate.

Shorty steered *Miss Abigail* around a group of sailboats anchored in a small cluster where they shouldn't be. Cursing them in his head, he said, "Make sure it's switched off. Wouldn't want to blind the two of us. Then go ahead and plug it into the auxiliary outlet." He took one hand off the wheel long enough to flip up the plastic shield covering the port.

"It's off," said Steve-O. "Plugging it in."

Shorty opened the sliding window to his left, stuck the spot outside, and lit up the sailboats slipping by a dozen feet off of *Miss Abigail's* port side.

The decks of the farthest two boats were cluttered with plastic bins and coolers, but devoid of life. Though he couldn't be sure, the half-dozen dark smudges on the bulkhead of the middle boat sure looked like handprints. Same general size. The splayed fingers of one particular print were abnormally long and tipped by foot-long crimson runners of what Shorty guessed to be dried-on blood.

On the nearest boat—a thirty-footer called *Vagabond*—a middle-aged man and much younger woman sat on deck chairs, smoking. Lying horizontal across the man's bare legs was some type of scoped long gun.

At once, the couple raised their arms to shield their eyes against the million-candle-power beam.

A noticeable slur to his words, the man said, "You're going to get yourself shot if you don't turn that shit off."

"Sorry, friend," called Shorty as he lit up the multitude of vessels at anchor in the waterway dead ahead.

Only a handful of the boats had any kind of lights burning above or below deck. Some of those were full of young people partying on deck. Others were ablaze only below deck, the light spilling from portholes and reflecting eerily off the bay water.

***

An hour removed from his namesake bait shop, and a full twenty minutes after having replaced Steve-O on the wheel, Shorty was a bundle of nerves from having to pilot the ungainly ferry through the maze of vessels at anchor in the dog-leg and narrows immediately preceding the exit to the Gulf.

Now, with nothing but wide-open water off the bow, Shorty made two executive decisions. First, he spit out the chewing tobacco and lit up a cigarette. Then, without consulting the siblings or turning to ask Steve-O his opinion, he steered to starboard, pointing the bow at the soft ambient glow thrown from the lights of dozens of cities.

Chapter 37

Sensing *Miss Abigail* shifting to a course that was a stark deviation from the agreed-upon line of travel, Riker stopped talking mid-sentence and snapped up his prosthesis.

"I felt it, too," Tara said. "Want me to go investigate?"

"Not after what he said to you earlier. Less time you spend alone with him, the better."

Finished snugging on his bionic, Riker rose and hugged Tara. "Thanks for listening," he said, then strode off for the pilothouse.

Arriving outside the closed sliding door, Riker's attention was immediately drawn to the horizon where, far off, north by west, a substantial swath of it burned orange and red. The way the light play shimmered and undulated like a volatile pool of magma reminded him of approaching Las Vegas in the dead of night. Whether arriving by air or land, the city that never sleeps was always enveloped in a similar bubble of light. Whereas he had seen the glow over Vegas as a beacon drawing him in, what he was staring at now was having the entirely opposite effect.

Tearing his eyes from the surreal sight, Riker knocked lightly on the glass.

As the pilothouse door slid open, Shorty shot Riker a questioning look.

All business, Riker asked, "Why are we hugging the shore?"

Voice taking the same tone, Shorty said, "Two words ... *maritime interdiction.*" Looking to Steve-O, he thanked him for his help, then asked him to put the throttles to idle and trade places with Riker.

"I'm tired, anyway," he said. "Think I'll go and rest my eyes."

"If you need to take a dump or something," Shorty said, nodding his head to the back of the boat, "there's one of those chemical RV porta-pottys in the aft locker. Locker's next to the receptacle you used to add the diesel to the internal tank."

"I'm a guy who needs his privacy," said Steve-O as he followed Shorty out of the pilothouse. "If it's all the same to you, I'll just hold it."

"Suit yourself," said Shorty. Stepping into the pilothouse, he invited Riker to join him.

Riker ducked his head as he entered. Reaching back blindly, he closed the door against a gathering wind.

For the first time since boarding the ferry, he got a real good look at the inside of the pilothouse. To say the place was cramped would be one heck of an understatement.

Above the front window was a curved mirror. Reflected in the mirror was the water they'd just transited. The surface close in was a churn of white aerated water. Farther off the stern, their wake was represented as a pair of slowly widening Vs.

Waist-high to Riker was a four-foot-long, wood-grained plastic dash. On the far-left side of the dash was a yoke like the kind found in an airplane cockpit. Next to the *wheel* in Shorty's capable grip, three identical throttles protruded from the dash.

STERN ENGINES was embossed on a plastic plaque stuck to the dash under the two nearest throttles. The third throttle was not labeled, which, of course, piqued Riker's interest.

"What's with the extra throttle?"

Smiling, Shorty said, "*Miss Abigail* has a secret hiding below deck."

"Inboard diesel to augment the outboards?"

"Other way around. Let's just say this old girl is the maritime equivalent of the Millennium Falcon."

Not getting the meaning of the little man's quip, Riker let his eyes continue to roam the dimly lit pilothouse.

Mounted to the bulkhead and sloping up and away from the wheel was a rectangular two-foot-wide flat-panel display. The unit was nearly as tall as it was wide. On the screen was a detailed digital map of the Gulf of Mexico. Included on the periphery was the Florida panhandle and good swathes of the southern shorelines of Alabama, Mississippi, and Louisiana.

Since there were no discernable buttons on the glass display, Riker figured it had to be a touch screen.

"What kind of radar do you have feeding data to that thing?"

"It's a Garmin Fantom open-array with about a ninety-nautical-mile reach. She has all the bells and whistles. Split-screen. Safety zone monitoring. It'll do everything and then some."

Technology, thought Riker as he walked his gaze across a shelf below the dash. On the shelf was a trio of radios, each outfitted with illuminated dials and sprouting its own handset.

"And the radios?"

Shorty looked up from the screen long enough to scan the sea around *Miss Abigail*. Satisfied there were no vessels lurking nearby in the dark, he said, "They're the best that money can buy. Let's just say I can listen in on most any conversation on any frequency."

Nodding, Riker continued his visual tour of the pilothouse.

Mounted on the wall next to Shorty and bristling with inspection tags was a red fire extinguisher. A holstered flare gun was affixed to the wall underneath the port-side window.

Finished, Riker asked, "What's your Garmin showing you?"

On the display, the map was still zoomed way out. Indicating a trio of wedge-shaped icons positioned a few miles offshore from Mississippi, Shorty said, "I've seen this before."

"What are they?"

"Coast Guard cutters *Cypress*, *Barbara Mabrity*, and the *Decisive* out of Pensacola, Mobile, and Pascagoula, respectively. That they're arranged equidistant to each other in a classic picket would normally tell me they're looking to catch runners bringing contraband to shore. However, due to the Romero bug, I think their mission tonight is containment. Which means they're supposed to round up squirters and send them back to shore. And that works in our favor. Can't help but think President Tillman has ordered his firewall moved west a few hundred miles."

"Thus the answer to my question," Riker said. "Staying close to shore keeps us off their radar."

"Yes, and no," said Shorty. "Hate to burst your bubble. But it's likely we're on their radar right now."

"Why the 'no' then?"

Shorty zoomed the image on the screen in a few stops. Pointing to one dot among dozens of small dots hugging shore from Pensacola to the first cutter's position, he said, "Because this little dot on the map is us. Which means we are basically a single needle in a haystack full of them."

Making a sweeping gesture at the dash, Riker asked, "Why all of this?"

"After Abby died, I deposited the life insurance money straight into Megan's college fund. The next day I started work on Miss A here."

"Who's Abby?"

Shorty didn't answer at once. When he finally did, his voice wavered. "My wife of twenty-three years. That's who."

Riker said nothing.

"About five years ago my Abby got diagnosed with the big C. She went all in with the preventative measures. Went ahead and let the docs lop off both of her breasts to stop it from spreading. That still didn't get it all." He went real quiet for a beat. "It spread all over her body. Finally took her from us two years ago Christmas day. Megan was shattered. She still wants nothing to do with the holidays from Thanksgiving to New Year's."

"I'm real sorry for your loss, Shorty. Still doesn't tell me why you need all this on an automobile ferry."

"I spiraled out of control trying to fill the void the loss of Abby left inside me. I started myself a little smuggling business. At first it was people who weren't supposed to leave Florida, for one reason or another. I did not deal in fugitives from the law, though. Then my moral compass got all twisted and I started moving stuff that comes packaged in big bundles. I guess I was hellbent on destruction." He shook his head slowly from side to side. "Wasn't thinking about Megan one bit … only about poor ol' Shorty." Covertly wiping his eyes, he said, "Enough about me. How'd you lose your left wheel?"

After making Shorty promise him there was no contraband onboard, Riker gave the man the short version of how he'd lost his leg, then steered the conversation back to the digital map, and where exactly on it he could expect *Miss Abigail* to make landfall.

Tracing the Alabama shoreline with a finger, Shorty said, "We'll follow this line, pass Mobile"—he looked up at Riker— "where *we* both agreed I would take you in the first place." Regarding the touchscreen, Shorty resumed tracing their course, saying, "Somewhere on either side of Gulf Port, Mississippi is probably our best bet. We'll cross that bridge when we get there."

"Mississippi," Riker said. "Just saying it makes me hear banjos."

"*Deliverance* was set in Georgia, my friend. *Mississippi Burning*, on the other hand …"

"Very funny," Riker said. "Put yourself in my shoes."

Looking down at Riker's boots, Shorty shook his head. "Both of my feet could fit inside one of those battleships."

Wrong analogy, thought Riker. "Imagine wearing my skin," he said. "While driving across *Mississippi.*"

"Parts of Mobile are burning," said Shorty. "That leaves us little choice."

Grunting, Riker said, "Mississippi it is. Just put us in somewhere quiet."

"You got it, boss."

"I'm going to heed Tara's advice and get some shuteye. If you think the Coast Guard is going to give us grief, please wake me up,"

"Copy that," said Shorty.

"And while Tara is on the forefront of my mind—"

Interrupting, Shorty said, "I know … you want me to stay away from her."

"Not what I was going to say, Shorty. She's a grown ass woman. Those are her words, not mine. You mess with her again, though, she'll likely grab you by your hair and underwear and make you go swimming."

Steve-O showed up at the sliding door.

Regarding the man, Riker slid open the door and stepped outside. Taking in a lungful of salty sea air, he said, "I was just leaving, Steve-O." Leaning in real close, mouth an inch from his friend's ear, Riker whispered, "Keep a close eye on him."

Steve-O nodded in understanding, then flashed a thumbs-up.

"Captain on the deck," said Shorty as he slowly nudged all *three* of *Miss Abigail's* engine throttles to their forward stops.

Chapter 38

With a Bolt coming at him from his left and right side, Riker threw the Sig's safety and leveled the semiautomatic pistol head-high to the one approaching from the right. As he did so, he was also bringing the Shockwave in his offhand to bear on the zombie charging hard at him from his left.

The boy and girl looked to be kindergarten-aged. Teeth bared, twisted faces glistening from the chin down with sticky blood, they converged on him with animalistic hunger in their eyes.

He closed his eyes again. Then, three reports—two sharp and one sonorous—sounded back-to-back-to-back. Before he could see the damage—if any—the speeding slugs had wrought on the zombies, he felt his body jerk and he was mercifully freed from the latest in a long string of very vivid nightmares.

Opening his eyes, Riker couldn't see an inch in front of his face. The black Pelican cases bracketing his body left and right were just heavy, sharp-edged objects with no visible outlines or discernable details.

He yawned, then drew in a deep breath. The briny nose of salt air tinged with the sweet smell of Hoppes Number Nine gun oil emanating from the Shockwave hit him first. Then, as he dragged the recently fired weapon from its place above his head and tapped its stunted grip two times against the box bed, the chemical odor of cordite clinging to it entered into the mix.

Less than a second elapsed before Riker's two taps were met by three more from outside. Two short, one long. The latter reverberating in the enclosed space as he exhaled sharply.

Next came a soft metallic click near his feet. A tick after that, as the tailgate was let down, he was bombarded with the angry cries of gulls and the bright, flat light of early morning.

"Come on out of there, *Nosferatu*."

It was Tara.

Voice a bit raspy, he said, "Do I have to?"

"You better," she said. "We have company."

"Where are we?"

"Offshore of Waveland, Mississippi."

About ninety miles from Pensacola, thought Riker. Hitting the light button on his watch, he learned he'd been asleep for about six hours.

Since the Shelby's load bed was long enough from the tailgate to the crew cab wall for Riker to lay flat on his back, that's how he'd slept.

Gripping one of the ribs running horizontal to the rigid tonneau cover, he pulled himself toward the rectangle of light pouring through the tailgate opening. Having shimmied in fully clothed and with his Salomons on, all he had to do now when his feet hit the deck was snug his Braves hat onto his head and wait for his eyes to adjust.

At once, he noticed they were no longer underway. Gone was the gentle rumble of the inboard diesel that had lulled him to sleep. Normally canted a few degrees to the stern when in motion, *Miss Abigail's* deck was now level with the horizon.

Now and again, gentle rollers caused the deck to loll front to back.

The shore lay a mile or so off the bow. Gone were the palm trees, mangrove, and magnolias. In their place were cypress, black willow, and water hickory, their branches drooping over swampy patches of shoreline that glowed bright green against the darker backdrop.

"Put some pep in your step, Bro. Someone wants to meet you." Seeing the Shockwave in his hand and the butt of the Sig protruding from the paddle holster in his waistband, she urged him to leave them both behind.

"Aren't you carrying your Glock?"

233

She shook her head.

"Where is it?"

Casting a furtive glance along the side of the truck, she said, "I stuffed it underneath the seat. Now come on, or they'll get suspicious."

Rising to full extension, Riker peered over the Shelby, toward the bow, where he saw Steve-O armed with the Nerf gun, Shorty by his side and holding an animated conversation with a man wearing a tactical helmet and outfitted in dark blue fatigues. Worn over the fatigues was a plate carrier and chest rig full of magazines. Strapped to the soldier's right leg was a drop-thigh holster containing a black pistol. In his hands was an M4 kitted out with some kind of holographic optics.

Stowing his weapons under the tonneau, Riker closed the tailgate and dropped to his knees.

"What the hell are you doing?" hissed Tara.

"Something that needs doing," he said. "Petty Officer *Tactical Tony* can wait an additional thirty seconds."

"How do you know his rank?"

"I don't. Just saw the Coast Guard cutter standing sentinel off of port. There's a number of classes of Petty Officer in the Coast Guard."

Under Tara's watchful gaze, Riker planted his hands on the steel deck, extended his legs, and began knocking out pushups, allocating the first twenty-two as a tribute to the number of veterans lost daily to suicide, then finishing the set for Murphy, Grayson, and Kincaid, all fallen buddies of his. Though nothing close to the number of pushups he'd performed while still a cog in the Big Green Machine, he never did more than twenty-five, thinking to do so would somehow jinx his buddies who still resided on the good side of the dirt.

As Riker was knocking out the pushups, Tara brought him up to speed.

"We're being turned back," she said as Riker rose. "Shorty's trying to talk his way past the blockade."

Thinking, *Here we go again*, Riker looked to Tara. Popping his neck, he said, "Beauty before brains."

No sooner had the words crossed his lips than he saw Tactical Tony craning in their direction and waving them forward.

The man was indeed a petty officer. The subdued insignia patch consisting of a shield above a single chevron put him at E-4—Petty Officer 3rd Class. A large rectangular patch affixed prominently to his plate carrier read *USCG*. His name tape read *Magee*.

Petty Officer 3rd Class Magee looked Riker up and down. Even giving up six inches, the Tactical Law Enforcement Team member struck an imposing figure.

Riker looked past Magee. Scrutinized the three additional crewmen aboard the rigid inflatable boat bobbing off *Miss Abigail*'s stern. All wore side arms. And all but the RIB's seated pilot held M4 rifles at a low-ready.

Steve-O said, "I gave him permission to board. Don't worry ... I got your back, Lee."

Shorty shrugged. "The commander of *Decisive* didn't give us much choice. She hailed as I was turning in to shore and ordered me to go dead in the water."

Magee said, "You'll need to reverse course. If you don't agree, I have orders to take you into custody and set your vessel adrift."

The dull roar of engines on a white and black vessel approaching from the east drew everyone's attention. It looked to Riker to be some kind of motor yacht. And for a thirty-footer, it was getting it on. The ocean under its bow was taking a beating, the water frothed and hued bluish-white. At the stern, its wake was a single V roiling away at an incredible pace.

Shorty and Riker exchanged knowing glances.

Noting there was no helicopter parked on *Decisive's* helipad and that the RIB was not sprouting an M240 Bravo machine gun from her prow, Riker said, "Sure, Petty Officer Magee. We'll turn back." Looking to Shorty, he asked, "Where to? Can't be Mobile. Tara says it was burning real good when you all passed it by last night."

Magee was watching the yacht's approach. It looked as if the speeding vessel would eventually cut between *Miss Abigail* and

Decisive. Split the goalposts, so to speak. Or in bowling parlance: totally flub a 7-10 split.

Shorty said, "We'll play it by ear. A good deal of Pascagoula and Biloxi were dark as well."

"Power outages?"

"Widespread outages," acknowledged Shorty.

Magee had dragged his attention back to Riker at just about the same time he received a call from *Decisive.* After listening to someone on the other end order him to check out the motor yacht, he turned back to Riker. "You are free to make landfall anywhere *east* of Mississippi. The President has declared a state of emergency. No doubt Martial Law is coming. If you're smart, you'll find yourselves somewhere safe to hunker down and ride this out."

Trying to, thought Riker. *Then you came along and plugged yourself into the equation.*

Tara said, "There *was* a marina west of Mobile."

"That'll have to do," said Shorty. Then, looking to Petty Officer Magee, he added, "Thank you for keeping the high seas safe."

If Magee heard the platitude, he didn't let on. The RIB was pulling alongside *Miss Abigail* and the petty officer was already throwing one leg over the rail and reaching for the helping hand offered to him.

Once aboard the RIB and strapped into a seat, Magee met Riker's stare and stabbed a finger to the east.

Message received.

Riker flashed a thumbs-up.

When the RIB pilot opened up the throttle, the rest of the crew braced and the twin outboards churned the water white.

Riker took his eyes off the retreating boat and looked to Shorty. "They are *not* the enemy," he stated. "We *do not* shoot at them even if they fire warning shots at us. Agreed?"

Shorty nodded.

"Then what's our play?"

Indicating the wide strip of sandy beach dead ahead, Shorty said, "I still want to put us ashore here at Buccaneer State Park. I've used it as a drop-off point before."

"So you're going to feint to the east just for appearances and then cut a hard left and charge ashore?"

The RIB was halfway to *Decisive*, its wake a long white crescent bending out to open sea, away from the ferry. Now a fair distance off the cutter's bow, the white and black motor yacht had slowed and was in the middle of a long, graceful one-eighty.

Inserting a fresh dip of chewing tobacco, Shorty nodded. "It'll be a little more than just a quick feint to the east, though." Wiping his hand on his pants. he added, "I want two things to happen. First, I want to sell our capitulation to whoever may be watching us from *Decisive's* bridge. Second, I want to give Magee and the boys aboard that RIB sufficient time to become preoccupied with their new detainee."

Tara asked, "Can we outrun them if they come back?"

"The cutter, yes," said Shorty. "By the time they start turning her around, we'll be well on our way to shore and have a good enough head start."

With a tilt to her head, she said, "How about the little boat?"

"No way."

Riker asked, "What's her top speed?"

"Best guess is that she can push close to thirty knots," Shorty said. "We can make a little over twenty if I peg all three throttles." He detailed his plan, assigning each person a role.

"We're going to have to time it just right," said Riker. "Even then, we'll be cutting it real close." Regarding Steve-O, he asked, "Did you follow all of that?"

Steve-O displayed a thumbs-up. "Affirmative. I got it all, Lee."

"Tara?"

Nodding, she retrieved the binoculars from Shorty and passed them to her brother.

Taking the wheel, Shorty fired up the outboards and started the ferry turning away from shore.

Raising a hand as a shield against the low-hanging sun, Tara made her way back to the Shelby.

With the ferry picking up speed, Riker lifted the binoculars to his face and trained them on the shoreline. Straight away he saw the reason Shorty wanted to motor a short distance east before committing their turn to the north.

Once used as a military base of operations by Andrew Jackson during the Battle of New Orleans, the flat expanse of treed land was now called Buccaneer State Park.

Instead of soldiers resupplying for a fifty-mile march to New Orleans, what was once known as Jackson Ridge was overrun with dozens of slow-moving walking corpses. The majority of the zombies wandered aimlessly amongst a half-dozen recreational vehicles parked on cement pads just beyond the beach. Past a picket of trees further ashore, shadowy forms traipsed between tents of all shapes, sizes, and colors.

Overturned camp chairs ringed one tent-site's fire pit.

At another site, an elderly man, his throat a mess of pulped flesh, planted both ashen hands on a camp cooler and struggled to stand. The zombie's vacant-eyed stare started gooseflesh to pop on Riker's ribcage.

Continuing the sweep, he came to believe the park had filled up pretty quickly. It looked as if all of the tent-sites were taken, with many more tents erected where they shouldn't be: On patches of common lawn. Entirely flanking grass beside an empty wave pool plastered with colorful fallen leaves. Some even erected on bare asphalt.

Clearly people had been desperate for a place to sleep away from wherever they'd come.

Yet strangely, only one in ten sites had a vehicle parked in its assigned slot.

People left here with the same urgency as they had arrived, thought Riker as he focused on some movement farther inland.

Through the trees he saw a square, one-story cement-block structure. It sat on a patch of vibrant green grass that contrasted sharply with its drab battleship-gray paint. On the side of the building facing Riker were two gray doors. The door on the left was labeled *Men*. The other, on the right, was labeled *Women*. Obscuring most of the wall between the doors was a Coke machine, its signage and buttons darkened.

Standing before the machine and seemingly pressing the raised buttons at random was a young girl. Barefoot and dressed only in floral print pajama bottoms, every inch of the girl's exposed skin was pale as the face of a full moon.

Sweeping the binoculars back to the RV camping area, Riker spotted a trio of corpses on the ground outside a thirty-foot Winnebago. Each had been shot multiple times in the torso. *Center of mass* is what the shooting instructors called the prime real estate between navel and breastbone. It was the spot on the enemy's torso he had been taught to aim for.

Copious amounts of pooled blood on the gray cement told Riker the three men weren't all the way dead prior to them receiving the headshots that fully punched their tickets.

In the cluttered background, he detected dead things moving among the crush of RVs. A flash of color. A leering face in an open door. Pale hands batting at drawn curtains inside an immaculate Itasca motor coach.

A hundred feet east of the RV-park-of-the-dead was a wide cement boat ramp. Compared to the docks and ramp at Shorty's establishment, this facility was fairly basic. Right of the algae-slickened ramp was a simple floating dock with a trio of unmanned sporting boats lashed to it.

Though Riker couldn't be sure, he guessed the dock extended out thirty feet or more over the water.

Beyond the dock was a parking lot crowded with dozens of pickups and SUVs, most of them still hooked up to empty boat trailers.

It was one hell of an exodus. He figured it probably took place shortly after the ominous Presidential Alert that went out the night before.

All in all, Riker counted more than thirty dead things—by far the most he'd seen in one place with his own eyes since witnessing from the air the hordes of undead amassed in Battery Park on Lower Manhattan.

Having seen enough to know Magee and his crew were now the least of their worries where getting ashore was concerned, Riker passed the binoculars back to Shorty.

"Could have warned me about what's waiting ashore," he said.

"Would it have changed your plan?"

"Nope," said Riker. "Not one bit."

"Good ... because we've been seeing those things moving on shore since Mobile."

Riker said, "Then we better be on our A-Game when we go ashore."

As *Miss Abigail* picked up speed and started to drift slowly to port, he returned to the Shelby, fetched his weapons from the load bed, and then climbed into the driver's seat.

Three minutes, he thought, inserting a fresh magazine into the Sig. *A hell of a long time to be stuck between the rock and hard place we currently face.*

Chapter 39

Riker's watch read 6:55. He felt the sun coming through the pilothouse window, warm on his left cheek. Though it was the middle of October, the temperature today would likely flirt with eighty degrees before noon.

Brought on by the scene ashore, the tension he was feeling in his neck and back was quickly translating into one hell of a banging headache. And as a result of having worn the prosthesis virtually nonstop for the better part of twenty-four hours, the nerves in the nub of scar tissue were irritated and letting him know.

Tara said, "This is a trip." She was in the passenger seat, staring out at the Gulf water rushing by not a dozen feet away. *Decisive* and the pair of smaller vessels were partially obscured behind the pilothouse. Inside the pilothouse, Shorty was dividing his time between watching the cutter off his left shoulder and the shore at his twelve o' clock.

Eyes glued to the rearview mirror, where the approaching shore was represented by mostly sandy beach, tufts of grass, and snippets of a cement walkway paralleling the Gulf, Riker said, "Reminds me of sitting backward in a moving subway car."

Steve-O said, "Reminds *me* of a rollercoaster. And I think I'm going to be sick."

Recoiling, Riker said, "Think you can hold it?"

Fingers pressed to his lips, Steve-O shook his head.

With all of the windows powered up and the doors closed, it was quiet enough in the cab so that rumbling sounds could be heard coming from the backseat.

Only half joking, Riker said, "Give him Shorty's dry bag to spew into."

"That's not cool," replied Tara as she emptied the store-bought junk food out on the floorboard and handed Steve-O the empty plastic sack. "Not quite as nice as the barf bags on the airplane," she said. "But it'll do."

Riker felt a tremor race through the Shelby. Taking his eyes from the rearview, he regarded Shorty, who was gripping the wheel two-handed and staring back at him with an *oh shit* expression on his face.

Now unobstructed by the pilothouse, Riker got a good look at the source of Shorty's worry.

The rigid-hulled inflatable boat was already disengaged from the motor yacht and charging hard across open water toward *Miss Abigail*. Behind the RIB, *Decisive* was underway, too, and just beginning to come around to port.

With maybe half a mile between *Miss Abigail* and shore, and a little more than that separating her from *Decisive*, Riker wasn't too worried about the cutter getting between them and freedom. The RIB, however, was another story. Already it had halved the distance from its interdiction stop and *Miss Abigail's* current position.

There was a crinkling of plastic and a retching sound in the backseat. It was followed immediately by Steve-O promising profusely that he got *it* all in the bag.

Feeling the ferry's speed picking up, Riker started the Shelby's engine. Regarding Steve-O in the mirror, he said, "Are you going to be able to do your part when the time comes?"

Steve-O said, "Yes." More retching followed. Dragging the back of his hand across his mouth, he added, "I will do my job, Lee."

The acidic nose of fresh vomit permeating the cab prompted Riker to drop all four windows a couple of inches. For added measure, he started the Shelby's A/C running.

Tara was holding her nose and watching Shorty's every movement. At the same time, she was working a problem in her head that consisted of her best guess of their distance to shore and their current speed, the former of which she figured was half a mile or so, the latter pushing up against twenty nautical miles-per-hour.

"We've got about ninety seconds before we make land," she noted. "Come on, Shorty. Put the spurs to her."

Riker was watching Shorty, too. The man reminded him of an owl. His head was on a constant swivel as he continually shifted his gaze between the RIB and shore. Finally, as if Tara's words had reached him, he pegged the throttles, stretched a bungee cord through the spokes of the wheel, and then anchored both hooked ends somewhere out of sight.

In the next beat he had exited the pilothouse and was hustling toward the bow as fast as his little legs would carry him.

Taking ahold of the grab bar by her head, Tara said, "The little boat is about to crawl up our ass." Flicking her eyes to the side mirror, she saw two things. Close in and already drenched by the fine spray rising over the bow, Shorty was kneeling by the ramp and working on getting it lowered.

Farther off, on shore, the zombies of Buccaneer State Park had taken a keen interest in *Miss Abigail*.

Having already turned toward the engine noises rolling off the bay, the handful of Bolts intermingling with the Slogs broke ranks and set off sprinting for the strip of white sand fronting the RVs.

Riker had also been watching Shorty in the passenger-side wing mirror. Seeing the man rise and turn back toward the Shelby, he said, "Steve-O ... *now!*"

Already free of his seatbelt, Steve-O lunged across the backseat and threw open the rear passenger-side door.

"Done," stated Steve-O ahead of a couple more dry heaves.

Voice rising an octave, Tara said, "Ten seconds," and started counting down.

Hearing his sister's count hit *eight*, Riker swung his gaze forward and saw the RIB quickly draw up alongside the ferry and then suddenly go low in the water. Imagining the pilot had just cut power to the outboards and drawn them from the water in order to preserve the props, Riker put the transmission into Reverse, engaged *Baja Mode* on the four-wheel drive selector, and then released the parking brake.

Keeping pressure on the brake pedal and his eyes on the beach looming in his wing mirror, Riker revved the engine a few hundred RPMs into the power band. At once he could feel the Shelby's 770 horsepower V8 and her huge Brembo brakes going to war with each other.

In the span of a couple of seconds, numerous things occurred.

The noise of metal grating against cement rose over everything as the ferry, still moving at top speed, ran aground.

A sound like a shotgun blast rang out and the Shelby's tailgate was pelted with sand and pebbles when the deployed ramp met the dry section of the sloping boat ramp.

Catching a bit of collateral damage on his backside, Shorty dove into the backseat. As he hauled the door closed behind him, Riker pinned the accelerator, let up on the brake, and returned his attention to the RIB.

In the next beat, with the rising whine of the Whipple supercharger under hood drowning out Shorty's smoker's rasp, the warnings being shouted through a bullhorn by Petty Officer Magee, and the awful sound of Steve-O filling up his barf bag, the Shelby lurched violently from the ferry's tilting deck.

When the truck's load bed cleared the edge of the canted ramp, Riker saw that Shorty's aim had been off by a degree or two. As a result, the ferry missed hitting the boat ramp square on. Still pushing water, *Miss Abigail's* screws propelled her stern clockwise to port and she slipped sideways off the edge of the partially submerged ramp.

When the ferry's slab-side smacked into the RIB, Petty Officer Magee and a second crewman were catapulted overboard. Then, like a flea flicked off a dog, the much smaller boat was sent spinning away from the multi-ton ferry. As the pilot worked to engage the props and get control of the RIB, a huge volume of water washed over its gunwales, causing the tiny craft to roll to port.

While all of this was happening, the Shelby was going airborne. As the big truck came down hard on the algae-covered ramp, its long travel suspension soaked up most of the impact.

Equal and opposite reactions being what they are, everyone aboard the rig Steve-O had just recently dubbed Dolly was thrown around like rag dolls.

The Shelby hadn't made it a dozen feet up the ramp when the off-road tires began to slip and all forward momentum was lost.

Cursing the state crew responsible for maintaining the ramp, Riker reined in the throttle and, to counter the fishtailing rear end, turned the wheel hard to the right.

There was a squeal from the power steering pump when the front wheels reached the limit of their travel.

A bang sounded near the truck's right rear quarter. A tick later, Tara was having a staring contest with a twenty-something male zombie. Unaware of the automotive glass separating it from fresh meat, the thing slammed its face hard into her window. Though teeth splintered and the door vibrated from the head-butt, the window held.

In his wing mirror, Riker saw a mixture of Bolts and Slogs converging on the truck from the east. On the beach, Magee and the other Coastie were busy rescuing the pilot from the overturned RIB.

When the Shelby finally started moving again, a Bolt flashed by them on either side.

Tara's zombie was still mashing its shredded lips against her blood-streaked window when the truck's tires again lost purchase. Instantly, the zombie was enveloped in blue-gray tire smoke drifting from all four wheel wells.

"Put your window down and shoot it," ordered Riker.

Before Tara could comply, the monster turned and sprinted off toward the RIB crew still wading ashore.

Chapter 40

"Come on, come on, come on," chanted Riker. He had the wheel turned against the slow downhill slide and was stabbing the accelerator.

Miss Abigail was sideways to the boat ramp, her engines still sending power to a trio of chewed-up screws, when the Shelby's rear tires finally burned off enough organic matter to catch hold of the pavement.

At roughly the same instant, Shorty was bailing out of the truck, his Glock in hand, screaming a warning at the waterlogged RIB crew.

One by one, the men became aware of Shorty. In the next beat, they saw what was bearing down on them.

With just seconds to react, Magee dragged his rifle around on its sling and engaged the nearest threats.

As the Bolts fell, their gaping head wounds turning the sand red, Riker was steering frantically to get the Shelby tracking straight.

A dozen feet from the Shelby, having dropped to a knee in the sand, Shorty was firing his pistol at the oblivious Bolts sprinting past him.

"What a tool," bellowed Tara as she pulsed her window down. "He's going to get himself killed."

"I don't know about that," Riker said as the truck was buffeted by a wall of wind. Wincing against the combination of harsh sunlight and wind-driven sand infiltrating his partially open window, he pointed to the orange and white helicopter coming at them low and fast out of the east. Though he wasn't certain if it was the same model chopper he had rented to scatter his mom's ashes over Niagara Falls, it bore a striking resemblance. Same tricycle landing gear tucked away in the fuselage. Same rounded nose and sleek fuselage that tapered back to a shrouded tail rotor.

A man wearing a bulky helmet and wielding a scoped and suppressed M4 carbine was hanging out the open starboard-side door. Turbine emitting a ferocious whine, the helicopter ripped over a still-struggling *Miss Abigail* with only a yard or two separating its flat underbelly from the radar antenna spinning lazily atop the ferry's pilothouse.

Once clear of the ferry, the helicopter flared hard to starboard, spun clockwise on axis a couple of degrees, and then adopted a level, steady hover over the beach.

Having been presented a clear shot at the zombies converging on his Coast Guard brethren, the crewman in the chopper opened fire on the runners.

Brass casings arcing from the rifle glittered in the sun as they tumbled groundward through the blowing sand.

Riker dragged his attention from the helo to Shorty in time to see the man shoot a teenaged Bolt pointblank in the face. As the runner dropped dead and plowed a berm of sand with its body, a dozen feet away Magee was kneeling on the beach and dumping rounds into the advancing dead.

Getting the Shelby pointed toward the parking lot entrance, Riker powered his window down, jabbed the Sig outside the truck, and started shooting at the Slogs angling toward Shorty and the others.

Above the fracas, the chopper was side-slipping left and dropping fast toward a clear patch of sand. In the door, tethered in place by a nylon strap, the crew member with the M4 was busy swapping magazines.

Seeing Magee check his fire as Shorty entered his sights, Riker laid on the horn, getting the attention of all parties involved.

The half-dozen Slogs cresting the grass berm between the beach and RV park turned in unison toward the new stimuli.

Realizing he was caught on the wrong end of a rifle, Shorty slowly raised both hands above his head.

Meeting Shorty's wide-eyed gaze, Magee lifted his cheek off the rifle stock and pointed toward the slow-rolling pickup. Then, just as the helicopter settled on the beach behind him, he repeated the gesture, bellowing, "Save yourselves!"

Shorty didn't need to be told twice. After reading the petty officer's lips, he shielded his face against the stinging sand, leaped over a head-shot corpse, and hustled back to the Shelby.

Nearing the pickup, Shorty saw a runner vectoring in on him from the campground. It was a young girl wearing only pajama bottoms decorated with yellow and blue flowers. Chest red with blood and arms pumping furiously, she was fixated solely on him until the Shelby's rear door opened and a steady stream of neon-green Nerf bullets cut the air directly in front of her.

The undead girl forgot all about Shorty and veered off toward the water, in hot pursuit of the colorful items. The moment her course changed, tiny geysers erupted in the sand in her wake and continued to walk the beach until the bullets responsible stitched a jagged pattern up her back. Slapped down face first into the sand, her arms and legs continued to move until a screaming hunk of lead split her skull wide open.

Hearing the door thunk shut behind him, Riker powered the Shelby up the beach toward a band of chest-high dunes.

Though he tried to blink it away, the image of the girl atop the crude sand angel decorated with a halo of her own brains would be forever seared into his memory.

Chapter 41

Tara had turned in her seat just as the Shelby's front tires rolled across the cement walkway bordering the beach. Bracing against the rocking she knew was to come, she addressed Shorty. "What were you thinking jumping out like that? It certainly wasn't in the plan."

Busy clicking into his seatbelt, Shorty said, "You and all your bloody plans."

In the rearview, Riker saw the last of the RIB crew scrambling aboard the helicopter. Arrayed all around them on the wet sand were more than a dozen corpses. As the craft launched skyward, black smoke pouring from *Miss Abigail's* dying engines was sucked up by the spinning rotor only to be sent roiling away like so many breaking waves.

Turning from the parking lot to the drive running through the RV camping area, Riker said, "Shorty ... you going to answer Tara's question?"

Tucking away the empty Glock, he said, "They've come to my rescue before."

Tara set her Glock on her thigh. Regarding Shorty, she said, "Those same three guys?"

"Here come some more Sickos," warned Steve-O as a pair of slow-movers emerged from between two older model RVs.

Shorty said, "Different crew, Tara. *Decisive* was busy somewhere else in the Gulf." Casting a wary gaze at the dead things, he went on to explain how, as a young man, he'd been foolish enough to flirt with a hurricane in a small open-bow boat.

He shivered when he recounted the time spent in open water with nobody around and having to watch his own boat sink.

"Reminds me of the sinking of the *USS Indianapolis*," noted Riker. "Being all alone out there with hundreds of hungry sharks below you." He shuddered. "That's some serious nightmare fuel."

Shorty shook his head. "Spent six hours out there without seeing a single dorsal fin."

"How'd you get rescued?"

"The crew chief in a Dolphin helicopter spotted me. Abby always insisted I wear the brightest life vest possible. Got me a puke-yellow one for my birthday a week prior. The rescue swimmer they sent in for me said if it hadn't been for the vest, the crew chief would have missed seeing me.

"Hurricane Elena was a real nasty one. She made it to a Category Three. Luckily my boat lost power on her trailing edge."

Steve-O announced the presence of more Sickos.

Riker spotted them the moment the drive began to curl to the north. He said, "Good eye, Steve-O. How many you think?"

"Twenty ... maybe more."

The one-way drive was wide enough to accommodate even the largest RV. Which was a good thing. Because the zombies facing them were spread out five abreast and four to five deep—a slow-moving knot Riker hoped to lure to one side or the other.

All ages were represented. Whereas the Bolts that stormed the beach and boat ramp hadn't been carrying with them the stench of rotting flesh, this motley band had the market cornered on it. Which led Riker to kick the A/C to High and posit an observation. "This is the third time I've seen younger, more fit specimens acting like slow-movers."

"Slogs," interrupted Tara. "It's fitting. If there are Bolts among them, we'd know it by now."

Continuing, Riker said, "And they smell like ass warmed over. Probably been dead a couple of days."

"At least," noted Shorty. "The one I killed yesterday died and then came back within an hour. He didn't stink."

"Yet," said Tara. "Was he young?"

Shorty said, "Late twenties, I'd guess."

As the Shelby rolled by the pack, the sound of palms slapping sheet metal and glass echoed throughout the cab.

Wincing, Tara continued her line of questioning. "Was he a sprinter?"

"Flo effin Jo," answered Shorty.

"She was *faaast* on her feet," added Steve-O. "Star of the twenty-fourth Olympiad. I watched every second of it at home with Mom and Dad."

A Slog mashed its bloated face against Steve-O's window. Something sharp had cut a deep fissure nearly ear to ear under the obese woman's chin. And as her mouth pistoned up and down, shiny white maggots dribbled from the mortal wound.

Pulling free from the clutch of dead, Riker steered through the open gate. After turning right and noting on a sign how to get to the park exit, he stole a quick glance into the back seat.

Behind him, Steve-O had removed his hat and was fanning himself with it. The man looked green to the gills and on the verge of resuming the spew fest. On the opposite side, Shorty was crowding his door, muscles tensed and watching Steve-O's every move.

Riker said, "You need a new barf bag?"

"Not yet," responded Steve-O.

"The one he has can't get any fuller," said Shorty.

Pressing her fingers to her lips, Tara said, "Great, now I think I'm going to be sick."

"Want my bag?"

"*No*, Steve-O. That'll surely make me hurl."

"Holy crap," blurted Riker. He pointed at the water park he'd spotted through the trees from the ferry. On the end of the facility not visible from the water, a large handwritten sign declaring the place *Closed Until Further Notice* was affixed head-high on the chain-link enclosure.

"Hate to break it to them," declared Shorty. "Further notice ain't coming." His eyes were glued to the north side of the wave pool where nearly a hundred former human beings stood staring at them through the outwardly bowing fence.

As the Shelby rolled by, the zombies in back shuffled forward, crushing the ones at the front hard against the stressed fence.

Skin and flesh and features on some of the leering faces were being peeled away by constant contact with the chain-link. Fingers intertwined through the holes in the fence were sheared off.

"So many Sickos," noted Steve-O.

"Outside of Manhattan, this is the most I've seen in one place," said Tara. "Mount Sinai, included."

A chorus of raspy hissing arose from the stirring corpses at the first sight of the Shelby. Now, with the fence barely a dozen feet from Steve-O's window, the eerie sound was replaced by a growing crescendo of guttural moans.

Gaze locked on one young girl being slowly cut to pieces against the fence, Shorty said, "Get us the hell out of here before that thing fails."

Nodding, Riker ignored the strategically placed speed bumps and sped off to the north.

They passed through the car camping area, nearly a quarter-mile stretch of flat ground where the zombies outnumbered the tents and the tents far outnumbered the cars left behind.

Nearing the park entrance where the drive took a sharp bend was a large wooden sign with *Buccaneer State Park and Campground* carved into it. The camping fees and a litany of campground rules were listed on the top half of the sign. The bottom two-thirds of the sign was thick with scraps of paper, napkins, and paper plates. The messages scribbled on the makeshift signs were mostly left by people fleeing the park and contained information pertaining to where they were going.

A barefoot corpse was sprawled out on the ground in the sign's shadow. It had on only blood-soiled cargo shorts. On the grass next to it was a tattered and torn tee shirt. Its bolt open, a long rifle lay on the drive.

Riker noted a distinct, unnatural curvature to the barrel. Clumps of hair and blood clung to the buttstock and rubber recoil pad.

Clearly, someone had brained this one with the rifle.

Fingers were missing from both of the corpse's hands. Nearly all of the flesh had been stripped from its arms. Skin and muscle on one side of its bearded face was peeled back. The row of molars exposed by the violent act were cracked and yellowed. It looked as if the only thing keeping the man's jaw from coming unhinged from his skull were a few thin strands of glistening muscle.

The gory sight reminded Riker of the anatomical model of the head in his high school biology class. That damn thing always creeped him out.

And this was no different.

"Looks like he's smiling," said Steve-O.

Shorty said, "After having his guts ripped out like that, he's probably happy to be dead."

The torso had been reduced to a hollowed-out chest cavity ringed by raised bite marks. Riker didn't see a single organ he could identify. He did, however, see the two fingers remaining on its nub of a left hand begin to twitch. He was back to looking at the mess of a face when the eyes snapped open.

Frozen with morbid curiosity, Riker straightened in his seat, staring and kneading the steering wheel as the corpse worked itself into a sitting position.

Seeing the corpse suddenly hinge up and a mess of bloody detritus sluice onto its lap hastened in Tara what the stench wafting from Steve-O's puke bag had started. Thrusting a hand over the seatback, she blurted, "Bag," and waggled her fingers for emphasis.

Taking the plastic bag bulging with warm sloshing liquid, Tara added chunks of granola bar and several ounces of yellow bile to the mix.

Seeing the corpse lose its balance and flop back onto its side, Riker turned his attention to the messages on the sign. Squinting, he read a few of the notes with the largest font. Most

253

began with: *It's not safe here.* Some detailed attacks by *dead things* or *walking corpses.* A few actually referred to their attackers as *zombies.*

The disemboweled zombie had found its way onto its stomach—or the remains thereof—and was dragging itself toward the Shelby, using its toes and bloody meat-hooks-for-hands as propulsion.

Riker looked to Tara. "When you're all done puking, Sis ... can you read some of the signs so we can get a feel for where everyone was going?"

"I got it," said Shorty. "Just had my eyes lased." He powered down his window and stuck his head outside.

In the wing mirror, Riker watched the crawler. It had reached the Shelby and was grabbing hold of the running board.

"Well?" he asked.

"All of them are going somewhere north or west of here. We got Jackson, Casper, Oklahoma City, Topeka, Omaha, Sioux Falls. Quite a few are setting their sights on places nearby. New Orleans, Albuquerque, Dallas, Houston, Santa Fe. Then there are a handful ranging out farther west. Colorado Springs, Pueblo, Salt Lake City."

"We're going farther west," said Riker. It was the first time he had voiced it out loud. In his experience, the longer he held his cards close to his vest, the better the ultimate result. "I'm guessing with *Miss Abigail* out of action, your mind just got made for you."

"Not entirely," answered Shorty. Changing the subject, he displayed his Glock and said, "I'll put the camp host out of his misery. But I'm out of ammo for this. Only had the two magazines."

Tara checked the Shockwave's safety, then handed it back to the man. With a smirk forming and a twinkle in her eye, she said, "Here, use this."

With a tilt of his head, Riker said, "That's cold-blooded, Sis."

Shorty looked a question at Riker.

Riker said, "That little thing has a recoil like you wouldn't believe. It's like a Blunderbuss on steroids."

Fixing his blue eyes on Shorty, Steve-O said, "He's a grown ass man, Lee."

"I can handle it," Shorty declared. He looked to Riker. "Question is ... do you know what a Blunderbuss is?"

"A short, shotgun-like rifle used mainly to repel boarding pirates," said Riker. "I confess. I used to watch that Vegas pawn store show run by the three generations of smart asses."

Shorty looked dumbly at Riker. Then he went to work, quickly cycling the shells from the weapon. After giving them a look, he reinserted only the slugs. "Got more?" he asked.

"If you need more than three," said Riker, "you deserve to be eaten by that sad sight."

"You have a point." Shorty dumped the extra shells in a pocket, exited the truck, and looped around back. Setting the Shockwave down on the ground, he grabbed the zombie by the ankles and dragged it away from the pickup.

Looking at the sky through the smoked moonroof, Riker said, "Divert your eyes, folks. We're all out of barf bags."

There was a single tremendous boom, then Shorty was climbing aboard and saying, "Go, go, go. My good deed came with unintended consequences."

Dropping his gaze to his wing mirror, Riker saw the dozen or so Slogs the report had stirred up. Most were a good distance away and posed no immediate threat.

"Sickos," said Steve-O. "I don't see any Bolts."

Thank God for small miracles, thought Riker as he got them moving toward the nearby feeder road.

They had only traveled a quarter of a mile or so and were coming out of the trees where the road widened when Riker began to curse under his breath.

"If it wasn't for bad luck," said Steve-O.

"We wouldn't have any luck at all," finished Tara.

"Someone didn't want to be followed," observed Shorty.

"Damn it," said Riker, pounding a fist on the wheel. "Looks like we have our work cut out for us."

255

Chapter 42

In the spot where the only road in and out of Buccaneer State Park widened to two full-sized lanes flanked by steel guardrails, a massive fifth-wheel trailer sat angled across two-thirds of the road. It was a newer model Jayco with pop-outs and a raised ceiling. No pickup was attached, and all of its tires were flat.

The fifth-wheel hitch was embedded into the dirt shoulder on the left side of the road where the front end of the trailer abutted the rust-streaked guardrail.

To the right, the opening between the rear of the trailer and guardrail was barely wide enough for a small pickup or passenger car to pass through.

Riker said, "No way Dolly is getting past that."

After craning to get a better view, Tara agreed with him. "Not enough Vaseline in the world to make that happen."

Sparing everyone the sexual innuendo hanging on the tip of his tongue, Shorty said, "We have to make it happen. This is our only way out."

"I've got an idea," said Riker as he let the truck roll closer to the trailer.

Gaining a better viewing angle, he saw that the trailer's rear bumper and opposing guardrail were streaked with all the colors of the rainbow. Which led him to believe the trailer had been nudged to its current resting place by smaller vehicles pushing through.

And if smaller vehicles could get the behemoth moving, he figured the Shelby could finish the job.

Issuing marching orders, Riker set the transmission to Park and exited the truck.

Working together, Riker and Shorty got the Shelby's bumper-mounted winch spooled out and attached to the trailer's grease-slathered fifth-wheel hitch.

Standing near the bend in the road and watching their backs, Tara heard the roar of the Shelby's big V8. A tick later a groaning of metal joined the mix of mechanical sounds coming from the ongoing operation. Tearing her eyes from dozens of Slogs approaching from the direction of the park's entrance, she regarded the vehicular struggle taking place on the road behind her. It seemed as if the scene from the boat ramp was being replayed. The Shelby's rear tires were spinning and its back end had started to waggle back and forth across the solid yellow centerline.

And the blue tire smoke was back, too. It billowed from the wheel wells and then drifted slowly across the two-lane as the tires put black marks down on the gray cement.

With another groan and a bang, the Jayco slid off the guardrail. Initially the fifth-wheel hitch carved a deep channel in the dirt shoulder. As it came into contact with the raised asphalt where the road started and the shoulder ended, the Jayco jumped up onto the smooth surface where friction was nearly nonexistent.

Inside the Shelby, with Steve-O calling the play-by-play for him, Riker sensed that the trailer was about to break free of the guardrail's hold before it actually did. And when it did, he was ready, simultaneously lifting his foot off the accelerator and loosening the cable tension with the push of a dash-mounted button.

Standing clear of the taut cable and supervising the affair, Shorty caught Tara peeking and promptly directed her attention back to the steadily advancing herd.

Once the trailer had started moving, its slow counterclockwise pivot didn't cease until it was parallel to the centerline.

"That'll do," hollered Shorty.

Riker selected Park, set the parking brake, then watched as Shorty loped over to the Jayco and went to work unhooking the cable from the fifth-wheel hitch.

Turning in his seat, Steve-O said, "Pretty lady is in trouble."

Peering into his wing mirror, Riker saw Tara with her Glock trained on the leaders of the herd and slowly backpedaling down the middle of the straightaway. At the rate she was giving up ground, he had a bad feeling the dead things would be within arm's reach of the pickup before Shorty could get the cable spooled up and secured in its housing.

Though the winch was still reeling in the cable, Riker ordered Shorty to coil it up as best he could and throw it onto the hood.

The cable and hook landed atop the hood with a bang.

"That's going to leave a mark," said Steve-O.

The door behind Riker's had opened and Shorty was scrambling in before Riker could answer.

Steve-O regarded Shorty. Nudging the brim of his Stetson up with a knuckle, he said, "You scratched Dolly."

The passenger door opened, Tara jumped in, and the truck started rolling forward at once.

Ignoring Tara's harried entry into the cab, Shorty said, "What's with you guys calling this pickup Dolly?"

A little short of breath, Tara said, "That's the name Steve-O gave this beast of a truck. Personally, I think it's a little too girly of a name."

"Lee likes it."

Riker flicked the switch to stop the winch motor. Getting the cable spooled all the way in could wait until later. Steering Dolly around the trailer, he said, "The name just kind of stuck. Besides, it does roll nicely off the tongue."

Tara checked the herd in the wing mirror. The dead things hadn't quite reached the pickup's tailgate when she made it to her seat. Now, however, they were occupying the patch of rubber-streaked road the pickup had just vacated.

Shorty said, "You named this rig Dolly? As in Dolly *Parton?*" As he uttered the surname, he pantomimed cupping a pair of Triple Ds.

Steve-O cracked a half-smile and winked at Shorty.

"No shit," said Shorty, smiling. "I'm a *big* fan of her, too."

"I wonder why," Tara retorted. "You should see Steve-O's tattoo. Let's just say, the artist didn't leave much for the imagination."

"Given the Texas-sized belt buckle, Stetson, and boots," Shorty said, "I already had you pegged as a country and western fan. Just not a *diehard* country and western fan."

Beaming, Steve-O said, "I have been to Dolly World."

Tara laughed and pretended to tweak her nipples. "Shorty sure wishes he was in Dolly's World. Don't you, Shorty?" Making a second risqué joke, she attempted to correct them on the theme park's name by asking, "Or is it just Dolly *Wood* that you desire?"

Shorty chuckled loudly and steered the subject back to the tattoo. "Let me see it."

Steve-O was rolling his sleeve up when Riker stabbed the brakes. A keening of metal raking metal came next as the cable shot off the hood.

Riker restarted the winch motor to reel in the rest of the cable.

In the backseat, Shorty was *oohing* and *aahing* over Steve-O's fresh ink.

"Best of the best reimagined as Mount Rushmore. Great idea," gushed Shorty.

A clunk and brief whine sounded when the hook snugged into the port on the front bumper. Shutting the winch motor down, Riker looked over his shoulder at Shorty. "Did you know who the black guy is?"

"Who doesn't? Best damn new-school singer to come on the scene since Garth Brooks."

Slowing down to cross some railroad tracks, Riker said, "He's still Hootie to me."

"Hootie *who?*" joked Shorty.

"Hootie and the *blow me*," answered Riker. Turning west on Railroad Avenue, he asked Tara to pull up the navigation screen and plot a course to the nearest car lot.

"*New* car lot," Shorty said. "A lot of miles between here and Chicago."

Tara shot Riker a questioning look.

He whispered, "Tell you all about it later."

Chapter 43

The navigation system indicated the closest new car dealership nearest to Buccaneer State Park was in Waveland, Mississippi. To get there required Riker to pull a U-turn on Railroad Avenue and drive a couple of miles east.

Getting the Shelby turned around on the road wasn't an issue. Just a quick three-point turn and they were on their way.

Traffic moving eastbound on Railroad Avenue seemed heavy for such an early hour.

Driving toward the sun becoming an issue, Riker donned his sunglasses and, for good measure, flipped his visor down.

"Sure it's a new car dealership?"

Looking back at Shorty, Tara said, "I heard you the first time."

"Just checking," Shorty said, raising his hands in mock surrender.

Tara crossed her arms over her chest and directed her attention to the narrow, crescent-shaped lake passing by on the left. The water shimmered silver at the edges from the morning light then darkened as it took a dogleg left into the trees.

Shortly after passing the lake, Railroad Avenue became South Street. Following Tara's direction, Riker turned left on Brown Street, which cut through a sleepy little neighborhood consisting of large houses separated by expansive tracts of treed land.

"Right at South Central," instructed Tara. "Then shortly after South Central becomes North Central, you'll hang a left on Nicholson. Keep straight for a couple of blocks and hang another left on Henderson. It'll spit us out on the dealer's doorstep."

Shorty said, "Please tell me it's a Chevy dealer."

"You said *closest* dealership," remarked Tara.

"Beggars can't be choosers," added Steve-O.

Sinking back into his seat, Shorty said, "Dogpile on the old guy, why dontcha."

"*Closest* is Charlie Henderson Ford. And that's where we're going," said Tara

Shorty said, "*Ford*. Fix ... or ... repair ... daily."

"You're sitting in a *Ford*," Riker shot. "Take it back or get out."

Though Riker had been joking, he still slowed down, moved to the shoulder, and popped the locks for effect.

"I take it back," Shorty said. "This is one fine vehicle you have here, Mr. Riker."

Smiling, Riker accelerated and moved back onto the road.

"I figured as much," said Tara. No sooner had the words left her mouth than her eye was drawn to a commotion in front of a two-story house a couple blocks ahead. A car was crashed into a large tree in the home's front yard. Its hood was buckled and steam billowed from a ruptured radiator.

The form at the wheel was shrouded by the remains of the deployed airbag and flailing its arms.

A woman in a bathrobe stood on the lawn. She was next to the car and peering inside. Seeing the approaching Shelby, she stood straight and waved.

Heading Tara off at the pass, Riker said, "I'm not stopping."

"Might be a Sicko in the car," said Steve-O.

Remembering how the house fire outside of Middletown had drawn the Bolt from the surrounding neighborhood, Riker agreed with the man's assessment.

***

They arrived at Henderson Ford a couple of minutes after passing the accident on North Central. The single-story building took up most of a city block. Its stone façade featured a number of arched porticos fronting twenty-foot-tall windows, all of them rounded off at the top. Resembling the Arc de Triomphe, the soaring stone grand entrance rose above the roofline by twenty feet or more. Continuing with the style of the windows flanking the dealership entrance, the top of the glass window in the grand arch followed its curvature.

Above the windows left of the entry was a twenty-foot-long sign that read *CHARLIE HENDERSON*. Positioned prominently on the grand arch, above the lightly tinted glass, was a second sign. It was the size of a billiard table and identical to Ford's ubiquitous blue oval.

The lot fronting the darkened building was home to a dozen compact cars sporting dealer sales invoices affixed inside the driver-side windows.

Though Riker was no expert, and all the new cars looked very similar to him, he guessed the econoboxes were Escorts, Fusions, and Fiestas based on the commercials he'd seen on television.

"Maybe they keep the trucks and SUVs around back," he said to nobody in particular.

"Shorty doesn't need an *Expedition*," Tara exclaimed. "He's just a little guy. Maybe a SMART car would do the trick."

"Hey," scolded Steve-O. "I'm a little guy, too." He unbuckled and planted his elbows on the front seat bolsters, a deadly serious expression on his face.

Shorty held his tongue. He could take it just as good as he could dish it out. In that way, he and Tara were alike. And that's why she was growing on him. *Hell*, he thought as he was asking to be let out at the corner nearest the side lot, *all of them are growing on me.*

"I want to take you around the block," Riker said.

"I'm good with that."

"The place sure looks like it's closed," noted Tara.

"All the better," said Shorty as he scooped his dry bag off the floor.

While Riker wheeled them around the corner, Tara shot Shorty a quizzical look.

In response, he said, "There's a lot about me you don't know, Tara." Smiling, he reached into the bag and came out with a two-foot-long piece of metal. It was thin as a bank card and roughly two inches wide. One end was notched, the other wrapped with silver duct tape.

"I know that's a slim jim," she said. "And I know it's used to unlock car doors."

"And SUV doors," replied Shorty, smiling.

Interrupting, Steve-O said, "Sickos, four o'clock."

More like two, thought Riker as he braked at the corner curb cut to let Shorty out.

Shorty didn't act right away. He sat there and looked each of them in the face. Finishing with Riker, he said, "I appreciate the ride. Probably didn't deserve it after how I price-gouged you."

Tara said, "How bad *did* you gouge him?"

"You don't want to know," answered Steve-O.

Raising a hand to silence everyone, Riker told Shorty they were square. Then he reached to the floorboard and came up with the Shockwave. "Take this," he insisted. "A fella gave it to me when I was in need."

After a brief protest, Shorty gave in. "I'll take it. But I had better go now. Those things are coming."

Tara said, "It's just a couple of Slogs. You can outrun them."

Shooting her the side-eyed look copied from their mom, Riker said, "Never assume." Shifting his gaze to Shorty, he added, "Beware the Bolts."

"I've lived this long on wits alone. I think I'll be OK."

Riker rummaged around inside the center console and came out with a pen and scrap of paper. He extracted Wade Clark's business card from his wallet, copied the number down on the paper, then continued to write for a few more seconds.

Shorty used the time to stuff the Shockwave and shells for it into his bag.

Finished, Riker handed the paper to Shorty, saying, "This guy runs a helicopter tourism outfit in upstate New York. Look him up after you do what you have to do in Chicago. He ain't cheap, but he's reliable."

Shaking his head, Shorty said, "My phone is back with *Miss Abigail*. Guess I could source a burner or something."

Reaching back into the console, Riker took out the bag containing the iPhone. "Take this," he said. "All you need to do is find a way to activate it."

Eyes a little misty, Shorty stuffed the phone into his dry bag, then thanked Riker and Tara. Turning to face Steve-O, he said, "You can be my first mate anytime, *Steve*. I'm going to miss chatting with you."

Smiling wide, Steve-O said, "Me too." He paused for a spell. Studied Shorty with his liquid blue eyes. Finally, he said, "Shorty, what's your *real* name?"

Without hesitation, Shorty said, "Jimmy Twigg." Pocketing the scrap of paper, he shook Steve-O's hand and was out the door with the bulging dry bag slung over one shoulder and his head on a swivel.

Riker powered his window down. Rising up off his seat, he inspected the vehicles on the side lot. Regarding Shorty, he said, "There's a silver Tahoe in the back row with your name on it. Sign on the window says it's a 2014 model. Think that'll do?"

Shorty flashed a thumbs-up and mouthed, "Thank you!"

Riker said, "I'm praying you find what you're setting out to. Now get going. We'll take care of the zombies while you cross T's and dot I's."

Hearing the Z word uttered froze Shorty in his tracks. He turned and opened his mouth, but nothing came out.

"I was speechless the first time I heard Tara say it, too. Until we meet again." Riker flashed the man a thumbs-up, then drove off toward the growing pack of slow-movers.

Chapter 44

After watching Shorty disappear into the Ford lot, Riker regarded the approaching zombie herd. To get their undivided attention, he toggled the Shelby's emergency flashers and laid on the horn for a solid three-count. As soon as the leader of the pack took notice and started a slow loping turn away from the Ford dealership and onto Henderson Avenue, Riker shifted into Reverse, eased his foot off the brake, and allowed the idling engine to propel the pickup away from Charlie Henderson Ford at walking speed.

To keep the Slogs interested, every twenty feet or so he toggled the high beams on and off and repeated the thing with the horn.

Drawing a strange look from the driver of a small compact arriving at a four-way stop, Riker ignored his sign, stopped the Shelby in the middle of the intersection, and threw the transmission into Drive.

Meeting the driver's gaze, he mouthed, "Get out of here. Now!" then spun the wheel hard counterclockwise and sped off west.

Tara spoke first. "Think one block is going to do it?"

"Shorty told me that while his wife was sick and couldn't work, he supplemented his income by repossessing cars for a group of dealerships in Tampa. If I was a betting man, I'd put money on him already being inside the Tahoe with its motor running."

"That's stealing," observed Steve-O.

"Yes, it is," said Tara. "But sometimes circumstances warrant breaking the law. We stole that Suburban from the high school lot right before we met you. Had to do it to get away from the Sickos."

Steve-O nodded in understanding.

"Throw our destination into the navigation thing," Riker said. "Pick a course that keeps us away from the larger cities."

While Tara typed on the touch screen, Riker wheeled west. A few blocks from the Ford dealership, they passed by a sign for Highway 607.

"Turn here?"

"Yes," Tara said. "About nine miles and you'll hit a cloverleaf. There you'll be taking the ramp to I-10 West." She settled back into her seat and asked her brother to make good on his promise.

***

With the interchange looming dead ahead, Riker finished recounting to Tara and Steve-O everything Shorty had told him when they were alone together in *Miss Abigail's* cramped pilothouse.

Indicating the I-10 West onramp, Tara said, "Here." Turning toward Riker, she asked, "How much money is in smuggling Cuban cigars to New Orleans?"

"Apparently enough to put his daughter through NYU."

"Where does she stay?"

"New Jersey."

Tara shook her head. "After what we saw in Lower Manhattan, I'd hate to still be in Jersey."

Steve-O said, "Lots and lots of Sickos."

"Thousands of them," said Riker as he merged into heavy traffic on the I-10 West."

Turning to face her brother, Tara said, "You going to tell me how Chicago fits into Shorty's itinerary?"

After a long pause, Riker said, "When we were alone in the pilothouse, Shorty confided in me that he has a grown son in Chicago."

Brows arching, Tara asked, "Where in Chicago?"

Riker accelerated and slipped over to the fast lane. Here the westbound lanes were flanked by trees so thick he couldn't see what was happening over on the eastbound lanes.

Settling into an easy seventy-miles-per-hour clip, he answered Tara. "We didn't get into that. All he said was that Matt is a metro cop and happens to be a huge Cubs and Bears fan. I guess Shorty gets up there a couple of times a year to catch a game with him. I didn't have the heart to tell him that, cop or no, not hearing from his kid for nearly a week with this Romero thing spreading was not a good omen. I did, however, let him know it all but assures his Cubbies aren't going to break their World Series drought."

Imagining the entire playing surface at Soldier Field covered with occupied body bags, Tara said, "First he loses Abby, then Romero happens and his daughter Megan goes incommunicado in Jersey. I'm afraid Matt being a first responder will prove to be strike three for Shorty."

"He insisted his boy isn't the type to fiddle while Rome is burning," Riker said. "I guess Shorty's a glass-half-full kind of thinker."

Shaking her head, Tara said, "Then I'm afraid his glass is half-full of zombies."

Apparently, Riker's earlier admonishment had no effect on Steve-O. He was back to hanging on the seatbacks. Taking advantage of the sudden lull in the front seat conversation, he said, "William Perry was my favorite Bear."

"What was his nickname? You remember, Steve-O?"

"Of course I do," he shot. "I was already a teenager."

Tara said, "Well?"

Steve-O said, "The Refrigerator."

Riker took his eyes off the road for a moment. "What's his jersey number?"

"Easy peasy, Lee Riker. Number seventy-two!"

"Great memory," Riker replied. "I was more of a Walter Payton fan."

"You sure you even watched football back then, Lee?"

"He has a point," said Tara. "What grade were you, Lee? Third, maybe fourth?"

"Third," said Riker.

Taking Steve-O's side, Tara said, "You were just rooting for whoever Dad was going for."

Stealing Shorty's comeback, Riker said, "Dogpile on the old guy, why dontcha? I still say Sweetness was the man."

They drove in silence for twenty minutes, passing through twenty-five miles of southern Mississippi without experiencing any of Riker's preconceived drama.

A half-dozen miles before the I-10 crossed the Pearl River at the Louisiana state line, Riker noticed a sign announcing NASA's John C. Stennis Space Center.

"Keep your eyes peeled, guys. You may be able to see the top of a gantry or rocket nosecone north of us."

"Which way is north?" asked Steve-O.

Tapping a finger on her window, Tara said, "That way."

As Riker kept his eyes on the road and drove, Tara and Steve-O craned and stared hard to see beyond the roadside trees.

The state line came up quickly with none of them seeing anything even remotely resembling the towering white gantries they'd all seen pictures of in history books or witnessed in action on television during the many televised Space Shuttle launches.

Sadly, all that was visible from the I-10 was a squat mirrored building on the south side. Planted beside the road shooting off northbound toward the sprawling facility was a tiny nondescript sign announcing the place's existence.

It was not the NASA Riker remembered. The demise that had begun with the stroke of a pen that assured a rapid defunding was only hastened by a West Coast visionary whose lofty goals seemed too far out there for Riker to embrace.

The once-proud program that put American boots on the moon was now a shell of its former self.

A quarter-mile from the bridge across the Pearl, brake lights flared and all lanes of traffic slowed to a crawl.

Fearing another roadblock in their immediate future, Riker swerved to the breakdown lane and drove with the Shelby's tires straddling the white fog line. All he could see was the top of the bridge and the long line of vehicles creeping steadily toward it.

Sounding hopeful, Riker said, "I think we're going to get across."

"No flashing lights?"

Shaking his head slowly side to side, Riker looked to Tara. "Not that I can see. If there was a police or military presence on the bridge, we wouldn't be moving at all."

"No Johnnys?"

"I doubt it, Steve-O. They're probably busy putting out fires in Florida."

"Fires?"

"Figure of speech," Tara said. "I think Romero is spreading faster than the authorities can stage resources and respond to outbreaks."

Riker said nothing. And his silence on the matter said volumes. Withdrawing inward was a trait of her brother's Tara knew all too well. She remembered their father, a drunk in recovery, doing the same. When asked about it, Riker was wont to parrot one of their father's favorite sayings.

"Practicing a little *wait?*"

Riker smiled at that.

Elbows hitting the seatbacks, Steve-O asked Tara what she meant.

Giving up on trying to get a grown ass man to stay belted in, Riker ignored the fact Steve-O was again sitting in a prime spot to become a human missile through the windshield should they get in an accident. Keeping his eyes on the road ahead, he said, "Why am I talking?"

Confused, Steve-O asked, "What does that have to do with what the Pretty Lady said?"

Tara met Steve-O's expectant gaze. She said, "W ... A ... I ... T. *Wait*. It's an acronym for *why am I talking?* Lee doesn't have anything important to add to my Romero observation."

Steve-O harrumphed and sank back into the rear seats.

Not entirely sure if Steve-O got the gist of what an acronym was, Riker focused on the traffic.

The vehicles in the fast lane ahead of the Shelby had been moving like a jerked length of chain: Speed up. Slow down. Stop for a spell. Speed up.

There was no rhyme or reason for it. And it continued that way for another twenty minutes, only returning to normal beyond the midpoint of the bridge, where, clear as day, the *reason* was presented to the occupants of the Shelby in the form of a black wall of smoke rising from what used to be New Orleans' east side.

Tara said, "Looks like someone pissed off Mrs. O'Leary's cow."

"Not funny, Sis. One of my Army buddies lives in New Orleans. His neighborhood is smack-dab in the center of all that mess."

"I'm sorry, Bro. It's just that I'm sort of becoming numb to it all."

"Right there with you, Sis."

Riker kept driving, staying on the I-10 West for another six miles, pushing the speed limit where he could, and sticking to the middle lane when possible.

Coming to an impressive feat of mechanical engineering, where multiple on- and off-ramps coalesced into what looked from a distance like cement laces worked into an impossible knot, Riker asked Tara for directions.

Setting her phone on her lap, Tara gave the navigation screen a glance, then lifted her gaze to the horizon.

A triangular-shaped body of standing water was coming up on the right. Bordered by trees on two sides, it appeared man-made. The interchange began at what would be the base of the triangle, with the westbound lanes of I-10 paralleling its longest side.

"You're going to want to get to the right lane," said Tara. "Then take the next exit."

"Interstate 59 North?"

"You got it. Then look for Highway 41 North. It'll feed you to Louisiana Highway 16. From there, just follow the signs to

Shreveport." Finished rattling off directions, she dragged her phone back up in front of her face.

Though he was curious as to what on that little screen was so captivating to her, he kept his questions to himself, figuring she would absorb all she could, then, like a wrung-out sponge, dump it on them all at once.

Such was her nature. Gather all the facts prior to dissemination. And in a way, save for possessing their own unique approach, they were both very alike in that regard.

***

Out of the blue, an hour north by west of the turnoff to Highway 16, Tara slumped back into her seat and tossed her iPhone onto the dash.

Here it comes, thought Riker. Looking sidelong at her, he said, "What's up?"

"We're *fucked*, that's what."

Riker didn't say anything. As the Shelby ate up another mile, he watched a half-dozen helicopters in the sky over what looked to be a base of some sort. Though he couldn't tell what model the ships were, based on their methodical flight pattern—a slow back and forth that took them across the base and then back again—he was certain they were mounting some sort of search.

After enduring nearly a minute of silence, intruded upon now and again by light snoring from the backseat, Tara said, "I've been reading the front pages of foreign newspapers."

"And?"

"The leading stories all paint the same picture. Romero has a firm foothold in the U.K. and Germany. Same in Russia. The English version of Russia's Tass newspaper says it's all our fault. Their president is quoted as saying that we *wanted* it to happen. Even intimated we orchestrated it."

"How about Asia?"

Tara shook her head. "Couldn't find any papers translated to English. There were some pictures of what looked like hospitals. Couldn't tell much from the captions. Just a bunch of squiggles and sticks, if you ask me. But if it's true what they say about a picture being worth a thousand words, these ones were worth a million. They're fighting the dead, too. And just like it's hitting ours hard here in the States, their medical facilities are becoming flashpoints of infection. Thing that really amazes me … they aren't even censoring what's being put out. Neither are we. There's so much content on social media and YouTube that they've stopped scrubbing it. It's almost as if they're giving up."

Checking his mirrors for trailing vehicles sporting anything resembling a light bar, Riker said, "When we left Jersey, my gut feeling was that it was going to take a miracle for them to get a handle on Romero. Come Philadelphia, where things seemed normal, I changed my tune a bit. Figured they'd have it all contained before we got to Miami."

"What's your gut telling you now?"

"As of this morning, I was thinking one of two things is likely to come of this. Either our armed forces would rally and get it contained."

"Or?"

"Or we'd finally get paid back for sparing the rest of the world a lifetime of speaking German. If I'm being honest here, I imagined our staunchest allies would already be charging to our aid." He shook his head. "I'm afraid after what you just said, none of that is going to happen."

Chapter 45

Crossing into Louisiana nearly six hours prior, Dolly's trip computer had indicated the full load of fuel in her tank would see them all the way to Shreveport.

In reality, thanks to all the stop and go driving leading up to the border crossing, with fifty miles yet to go to Shreveport, the Ford's high-performance V8 had nearly sucked the thirty-six-gallon tank dry.

Steve-O and Tara had been asleep for a majority of the trip north, missing out on Louisiana's pines and rivers and lush green landscape, and leaving Riker alone with his thoughts.

Which was a lot of time to second-guess the decisions that had led up to where they were now, sitting in the cab, hoping to see a gas station with an OPEN sign ablaze, and cartoons suddenly their topic of conversation.

Steve-O was back to hanging off the front seats and polluting the entire cab with energy-drink breath. To say he was wired after slamming two large cans of the stuff in the ten minutes he'd been awake would be a massive understatement.

Regarding Riker, Steve-O said, "What's your favorite cartoon of *all* time?"

After spending a moment reeling in the years, Riker said, "Donkey Kong and Dragon's Lair. Dad was too cheap to give me quarters for the arcade, so I watched the cartoons and pretended I was playing the game."

Steve-O laughed and clapped his hands.

"I even resorted to using one of Mom's wooden spoons as a make-believe joystick."

"I don't remember any of that," admitted Tara.

Squinting to see a cluster of buildings a ways off the Shelby's right-front fender, Riker said, "You were like four years old and big time into your dolls."

Subjecting Tara to a face full of bad breath, Steve-O said, "What's yours, Pretty Lady?"

"Garfield and Friends."

Bouncing on the edge of his seat, Steve-O said, "Garfield loves lasagna." Then, all of a sudden, he settled down and declared, "I'm starving."

Consulting the navigation screen, Tara said, "There's a couple of options up ahead. Whichever one of them has the cheapest gas *and* hot food gets my vote."

Nodding agreeably, Riker addressed Steve-O. "What's your favorite cartoon, big guy ... Steamboat Willy?"

Tara broke out in laughter. Finally composing herself, she looked to her brother, saying, "He's old, but not that old."

Without missing a beat, Steve-O said, "Age is only a number."

Wiping a stray tear, Tara urged him to answer the question.

As if he'd crossed this bridge before and expected ridicule for what he was about to say, Steve-O adopted a real serious expression and said, "South Park is my favorite cartoon of all time."

The inside of the truck got real quiet.

After a few seconds, Tara said, "Next exit. There's a couple of minimart, slash, gas stations to choose from."

"Terrance and Phillip are my favorite characters," Steve-O said. He laughed again, adding, "Marcy at the home says that they're fart machines, just like me."

Chuckling, Riker said, "She got that right." He threw on his signal and started the process of getting over a lane.

Vehicles around them here were moving a few miles over the limit. A nice older lady in a Volvo wagon let them over.

Riker had noticed, as he drove and contemplated things, the farther west they got from the border, the less frantic people seemed to be with their driving.

Was *out of sight, out of mind* at play here? Or was he just witnessing blissful ignorance on the part of the residents of Northwest Louisiana?

Throwing the blinker on again and gliding up the ramp, Riker said, "Sooo funny how the tops of the Canadians' heads move up and down when they talk."

"Don't forget Token Black," Tara said. "Blew me away when they introduced him. Also stunned me when it was revealed he's the richest kid in South Park. Kind of like us, huh?"

Ignoring the last part, Riker said, "Remember Jimmy and Timmy, the disabled kids? *Timmmmy, Timmmmy, Timmmmy.*" He started to laugh but quickly checked it, stealing a side-eyed glance at Steve-O. If the older man was pissed, or even slightly offended, he wasn't letting on.

Acutely aware of the awkward silence, Tara said, "Yeah, the guys who made that show sure are equal opportunity ballbusters."

"At least they *included* Timmy and Jimmy," Steve-O said. "Most special needs people are never even mentioned on television shows. Dad said they just use us as background props."

Riker looked to Steve-O. "I am truly sorry for mimicking Timmy the way I did."

"So funny I forgot to laugh."

"I noticed," admitted Riker.

Turning away from her window, Tara said, "Looks like the Chevron is out of the running. Keep driving."

Riker saw that the main sign was dark, and every pump was fronted by an orange traffic cone.

All out of gas.

Better luck next time.

The mom and pop establishment a quarter-mile down the road paralleling Highway 71 showed some promise. And *Gas Fast's* price per gallon was nowhere near the *arm and a leg* Enrique back in Fort Myers was charging.

An arm, yes. But well worth it, considering only three of the five-gallon-cans in back still contained fuel.

Fifteen gallons, to be exact.

Parking partway on the curb cut, behind three other vehicles waiting to fill up, Riker set the brake, stilled the engine, and gave his food order to Tara as she and Steve-O piled out of the Shelby.

Then Riker stepped out and stretched. To kill the time while waiting for the line to advance, he popped the tonneau cover and came out with a couple of boxes. One was cube-shaped and the size of a volleyball, the other a yard long and roughly the width and thickness of a wordy hardcover novel.

Steiner was printed on the former, *Allen* on the latter.

He placed the Steiner box on Tara's seat and went to work opening the box containing the items produced at the Allen factory.

Riker had the adjustable gun rack placed in the back window in less than five minutes. The Allen Company was true to their word. No tools were required and the newly installed dual-rifle rack barely budged when Riker jiggled it.

He threw the packaging in the trash and hopped back in to move the truck ahead two spots. With another few minutes to burn, he fished a Benchmade single-tang blade from one of the Pelican cases in the bed and proceeded to cut away the temporary dealer plates installed at Bell Ford in New Jersey.

Tara and Steve-O had been inside the *Gas Fast* for close to fifteen minutes when it was Riker's turn at the pump.

When Riker squared up to the pump and went for the nozzle, he saw the price listed on the pump's digital display didn't jive with the price on the reader board out front. It was nearly two dollars more. Which didn't make a blip on his give-a-shit radar. He happily ran his card into the machine, selected Premium, and started gassing up the Shelby.

Finished filling the pickup's tank, and the spare can in the load bed, Riker tore off his receipt.

Locking the Shelby, he adjusted his Braves cap and went to look for Tara and Steve-O.

Chapter 46

Pushing through *Gas Fast's* grimy glass door, Riker passed Tara just as she was coming out. She was lugging four very full bags, two to a hand, and had used her backside to open the door opposite him.

"Steve-O's in the john." Showing off her full hands, she asked Riker to unlock the truck.

Holding the remote at eye-level, Riker hit the Unlock button. Without checking for success, he entered the store and went straight for the short checkout line.

The store was busy, which explained Tara's fifteen-minute disappearing act.

Travelers were stocking up on chips and sodas and candy. A couple of men in their fifties, wearing jeans and tee shirts and trucker's hats, stood before a small television at the end of the counter. On the screen was President Tillman. His head filled up the screen and his mouth was moving. Due to the volume being rolled most of the way down, Riker couldn't hear what was being said over the steady beeps coming from the cash register.

The clerk behind the register was a tall Asian man with a ruddy face and ready smile. Displaying nearly every tooth in his head while speaking rapid-fire, the clerk asked Riker what he needed. "Smokes? Snuff? Rolling papers?"

"A new hat," said Riker, pointing at the display behind the clerk.

"All football. Saints or Saints?" shot the clerk, smile unwavering.

"Texans or Cowboys?" said Riker. "Who had the best record before the season got suspended?"

The clerk shook his head. "Only follow Saints."

A voice from behind said, "Since you're sporting a Braves hat already, why don't you be consistent and go with the Falcons hat? I hear they're in the running for a Super Bowl berth this year."

Regarding the forty-something Caucasian offering advice, Riker shook his head. "No chance in hell the Birds are going to go that far. I'm looking for either Texans or Cowboys?"

A younger man directly in line behind Riker said, "I'm pretty sure the Cowboys had a game, maybe two up on the Texans before the shutdown."

"Then give me the Texans hat."

The clerk took the hat down and rang it up. "Anything else?"

"That's it," said Riker. Paying for the cap, he thanked both of the men for their input.

Shooting Riker a thoughtful look, the older man urged him to not count out the Falcons this season, adding, "Their offense is real close to firing on all cylinders."

Riker said nothing. *My ass*, was what he was thinking as he stalked off to find Steve-O

The bathrooms were down a brightly lit hall angling away from two rows of beer coolers. The doors were on the left. Nothing fancy. No cute play on words. They were labeled accordingly with peel-to-stick letters spelling out HIS on the left door and HERS on the right, which was next to a tiny office, its door cracked open just enough to let Riker see a wooden desk and pair of matching chairs.

Stacked on the right side of the hall opposite the bathroom doors was a chest-high row of split firewood, each bundle individually wrapped in clear plastic film. Beyond the firewood, standing on end and lined up against the wall near the office door, was a trio of commercial CO_2 tanks.

Standing before the *HIS* door was a twenty-something man. He was thin and tall, but not nearly tall enough to be able to look Riker eye-to-eye. His face wore several days' growth of red facial hair. On his feet were muddy work boots. And tucked into Levi's nearly worn through in the knees was a short-sleeved black tee shirt bearing a massive white sweat ring on the chest and two smaller ones under the arms.

Sour look on his face, the man regarded Riker. "You might want to use the ladies' room."

Riker prickled, then shot the man a questioning look.

"Fucking retard cowboy wannabe has been in there for ten whole minutes."

Pulling up his pant leg, Riker showed the man his prosthesis. "So what would this make me?"

A tick started in the man's left eye. Then his Adam's apple shot up and down a couple of times. Finally, after having run some kind of cost benefit analysis where saving face or having it punched in was concerned, he said, "A crippled nigger?"

Having already started as a dull throb behind his eyes, the man's response ratcheted Riker's growing headache into a Category-5 migraine.

Just as Riker raised a fist, with every intention of making the man eat his words, and a few teeth, the door swung outward, its metal skin totally cutting off any kind of avenue for him to follow through on the impulse.

Out came Steve-O, waving the wall of noxious air preceding him in all directions with his white Stetson.

"Oh," he exclaimed, sounding a little startled. "I didn't think you were the one banging and cussing, Lee. Looks like you're next. Better breathe through your mouth until the fan catches up."

Riker said nothing. Just held the door in place between him and the trapped racist asshole and watched Steve-O head for the front doors.

The brief cooldown period, with the open door blocking his view of the racist, did absolutely nothing to tamp down the dormant rage the man's caustic words had just resurrected.

Out of sight, out of mind wasn't at play here.

Riker took a quick step back and slammed the door closed.

The racist had backpedaled and was standing in front of the door marked HERS. In his hands was one of the Co2 bottles. Body squared in the narrow hall, a wicked scowl on his face, the man said, "Best get to stepping, peg leg."

"Or what?"

"Or I'll bash your *coon* teeth in. That's what."

Close to hurling from inhaling Steve-O's gas, Riker said, "How are you going to get that over your head and swing it at me in this narrow-ass hall *before* I lay hands on you?"

As the man shrugged, the bottle jerked up and down in his partially bent arms.

The ease with which he had hefted the bottle told Riker that it was empty. Which meant he had less of an advantage than he had initially thought.

He looked down the hall behind him.

Clear.

With the reach of an NBA power forward, and hands the size of dinner plates, Riker figured disarming the racist in such close quarters wouldn't be much of a chore.

A simple head fake got the man starting the process of bringing the cylindrical item on an upward trajectory.

Acting against his every impulse, Riker willed himself to not immediately react. He waited until the cylinder had cleared the man's nose and was blocking his field of vision. No longer able to see the whites of the racist's eyes, Riker took one step forward, slapped both palms atop the cylinder, then left his feet, adding all of his two hundred and forty pounds to the equation.

If the cylinder weighed twenty pounds empty, Riker guessed his action upped that twenty-fold.

The sudden realization that he was in big trouble erased the scowl from the man's face. In the next beat his eyes had flicked up and acquired the smooth metal cylinder now poised a half-foot over his head and coming down fast and hard.

While a person's first instinct to ward off injury is to raise one's arms in defense, Racist didn't have the option. Face fully exposed, the tank hit him squarely on the nose and forehead, instantly breaking the former and leaving a peculiar indentation on the latter.

The man fell to the tiled floor as if his power had just been cut.

Only thing Riker detected as the man turned ragdoll was his eyes rolling back into his head.

Suddenly gone numb, the man's fingers let go of the bottle a millisecond after his eyes closed.

Bad for him. Because gravity was pulling the cylinder to the exact spot on the floor his crotch would soon be occupying.

The man and cylinder hit the floor one after the other. Nearly so close together that any kind of lapse between the two was lost to the human eye.

Drawing a deep breath, Riker bent down, grabbed a handful of the man's shirt, and slid him into the tiny bathroom feet first and back against the floor.

As the man's body settled next to the toilet, arms and legs all akimbo, Riker noticed his chest rising and falling.

In one fluid motion, Riker hinged up, reached around and flicked the lock on the inside of the door handle, then pulled the door closed.

Exhaling, he said, "Enjoy your stay."

Seeing only a couple of guys with well-earned beer bellies perusing the offerings in the distant beer cooler, Riker replaced the CO_2 cylinder, yanked open the door labeled HERS, and stepped inside.

Finished with his business, Riker washed up and adjusted the Texans hat in the mirror.

Exiting the ladies' room, he came face-to-face with one of the beer connoisseurs.

Without missing a beat, Riker said, "I walked in on a guy a minute ago. Bet he's still in there. I'd use this one here."

The man looked at him and cocked his head.

Clearly the ladies' room was a *no go* proposition for this guy.

So Riker upped the ante.

"I walked in on the guy and caught him pleasuring himself. No telling how long it'll be *occupied*."

Just in case the beer-bellied fella needed a visual clue, Riker pantomimed the act he had supposedly witnessed.

Flashing a sad smirk, the man pushed past Riker and disappeared into the ladies' room.

Chapter 47

When Riker stepped from the *Gas Fast*, Tara was hanging out her window and urging him to hurry up.

Reaching the truck, the sharp, continuous blast of a blaring horn joined the tinnitus and low-grade banger already assaulting Riker's brain.

"These dudes in the Subaru are getting antsy."

As if on cue, the horn went quiet and a twenty-something with a mop of unruly blond hair started giving Riker shit for being inside for so long.

Rounding his side of the pickup, Riker stared the driver down. "Nothing stopping you from driving around and gassing up at the next pump."

That only enraged the kid and the horn started up again.

Live and learn, thought Riker, purposefully taking his own sweet time opening his door and climbing in.

Talking loud to be heard over the blaring horn, Tara said, "What's with the Longhorns hat?"

"Close," he replied. "This is the Houston Texans logo."

As he buckled in, she looked a question his way.

Massaging his tight neck muscles with one hand, Riker said, "I figured since we're going to be driving in Texas, might as well look like we *belong* in Texas."

"Ahhh," said Tara, nodding. "That would explain the temporary plates I saw in the garbage can and the impossible-to-miss gun rack that just *appeared* in the back window."

Instinctively, Riker peered over his shoulder. His eyes fell on Steve-O first. The older man was belted in, arms crossed, and wearing a hard to read expression.

As Riker lifted his gaze to the rear window, he saw the reason for Steve-O's strange demeanor. Snugged firmly in the gun rack's lower set of hooks was one of the NERF guns, complete with its stock extended and clear plastic magazine loaded to capacity.

"Perfect place for it," Riker said as he started the truck and selected Drive.

"Lee Riker approves," said Steve-O, adding an abbreviated fist pump.

As Riker let off the brake and slow-rolled past the open gas pump, he stuck his hand out the window, middle finger fully extended.

The honking stopped and insults equating the size of a pickup to the size of its driver's penis started to fly.

Tara regarded Riker. Noted the clenched jaw and white knuckles. "Let it go," she said. "Those dicks don't know the real you."

And neither do you, he thought, the visage of the unconscious man—blood trickling from his broken nose, extremities twitching subtly—front and center in his mind's eye.

Shortly after leaving the *Gas Fast*, they passed west through Coushatta, crossed the Red River near Armistead, and were motoring north by west on Highway 1, toward the Texas line.

Conscience gnawing at him, Riker finally spilled about what he had done inside the *Gas Fast*.

"He called you a nigger *and* peg leg coon?" Tara said, slapping the dash. "Not very original. Still kind of funny."

"He had it coming," Steve-O sneered. "I wish you would have did to him same as you did to that Sicko."

"That's savage," Riker said. "But I like the way you think."

"Steve-O's channeling Carol. Look at the flowers, *racist*."

"I have no idea what that's supposed to mean," admitted Riker.

"It's from a television show about *zombies* they run on my old favorite station. The station that *used* to run only old classics."

"Still," said Riker, pretending he didn't hear the Z word. "I should have restrained myself. Sticks and stones and all that."

"He was going to brain *you* with the air tank," reminded Tara. "I'm glad the reverse happened."

Riker nodded, then went silent.

To fill the void, Tara flipped on the radio and started surfing the dial for information.

***

Fifteen minutes later, roughly ten miles from Armistead, where the 1 shot off laser-straight due north, Tara silenced the worthless radio.

She said, "I can't believe they don't update those recordings more often."

Riker said, "No news is better than more *bad* news."

Steve-O stuck his head between the front seats. Head cocked at an impossible angle, he stared at Riker for a long three-count. "Is it true what that guy said? Do you have a small penis, Lee Riker?"

Thankfully Riker was gripping the wheel with both hands when the question was posed. It was the only thing that kept the Shelby on the road. His first instinct had been to throw his hands up and ask Steve-O why he thought the size of his unit was fair game for normal conversation. Which was a bad thing to do in a high-clearance vehicle traveling twenty over the speed limit on a road owed a good deal of TLC by whoever did that kind of thing in this neck of the woods.

A beat after being blindsided by those six words, Riker came to realize what *guy* Steve-O was referring to and took the proverbial high road.

Fearing *any* response to the question would steer the conversation down a rabbit hole, he kept his hands at the proper ten and two on the wheel, focused all of his attention on the gray stripe of asphalt ahead of the Shelby, and said absolutely nothing.

In the passenger seat, Tara turned her head toward the window and focused her attention on the sunlight shimmering off the distant Red River. She was doing a pretty good job of holding it together when Steve-O said, "I'm *sure* Shorty has a small penis." He paused for a moment with a thoughtful expression on his face. "That's why he wanted the big truck instead of a small car."

Tara leaned forward, buried her face in her hands, and burst into an uncontrollable fit of laughter.

"Are you OK, Pretty Lady?"

Hinging up, Tara dabbed at her eyes with a *Gas Fast* napkin. Somewhat composed, she said, "First off, Steve-O, you don't ask those kinds of questions in mixed company. Secondly, the type of vehicle a man drives has zero correlation to the size of his ... *penis*."

On the verge of losing it himself, Riker said, "How about you give us some examples, Sis."

Now Tara was speechless.

"Well ... let's hear it," said Steve-O, inching even further into the cab, his face turned toward Tara.

She fell back into her seat, laughing. Catching her breath, she said, "I've got nothing."

"How about past boyfriends? What did *they* drive?" Riker asked. "We *need* empirical proof."

"Don't put *me* under the spotlight," shot Tara. "He asked *you* the question."

Solemnly, Steve-O said, "If I could drive, it would have to be a tiny car."

"Tara knows all about tiny cars," quipped Riker. "Ask her about Thumbelina."

Easing back into his seat, Steve-O said, "What about Thumbelina?"

Grateful for the diversion, Tara retold the story of getting the little SMART car hung up on the light pole in Middletown. As she was lamenting the fact the car was probably still languishing away in the high school parking lot, Riker interrupted her.

"Would you look at that," he said, pointing to the lead engines of a southbound train. The tracks it was riding on were slightly elevated and paralleled the highway off to their left. At the moment, the highway and train tracks were both making a slight left-hand bend.

Because of the bend in the track and enormous number of cars stretching away north by west behind the three engines pulling them, the train wasn't exactly clipping along.

As the highway went straight again, Riker was afforded a better view of the flatcars. They were low-slung items loaded down with all manner of military equipment. Lashed to the first couple of train cars were a number of generators the size of garden sheds. Along with the dozens of portable light standards laid flat on the next flatcar were a pair of empty fuel bladders—both matte-black and, when expanded, larger than a Volkswagen Beetle.

Next came the vehicles. Two to a train car. Humvees occupied the next ten or so cars. There must have been twenty of them, all up armored, nearly half equipped with roof-mounted turrets inset with green-tinted ballistic glass. A few of the turrets sprouted Mk-19 grenade launchers, the rest M2 Browning or M240 Bravo machine guns.

The last twenty or so flatcars were transporting an assortment of Stryker APCs and high-riding Cougar MRAPs—all equipped with CROW roof-mounted remotely operated weapon systems.

All of the staging gear and vehicles were desert tan and bore stenciled markings much too small for Riker to read.

"I didn't see any ambulances or command vehicles," he noted. "Makes me think these are reinforcing and resupplying an already established operation."

"Romeo Victor?" said Tara, equal parts sarcasm and humor in her tone.

"That ship sailed. This is the real deal."

"Then where are they going?" Steve-O asked.

"My best guess," answered Riker, "is somewhere southeast of here. Maybe Mobile or New Orleans."

"Must be a lot of Sickos where they're going."

"I'd rather be here than there, any day," said Riker as they reached the tail end of the train.

"We haven't seen any Sickos for some time now," noted Tara.

Riker shot his sister a serious look. "Better find some wood to knock on. Because I'm afraid the wave of infection is picking up steam, rather than ebbing."

Looking around the cab, Tara said, "There's no wood in here. Maybe you should have bought a Mercedes or Escalade."

"I can pull over and let you knock on a sign post."

"My dad was superstitious," Steve-O added. "He was afraid of black cats. He *never* walked underneath a ladder. And if he spilled salt, he *always* threw some over his shoulder."

Tara's first inclination was to ask Steve-O what good throwing salt over one's shoulder was supposed to do. Instead, she said, "I don't believe in all that mumbo jumbo. If something is supposed to happen, it just does."

Other than the loaded-down train, and a couple of military convoys on the 1 that Riker was convinced were made up of units from places further west than Texas and Louisiana, southbound traffic was nonexistent.

Wondering what oddball topic Steve-O was going to toss into the ring next, Riker set the cruise control for seven over the limit, ran his seat back all the way to the stops, and began to mentally unpack the events of the last twenty-four hours.

Chapter 48

An hour after crossing the Red River, Riker had them skirting Shreveport on the Inner Loop Expressway. It hooked around south of Louisiana's third-largest city before meeting up with Interstate 20—a fifteen-hundred-mile stretch of the Interstate Highway System connecting Reeves County, Texas to its terminus in Florence, South Carolina.

Nearing the turnpike where Tara wanted him to merge onto the 20 West, a large expanse of flat paved ground flanked by metal hangars and glass terminals caught Riker's eye.

"That's Shreveport Regional," said Tara. "Got diverted there once. Compared to Atlanta International, there's not a whole lot to it."

The crew cab window on Tara's side pulsed down. Holding onto his hat, Steve-O said, "Where are all the airplanes?"

Tara said, "A guy on CNN was saying that all air travel has been suspended for seventy-two hours. I saw the clip on YouTube, so there's no telling when the countdown started."

"It's still in effect," Riker said. "I don't see any workers or vehicles doing their thing." Slowing the pickup and slipping to the right lane, he motioned toward the floor. "You know that box you've been kicking around like a soccer ball for the last sixty miles? Pick it up and tear into it like it's Christmas morning and it's your only present."

Hefting the box, Tara read the writing on the side facing her. "What's a Steiner M1050 LRF 10x50?"

Steve-O's inquisitive nature propelled him back to his spot between the seats.

As Riker powered Steve-O's window closed, he nodded at the box. "Turn it over and look at the picture."

"Oh goodie. Santa brought us binoculars," said Tara as she picked at the clear tape atop the box.

"Oooh," exclaimed Steve-O. "Those look like the ones Han and Luke used on Hoth in Empire Strikes Back. And in case your mom and dad didn't tell you … Santa isn't real."

"What?" Riker exclaimed, acting stunned and moving the wheel left and right to add to the feigned shock. "He keeps eating my cookies and drinking the milk I leave him."

"Lee is pulling your leg, Steve-O. He knows Santa only lives in the hearts and minds of kids the world over."

"As does Star Wars," Riker said, drifting all the way onto the shoulder. "Guess our man here is still a kid at heart."

Smiling at that, Steve-O said, "I just thought you should know."

"Thank you, Steve-O," said Riker as he braked and brought the truck to a halt on a wide spot on the shoulder. Going by the navigation unit, they were still a quarter-mile from the ramp he needed to take to access I-20 West. Directing his attention back to the unboxing taking place, he added, "Those aren't just any binoculars. They're similar to the ones we used in Iraq. We were always on the lookout for IEDs and insurgents in Iraq. Except these Steiners are much better."

"How so?"

"They have a laser rangefinder," Steve-O said. "Says so on the box."

"Steve-O's correct. Plus, once you get the lenses dialed in for your eyes, you don't have to touch them again. They autofocus for you. And the image stabilization is on par with any high-end digital camera."

Tara hefted the items once to gauge their weight and then brought them up to her face. "Pretty light considering they look to be wrapped in tank armor."

"Don't be fooled by that. Give a grunt long enough and he'll figure out how to break 'em."

"How do they work?"

Going somewhere in a hurry, a trio of black Suburbans tore by in the fast lane, buffeting the Shelby with a wall of wind.

"Johnnys," noted Steve-O. "I'm glad they didn't stop."

"I'm not so sure if those were the men in black," Riker said as he watched them edge over and take the 20 West exit. He didn't respond to Tara's question until the big SUVs were nearly out of sight.

Confident the mysterious convoy wasn't going to return, Riker leaned over the center console. Making sure Steve-O was paying attention, he pointed out the diopter rings just ahead of the rubber eyecups. "These adjust the focus for your eyesight. Pick something out there and turn them, one at a time, until you see the object clearly."

When she was finished, Riker moved her right pointer finger for her, repositioning it over one of the pair of top-mounted buttons.

"What's that for?"

"Turns on the laser for range finding. Go ahead and power it on."

She depressed the button.

"See a red dot and some numbers?"

She nodded.

Moving her finger to the second button, he said, "This one switches between yards and meters. Cycle to yards and then hold it down for a few seconds to enter a mode that lets you continuously lase a target. It's mainly good for gauging the distance to a moving vehicle."

Tara took to the binoculars rather quickly. She glassed the airport, reporting back her findings as she walked her gaze from left to right.

"The parking lots are all full to capacity. Long term and short. Lots of people left their cars on the shoulders of the feeder roads, too."

Thinking aloud, Riker said, "Some kind of mass evacuation?"

"That's the only thing I can think of," Tara said. "And this is a trip. They left firetrucks parked on both runways.

Flattened their tires to make sure they stayed put." Addressing Steve-O, she added, "I found the planes you were wondering about. Just a couple of smaller business-type jets parked at the far terminals. Looks like the big carriers' jets were diverted elsewhere."

Riker said, "They blocked the runways because this *used* to be outside the quarantine zone. Last thing you want if you're trying to minimize the spread of potential Bolts and Slogs is to allow planes fleeing the hot zone to land and stick zombies in your midst. One has to assume that's how Romero jumped their initial containment response."

Tara said, "Where is the fire crew? The baggage handlers and other ground personnel? The guys who guide planes with the flashlight thingies? And where did all the people go who left their vehicles behind?"

"Scared people," Steve-O said. "That's who. They were doing what we are trying to do."

Simultaneously, the siblings turned and looked questions at the older man.

"Duh ... they were trying to outrun the Sickos."

With more questions than answers cycling through his aching head, Riker pulled back onto the expressway, stayed in the right lane, then quickly signaled for one of the cloverleaf's many banked ramps.

As the Shelby nosed back around west on the turnpike, more of Shreveport was revealed. Far off in the distance, black smoke from a number of fires leaked skyward.

Closer in, Riker saw police cars blocking the arterials leading to the cloverleaf. Strangely, their roof-mounted red and blue lights were not activated.

Tara was sweeping the nearby neighborhood with the Steiners.

Riker asked Tara what she was seeing.

Lowering the binoculars, she said, "You're driving too fast. But I did see some movement on the side streets. People on foot. *Slow-moving* people on foot."

"More Sickos," said Steve-O.

Though Riker agreed with the man's assessment, trying to remain optimistic he said, "Now let's not go jumping to conclusions."

"I'm on Steve-O's side," Tara declared. "Since we're only ten miles from the Texas border, I have a feeling we're going to find out one way or the other, real soon."

Looking over his shoulder as he merged onto the 20, Riker saw several shadowy forms trudging across the field of grass in the middle of a sweeping turnpike devoid of traffic.

Feeling the cold finger of dread tracing his spine, he matted the pedal and said, "That's what I'm afraid of."

Chapter 49

The Texas border was still roughly two miles ahead on I-20 West and showing on the navigation screen as a vertical yellow line when Tara's reluctance to knock on wood came back to bite them.

They had just exited a gentle curve when they saw the Louisiana Department of Transportation and Development reader board ordering all vehicles with more than three axles to exit at the upcoming weigh station.

Riker had just finished reading the sign when, rather abruptly, the I-20 went from two lanes down to one.

Almost immediately the Shelby was caught in a narrow chute bordered by cement Jersey barriers on the left and dense forest on the right.

As Riker slowed the Shelby, he examined the Jersey barriers scrolling by outside his window. They were bigger than most he had seen. Roughly thirty feet in length and a couple of feet tall. He figured they had to weigh a couple of tons each. And the way they were deployed, end to end along westbound I-20's interior breakdown lane, getting the Shelby turned around here wasn't going to happen.

For a brief second, he considered jamming on the brakes and reversing out of the narrowing funnel. One look in his wing mirror dashed that notion. There were already a couple of vehicles behind him that'd been caught up in the same trap.

Craning out his window, Riker saw brake lights flaring way off in the distance, but no end in sight to the one-way chute.

On the right side of the Shelby, the weigh station was coming up fast. It was located on a paved parcel of flat land at the end of an exit with a lane long enough to accommodate three or four eighteen wheelers. The paved area was flanked on three sides by forest, with the interstate pushing up close on the south side.

The weigh house was a brick structure with small windows and a black tile roof. It stood all alone beside a rectangle of pavement several shades lighter than the single-lane drive leading up to it. Situated twenty-five feet above the weigh scale, mounted on a metal lattice crossbar running horizontally between two vertical poles, was an electronic sign the size of a snooker table.

On the sign was a simple message: WEIGH STATION CLOSED - PULL AHEAD - SHUT DOWN MOTOR AND WAIT FOR ASSISTANCE.

The weigh house was crowded on all sides by trucks and trailers belonging to the drivers who had heeded the message on the sign. Beyond the paved lot, sitting idle on another couple acres of land that looked to have been recently cleared from the forest, were even more multi-axle vehicles.

Lined up along the western edge of the clearing was a bulldozer, a front loader, a grader, and a dump truck. All of the equipment was desert tan. Thick, dark mud coated their tires and tracks and blades.

As usual, the Army engineers had done their jobs to perfection. Riker didn't see any evidence of the trees and brush. Just the flat edges of the perfectly graded dirt parking lot.

Parked before the front row of static eighteen wheelers were a half-dozen tan Humvees.

Riker started counting the big rigs in his head, finally stopping at thirty, with maybe half as many left uncounted. They were packed in like sardines—bumper-to-bumper and door-to-door. They created a sea of paint and chrome and glass, throwing their long shadows on the military vehicles and reflecting wan light of the westering sun in all directions.

Strange, thought Riker. *Not a single driver milling about.*

As the Shelby drew even with the graded area, Riker did see movement. Some didn't worry him. The rest sent a chill up his spine.

The former was the squad of armed soldiers clad in the newer brown, green, and tan MultiCam fatigues. They were dismounted and spreading out flat on the ground sheets that looked to be made from canvas or nylon. Whatever the material, the swaths were large enough to act as mainsails on a sailboat.

Pointing to the source of his unease, a massive fenced-in enclosure erected a stone's throw from the interstate, Riker said, "*That* is why you always knock on wood, Tara."

The rectangular pen was maybe fifty feet wide by seventy-five deep. It was constructed of twelve-foot chain-link fencing topped with concertina wire. The base of the fence was reinforced on the outside by four-foot-tall safety-orange HESCO barriers.

The pen was teeming with zombies.

They were packed in shoulder-to-shoulder, probing the chain-link with pale fingers and hungrily eyeing the soldiers just beyond their reach.

There were kid zombies and adult zombies. Old zombies and young zombies. Some were fully clothed and showed no obvious signs of injury. Others were nearly naked and sporting blood-stained bandages on their stark white extremities. Even from fifty feet, it was obvious to Riker the front row of living corpses was being slowly crushed against the fence by the press of dead flesh at their backs.

Tara's jaw hung open.

Still occupying his perch between the seats, Steve-O was struck speechless.

Riker slowed the rig and, using his master switch, ran Tara's window partway down.

Thick in the air, the sickly-sweet stench of death wormed its way inside the cab. And rising over the thrum of the off-road tires, the moans of the dead followed in after.

"Damn, that's awful," Tara said. "Run it back up, Lee."

Riker was powering up Tara's window when the vehicle ahead slowed and then came to a full stop.

Suddenly, like a thing alive, a ripple ran the length of the zombie pen and started the concertina wire swaying.

Concertina wire. A bit of overkill in Riker's opinion. As far as he knew, Slogs and Bolts couldn't scale fences.

Or could they?

Right then and there, as Riker stopped the Shelby broadside to the pen, he realized he really didn't know jack shit about the things it was holding at bay. Throwing a shiver at the prospect of an intelligent zombie with parkour skills, he looked to the rearview mirror, where he caught Steve-O studying him.

As soon as eye contact was established, Steve-O said, "We have a Sicko sighting. I told you so, Lee."

"Yeah ... lots of Sickos. You should have put money on it," Riker said. "You'd have been a winner."

Steve-O slapped a hand on Riker's seat back. "Winner, winner, chicken dinner."

Shooting Steve-O a sour look, Tara said, "Nothing winning about a mosh pit of death. Damn thing looks like a scene torn straight out of the Jewish Holocaust." Addressing Riker, she asked, "Do you think that fence will hold up if they all happen to surge forward?"

"This fence looks much sturdier than the one around the wave pool. I wouldn't worry about it," answered Riker. "My guess is they'll calm down once the soldiers get those blinds rigged up." Addressing Steve-O, he added, "Kind of off-topic, but ... can we retire that *chicken dinner* saying?"

In response, Steve-O ran a finger across his lips and pretended to close an imaginary lock.

"Keep the key," said Tara. "We still need our eagle-eye Sicko spotter to be able to call out Bolt sightings."

Nodding, Steve-O pretended to stash the imaginary key in his pocket.

The vehicles ahead moved forward a few car lengths.

"We're moving," Tara said. "Thank God. I can't stand how those things are looking at us."

Soon the trees beside the makeshift parking lot were blotting out the horror show.

Glancing at the rearview, Riker saw more vehicles changing lanes and slowing and merging into the single-file line back where the barriers began.

All those drivers unwittingly falling into the same trap as us.

As if she had been reading his mind, Tara said, "Nowhere to go from here but forward. What's the worst that can happen when we finally reach the head of the line? You think they'll turn us back for some reason?"

Riker didn't have an answer to that. Not enough intel. In fact, he wanted to take a look through the binoculars if the opportunity arose. What he did know, however, was that there was no ferry ride in their future, and he let the others know it.

Tara said, "So what you're saying is that you're done keeping secrets?"

"At least for today I am."

Tara shook her head.

Steve-O said, "Marcy and Darren never asked me to keep secrets. They were real nice people."

Riker said, "I'm sure they were," then winced as he realized he was speaking about them in the past tense.

If Steve-O grasped the nuance, he didn't let on.

After slow-rolling the Shelby down the chute for almost a half a mile, brake lights flared red and stayed red as the long line of vehicles ahead of them ground to a complete halt.

Leaving a half-truck-length buffer between the Shelby and small compact car to their fore, Riker put the transmission into Park and set the brake. He gave the line ahead of them a minute to move again. When it didn't budge, he shut down the motor to save fuel.

Though the Shelby's oversized tank was over three-quarters full, and the four backup cans held twenty gallons of fuel, Riker was afraid that if they made it into Texas, they'd be searching for gas before morning.

Tara peered through the Steiners.

Riker asked, "See the front of the line?"

"I think so."

"What's the range finder show for distance?"

She activated the laser. Saw the red numbers in the right eyepiece jumping all over the place. "Can't get the numbers to stop," she said. "I think it's around a mile. And there's lots of stuff going on up there."

Holding out his hand, Riker said, "May I take a look?"

Tara placed the binoculars on his upturned palm.

Riker put the Steiners to his face. Choosing a tan Humvee taking up most of the median near the head of the line, he activated the laser. Keeping the Humvee painted with the laser returned a good reading.

"Thirteen hundred and fifty yards is what I get. That's probably three or four hundred yards short of the head of the line, too."

Crunching the numbers in her head, Tara converted yards to feet. Then she compared her finding to the number of feet in a mile. Finally, she said, "I was close. We're about nine tenths of a mile from where it all starts."

Riker was happy she had taken it upon herself to do the computations. The low-grade headache that had been kicking his ass since the events at the *Gas Fast* was showing no sign of letting up.

Twenty seconds spent glassing the scene from front to back told him the first fifty or so vehicles at the head of the line were stopped bumper to bumper in a chain-link enclosure. The drivers remained at the wheel while soldiers with dogs walked the length, stopping at each vehicle to interrogate the civilians.

He also learned that select people were being taken from their vehicles and escorted toward the forest, some of them forcibly. Finished, he told Tara and Steve-O about the K9 detail and chain-link cage. The rendition of drivers and passengers to whatever awaited them in the forest, he chose not to share.

Fifteen minutes had gone by when the chain reaction of brake lights coming to life caught Riker's attention. The first to flare were at the front of the row and hard to see with the naked eye. A beat later the red lights were seemingly flying down the line straight at him.

A handful of seconds elapsed between the first brake light sighting and when the driver of the compact Elantra in front of the Shelby finally caught on and instinctively depressed his pedal.

Tara said, "Think the line's going to move?"

Riker shrugged. "I'm not starting the engine until it does."

Tara dragged a plastic sack off the floor, fished out a red tin the size of a pack of cigarettes, tore away the plastic wrapper, and passed the tin back to Steve-O. "Since it looks as if we have nothing but time on our hands, maybe pop a couple of those bad boys in your mouth. They're advertised to be curiously strong."

Steve-O said, "Breath mints? Are you trying to tell me something, Pretty Lady?"

"Those are for *both* of you. And I'm not done talking." She pulled a stick of deodorant from the bag. "Apply this, fellas. It's *Fresh Ocean Surf.* Hope you both approve."

"Me first," Riker said, grabbing it out of her hand.

Tara chuckled. "You got a problem sharing a pit stick with another dude? What ... you don't want one of Steve-O's red pit hairs invading your deep, dark thicket?"

Finished running the stick under his arms, Riker capped it and traded Steve-O for the tin of mints.

"It's just pit hair, for crying out loud. Not like we're talking about pubes." She shuddered. "Those give *me* the heebs."

Dodging the question, Riker said, "The line is moving," and started the motor.

Chapter 50

As Riker pulled the Shelby forward, creeping along at walking speed, he counted the Jersey barriers scrolling by on the left. When the Elantra ahead of them finally stopped again, Riker's count had reached eighteen, and the front of the line seemed no closer than before.

Setting the brake, Riker looked to Tara. "Help me out here. What's eighteen times thirty?"

"Five hundred and forty," answered Steve-O.

Tara nodded.

"How long is an average car? Fifteen feet?"

"Less," said Tara. "Got to take into account cars like my old one and that little gold thing ahead of us."

"Let's call it fifteen and not worry about the distance between cars."

"OK," said Tara. "You're trying to calculate how many vehicles just got waved through, right?"

Riker nodded as he shut down the motor.

"I'm a step ahead of you," she said.

"How many?" Steve-O asked. "Twenty?"

Tara hiked her thumb toward the roof.

Riker said, "Twenty-five?"

Again with the thumb.

Voice conveying a bit of skepticism, Steve-O said, "Thirty-five?"

Tara reached back and bumped fists with the man. "We have a winner."

Kicking his seat back, Riker said, "And I'm willing to bet you have already estimated when we'll be in the front group."

Tara smiled and nodded.

"That smile tells me it can't be that bad."

"Right now I figure we're in the ninth group out."

"Fifteen minutes a group."

She said, "More like twenty."

"We'll be in Texas in about three hours," Steve-O declared.

Simultaneously, Riker and Tara turned toward the backseat.

"He's good," Riker said.

"Rain Man good," Tara added.

***

During the next hour, Riker drove the Shelby ahead in the line two times, counting out a total of thirty-three Jersey barriers in the process.

As soon as he had shut the motor off after the second slow-rolling surge forward, the unmistakable engine roar and exhaust burble of Harley Davidsons on the move invaded the cab through his open window.

Tara lifted off her seat and peered out the back window. After craning around, she picked up the source of the noise. It was a group made up of about thirty motorcycles. The riders wore a mixture of traditional black and multi-colored riding leathers. Some wore helmets. Most did not, opting instead for a simple bandanna, or nothing at all.

Tara said, "Oh shit!" and twisted back around in her seat. Then, recalling a scene from a Brad Pitt movie in which a passing motorcycle shears the wing mirror from his Volvo, she ran her window down and reached for the Shelby's oversized wing mirror.

Beating his sister to the punch, Riker hit a switch that started both side mirrors to fold back under power.

There was a soft whirr and a couple of seconds after they began to move, the mirrors were flush with the windows. Just in time, too, because there was maybe six inches clearance between the pickup and riders as they blipped by, pushing a wall of wind and leaving a sonic tempest in their wake.

Warding off exhaust fumes with one hand, Tara ran her window up with the other.

"Were those Hell's Angels?" Steve-O asked.

"Nope," answered Riker, sounding amused. "I'd guess it's a few wannabes and a whole mess of professionals playing weekend warrior."

Tara said, "What do you think the soldiers are going to do?"

Riker imagined the E-6 or E-7 who was running the show, likely a Staff Sergeant or Sergeant First Class standing in the way of the oncoming bikes. M4 carbines at the ready, a couple of soldiers would have their superior's back.

Out loud, he said, "My money is on the bikers getting an ass chewing for cutting the line."

And he was right. Three minutes after zipping by, the bikes returned. Only this time it was in the form of a slow-moving procession. Engines barely revving above idle, the bikes weaved and bounced as they puttered along the shoulder. Exhaust pipes no longer emitting the ear-splitting notes, the pack seemed whipped.

Tara stared down the repulsed riders as they filed by. To a man they wore on their faces the expression of a scolded dog.

"Looks like the white-collar brotherhood failed to make their case," joked Riker.

Steve-O said, "Mom always said that cutting in line is bad."

"I agree with her wholeheartedly," Tara said. Reaching over the seat, she asked for the Rand McNally Atlas she'd bought at a truck stop outside of Philadelphia the week prior.

"Trade you for your iPhone."

Nodding, she handed over the smartphone and earbuds for it.

***

In a little less than two hours, Riker had driven the Shelby forward five times.

Over the course of those two hours, the trio had learned nothing new from the radio and eaten all of the junk food Tara had picked up at the *Gas Fast*.

"I'm hungry for real food," declared Steve-O.

"So am I," Riker said.

"I have to pee again," added Steve-O.

Grimacing, Riker said, "Me too."

"I can wait to eat *and* I can wait to pee," announced Tara. "So clamp it off, guys. I don't care how you do it. Just make it happen." As she spoke, she had been facing her window. And though it was just south of seventy degrees outside the truck, and pushing eighty inside, her window remained up and her door locked.

Sounding rather sure of himself, Riker said, "They're not going to escape, Sis."

Without taking her eyes from what she knew to be another zombie-choked enclosure—the third one set up beside the road in less than a mile—Tara said, "So tell me, then, exactly why do you have that pistol of yours in your other hand."

Riker said nothing.

She said, "That's what I thought."

"At least it keeps the smell out," noted Steve-O.

"Keeps the smell in, too," Tara replied as she handed the mint tin to her brother.

***

Now and again while they waited in line, Riker had employed the Steiners to watch the K-9 handlers as they made continuous laps around the front third of the line. Now, from the cab of the Shelby, parked three vehicles back from what he guessed was the demarking line of the front third of the queue, he spotted a squat, muscular soldier coming straight for him from across the grassy median.

On the end of a short lead was a similarly proportioned dog. It looked to be either a Bulldog or Pitbull terrier.

Letting the dog choose the route, the soldier stepped between a pair of barriers next to the Shelby and issued a command to the dog.

At once, the dog sat on its haunches. As the handler waited for backup, the dark brindle pooch's purposeful gaze never strayed from the Shelby.

The entire time Riker had been on the outside looking in, the handlers hadn't removed anything from any of the vehicles they had inspected. Not weapons. Not parcels. Nothing. They were only interested in removing people. And there seemed to be no rhyme or reason to it until Riker saw a man who had been pulled from a minivan turn and lunge for a handler.

The consequences had occurred instantaneously and without warning.

Somewhere to their left an unseen long rifle roared and the man went down. Just crashed vertically to the road and lay there still as a cadaver.

The handler had barely flinched. This was obviously not the first time the sniper overwatch had been forced to intervene on his behalf.

As the echo from the single gunshot toured the woods around the roadblock, the pink mist that had haloed the man's head drifted slowly to the road, landing away from the handler and his disinterested four-legged partner.

In the backseat of the Shelby, plugged into the iPhone and singing along softly to what sounded like a Keith Urban ditty, Steve-O had remained head down and oblivious to the entire event.

Hearing the shot as it happened, Tara had dropped the atlas to her lap, clasped her hands atop her head, and uttered a prayer for the fallen man.

Now, ten minutes removed from that event, Riker was being stared down by the same handler. Attached with Velcro to the handler's MultiCam fatigues were a number of patches. The stacked chevrons told Riker the soldier was a Staff Sergeant. The name tape on his blouse read *Hawkins*. The white band encircling one arm bore the letters *MP*. And unlike the Johnnys and contractors Riker had crossed paths with over the course of a week, this soldier's uniform featured both the American Flag and a unit patch. On the unit patch was a golden gauntlet clutching what looked to be a man. Rendered with all the detail of a stick figure, the man was being held upside down above the ground. Stitched in black on a scroll at the bottom of the patch were the words *ORDERLY REGULATION*.

Turning to Tara, Riker shielded his mouth and whispered, "This is probably the precursor to Martial Law, Sis. The Sergeant here is Army from some MP unit likely operating out of Fort Hood." Shaking his head, he said solemnly, "The Big Green Machine has entered the ball game. Stuff's about to hit the fan."

When Riker turned back, Sergeant Hawkins was standing just outside his window and motioning for him to open the door.

A blast of wind carrying the stench of spoiled flesh infiltrated the truck's cab as Riker complied.

"What can I do for you, Sergeant?"

Speaking with a heavy Boston accent, the sergeant said, "I need to have you open all your doors and remain seated."

Chapter 51

While Sergeant Hawkins was issuing his orders, Tara had been leaning across the center console.

Fixing the sergeant with her best *perturbed* look—a half-squint with one brow cocked— she asked, icily, "What's going on here?"

"Just open your door," Riker growled. "The sergeant has a job to do."

Once all four doors were hanging open, Hawkins released the dog to do its thing.

The dog's *thing* was to jump into the backseat with Steve-O and nose around, stepping all over the man as if he wasn't even there. Finished, the dog leaped down to the road on Tara's side, stood in front of her door on its hind legs and, its wide head bobbing and lolling about, gave her and everything around her a thorough sniffing.

Riker was last. For some reason the dog keyed in on his bionic.

Noticing the titanium-and-carbon-fiber prosthetic, the sergeant asked Riker where he'd lost his leg.

Hoping to pull the former-Army card and probe Sergeant Hawkins for information, Riker told him about the day the IED planted on Route Irish sent him home from the war early.

Seeing vehicles down the line receiving the same K-9 treatment, Riker said, "Can you share any intel?"

"Just that you're in the last group we're allowing into the Green Zone."

Green Zone. That's original.

From the backseat, Steve-O asked, "What's his name?"

Hawkins seemed to soften. He said, "*Her* name is Ruby."

"Can I pet her?"

Shaking his head, Hawkins said, "No. Sorry. She's a working dog."

"What's her job?"

"She sniffs out dead bodies."

"A cadaver dog," Riker said. "All of our dead bodies are in the load bed."

Posture firming up, Hawkins said, "Is the tonneau cover locked?"

Wishing he hadn't uttered the smart-ass remark in the first place, Riker nodded. "Want me to unlock it?"

Glancing at the exposed prosthesis, Hawkins shook his head. "Give me the key. I'll lock it once Ruby's done her thing."

"I know you're just crossing Ts and all that," Riker said, "but I figure you ought to know that I'm transporting a few rifles and pistols back there. They're unloaded and secured in a Pelican case." Hooking a thumb at Steve-O, he added, "We're careful to keep them out of my brother's reach."

Hawkins didn't seem at all interested.

Riker handed over the keys. As he did so, out of the corner of one eye he spotted a female soldier standing on the road two vehicles ahead of the Elantra. Strangely, the soldier wasn't wearing an MP band. On her shoulder was a different patch, one that Riker had never seen before.

The female soldier wore a pistol on one hip and carried in her dominant hand what looked to be a TASER.

As Hawkins looped around back of the Shelby, with Ruby stretching out her lead, Riker nudged Tara and pointed at the female soldier.

Together they watched as the soldier leaned into the vehicle and walked the device over the driver's face and neck. Saw her hold a brief conversation, then move on.

After witnessing the female soldier employ the device on a trio of people crammed into the cab of a small pickup, it was clear the item was intended for something other than incapacitating a person. In fact, it didn't seem to be doing anything at all *to* them.

When Hawkins returned with the keys, declaring the Shelby's bed "cadaver free," Riker nodded toward the female soldier approaching the Elantra.

Beating Riker to the punch, Hawkins said, "When Captain Long gets to you, she's going to read everyone's temperature with a no-touch body scanner." Regarding Steve-O, he added, "Don't worry … no one is going to get poked or prodded. We just need to be certain the infection does not cross over into Texas. If the captain's device says you're all below 100.4, you are good to go when the block opens up."

Since the sergeant had broached the subject, Riker said, "Romeo Victor was mil-speak for Romero Virus, *not* the name of the op, am I right? And I'm guessing branding that unnamed op as just a training event was cover for the initial thrust at containment. Am I still hitting the nail on the head?"

Sergeant Hawkins said nothing. He just stood there watching Captain Long wave her device over the Elantra driver's face.

As it turned out, Captain Long's work would entail more than just checking the Elantra driver's temperature. Finished with the business at hand, she stepped back and ordered the man from the car.

When the middle-aged man stepped from the car, he jammed a misshapen Panama hat atop a shock of unruly black hair and unloaded with a barrage of verbal insults.

Standing her ground, the captain pocketed the thermal scanner and, in an authoritarian voice full of Southern twang, ordered him to his knees.

Instantly Riker noted that the man was way too big for the Elantra. Dressed like he'd just boarded a cruise ship—floral-print shirt, khaki walking shorts, and white boat shoes—the man looked wildly out of place standing on the road beside the beat-up compact car. And though the interaction was taking place a handful of yards away, Riker noticed that the man's boat shoes were stippled with what looked to be blood.

Captain Long repeated her order.

The man balked. Just stood there looking down on her. And though the man had a good half a head on the captain, she showed no signs she was intimidated by him.

When the man didn't immediately comply, Hawkins called out, "Captain Long?"

Long answered Hawkins with an open hand.

The Elantra driver followed the captain's empty hand with his eyes.

Bad move.

Like a magician's sleight-of-hand trick, with the other hand the captain slipped a slim black device from a case on her belt, brought it around in a slow left to right arc toward the driver's exposed neck, and thumbed it on.

By the time the driver realized what was happening, blue/white bolts of electricity had bridged the short distance from device to skin and he was dropping to the road as if the rug had been pulled out from under him.

The captain left the incapacitated man to twitch on the road as she pulled a pair of zip cuffs from her pants pocket. She bound the man's wrists and ankles together with the thick nylon ties, then rolled him over and quickly inspected his neck and extremities.

Looking in Hawkins' direction, she said, "He's got a fresh bite wound … upper thigh. Temp's spiking pretty big."

Sergeant Hawkins craned and spoke into a radio handset riding atop his left shoulder.

A beat later two soldiers showed up and whisked the driver away.

"What *not* to say to a lady with juice," Tara declared ahead of a soft chuckle.

As the captain approached the Shelby, another soldier who had shown up with the security detail hopped in the Elantra and drove it to the breakdown lane.

Pissed he didn't think to start the Shelby and run its air conditioning prior to what appeared to be a test that held the metaphorical key to them getting across the border and away from the noose rapidly tightening around them, Riker resorted to urging Tara and Steve-O to imagine they were enjoying a cold glass of sweet tea … in Antarctica.

Tara said, "Have you gone crazy, Lee?"

Riker adjusted his Texans cap. Then, wearing a sheepish look, he said, "Best I could come up with. If any of us are running a temperature, we'll be separated. Probably for good."

Steve-O said, "It'll be OK, Lee Riker. I'm sure of it."

The captain was at Riker's door and staring in at him. Riker whispered, "Obviously, Steve-O, your glass of sweet tea is half-full," then turned toward the captain, wearing a fake smile and thinking of all things cold.

Chapter 52

Riker, Tara, and Steve-O sat there, through the last of the afternoon sun, while Captain Long did her thing.

She started with Riker. Made him remove his hat and ran the thermal scanner over his forehead. Remaining tight-lipped, she glanced at a screen on the instrument. Clearly not satisfied, she repeated the procedure.

Tara called out, "Better go easy on my brother. I can assure you he is *not* infected."

The captain paused for a tick and fixed Tara with a glare that could only be interpreted as a silent order for her to stand down.

Hoping to head off any response from Tara, Riker asked, "How far north does the Green Zone stretch?"

The captain paused, shot him an *I'll pretend I didn't hear that* look, then moved on to Steve-O, who preempted her test by saying, "Mom always told me I run hot. Just thought you should know."

"Hat," said the captain, all business.

Steve-O removed his Stetson, then remained still as he was subjected to the same test as Riker.

For Steve-O, there was no second pass with the medical instrument.

Coming up to Tara's side, Captain Long said, "I like your spunk."

Glare softening, Tara said, "I'm sorry for being such a bitch."

Running the scanner over Tara's face, the captain said, "If I were in your shoes, I would have likely pulled that Glock you have trapped underneath your left thigh and shot my way out of here."

Brows dropping half an inch, Tara said, "Really?"

"No," replied Long. "That would have been a suicide mission. However, know that you three are the luckiest folks in Louisiana today. Best advice I can give is you should scoot across Texas as fast as you can. Go somewhere remote and—"

The rumble of an eastbound military convoy drowned out the captain's words as she turned and motioned to Hawkins.

Tara asked the captain if she'd passed the test. Getting no response, she looked askance at her brother.

Riker leaned in and said, "No doubt you did. That gesture Long just gave Hawkins. Spinning her finger in the air. It means get the show on the road ... sort of. Or, in mil-speak, we're going to be Oscar Mike any minute now."

As if confirming Riker's hypothesis, the lights atop the portable standards began to flicker on.

Seconds later, the pickup beyond the patch of road vacated by the Elantra fired its engine. Then, like a thing alive, the entire line of vehicles stretching west toward the setting sun began to inch forward.

They were Oscar Mike, indeed.

The forward surge was slow at first, then picked up, the lead vehicles shooting through the chain-link tunnel like water penetrating a fissure in a dam.

When the lane opened up from one to two, the drivers out front accelerated. Not to be outdone, several vehicles in the middle of the queue made their move, sprinting to get to the front of the pack.

When the Shelby exited the chute, Riker couldn't help but think of the one start to an Indianapolis 500 he had ever watched. Not wanting to get caught up in anything resembling the pileup he had witnessed that day at the races with his dad, he eased off the pedal and stayed in the right lane.

In the backseat, Steve-O launched into a pretty damn good rendition of Willie's *On The Road Again*. Riker was still blown away at how good the man was at mimicking country crooners—especially Willie Nelson.

This got him to thinking about where the old guy was holed up. Probably in a compound somewhere in Texas, strumming a guitar and surrounded by a nice supply of *medicinal* marijuana.

Tara pointed off to the left.

Across the median, Riker picked up the large convoy of tan military vehicles coming at them from the west. Headlights ablaze, they were moving slowly, two abreast, and maybe twenty deep. Save for an M1 Abrams main battle tank, seemingly every piece of armor in the United States' inventory was represented. And like the earlier convoy, the red and yellow flags of the 1st Cavalry Division flew from some of the vehicles' antenna.

"That's not a good sign," Tara said.

Failing to imagine the number of infected that would warrant the better part of a combined arms division to move into the Red Zone, Riker stated the obvious: "Then it's a good thing we're going in the opposite direction."

With the main body of the eighty or so vehicles released when the roadblock was opened up clipping along I-20 well above the posted seventy-five-mile-per-hour limit, Riker kicked his speed up to eighty. A beat later a sign emblazoned with the red, white, and blue state flag of Texas and the words *Welcome To Texas* flitted by. Strangely, considering the circumstances, it was the only indicator a border was being crossed. And it was also the only thing welcoming about a surrounding landscape quickly being swallowed up by a fast-moving shroud of darkness.

Steve-O suddenly stopped singing. He said, "When night falls around here, it really falls."

Tara agreed. "With all the clouds and a waning moon, it's going to be impenetrable before long."

Taking a cue from them both, Riker flicked on the Shelby's headlights. For good measure, he also toggled on the bank of LED driving lights housed in the Shelby's massive front bumper.

The gray strip of two-lane being sucked under the fast-moving Shelby was instantly lit up like a perp under interrogation.

"We need to eat," Steve-O said. "You promised, Lee."

"I second that," was Tara's reply.

Passing by a deserted rest stop, Riker grumbled something about not stopping until they were low on gas and needed to access the spare tanks in back.

To Steve-O's delight, Tara nixed that idea.

When Riker pressed the issue of continuing on and pulled a couple of cereal bars from a pocket to stave off their hunger, Tara resorted to the one thing that had always made their dad capitulate when she and her brother found themselves on a road trip and in a similar position.

She said, "Are we there yet?" and continued to repeat the question until Steve-O caught on and joined her.

After hearing 'Are we there yet?' for what seemed like the hundredth time in less than a minute, Riker's resolve crumbled like a house of cards in a hurricane.

Shooting Tara a sour look, he said, "*Fine.* Find us a place to eat. And it better not have a drive-thru."

Tara thumbed on her phone. Almost at once, she shut it down, saying, "No service."

"Try the navigator thing," urged Riker.

She pulled up the screen. Tapped the zoom-out button a few times, making the image shrink down so that a good chunk of the Texas/Louisiana western border filled the entire screen.

"Do you see a greasy spoon?" Steve-O asked.

"Here," Tara said, tapping on a location that was ahead of them and on the right side of the interstate.

Seconds later, the trees flanking I-20 West thinned out and the lights of Waskom, Texas dominated the new vantage. Especially alluring to Steve-O was the illuminated yellow M a short distance beyond the next exit.

Steve-O knocked on his window. "Is that it?"

In unison, Tara and Riker said, "No way!"

"Where then?"

"A place with greasy spoons," quipped Riker.

Steve-O had to wait five long minutes to see what Tara had chosen off the navigation screen. To everyone's delight, it was open. Behind the squat baby-blue building was an enormous pond. Halide lights rising up from the mostly empty parking lot bathed the building and vehicles in a ghostly orange hue that didn't quite reach the body of water bordering the restaurant to the north.

Rectangles of light spilling from the many windows flanked the building's west side. On the south elevation, a glowing neon sign that read *Catfish Corral* painted the ground all around the front door a vivid red.

Before Riker could find a spot under a light to park Dolly, Steve-O was giving Tara's selection two enthusiastic thumbs-up and unbuckling his seatbelt.

Chapter 53

Riker parked the Shelby on the corner of Catfish Corral's lot nearest to the pond. He chose a lined spot awash in the spill from a bulb high above, where the pickup containing all of their worldly possessions could be seen from any one of the restaurant's large, west-facing picture windows.

The trio entered through the front doors and Tara asked the teenaged hostess to seat them where they could see the parking lot.

The hostess summoned a gangly redheaded server whose nametag read *Chad*.

As usual, Riker got most of the attention from both the hostess and Chad. Hard not to thanks to his pro-football-player's physique.

Chad showed them to the booth Riker had hoped for. It was in the corner by a window that faced the lot. It also had a great view of the pond.

A large boathouse sat on the bank less than a hundred yards away. The pond was ringed by scruffy plants and looked like a place the Creature from the Black Lagoon might call home.

As Chad set out the menus, Riker asked, "You farm your own catfish out there?"

"No, sir. That's just a water feature for lookin' at. Catfish we serve is farmed in New Orleans. Dick has it flown in fresh every other day."

Crestfallen, Riker said, "What are you drinking, Sis?"

"Sweet tea."

"Me too," Steve-O said, pushing his menu aside.

Riker asked for the same.

After letting his gaze linger on Riker for an extra beat or two, Chad set off toward the kitchen.

Categorizing the extra attention as a byproduct of either his stature, skin tone, or both, Riker swept the room with his eyes. The booths were upholstered with glitter-infused red vinyl. Even under the low lighting, they sparkled a bit.

On the table tops were pages from old newspapers. The shellac used to seal them in was scratched and yellowed, making the stories accompanying the headlines near impossible to read.

Seeing Chad push through a pair of swinging doors behind the host stand, Tara said, "I was hoping the same thing about the pond."

"Can't beat wild line-caught catfish," Riker declared.

Chad was back in a flash with their drinks. As he navigated the room, his eyes never left Riker.

Of course, Riker got his tea first. Then Chad passed teas to Tara and Steve-O and came back for Riker's order first.

Motioning to Tara, Riker said, "Ladies first."

Tara and Steve-O ordered nearly identical plates: Cajun catfish strips with tomato relish, hushpuppies, coleslaw, and cornbread with honey butter.

Riker went with the same, but added a rare ribeye steak and baked potato with all the trimmings.

When Chad walked away, Tara said, "Methinks he's got eyes for you."

Steve-O was in the middle of taking a drink. Upon hearing Tara's declaration, a stream of iced tea shot out of his nose. Composing himself, he said, "Lee Riker has a not so secret admirer."

Speechless, Riker shook his head, then rose and struck off for the restroom. Along the way, he pulled Chad aside and jokingly said, "We need a cleanup on aisle one. Seems my brother has a hole in his lip." Then, all business, he turned his back toward the booth, and whispered, "Have you been here most of the week? Working, I mean."

Chad nodded.

"Serve lots of guests?"

Again with the nod.

Riker quickly shared most of what he'd seen and done over the last thirty-six hours. He started with the dead coming ashore in Miami, him and the others coming ashore at Buccaneer State Park, and ended by describing the pens full of living dead at the border, just six short miles away.

When Riker stopped talking, Chad's face was blanched and bore no discernable expression.

Shell-shocked was the only word Riker could think of to describe Chad's affect.

Feeling awful for heaping all he knew about the outbreak on the young man's shoulders, Riker apologized. After looking around the restaurant to see if anyone was listening in, he asked Chad if he'd heard any of his guests talking about living dead things.

"You mean *eaters?*"

Riker said nothing.

Chad swallowed hard one time, then told Riker all that he could remember.

Riker listened, never once interrupting. Once Chad had finished, he thanked him and continued on to the restroom.

From her spot in the booth, Tara had watched the entire interaction. The look on the younger man's face when her brother turned and walked off worried the hell out of her. It was a mixture of confusion and incredulity. Surely Lee hadn't mentioned her half-joking observation to the twenty-something. That wasn't Lee at all. He wasn't one to make someone feel uneasy for no good reason. And he certainly wasn't a homophobe. Or racist. Or any of those other awful things people seemed to be so quick to foist on people they don't agree with.

However, worrying Tara more than someone she didn't know getting their feelings hurt was her brother's pronounced limp. She'd noticed it earlier at the *Gas Fast* but hadn't said anything.

The food was arriving at the table when Riker returned.

Face still a bit pale and devoid of emotion, Chad asked if he could bring anything else for the table.

Saying they had everything they needed, Tara waved the man off.

Once Chad was out of earshot, she said, "You're limping, Bro. You OK?"

"It gets irritated after awhile. Just a thing that happens. Plus, all the sitting and driving is taking a toll on my lower back."

Spoonful of slaw poised in midair, Steve-O said, "Let Tara drive. I will be her wingman."

"I bet you will," Riker said.

Ignoring her brother, Tara sipped her tea. Dabbing her lips on a napkin, she said, "We'll move stuff around back there so you can stretch out."

Riker said, "I'd need a limousine to do that." He handed over the remote fob. "You kicked ass being backup driver on the way down from Jersey. Just remember, speed limit is seventy-five in Texas."

"Means I can drive eighty-five if I want, right?"

"Better watch out for tumbleweeds," Steve-O said, throwing his napkin on his plate.

Half-finished with his meal, Riker looked at the other man's clean plate. "Damn, Hoover. You sucked that down."

Tara put her hands to her face. "Hoover. That was good."

If Steve-O got the joke, he didn't show it. "I'm going to the grown ass men's room. Be right back."

Turned out Steve-O's idea of "right back" was ten minutes. When he returned, the plates had been cleared and the check dropped off.

Tara said, "Ready?"

Steve-O said, "What, no desert?"

"Grab a mint on the way out," said Riker as he took the wad of bills from his pocket and peeled off a pair of crisp hundreds.

Waiting by the edge of the table, Chad scooped up the check and cash and said, "I'll be right back."

Riker called out, "Keep it," and rose from the booth.

"A hundred-dollar tip?"

"Don't make me change my mind, Chad."

Thanking Riker profusely, Chad looked to Steve-O. "You take as many mints as you like, sir," and disappeared through the pair of swinging door leading into the kitchen.

At the Shelby, as discussed, they changed seating arrangements, with Tara behind the wheel and Steve-O riding shotgun.

With both front seats run nearly to their forward stops, Riker had an ample amount of room from front-to-back. Side-to-side, however, was the issue. The space was maybe five-and-a-half-feet from armrest to armrest. Which meant to sleep on the bench seat, he was going to have to lie on his side with his knees drawn up to his chest.

For all of its plusses, good ol' Dolly was far from a limousine.

Before firing the engine, Tara fiddled with the navigation unit. Finding it a bit glitchy, she turned on the dome light and traced their route the old-fashioned way—on the wide pages of the Rand McNally atlas.

Still sitting up in the backseat, Riker said, "Chad wants us to steer well clear of Dallas."

"That's going to take us way off course," she said. "Either direction we skirt it, south or north, we'll be burning up precious fuel."

"You have a full tank. Plus twenty gallons in back. Fifty-six gallons ought to get us most of the way to where we're going."

Tracing her finger across two pages, Tara said, "I think you're right." She tossed the atlas to the floor, then took her Glock from the console and put it underneath her right thigh.

Looking at his watch, Riker said, "If we're lucky, we'll be hitting Amarillo by morning."

Hearing those last three words straightened Steve-O up in his seat. Smiling, he cracked open a bottled water and took a sip.

Here we go, thought Riker, just as the man in the front seat launched into the song *Amarillo By Mornin'* popularized by George Strait in the early '80s.

As Tara steered for the nearby interstate, Riker shed his prosthesis, balled a jacket up to use as a pillow, and stretched out on the seat as best he could. His watch, wallet, wad of cash, and bag of gold coins and ingots went into the door's lower side-pocket. Feeling the Sig and holster digging into his side, he tugged the holster free and placed it and the pistol on the floor within easy reach.

In a matter of seconds, serenaded by the unlikely combination of the Shelby's exhaust note, the hypnotic thrum of off-road tires rolling up the ramp to I-20, and Steve-O's near perfect cover of an oft-covered song, Riker drifted off to sleep.

Chapter 54

Riker awoke in the backseat of the Shelby, totally disoriented. Gone was the sensation of movement that had lulled him to sleep and kept him there. It was totally quiet and he couldn't see his hand in front of his face. Put together, it was as if he'd been deposited on the dark side of the moon. Or had been kidnapped, hooded, and folded into the trunk of a tiny Hyundai Elantra.

He was on his right side with his head still resting on the jacket. The cool leather of the seatback against his forehead assured him he wasn't in a car trunk.

Voice a near whisper, he said, "Tara? Steve-O?"

Nothing.

For a half-beat he thought maybe Tara had gotten drowsy and pulled over. Maybe the pair were slumped down in their seats and conked out like he had been.

If so, why wasn't he getting an earful of Steve-O's snoring?

A couple of things he did know. As if Dwayne "The Rock" Johnson had put him out with a choke hold, there was a terrible pain in his neck. In addition, his entire right arm was useless. Fingertips to shoulder, he couldn't feel a thing. No sensation at all. Only when he sat up did the sudden eruption of pins and needles let him know the arm was still attached to his body.

On the plus side, his stub no longer possessed a heartbeat of its own. Staying off of it for an indeterminate amount of time had done him good in that department.

With his left arm, he probed the front seats, finding only empty space and more cool to the touch leather.

Beginning to worry, he looked out the windows. Slowly scanned all points of the compass.

Still no signs of life.

If there was anyone out there, the impenetrable darkness was concealing their movements.

Riker quickly gunned up and snugged on the bionic.

To maintain any type of advantage he might have over anyone watching while preserving what little night vision that might be building, he slid the switch on the dome light to OFF.

As he pushed open the door, he noticed a big drop in temperature. Whereas it had been around seventy degrees outside of the Catfish Corral, here the air had a mid-fifties chill to it.

Riker opened the door slow and smooth. When he stepped to the ground, he felt the soles of his Salomons sink in what he thought was very fine dirt. Or sand. He couldn't be sure.

Leaving the door open, he looped around front of the Shelby. Pausing by the right front fender, he placed his palm atop the hood.

It was still warm.

As he stood there, staring away from the pickup, slowly he began to see shapes. Just lighter outlines of things in the foreground, really.

Close in were what he took to be low bushes or scrub brush. In the middle distance was a car-sized hole in the dark. A sedan. Bigger than the Elantra, but smaller than an old American car.

Behind what he took to be a car was a second hole in the dark. It rose twenty feet above the car's roof and rambled off left and right.

Trees?

Though he wore a long-sleeved shirt buttoned up to his sternum, the cold still raised goose flesh on his arms.

Sig held at a low-ready, he advanced toward the car, taking slow, tentative steps. Kicking up unseen puffs of dust, he crossed the distance, the only sound the soft squelch of the talc-like dirt moving underfoot.

To give him a little warning lest he come up against someone or something waiting for him in the dark, he swept his off hand back and forth in front of him as he moved. Having covered what he guessed to be half the distance to the car, he picked up the scent of decaying flesh.

The odor was eye-watering by the time Riker felt his fingers brush cool metal. Running his hand over the surface revealed the raised ridges of what had to be some kind of metal emblem. Perhaps a badge denoting make or model. Moving his hand left introduced some kind of metal trim, then the unmistakable smooth surface of window glass.

Suddenly, something hit the glass with tremendous force, the strike causing it to flex against Riker's palm. Then there was a clacking sound. Next came a noise like that of a gas station squeegee being dragged across a dirty window.

In his mind's eye, Riker saw the dead thing tonguing the window from the inside. Saw the window clouded by long wet streaks of whatever fluids wept from the putrefying body.

Screw tactical advantage, he thought, dragging the Scorpion from his pocket. Last thing he needed was to bump into another one of these in the dark.

He averted his eyes and thumbed on the tac-light.

Squinting against the brilliant white cone of light, Riker held the flashlight hip-high to him and walked the beam left to right, beginning at roughly his nine o'clock and ending at a point directly off his right shoulder.

All of Riker's earlier conclusions were confirmed. The ground under his Salomons was covered with a thin layer of khaki-hued dirt the consistency of baby powder. Low scrub that he thought might be mesquite formed a low barrier in front of a picket of mature trees split down the middle by a narrow dirt track.

Parked broadside to the trees was a late model Chevy Impala. Somehow the black four-door sedan had become a tomb for a badly decomposed female zombie.

Reacting to the light sweeping across the car, the zombie seated behind the wheel bashed its face repeatedly against the window glass. The nonstop pounding quickly turned its already split lips into a pinkish gray paste that coated the window with a cataract-like film.

Focusing the beam on the ground behind the car revealed footprints other than his. They were two different-sizes and left there by two very different style of footwear—the smaller of the two definitely possessing a squared-off boot heel.

Riker thought about calling out for the pair but quickly decided against it. If a flashlight beam wasn't bringing zombies out of the woods, no sense in ringing the proverbial dinner bell for them.

Instead, he turned the flashlight bezel until the wide cone of light was a focused beam. Lighting up the side-by-side tracks, he followed them to the break in the trees, where he paused and listened hard.

Hearing nothing but leaves chattering from a light gust, he continued on down the narrow, wheel-rutted track.

About twenty feet from the clearing the Shelby was parked in, Riker came across a wooden sign. It was low to the ground and affixed to two four-by-four posts. The sign was so riddled with bullet holes that the only words on its face legible to Riker were, *Camp, Pack, Out,* and *Trash.* Below was a string of smaller numbers and letters that didn't make much sense to him. Strangely, they had gone largely untouched by the gunfire directed at the sign.

Best guess was the last line was some kind of municipal code. Maybe a reminder of the penalty one could receive for camping here and not taking their trash home with them.

Fair policy.

While Riker pushed further down the track, he wondered what the penalty would be for whoever shot up the sign. Surely not stiff enough.

As the tree-lined track spilled out into what appeared to be a second unimproved parking lot, the red and yellow side reflectors on a high-riding, hunter-green SUV across the way grabbed the light and refracted it back at him.

Stopping to expand the beam, Riker heard two people talking. Leveling the beam on the full-sized SUV, he saw a fleeting movement near the right rear wheel.

He called out, "Tara," and heard a cough. After a half-beat of silence, during which the answer he expected to hear never materialized, the coughing resumed.

To maintain any kind of advantage afforded him by approaching the scene from the blindside and with the noise to mask his footfalls, he extinguished the light and immediately set off across the lot.

Sig leading the way and every nerve ending in his body crackling with pent-up energy, Riker walked with purpose toward the foreign sounds.

Chapter 55

The coughing fit continued as Riker heel and toed it across the lot, toward the squared-off SUV. As he made it to the driver's side rear quarter, the fit was replaced by a retching sound that went on and on and showed no sign of letting up.

All in all, when put together, Riker was coming to the conclusion he was hearing the life being choked out of someone. Or, as his imagination began to run, maybe he was listening to a zombie rending the esophagus from Tara's dying body.

As he rounded the rear of what the prominent badging told him was a Land Rover Discovery, the choking sounds ceased and his gaze was drawn to a spill of weak light angling down and away from the rig's rear bumper. The illuminated patch of ground was split down the middle by the shadow of a slender woman on her knees. A ball cap was perched backwards on her head and, judging by the long, slender object bridging the gap between her clasped hands and mouth, Riker feared he had just caught a woman and a very well-endowed man in a compromising position.

Riker was trying to decide how he should go about announcing his presence when a familiar masculine voice said, "Keep going," and then at once a raspy feminine voice replied, "I'm sucking as hard as I can."

With a familiar heady scent hitting his nose, Riker came to realize what was *really* going on just out of sight behind the Land Rover.

On the verge of laughing out loud, he holstered the Sig, stepped into the light spill, and cast his gaze along the length of the slab-sided vehicle.

He saw exactly what he'd expected based on the shadow and brief snippet of heated conversation.

On her knees and facing the SUV's quarter panel was an oblivious Tara. Trapped between her teeth was a short length of garden hose whose opposite end disappeared behind the SUV's open filler door.

Steve-O, the owner of the masculine voice, was standing a little hunched over opposite Tara and holding an iPhone. The device's flashlight feature wasn't great; however, it still produced a beam sufficient to cast a damn funny shadow.

If a picture is worth a thousand words, thought Riker, then the mental image he was storing for later was going to make for one hell of an *Aunty Tara* story to tell future nieces and nephews. Assuming she finally found the elusive *one* before her biological clock shut that window for good.

Pushing from his mind the crazy notion of one day becoming an uncle, Riker cleared his throat.

With nothing to compete with, the grating noise emanated from Riker's throat much louder than he had intended. It almost sounded like a wild cat issuing a warning.

Engaged in the task of trying to liberate the Discovery of any gas left in its tank, both Tara and Steve-O started, the former spewing gasoline and a couple of curse words, the latter kicking over the three empty gas cans lined up behind him.

Like she'd just sat down on a thumbtack, Tara rocketed up from her crouch. On her face was a stunned expression. On her head was Riker's Braves hat. Hose in hand, she said, "Good morning, asshole. Don't *ever* do that again."

Voice quavering, Steve-O said, "You scared the crap out of me, Lee Riker."

"That makes two of us," Tara shot. "But who's counting?"

Riker looked around. "First off, you should have woke me up so you'd have someone to watch your backs. Secondly, it's not morning yet. And if I wasn't just hearing things earlier, Pretty Lady here promised—"

Finishing the thought for him, Tara said, "I promised that we would reach Amarillo by morning. And that's still a possibility, with a little more fuel." She pointed the end of the hose at him. "Now how in the hell is this supposed to work?"

Recalling her shadow, he said, "While I've never done it myself, some say it takes a lot of practice."

"You just went *there*, didn't you, Lee."

Without missing a beat, Steve-O said, "And you know what they say, Tara. Practice makes perfect."

Ignoring the last comment, Tara stared daggers at Riker. "You guys are *naaaasty*."

Changing the subject, Riker said, "Your gas mileage suffered a bit, eh?"

"I was driving a little lead-footed," she conceded.

Riker said, "Hard not to in that beast."

Tara thrust the hose in Riker's direction. "So show me how it's done."

Shaking his head, he took the hose from her and started to suck. He continued until he felt the hose go heavy in his hands. As the first drop of gas hit his tongue, he quickly thrust the hose into the can Steve-O was tending for him.

He said, "And that's how you do it."

She said, "Tastes like shit, doesn't it?"

He coughed once and spit on the ground. "It's definitely *not* sweet tea."

Steve-O rooted around in a pocket. Came out with a handful of white mints. "Altoid?"

Looking the pile over and seeing a good deal of lint and other unidentifiable fibers clinging to the mints, both siblings declined the offer.

Addressing Riker, Tara said, "I made it the three hundred and forty miles to Seymour on that first tank. It was a little after one a.m. and no gas stations were open."

"*Nothing* was open," added Steve-O.

"That's where you dipped into our reserves?"

Tara nodded. "Had no choice. Pulled off on a side street. I stood guard while Steve-O did most of the work. Those twenty gallons saw us to this lonely little slice of Texas."

"Where are we and what time is it?"

Tara said, "Check your big ass watch?"

"I don't have it."

She asked, "Where is it?"

"In the truck with my coat and *other* hat."

Steve-O thumbed on Tara's iPhone. He said, "It's 3:18 a.m."

Tara said, "We're a few miles shy of Amarillo. Probably a couple of hundred more to go before we reach our final destination. Assuming it's still there."

Riker said, "Glass half-full, Tara. Two hundred miles, huh? You know what that means."

"What does it mean, Lee?"

"It means we *will* be at Casa de Riker by sunup." He looked at Steve-O. "You got a song that fits that?"

The brim of Steve-O's Stetson cut the air. "Nope. I got nothing, Lee Riker."

Riker slapped the Discovery's roof. "Hot damn," he said. "Steve-O finally got stumped."

In response to the gong-like noise, something moved inside the SUV, causing it to sway to and fro on its suspension.

"There's a Sicko in there," Steve-O said. "We didn't bother looking. Tara says you've seen one, you've seen them all."

Hooking a thumb over his shoulder, Riker asked, "What's beyond the lot?"

Crossing her arms, Tara said, "A few walk-in campsites. You don't want to go back there."

The look Riker gave her was a plea for more information.

"I didn't see what's back there," she said. "Steve-O went back there to pee." Looking to Steve-O, she said, "Tell him what you told me."

Jaw taking a firm set, Steve-O said, "Zippered tents with hands and faces coming out of them."

Riker looked up from his task. "Were they ripped? The seams coming apart?"

Steve-O shook his head. A pronounced motion that had his Stetson wobbling on his head. "The hands were pushing out at me. Mouths were opening and closing against the tent. I think it was kids."

"Just kids playing? Maybe they couldn't sleep. Being out here in the sticks on a moonless night does that to a person."

Tara said, "That's wishful thinking, Lee. And you know it."

Voice taking an ominous tone, Steve-O said, "They were already Sickos. But they couldn't see me. So they didn't follow me back."

Riker's mind conjured up an image of tiny faces bulging the nylon, the continuous movement of their unseen mouths opening and closing. Throwing a shiver, he shifted his gaze to the beaten path leading to the walk-in sites, pulled the hose from the full can and, with his thumb, staunched the flow of gas.

Fully intent on steering the conversation away from the unknown horrors lurking in the surrounding woods, he asked, "How'd you two get the filler door open?"

"With your multi-tool," answered Tara. "Just required a little bit of prying."

"Firing on all cylinders, Sis," said Riker as he stuffed the hose into the neck of the second can. After the fuel started flowing, he asked for the tool.

She handed it over.

Ordering Steve-O to watch out for Sickos, he immediately went to work removing the Land Rover's plates.

As license plates went, these were pretty cool looking. A stylistic red sun floated on a field of turquoise. Horizontal writing above the sun read **Centennial 1912-2012**. Below the sun, spelled out in larger block letters, were the words **New Mexico**. In smaller lettering below the state of origin was the state motto—**Land Of Enchantment**.

***

Twenty minutes after starting the siphoning project, they were all headed back to the Shelby.

Riker led the way. In one hand was the Sig, in the other the tactical flashlight, its beam alternating between illuminating the pair of worn ruts at their feet and the trees and scrub lining the dirt track.

In case some of the things had escaped their tent tombs and had somehow flanked them, he had insisted they maintain noise discipline until they were back to the roadside pullout.

A couple of steps behind Riker, Tara had the fingers of her left hand looped through the handles of two empty gas cans. Though she tried hard at keeping them away from her body, now and again they would strike her leg and bang together. The hollow noise created carried a long way in the night. Clutched in her right hand was a five-foot-long stick as thick around as her wrist.

For quietly braining the first Sicko we see, was her justification for scooping up the stick. The periodic warning rattle of a nearby diamondback was what Riker chalked it up to.

Steve-O brought up the rear. In each hand was a nearly full five-gallon can. Riker guessed each one weighed about forty pounds. The man had lifted the cans with ease. So it wasn't so much the weight that was the problem, it was the gas sloshing around inside that was throwing off his equilibrium.

And the heels on the man's boots.

And the rutted track.

All of the things conspiring against Steve-O caused him to walk with a side to side sway and stall out completely every third or fourth step. The loss of forward momentum usually lasted a half-beat before he got it going again.

Riker had teased him along the way, saying he had the penguin walk down and all he needed to complete the look was a black and white tuxedo.

Steve-O said, "Eff you, Lee," and dropped the cans in the dirt.

Riker stopped in his tracks.

"Take it back," demanded Steve-O.

Having been the butt of many a joke about his gait, Riker issued a sincere apology. He even offered to carry the cans the remaining hundred feet to the Shelby.

In the end, the apology was sufficient. Steve-O picked up the cans, lugged them to the Shelby and, without another word, leaned inside and pulled the lever to open the fuel door.

Working by feel in the dark, he transferred the siphoned fuel into the Shelby.

While Steve-O went about his task, Riker clamped the tactical light in his mouth and used the multi-tool to install the pilfered plates.

Finished, he called out for Tara.

No response.

Swinging the beam toward the Impala, he saw Tara flanked by the pair of cans she'd carried back from the parking lot, busy siphoning fuel from the Impala. A few feet to her left, illuminated by the outer ring of light, the zombie at the wheel was craning in her direction and smashing its pulped features against the detritus-slimed window.

***

Returning to the Shelby a few minutes later, Tara's gait was nearly identical to Steve-O's when he had been loaded down.

Setting the cans next to the Shelby, she said, "That's about seven more gallons to add to our haul."

"Haul is right," Riker said, hefting the fuller of the two cans. Looking to Steve-O, he added, "*Never* let anyone try to tell you that you can't pull your own weight, Steve-O. Because you can. In more ways than you may know." He paused for a second, then added, "And I'm sorry for poking fun at you."

Offering a fist bump, Steve-O said, "Apology accepted."

To seal the deal, Riker rapped knuckles with the man.

Chapter 56

Once Riker had steered the Shelby through a big U-turn across the dusty pullout, Tara called out the turns until they were back to Highway 287 West.

Ten minutes after topping off the Shelby's tank, Riker had her clipping along in the slow lane at a conservative five over the posted limit.

Though the high-intensity headlights and bumper-mounted LED light bar illuminated a wide swathe of the shoulder and road ahead, Riker wasn't able to see much of anything beyond the fence bordering the deserted two-lane. Aside from the tangle of wiry scrub crowding the fence, and random tumbleweeds picked up by the blue/white headlight wash, he was totally in the dark, both figuratively and literally, as to the makeup of the landscape beyond. For all he knew, there could be a mountain or canyon or mesa somewhere out there.

He couldn't answer whether the dirt of the Texas Panhandle was tan, red, ochre, or a combination thereof.

"I feel like I'm still staring at the insides of my eyelids," he announced.

"I am staring at the insides of mine," Steve-O declared. Which was true. He was leaning against the passenger-side rear door, eyes closed, glasses perched atop the Stetson sitting on his lap.

Riker regarded Tara. "What did you make of the rest of Texas?"

"Not much," she answered. "Just lots of neon beer signs and lit-up gas station reader boards telling me I was shit out of luck if I needed gas."

"How about Dallas/Fort Worth? Was the lady captain blowing smoke, or does Romero have a foothold there, too?"

"Like you chose to do when we got close to Shreveport, I took a route that kept us south. We saw people looting. Lots of broken windows. Cops everywhere, speeding this way and that way." She went quiet for a few seconds. "Lee ... parts of Dallas were burning. Farther north, huge sections of the city were completely dark. Even the skyscrapers were just black obelisks."

"Sounds like they were experiencing rolling blackouts. That'll cause unrest among the locals. Nothing says government is failing you like a prolonged power outage."

Tara drew in a deep breath and then exhaled sharply. "You OK?"

Shaking her head, she said, "Not really. You want to know why I didn't wake you?"

Riker said nothing. Kept his attention on the road.

"The locals in the small towns between the Dallas suburbs and Seymour, where we fueled up from the cans, were doing the same thing as the folks in Florida."

"Standing guard at their freeway ramps."

"Yep," she said. "And the silver lining to that cloud is that every single one of the military vehicles we saw were rolling east."

"Towards what I imagine is a rapidly shifting front line in what's looking more and more like a losing battle being waged against our own population."

Throwing a hard shiver, Tara asked, "How much fuel do we have?"

Glancing down, he said, "Half a tank, give or take."

She did the math in her head. "If you don't drive erratically like me, that may get us all the way there."

He said, "Is that the *plan*?"

She said, "The *plan* was blown the second we got on that ferry."

He said, "Tara, you know I wasn't on the tip of the spear over there in Iraq, but whenever I *was* around the guys who saw a lot of combat, I kept my eyes and ears wide open. I was just trying to learn what to do and what not to do in order to stay alive in a war zone. That's all. I wasn't trying to live vicariously through them, or anything like that. To be honest, I felt like I was doing my part over there. Mostly when I was driving for my brothers, though. For fellow soldiers. Ground pounders as we called them."

"What's your point, Lee? You're kind of rambling."

"The guys who see the action have a saying."

"What's that?"

"No plan survives first contact with the enemy."

Tara remained tightlipped.

Riker went on, "Getting away from Southern Florida when we did was just plain luck. After that, we *kind of* stuck to the plan. What I'm getting at is we have to be flexible. The Marines have a saying—Improvise, Adapt, and Overcome. I think we're all doing a great job at all three of those things." He craned as if trying to get a better look at something off in the distance.

"You see something?"

"Thought I saw city lights reflecting off the clouds. Probably just wishful thinking."

"God, I hope Amarillo isn't showing signs of zombie activity."

"Hope for the best. Prepare for the worst."

"You're full of sayings, Lee,"

"That's not all I'm full of."

For the first time in a long while the siblings shared a laugh.

Ten minutes after getting underway, with Steve-O sawing logs in the backseat and Tara perched on the front edge of her seat, Amarillo presented as a faint bubble of light hovering above the road just off the Shelby's right-front fender.

Five minutes later, they passed a sign cluster rising up from the right shoulder. The largest was a welcome sign. **AMARILLO** was spelled out in big uppercase lettering, the double Ls in the word represented by a pair of red cowboy boots. Below was a tag line written in cursive that read **Step Into The Real Texas**.

338

A second sign announced Amarillo as home to Rick Husband International Airport.

Riker steered onto a ramp that took them off Route 287 and onto Interstate 40 West.

To their right was Rick Husband International. It was a single runway affair, the long white strip of cement hard to miss from the elevated vantage. Fronting the runway and lit up like a toppled Christmas tree was a row of squat glass-and-steel terminals bearing a number of colorful signs. On the side opposite the runway was a patchwork of car-choked parking lots.

All of it rambled away from the city, north by east. A few planes were sucked up against darkened jetways. Others sat idle on the far east side of the airport, where the orange oval spills from halide lights on stands made it impossible to tell to which carrier they belonged.

Nothing moved on the runway. And like all of the other airports they'd passed so far, heavy equipment was positioned on this runway.

Riker said, "Who is Rick Husband?"

Tara was already tapping away on her iPhone.

"You have service?"

She looked up and nodded. "It's real slow, though." Pointing out across the hood, she said, "Whoa! Looks like we found Viagra World Headquarters."

As the off-ramp curled around, making a gradual transition to I-40, the airport was replaced out the Shelby's windshield by downtown Amarillo.

Standing out in the middle of the dimly lit city was a twenty- or thirty-story building. It was a rectangular slab of cement inset with long vertical windows. The monolith looked out of place amongst the dozens of surrounding buildings, most of which barely rose to a third of its height.

Illuminated signage graced the corners of the building facing Riker. Reading a sign, he said, "I'm pretty sure that says Plains Bank, not *Viagra*, Sis."

"Both have something to do with people getting screwed."

Saying, "That they do," Riker signaled, pulled around a slow-moving Volkswagen Vanagon, and jumped back into the fast lane.

Interstate 40 cut through Amarillo's primarily residential south side. The city blocks here were set out in a neat grid pattern that mostly paralleled the interstate.

Following the same general tack as the famed Route 66, the interstate continued on, due west for seventy miles, passing by Wildorodo, Vega, and Adrian—all sleepy railroad towns whose origins could be traced back to when the west was still wild.

Crossing the imaginary state line separating Texas from New Mexico, they entered the Mountain Time Zone.

Seeing the time change already reflected on her iPhone's display, Tara said, "Thanks to entering the great state of New Mexico, we all just gained another hour."

Riker exclaimed, "Man, oh man. I suddenly feel refreshed. Like I just downed a triple shot espresso." A lie, because he was growing weary again from non-stop driving. And like the clock rolling back an hour, seeing Steve-O still conked out in the backseat did nothing to alleviate the fatigue setting in. In fact, if it had any effect on him at all, it only served to remind him how badly he wanted to reach their destination, to lay down in a real bed—not a truck bed—and try to forget everything happening in the real world.

Chapter 57

Blown away by the lack of a roadblock at the border, Riker exchanged a knowing look with Tara. Afraid giving voice to what he knew they were both thinking might reverse their good fortune, he kept his mouth shut. Instead, he matted the pedal. Once the speedometer needle hit eighty-five, he engaged the Shelby's cruise control.

Quickly putting ten miles behind them, Riker hauled the Steiners from the center console and handed them to Tara.

She said, "It's still dark. What good are these going to do?"

"We're all alone out here. We have been since Amarillo. I figure the closer we get to Santa Fe, the more likely we'll come up on a state patrol cruiser or the Santa Fe PD ranging to the edge of their jurisdiction."

"You want me to keep these up to my face for the next two hundred miles?"

"No," Riker said. "Just scan the road front and back every couple of minutes. Be on the lookout for parking lights off to the side of the road. Really key in on any overpasses you see coming up on the navigation unit."

Grimacing, Tara cracked open an energy drink and settled into her seat.

***

Ninety minutes later, having covered nearly half the distance to Santa Fe, Tara's diligence paid off.

"Shit," she exclaimed, "there's a black and white entering the interstate on the next ramp."

Tearing his gaze from the eerily quiet Santa Rosa airport, passing by just off the interstate on their left, Riker picked up the police cruiser. It was awash in light from the standards beside the cloverleaf and sweeping onto the two-lane up ahead, where a second major thruway crossed paths with I-40.

The car was low-slung and wide at the hip. It rolled on performance tires wrapped around basic black rims.

He said, "Looks like a Dodge Charger."

As the cruiser accelerated and slipped into the fast lane, the Shelby came even with what appeared to be Santa Rosa's city limit.

Riker couldn't help but notice the large number of eighteen wheelers sitting idle on vast plats of brightly illuminated blacktop surrounding a cluster of businesses near the freeway interchange. Compared to what they'd seen so far, and that it was four in the morning, the place was hopping.

Tara tapped on the navigation screen.

Stomach growling, Riker eyed the signage coming up on the right. The golden arches of a McDonalds rose above a darkened PaPo's Pizza joint. A restaurant called Route 66 sat on a short block wedged between the La Quinta Inn and Santa Rosa Econo Lodge Inn and Suites. And really catching his eye was the red Dairy Queen sign looming large just off the interstate to their left.

God, what he wouldn't give for a bacon cheeseburger and some onion rings right now.

Instead of answering to the hunger pangs, he said, "How far of a lead do you think the cruiser has on us?"

She lowered the Steiners. "Half a mile by now. Maybe a little less."

Hoping to avoid the State Patrol cruiser, Riker disengaged the cruise control and threw on the right signal.

Tara said, "Looking for gas?"

"That and to let the cruiser get a bigger lead on us."

"We have enough gas in the tank to get to Santa Fe, don't we?"

SHAWN CHESSER

"What's between here and our next waypoint?" Riker asked.

Tara pinched and swiped the image on the nav screen. Finally, she said, "Santa Rosa's downtown core ... if you can call it that, is off to the left. There's a second interchange serving the city. After that, nothing but desert for sixty or seventy miles."

"After that?"

"Santa Fe is forty miles north by west."

Regarding the gas gauge, Riker concluded they'd be cutting it real close if they didn't hit a station now. Eyeing the sprawling truck stop, he said, "Let's kill two birds with one stone."

Nodding, Tara said, "Looks like we have our choice of stations. Where do you want to eat?"

Appearing between the front seats all of a sudden, wisps of reddish-gray hair going this way and that, Steve-O said, "I spy with my little eye ... a McDonalds."

Bowing to convenience, Riker again let the man have his way. Steering toward the ramp opposite the one the cruiser entered the interstate, he said, "Breakfast sandwiches it is."

Steve-O's golf clap was priceless. He donned his glasses and looked to Tara. "What's new?" he asked.

"You missed *nothing*. There were no Sickos. No roadblocks. Zero. Zilch. Nada."

Steve-O smiled big and looked to Riker. "I saw the insides of my eyelids. If it's good enough for Lee Riker, it's good enough for me."

Smiling at the solid endorsement, Riker looped them back around to the McDonalds. Slalomed through light standards on an otherwise empty lot. Then nosed the Shelby into the single-lane drive-thru.

They encountered the kind of crowd one would expect to find at four in the morning in a town with no discernable nightlife. No crowd at all. The place seemed deserted. Not a single car in the lots, front or back.

After waiting patiently for a few seconds, no kind of greeting spilled from the speaker. Riker glanced at the menu board. Taped to the board above the speaker grille was a sign he'd missed the first go-round. **Please pull to the second window** was written in black ink on back of a strip of blank receipt paper held in place by clear tape.

Riker craned to see what he was getting into as he pulled forward.

The bi-fold doors parted and out popped the cherubic face of a young woman who looked to be a year or two away from her first legal drink.

She said, "Sorry to have you pull ahead, it's just easier this time of night."

The tag on her uniform blouse said her name was Bethany.

Bethany had a point, thought Riker. Hard enough to understand through those speakers what the person inside was saying. From a reverse perspective, a potential customer with a few drinks under their belt slurring an order through the same connection likely came across sounding like Charlie Brown's teacher.

"No worries," he said. "I completely understand." Without a menu to consult, he ordered from memory. "We'll need five sausage egg McMuffins. Two black coffees. Why don't you add two orders of pancakes with syrup and butter to that." He craned toward the backseat. "Whatcha drinking, Steve-O?"

"Hot chocolate."

Wearing an expression that clearly said *Finished?* the drive-thru girl tapped a chewed-on fingernail on yet another handwritten sign. It was partially hidden on one of the bi-fold doors. On the sign were exactly six items.

It was at this point Riker noticed two employees standing some distance behind the drive-thru girl. Arms folded across their chests, the man and woman, both in their twenties, were looking at Riker and Tara as if the siblings were visitors from another planet.

After reading the *menu*, Riker said, "Give us five apple pies, five hash browns, and two coffees." He paused. "Sure you don't have hot chocolate?"

344

Bethany shook her head. "Just coffee, sodas, and water. More bad news … we're out of apple pies. Only flavor we have left is pumpkin. Is that going to work for you?"

Nodding, Riker said, "It'll have to do. Add a coffee. You have chocolate syrup or hot fudge?"

Though her face wore a vacant expression, Bethany nodded as if the question had registered.

"That's called a mocha," she said. "We can do it," and banged out the order on an iPad-type device attached to a till.

In a matter of seconds the rest of the skeleton crew was crowding Bethany at her window. The twenty-something man with dark bags underneath his eyes handed over a paper sack smelling of pumpkin spice and hot grease. "Sorry about the limited menu," he said. "We haven't received anything from the central warehouse in two days. I guess stations from here to Arkansas are having a hard time getting fuel for their pumps. Trucks are just sitting while product spoils."

Pointing in the truck stop's general direction, Riker asked, "How about the plaza? Do they have any fuel?"

The man shook his head. "Nothing. Been about three days since their last tanker showed up. I hear there's a lot of stranded truckers sleeping in their rigs."

The woman who had been hanging back and pouring coffees craned around Bethany.

She was waifish, with pink locks of once-blonde hair tucked under a restaurant-issue cap. *Heroin-chic* was what sprang to mind as Riker got a better look at her.

She shot a nervous glance at the darkness crowding in on the Shelby. "What's it like out there?" she asked.

Riker thought he detected a touch of fear in her tone, but before he could respond, Bethany added, "Have you guys actually seen a … *zombie?*"

Riker was a little taken aback. It was the first time he'd heard a stranger call the living dead anything but Bolts, Slogs, Zips, or Sickos. After taking another beat or two to compose an answer, he said, "It's real bad back East. All the way through Louisiana, actually. As far as *zombies?*" He shrugged. "I'll just say that I've seen things I cannot easily explain, and leave it at that." Hooking a thumb at Tara, he added, "She saw them first. Little over a week ago. Back in Indiana."

Leaning across the console, Tara established eye contact with Bethany. Voice taking a serious tone, she said, "*Zombie* was the first word that came to mind when I saw a dude die and then come back to life. One second he was flopping around and bleeding out. The next thing I know, he was sitting up and tearing a woman's throat out. Call 'em whatever you want to call them, just remember that they're deadly as hell."

The man slapped a pile of napkins on the stainless-steel ledge between the bi-fold doors.

Taking the napkins, Riker said, "Some of them we've seen are fast. Others are slow. Seems like the younger and more fit ones among them fall into the former category."

Bethany's head tilted to the side. "Former?"

"The younger and more physically fit zombies are the fast ones," Tara said. "We call them *Bolts*."

The other female employee passed Bethany the hot drinks.

As Bethany went about snugging the drinks into the beverage carrier, the man leaned in and stuck his face close to the window above the bi-fold doors. Breath fogging up the glass, he said, "You two are full of shit. There is no such thing as zombies or dolts or ghosts or the effin Blair Witch. You all are just feeding the rumor mill and these two are eating it all up."

Riker took a twenty from his cash wad. Handing it to Bethany, he locked eyes with the man. "I saw the state patrol headquarters down the road. How many are working the interstate any given night?"

Bethany took the twenty and answered the question. "One on the weekday nights. Two days and weekends."

The other woman added, "They have six or seven working most holidays."

Though he thought he knew the answer, Riker said, "How about tonight?"

"Vern's all alone tonight," said the man. "He just left here with coffee and food a few minutes ago."

From the backseat, Steve-O said, "I'm eating while it's still hot."

Tara said, "Go ahead."

The sound of paper being torn filled the cab.

Riker said, "To prove we're not *full of shit*, I want you to go back to the office and call Dispatch. Tell the person who answers that you just saw a *zombie*. I guarantee you the person will not think you're *full of shit*."

Bethany shot a look to the man. She said, "Do it, Kyle."

He said, "It'll come up 'McDonalds' on their caller ID and we'll all be fired."

Tara said, "Use one of your phones."

Kyle said, "Same thing happens when you use a mobile. And there's no way I know of to block it."

Figuring the gaunt-looking man had experience in the matter, Riker said, "There's a pay phone out front of the restaurant a block down. I'll give you the money so you can go down there and make the call."

Kyle seemed hesitant.

Bethany tried handing Riker the change from the twenty.

Riker said, "Keep it. Go ahead and give Kyle what he needs from it." He peeled a hundred from his cash wad. Slapped it on the counter. "If Kyle is told he's full of shit and Vern isn't dispatched, Kyle gets the money for his troubles."

"What if Vern shows up?" asked Bethany.

All business, Riker said, "Means the infection or whatever it is has crossed over into New Mexico and we all have something to worry about."

Staring Benjamin Franklin down, Bethany said, "The hundred?"

"You all split it," Riker said. "Call it an early Christmas present." He saw Kyle back away from the window. Through a sliver of space between Bethany's shoulder and the wall to her left, he saw Kyle shuck his apron and don a navy-blue windbreaker.

Riker said, "Ladies, looks to me like Kyle is accepting the challenge." Gesturing to the edge of the lot, where the spill from overhead lights was mostly nonexistent, he added, "I'm going to park over there so we can eat."

Easing the Shelby against a picket of medium-sized trees about fifty feet from the drive-thru window, where they all still had a clear view of I-40's westbound lanes, Riker shut the motor down.

Saying, "What now?" Steve-O passed the sack of food forward.

"Yeah, good question," Tara said. "What now?"

Taking a long pull from his coffee, Riker said, "Now we sit back, eat our food, and watch the show."

Chapter 58

Riker was starting in on his hash browns about the time Kyle was sprinting diagonally across Historic Route 66, toward the Santa Fe Restaurant and, hopefully, for everyone watching, a well-earned C-note.

Tara folded an empty pie box and stuffed it back into the bag. After washing the pie down with a swig of coffee, she said, "Think Vern is going to respond?"

Riker said, "One million percent, yes. Question is, how long will it take him to arrive?"

Taking her hash browns from the sack, Tara asked, "How fast are those cruisers?"

"Quicker than snot."

Steve-O said, "Faster than Dolly?"

Across the street, Kyle was pressing the receiver to his ear and appeared to be placing a call.

Seeing Kyle hang up and start back for the two-lane separating the two entirely different restaurants from one another, Riker said, "Dolly would hold her own in a straight line against the Charger and its HEMI. While Dolly excels in the horsepower department, the cruiser has her beat when it comes to handling and stopping."

Tara said, "So what's the over/under on Vern's arrival time?"

Riker consulted his watch. Estimated they had burned five minutes in the drive-thru and another two eating and playing voyeur. So, rounding up, he deduced Vern had been gone eight minutes.

Assuming Vern had kept to the speed limit after entering the interstate and motoring west, Riker figured he was somewhere between eleven or twelve miles distant. Plugging this into an equation that allowed for thirty seconds to get turned back around and had Vern racing back to the location of the zombie sighting at near maximum speed, Riker set the over/under of his arrival at six minutes.

"Six minutes to drive twelve miles. No way," Tara said. "I'll take the over on that all day long."

Knowing how much *he* had enjoyed racing souped-up luxury SUVs at top-speed on the rare occasion he found himself without a VIP aboard, Riker rather confidently accepted the *under* line.

Steve-O said, "I'm with Lee on this one."

Tara said, "Of course you are, Steve-O. You're always with Lee." Then, regarding her brother, she asked, "So, what are we betting?"

"Loser does the dishes at Casa De Riker for thirty days."

Brows meeting in the middle, Tara said, "You think we'll be there that long?"

"What planet are you on, Sis? Haven't you been taking notes?"

Steve-O said, "Won't be long before the Sickos are everywhere."

Tara said nothing for a long while. Finally, when she did speak, her eyes had gone glassy with tears and there was a noticeable waver in her tone. "I wanted to travel, Lee. To places warm and cold and in between. I've never been rich. Now that I am, this shit has to happen. Seems like I never win in life."

Riker had known this was coming. He had noticed the slight change in her demeanor the moment they left the mansion in Miami. She was a bit edgier to him than normal. She'd even snapped at Steve-O, an action that was definitely not in her nature.

It's going to get worse before it gets better, he thought.

But out loud he said, "You did good on the mansion. We got a few days to get stuff in line. You got some sun. Steve-O got *too much* sun. I got stuff done I needed to get done. All in all, it was a nice little vacation." Peering over at the drive-thru window, he saw the three skeleton crew members filling up the rectangle of lightly tinted glass.

Suddenly an unfolded napkin filled up the space between seats.

Tara took it from Steve-O, thanked him, then dabbed at her eyes with it.

"Look at it on the bright side, Tara. You're not wearing mascara. Therefore you don't look like Tammy Faye Baker. Remember those raccoon eyes leaking black tears?"

"How could I forget?" Pointing at the drive-thru, she said, "Kyle was rocking raccoon eyes. Wonder if that dude *ever* sleeps."

As if he knew he was subject of conversation, the man placed his hands on the window and stretched to full extension.

Bethany and her unnamed co-worker slipped away from the bi-fold only to emerge a few seconds later through a windowless door at the rear of the restaurant.

Tara ran her window down. "Hear that?"

Riker nodded. He definitely heard the rising and falling blare of the rapidly approaching siren.

Tara said, "We better go now."

Without a word, Riker buckled up and got the Shelby started and rolling forward.

Turning right onto Old Route 66, he saw, still maybe a mile distant, the diluted glow of the blue and reds popping off in the light bar atop Vern's patrol Charger.

"Five minutes and ten seconds," Riker said, turning onto the ramp that fed back onto I-40 West.

As Riker merged the Shelby onto the interstate and took up station in the right lane, the Charger blipped by, a furious flurry of quivering needle antennas and wailing sirens and blinding lights.

Face and upper chest lit up by the soft glow from the computer and radios making up an elaborate electronics suite, the hatless trooper sat hunched over the wheel, radio handset pressed to his mouth, eyes no doubt scanning ahead for the exit.

In his side mirror Riker witnessed the single bank of LED lights set above the cruiser's rear bumper go solid red as the black and white braked hard to negotiate the exit ramp.

Riker said, "Fish on!" and accelerated to ten above the limit.

Clearly not happy at the prospect of a month's worth of dish duty, Tara said, "How'd he get here so quickly?"

"Question is, what do we do if we run out of gas before we make it to Santa Fe?"

Steve-O said, "We can suck-steal some more gas."

Got to hand it to the man, Riker thought. *He calls them like he sees them.*

But out loud he said, "Let's hope for Tara's sake we don't have to do that again."

The thought alone caused Tara to again taste and smell the gasoline. Her salivary glands kicked in, causing her to gag a couple of times.

She said, "I'd rather push this thing a mile than swallow another drop of unleaded. Even the pumpkin spice in the pie, which I fuckin' hate after making thousands of pumpkin-spiced lattes, couldn't cleanse my palate of the chemical taste."

Steve-O said, "Suck, Tara, don't swallow."

Aware the man wasn't *going there*, she said, "Duly noted," and tapped the zoom-out icon on the navigation screen until their general vicinity had shrunk down to a small, centrally located square on the display.

On the screen, I-40 was a squiggly green line tracking gradually north by west, to an eventual rendezvous with U.S. Route 285. That split off on a near ninety-degree northerly tangent toward Santa Fe and the route's eventual terminus in Denver, Colorado, nearly four hundred miles beyond.

Tracked by a web of GPS satellites high overhead, the Shelby was represented as a red triangle within a red circle. At the moment, the icon was equidistant from all four corners of the digital map and tooling west on I-40.

Tara said, "Want to wager?"

Riker said, "Maybe. What's on the line?"

"Double or nothing on the dishes."

As the headlights picked up a sign indicating that the nondescript span ahead crossed over the Pecos River, Riker asked what they were wagering on.

Tara said, "I'm betting that *you* will be siphoning gas before we reach Santa Fe."

Seeing the wager for what it was, a pretty good indication she'd been mulling over how to get out of her turn on the hose, he said, "I'd take that in a heartbeat. However, I can't in good conscience accept the bet."

Tara shot him a queer look.

"Kyle said Vern just got coffee and food, right?"

She said nothing.

"Would *you* resume your patrol, or find a cozy hiding spot near your beat to enjoy your food and drink before it gets cold?"

Gaze fixed on the dark void ahead, she downed her coffee, stuffed the cup in the sack, then folded her arms across her chest.

"If it's any consolation, I'll release you from dish duty."

Tara shook her head. "I'll do the dishes. You do the sucking."

Having watched the entire back and forth with rapt attention, Steve-O said, "Don't you fret, Pretty Lady. I will help you with the dishes."

Tara looked to Riker and stuck her tongue out. Addressing Steve-O, she said, "Deal."

Chapter 59

Between Santa Rosa and the I-40 junction with U.S. Route 285, a total of fifty-eight miles of lightly traveled two-lane, there had been no shortage of billboards advertising Clines Corners. As the odometer ticked off the final miles, expectations among everyone inside the Shelby kept pace with the substantial elevation gain between the two waypoints.

A couple of miles and change from Clines Corners, everyone had already given voice as to what the place would be like when they finally got there.

Steve-O was certain the gift shop would be huge, with aisle after aisle containing shelves full of Route 66 memorabilia. He was also set on finding a jade and silver belt buckle as big as Texas and as garish as the stolen New Mexico plates on the Shelby.

Adopting a pessimistic stance, Tara figured either her big brother would find some way to get into trouble at the world-famous Clines Corners. Or, more than likely, trouble was going to find him.

Always has, always will, had been her final words on the matter.

Riker's bar was set somewhere between possible fisticuffs and encountering the mother of all gift shops. That the first billboard outside of Santa Rosa—likely the billboard trooper Vern had parked behind in order to enjoy his breakfast—touted the combination Travel Center/RV Park as a Route 66 historical site established way back in 1937, he was expecting to see little more than a squat adobe building with multiple fuel islands, a couple of restaurants, and ten-dollar gas.

Supposedly open 24/7, and no doubt lit up with a copious amount of neon signage, he also thought that by now they should be seeing Clines Corners as a colorful bubble of light on the western horizon.

"Where is it?" Steve-O asked from his usual perch, elbows firmly planted on the seatbacks.

"I just had the same thought," Riker said, slowing considerably in anticipation of an upcoming exit. Suddenly he pointed across the dash at a point in space. "I see it now. There, behind the overpass."

"It's completely dark," Tara said. "No way it's closed. The last billboard said it's open twenty-four-seven, three-sixty-five."

Riker took the exit, then braked at a four-way stop to let a minivan go through. Crossing the two-lane, he nosed the Shelby onto the Clines Corners lot and learned he was mostly correct in his blind assessment of the place.

There were, indeed, two restaurants. Clines Corners was a full-service operation on one end of the dining experience spectrum. On the other was a Subway sandwich shop.

As close to the good old Route 66 days as Riker was going to get was the darkened Phillips 66 sign above the truck plaza fuel islands.

On the south side of the building, sitting atop a thirty-foot pole, was a V-shaped sign. Spelled out in yellow letters stacked vertically atop one another were the words **TRAVEL CENTER**.

A second sign sat horizontal on the roof, directly above the entrance. Spelled out in three-foot-high yellow block letters were the words **CLINES CORNERS**.

Where Riker had erred in his blind assessment was his assumption that the place would be lit up like a Vegas casino.

Nothing could be farther from the truth. Though the massive signs and key design elements on the building were adorned with hundreds of feet of bent-glass-tubing, the neon gas inside was inert.

Steering for the fuel island, he said, "A little underwhelming, huh?"

Steve-O said, "Maybe they didn't pay the electric company. Happened one time at the home."

Tara said, "Your caregivers didn't pay the bills?"

"Ted told the man on the phone that the mailman lost the check."

"Likely story," Tara said. "I think Ted was drinking."

Riker said, "Or gambling."

"Or both," Tara added.

After looping counterclockwise around the far island, Riker stopped the Shelby beside the nearest pump. Expecting to see a hand-lettered sign informing him the pumps were dry, he instead saw only dark-gray LCD screens and padlocked pump handles.

"That does nothing to shed *light* on this mystery."

"Pardon the pun, right, Sis?"

"Inadvertent pun," she said. "Still pretty funny."

Smiling at that, Riker steered a big circle to the north edge of the plaza. Looking west, he detected no movement in the expanse of gravel bordering the paved lot. Just a few eighteen wheelers parked there. Reflected back at him in the tractors' window glass was the strobing red and blue lights of an indeterminate number of emergency vehicles.

Steve-O said, "Are we going to park and go inside?"

Riker said, "I don't think they're open for business."

Pointing at the south-facing entry, Tara said, "There's a sign on the doors and some tape or something blocking entry. Drive closer so we can see what it says."

Riker rolled forward and stopped a truck-length short of the entry. Slivers of light peeked around the edges of the mirrored film covering the double doors. Taped to one of the doors was a square of paper. Scrawled in black ink on the paper was a simple and succinct message: **Closed Until Further Notice**.

Woven through both door pulls and tied off on a pair of waist-high cement poles meant to protect the doors from poor drivers was a length of yellow tape emblazoned with the words **CRIME SCENE - DO NOT CROSS**.

Tara said, "Well, that seems to explain the flashing lights around back."

Preoccupied by the battle raging inside of him between morbid curiosity and the all-encompassing need to find fuel for the Shelby, Riker said, "What do you want to do?"

Hooking a thumb over her shoulder, Tara said, "Let's go back there and take a look."

That was all it took for Riker's curiosity—morbid or otherwise—to come out on top. In the next beat he was wheeling them around back and telling Steve-O to look away until they knew the nature and severity of the crime.

As the Shelby rounded the building's northwest corner, the scene was revealed in tiny slices.

First, they saw a white panel van with the words County Coroner plastered on its slab side. It was sitting on the far edge of the parking lot, partially blocking a much taller van wrapped with vinyl graphics identifying it as belonging to a news outfit headquartered in Albuquerque.

On the ground next to the county meat wagon, their limbs bent at impossible angles, was a pair of bullet-riddled bodies. Both were males. And both had lots of gray facial hair on their upturned faces.

A yellow Versa-cone sat next to a tire iron still clutched in one corpse's hand. A dozen smaller yellow cones were spread out to the right of the bodies. Their spacing and placement seemed totally random.

Riker guessed the crime-scene cones were marking the locations of spent brass. The absence of blood halos around the corpse's heads led him to believe that prior to death they weren't zombies. Most likely, they were just a couple of long-haul truckers caught in the middle of an armed robbery.

A classic example of wrong place, wrong time.

Parked broadside to the crime scene was a black Chevy Silverado from the Torrance County Sherriff's office.

Working in the splash from the blue and reds spinning lazily inside the pickup's roof-mounted light bar was a portly, balding man. He wore black slacks, a blue windbreaker with

"Albuquerque ME" printed in yellow on the back, and comfortable looking, thick-soled shoes. At the moment, he was crouched next to the corpse with the tire iron and snapping pictures with an expensive-looking camera.

When the Shelby's lights washed over the scene, the man stopped what he was doing and looked in their direction.

Tara directed Riker's attention to the rear doors on Clines Corners' west-facing wall. They were identical to the pair up front, only these were standing open. Streamers of crime scene tape tied to the door pulls stretched around an identical set of cement poles to create a makeshift barrier.

Now and again a light would flash inside Clines Corners, revealing yet another bloodied corpse laid out in the middle of a long, darkened hallway.

"Looks like a robbery gone wrong," proffered Riker. Seeing the sparkle of broken glass on the floor near the dead body, he added, "They shot out the lights on their way to the parking lot. Which makes me think they were pumping warning shots into the ceiling."

Tara said, "How do you explain the bodies?"

Steve-O said, "I bet the Sickos beat us here."

"I don't think so," Riker said. "These guys likely tried to intervene and paid the ultimate price. Too bad there wasn't a good guy with a gun here when all this went down."

While Riker was speaking, the coroner approached the Silverado, spoke to the deputy inside, and then pointed at the Shelby.

At the exact moment Riker finished voicing his theory, the Hispanic deputy exited his pickup. He was tall and well-muscled. Looked like he could hold his own with the best of them. Riker figured if he and the deputy were standing toe-to-toe, they'd be looking each other in the eyes.

The deputy donned his Smokey the bear hat, smoothed out his coyote-tan uniform pants, and started a slow-walk toward the Shelby, all the while waving them away with one hand and mouthing, "Clines Corners is closed until further notice. You can't be here. Move along now."

Nodding, Riker flashed the deputy a thumbs-up.

Message received.

Mind full of unanswered questions, and with the prospect of the Shelby's tank going dry prior to reaching Santa Fe a very real possibility, Riker wheeled the Shelby around to a rendezvous with U.S. Route 285 northbound and whatever fate awaited them.

Chapter 60

Riker set the cruise control for seventy-five and settled in for what looked to be a quick forty-minute jaunt between Clines Corners and downtown Santa Fe.

Flanked on both sides by unseen desolate terrain, U.S. Route 285 meandered north by west for forty miles before merging with Interstate 25.

Bypassing the ramp to I-25, Riker followed Tara's direction and steered onto a two-lane she had called Old Las Vegas Highway.

"We are nowhere near Las Vegas," he insisted.

"There you go thinking again," quipped Tara. "Nevada doesn't hold patent on the name Las Vegas."

"So there's a Las Vegas in New Mexico?"

Before Tara could reply, Steve-O dove into a syrupy performance of *Viva Las Vegas* that sounded suspiciously like the bloated Elvis whose last years were spent onstage as a barely moving target for women hell-bent on pelting him with their panties.

Tara tapped the navigation screen. After it flared to life, she maneuvered it around then tapped it again.

"It's right here," she said. "As the crow flies, it's about fifty miles due east of us."

Riker looked off to his right. All he saw was the first hint of day far off to the east. It was a faint sliver of dark purple that seemed to lighten during the handful of seconds he spent staring at it.

"Only thing I see is day thinking about breaking."

"Good," Tara remarked. "That'll make walking to look for gas much easier on you. Would be a shame if you ran into a rattlesnake in the dark."

The moment Tara said *rattlesnake*, Steve-O halted his Elvis impersonation. Leaning forward to look her in the face, he said, "Or something worse than a snake."

Tara said, "What's on your mind?"

"Lee could encounter a whole bunch of Sickos. Maybe as many as we saw after the building fell down."

"Let's pray it doesn't come down to that," Riker said. He consulted the fuel gauge, then regarded Tara. "That light is about to come on. I can feel it. How far until we get to Santa Fe?"

She manipulated the screen, then pointed at the icon representing the Shelby. "We are here." Tracing an inch of Old Las Vegas Highway with her finger, she tapped the glass. Under her nail was a pixelated squiggle of lines snaking through what could only be neatly arranged city blocks. Looking at Riker, she added, "And Santa Fe is here."

Sounding annoyed, Riker said, "That tells me nothing."

Having already finished a long stint of driving across Texas in the dark, Tara had developed a good feel for gauging distances with a quick glance at the navigation computer.

"We're six or seven miles out," she stated confidently. "And from here, we should already be seeing the lights of Santa Fe." She paused and grimaced in the dark. "I don't like the looks of this, Lee."

Just as she went quiet, a sign announcing *Santa Fe - Population 66,678* blipped by on their right.

A half-beat later, numerous things happened all at once.

Dragging Riker's gaze to Tara's wing mirror was a brilliant flare of orange and red.

As the sun made its first appearance of the day, quickly imbuing the low clouds in the east with a muted shade of orange, a warning icon nearly identical in color appeared on the instrument cluster.

With the sun's rays chasing the shroud of darkness playing out as more of a slow and steady march west than a flick of a switch kind of thing, Riker's gaze was drawn from the low fuel indicator to the landscape ahead, where he saw a hundred points of light identical to the one rising steadily behind him.

He said, "We have a Santa Fe sighting."

Tara said, "Land of enchantment, my butt." Shielding her eyes, she added, "Should have called Santa Fe the land of *east-facing windows*."

The glare quickly dissipated when the sun's azimuth changed.

In a matter of seconds the foothills rambling away from Santa Fe north by west went from a dusty-brown to almost blood-red in color. Which was a bit unnerving in the superstition department.

Signaling for the upcoming Santa Fe exit, Riker said, "Wonder what caused the power outage."

What was really on his mind, though, was from where the city drew its power. For when he gave Tara his wish list containing locales and other things he wanted her to consider while scouting places for them to ride out Romero, he hadn't figured into the equation the proximity of nuclear reactors to his version of Shangri-La.

A slight tremor in her voice, Tara said, "You think Santa Fe's suffered a zombie outbreak?"

Steering the Shelby onto a northbound two-lane called Old Pecos Trail, he said, "If so, Romero is picking up speed exponentially as it moves west."

Tara said nothing. But her actions spoke volumes. Simultaneously, she plucked her Glock from the console with her left hand and confirmed her door was locked with her right.

Doing his big brotherly duty to calm her, Riker said, "I'm sure it's nothing, Sis. Maybe a squirrel climbed inside a transformer or something."

"There are no squirrels in the desert," insisted Steve-O.

Turning toward the backseat, Riker said, "Lot of *help* you are."

Steve-O smiled and flashed a thumbs-up.

As Old Pecos Trail cut through blocks of residential and passed by a golf course with water-starved greens and fairways, Tara messed with the navigation system.

Locating a nearby cluster of gas stations, she said, "Where this street splits off to the right, you go left. Another mile or so down Saint Michael's Drive and you'll have a couple of stations to choose from."

Though as a rule Tara didn't trust gas needles once they entered the quarter-full range, seeing it pegged *below* E prompted her to cycle to the SYNC's fuel consumption screen for a second opinion. No sooner had the display filled up with information regarding fuel consumption, average speed, and trip time than she saw the single digit indicating range remaining.

And in the blink of an eye that digit changed from 1 to 0.

Raven Rock Mountain Complex

President Tillman had only left his chair in the simulated Situation Room on two occasions since okaying the first Presidential Alert many hours ago: once to use the restroom, and another time to retrieve a second bottle of Knob Creek from a nearby cabinet.

Standing guard outside the open door was Special Agent Kite.

Frozen on the massive display across the room from the President was the final result of a twenty-second video clip recorded about the same time he had started in on the first bottle of Knob Creek. The crystal-clear footage had been taken by one of the DoD's Keyhole military satellites parked hundreds of miles above the District of Columbia. The smoking wreckage of Executive Foxtrot Two lay at the end of a dark furrow carved into the grass on the periphery of the Air Force Memorial, a stone's throw from the Pentagon.

Though he'd already watched the fiery collision between the CNN news chopper and the MV-22 Osprey with his entire family aboard, he aimed the remote at the cabinet and started the footage anew.

Breaking several FAA rules regarding restricted airspace put in place after the 9/11 attack on the Pentagon, the chopper flew in screen right. It was moving low and fast and side-slipping parallel to the nearby multi-lane highway. After seeing the accident for the first time, Tillman was certain the pilot and camera operator aboard the news chopper were no doubt preoccupied with trying to get the best shots possible of the mayhem taking place in and around the jammed-up vehicles a hundred feet below.

At first, the glancing blow the Bell chopper inflicted on the Osprey appeared survivable.

Instantly, the chopper was sent spinning away toward the eight-lane highway. Agent Kite would later tell the President that the pilot was likely trying to auto-rotate the powerless helicopter to a suitable landing spot. It hadn't ended well. The Bell came to rest on its rotor mast with blade fragments littering the grass and the airframe a hunk of compacted metal. The fire broke out a millisecond later, consuming the chopper and then spreading amongst the static vehicles and hundreds of newly turned zombies.

Rubbing his temples, Tillman watched the Osprey wobble in air, straighten out for a moment, and then go nose down.

If Tillman believed Albert Einstein's definition of insanity—doing the same thing over and over again, expecting different results—then what he was doing fit the Nobel winner's assessment like a glove.

Tillman shouted, "Pull up, damn it," as he slammed a fist on the table. Once again, his plea went unheard as the Osprey cartwheeled to earth. For a millisecond, exotic alloys and sheet metal were reshaped as the aircraft bent into an inverted V. Then, with a sudden flash of light, ignited aviation fuel irrevocably changed his world.

"Hank?"

Tillman shut off the display. Looking over his shoulder, he saw his SecDef standing in the doorway.

"What is it, Tank?"

"We need to get you in the chair for a quick cut and shave. A little makeup wouldn't hurt, either."

"I'm not addressing the nation on television. Can we do it another way?"

"We can do a series of Presidential Alerts. Rely on word of mouth to spread the information to those without operable devices."

"The Tupolev bombers?"

The SecDef moved into the room to allow Chairman Dunlap to enter.

Addressing the President, Dunlap said, "The Bears are still coming. NORAD has them about twenty miles off the Aleutians. F-22s out of Elmendorf are wheels up and scrambling to intercept. Sir"—he paused for effect—"I and the other Joint Chiefs recommend we jump from Round House to Cocked Pistol. Show Volkov we're not taking any shit from him."

Nodding, Tillman said, "Make it all happen. And, Tank."

"Yes, sir?"

"Have our boys splash those Bears if they so much as brush our airspace. That'll be the cherry to the new defense condition."

Both the Chairman and SecDef hurried off without another word.

Tillman poured more bourbon into his glass. Sitting there by himself, he powered up the display and renewed his sad attempt at changing the recent past.

Chapter 61

The first sign the Shelby's big V8 was being starved of fuel came as a knocking sound under the hood. Immediately thereafter, the truck began to lurch.

Confirmation the engine had stopped running was relayed to Riker visually as the needle on the engine RPM gauge crashed to 0.

Instantly, the steering became a chore, a response from the brakes nearly nonexistent, and Riker a loser of the bet he'd made with Tara.

All alone on the stretch of two-lane, just beyond the split, Riker slammed the transmission to Neutral and steered toward a patch of shoulder adjacent to a multi-unit apartment complex. Under intense scrutiny from Tara and Steve-O, he wrestled the truck all the way to the curb, stomped hard on the brake to get it stopped completely, and ran the shifter into Park.

"Well, shit," were his first words. "Looks like I'm doing some walking," was his follow on-statement.

"Through the valley of fuckin' death," Tara said, showing him on the navigation screen what lay between their current position and where they needed to be.

On the right, maybe a quarter-mile ahead, depicted by a smattering of digitally rendered buildings ringed by parking lots, was Christus St. Vincent Regional Medical Center. Directly across the street, albeit a much smaller group of buildings with only one parking lot, sat Santa Fe Presbyterian Urgent Care.

Tara said, "We could call Triple A."

"We don't have Triple A."

"We could set up an account."

"We're going to apply for roadside service in the Green Zone using an address in the Red Zone?"

Tara thought for a second.

Then she said, "We can use Casa de Riker."

Riker said, "Our names won't be attached to the paperwork until the county registrar and whoever else needs to validate the transaction pushes all the proper buttons." He shook his head. "Now you're the one thinking too much."

"At least let me to scout the road ahead for you with the binoculars."

Riker shook his head. Snugging the holstered Sig onto his waistband and smoothing his shirt over top of it, he said, "I have to make the walk regardless of what you may see up ahead."

She said, "Take your phone with you."

He said, "I gave it to Shorty, remember?"

"I was talking about your flip phone."

"There's a problem."

"What problem?"

"In all the commotion during our flight from Villa Jasmine, I forgot all about it. Left it in the kitchen next to the bottle of Ibuprofen I should have grabbed."

"Now you don't have any kind of phone?"

Nodding, he said, "I've gone radio silent," and then pushed open his door.

She said, "Be careful, Lee."

Steve-O said, "Don't worry, Lee Riker. We'll hold the fort down until you get back."

"I know you will."

With that, Riker zipped his jacket up against the morning chill, stepped onto the street, and shut the door behind him.

A car drove by real slow. The driver watched him as he opened the tonneau cover and took one of the empty gas cans from the load bed.

The car didn't stop.

Securing the tonneau, Riker looked the length of Saint Michaels Drive.

Aside from the retreating compact car, he was all alone. So, wondering when rush hour started on a weekday in Santa Fe, he stuck his thumb out and set off walking with the sun at his back, down a deserted road cutting through the heart of what had to be the city's medical district.

By the time Riker made it to where the medical facilities dominated the better part of six city blocks, five minutes had slipped into the past, and the Shelby was looking about the size a Hot Wheel car.

Surveying his surroundings, he saw that the signage on the buildings was dark, but inside, weak light splashed against the walls and floor. Which led Riker to believe both facilities were operating on backup power.

On Riker's left, the smaller of the two, Presbyterian Urgent Care, was doing a little business. There were a dozen cars in the lot and a couple of people out front, smoking.

Across the street, the lots of Christus St. Vincent were mostly empty. As he drew even with the west side of the next block, he watched a lone ambulance swing off the main drag and tool down a one-way drive he suspected fed to the back, where most likely it would stop under a covered entrance labeled EMERGENCY.

Though he had no way of being certain what was back there, nearly every hospital he'd ever been to used the same setup. Who wants to have the fully healed or recently patched-up rubbing elbows with the newly arrived?

Nobody.

That's who.

It was bad for optics.

And morale.

The one thing he was certain of as he put both facilities behind him was that this supposed *Valley of Death* of Tara's had nothing on Mount Sinai Medical Center back in Miami.

There were no rows of body bags containing living dead. There were no orderlies or ambulance personnel fighting off the newly risen dead.

It was night and day.

If Romero was gaining a foothold in Santa Fe, it certainly wasn't evident based upon what he saw here.

***

Twenty minutes after setting out walking, Riker was standing at an intersection where he had to make a choice between the pumps outside the Smith's at the Plaza Del Sol or the Shell station across the street from it.

He picked the latter. The choice had been an easy one to make.

For one, to get to the Shell station there was one street to cross, versus two. Secondly, the Smith's had four cars parked before the pumps, waiting. The Shell station had only one.

In the handful of minutes Riker had been away from the others, the morning commute had gone from the lone compact to a steady stream of vehicles. Riker was amazed at how orderly things were going, considering the traffic lights were all down. Approaching the corner, he watched drivers stop dutifully at the nearby intersection, wait their turn, then motor off to wherever they were going.

Seeing an opening, Riker crossed in front of a car driven by a middle-aged woman with a ready smile and sparkle in her eye.

Returning the smile, he resisted the urge to stop in the crosswalk and ask her all she knew about the power outage. Instead, he kept walking, then mounted the curb on the other side, his sights set on the attendant standing sentry before the Shell station's glass double-doors.

Waving the empty gas can in the attendant's general direction, Riker called out, "Are your pumps working?"

The attendant called back, "Nah, mate. Power's out. Been out for a couple of hours now. And me pumps run on electricity."

The man looked to be in his mid-fifties. Neither short or tall. He wore his silver hair in a tightly bound ponytail that fell halfway down his back. Though he resembled Willie Nelson, he spoke with an Australian accent.

369

Waiting until he was close enough that he didn't have to shout again, Riker asked the burning question. "Why's the power out?"

"You hear about the bloodshed down at the Corners?"

Riker was close enough now to see that *Clay* was embroidered in yellow above the left breast of the Aussie's black polo-style shirt.

Playing dumb, he said, "Not yet, Clay. What happened?"

"A bloke and his Sheila went Mickey and Mallory on the night crew down there."

Now really in the dark, Riker asked, "Mickey and Mallory?"

"The lovers from Natural Born Killers. The movie, mate."

Riker shook his head.

"They made like rabbits. Coppers picked them up east of here and gave chase. Roared right by me station." He pointed east, then swung his arm on a flat plane, left to right, a full hundred and eighty degrees. "I heard the engine and pipes and saw a green blur. Then the coppers' interceptors scream by like they're chasing O.J. fuckin' Simpson all over again."

Knowing the O.J. chase had been a slow-speed affair, Riker asked, "How long have you lived in the States, Clay?"

"Twenty years here in Santa Fe. Twenty-five total, in the States."

Riker nodded. "That explains it."

If the statement registered, Clay didn't let on.

"So why the widespread power outage?" pressed Riker. "Did they hit a pole or something?"

Clay shook his head. "Worse. Me mate who drives Uber rang me and said the runner made the turn. Two interceptors following him did not. He says the coppers crashed into an electrical substation on the western edge of town. The remaining copper, likely in the name of public safety, broke off their pursuit."

Likely to render aid, Riker thought.

But out loud he said, "One would think with the hospital down the street operating on backup power, getting the lights back on would be job number one."

"Saw this back in August. Lightning strike cut power to all of Santa Fe and on down to Albuquerque."

"How long was the power out that time?"

"Couple of hours."

Suddenly, coinciding with Clay's reply, the lights in the pumps, fluorescent tubes in the ceiling above the island, and just about every bulb in the darkened store flared on all at once.

Without missing a beat, Riker handed Clay a hundred-dollar bill and said, "I'll take five gallons of premium."

"Help yourself, mate. Be right back with your change."

The man waiting in the lone car stepped out and stuck his card into the reader.

As Riker pumped gas into his can, the man called across the distance with the offer of a ride back to his car.

Tapping his prosthetic, Riker said, "I don't *need* the ride. But I will gladly accept your kind offer."

Clay returned and placed seventy-three dollars and some coins in Riker's upturned palm.

Riker said, "Take whatever you need out of this to cover the man's gas."

Glancing at the other pump, Clay said, "I reckon it's going to take more than that, mate."

Riker peeled off a fifty, handed it over, then lugged the five gallons of gas over to the waiting ride.

After a bit of small talk, Riker and the man calling himself "Hal" were on the road, the full can in the back seat of the little Honda, and the morning traffic around them picking up exponentially.

Chapter 62

The white compact car sliding in behind the Shelby seemed to catch Tara by surprise.

Riker saw the stunned look was still parked on her face as he unfolded himself from the front seat and exited with the gas can in hand.

After thanking Hal and watching him pull away, Riker went around back and emptied the can into the Shelby's tank.

Entering the cab, he said, "Mission accomplished."

Outside the pickup traffic had picked up a certain rhythm. Gone was the courteous *you go first — no, you go first* attitude he had observed when the traffic lights were down. Now, the dog-eat-dog mentality he'd seen on display among morning commuters in every big city he'd set foot in was back.

Still wearing the look of concern, Tara said, "The police are searching for someone, Lee. We saw them cross the street ahead and then return on the one behind us."

With a smile, Steve-O said, "But we held the fort down."

Now the one showing concern, Riker said, "Did they notice you guys?"

Tara said, "We ducked down when they passed by behind us."

"Good," Riker said. "It'd be catastrophic if they run these plates."

"Then let's take them off."

He shook his head. "It'd look suspicious us taking them off here." He paused in thought for a moment. Finally, he asked, "How far to the place?"

Tara took a scrap of paper from her pocket and plugged the address written on it into the navigation computer. Reading off the screen, she said, "From here, about fifteen miles." With a twinkle in her eye, she asked, "Why? Are we going there now?"

"Soon," he said, signaling and pulling into traffic. "We still need to gas up and buy food. And I know just the place."

During the five-minute drive, Riker shared all that he'd learned from Clay.

Riker had pulled the Shelby onto Plaza Del Sol and was steering for the gas pumps fronting the Smith's about the same time Tara had finished her synopsis of Natural Born Killers. "Pretty crazy movie. I think I prefer Woody's character in Zombieland over Mickey."

Riker didn't ask her to explain.

From the backseat, Steve-O said, "I like Tallahassee, too."

Further confused, Riker parked broadside to a pump and shut the truck down.

Seeing the price per gallon for premium, Tara said, "Five bucks a gallon?"

"Cheaper than across the street," Riker said, dragging his wallet from his pocket.

He ran his card into the reader and then filled the Shelby's tank. Finished, he dropped the tailgate and took out the empty cans.

Receiving a good dose of stink-eye from the woman motorist who'd pulled in behind the Shelby, he finished the task, stowed the full cans, then made a point of printing out a receipt.

He smiled at the lady and mouthed, "Thanks for your patience" as he looped back to the driver-side door.

As soon as Riker buckled in and started the motor, Tara said, "One of us is going to have to stay with the truck while the others do the shopping, right?"

Riker took his time to answer. He pulled a U-turn, drove two hundred yards across the mostly empty lot, and parked again in a yellow-lined handicapped spot close to the grocery store's front entry.

Setting the parking brake, he said, "I'll stay."

"Anything special you want me to get?"

"Ibuprofen, Rocky Road ice cream, milk, and Doritos."

"Flavor?"

"Nacho Cheese."

Steve-O said, "Spicy or regular?"

Feeling a little annoyed, Riker said, "Use your best judgment." Regarding Tara, he asked her to unlock her phone and leave it with him.

She thumbed it on, tapped the screen, and tossed it onto the seat next to him.

"Traffic just got a lot busier back there," Riker said. "Both gas stations are filling up with cars. I want you to make it quick. And be careful."

She shot him her patented *I'm a grown ass woman* look and hustled toward the entrance with Steve-O hot on her heels.

Riker watched the doors part and the pair disappear inside. No sooner had the doors closed behind them than Tara's phone emitted a familiar tone and he was reading a new Presidential alert containing a very dire message.

Inside the Smith's, Tara grabbed two full-size shopping carts. Pushing one over to Steve-O, she said, "Divide and conquer. And, Steve-O … don't just load up on junk food. OK?"

Flashing a thumbs-up, Steve-O hustled away.

***

Tara arrived back at the lone checker before Steve-O. As she loaded meat and bread and vegetables onto the conveyer, the clerk asked her if she was shopping for the apocalypse or something.

"Or something," Tara replied.

Boot heels clacking on the floor as he walked, Steve-O emerged from a nearby aisle and parked his overloaded cart behind Tara's.

Taking visual inventory of the contents of Steve-O's cart, Tara noted he had done exactly the opposite of what she had asked him to do.

It was as if she had been speaking Swahili when she said to him *Don't just load up on junk food.* Because all that was in the cart *was* junk food.

Arranged neatly in the bottom of the cart, colorful ice cream cartons provided a solid foundation for an unsteady pile of junk food.

Settling atop the ice cream was what looked to be every imaginable brand and style of chip, including at least three bags each from every flavor in the Dorito line.

It was instantly clear to her that he had thoroughly sacked the cookie aisle. In addition to multiple bags of two different flavors of Oreos, all of the offerings from Pepperidge Farms and Nabisco were accounted for in the cart.

Exasperation evident in her tone, Tara said, "All that you have in your cart is junk food."

Steve-O smiled wide. Sticking a hand into the pile and coming out with a cluster of ripe bananas, he said, "This isn't junk food."

"Well, that puts a little balance back into your food pyramid."

Steve-O said, "Your sarcastic remark is not appreciated."

The clerk said, "Start loading, young fella."

The clerk had every license to call Steve-O young. She looked to be at least a decade past retirement age.

"Why no nametag?" Tara asked.

"Cause I'm the damn owner," barked the lady, blowing a stray wisp of gray hair out of her eyes. "And this is what owners do when a bunch of snowflakes call out because of a blackout."

Waiting for the lady to launch into the old *in my day* routine, Tara helped Steve-O unload his cart. When the owner stayed quiet, Tara sent Steve-O back for some select toiletries and more of what fit her idea of real food.

As Steve-O meandered down the canned food aisle, the owner said, "So what are you really doing with all of this?"

"We're going to donate it to the Boy Scouts. So they can go on a long retreat."

"Bullshit," said the owner. "Besides, there is no Boy Scouts any longer. It's the *they* Scouts or something ludicrous like that."

More to push the owner's buttons than to take a stance, Tara said, "Change is inevitable, you know."

Lips pressed into a thin white line, the owner scanned and bagged. She even remained tightlipped as she scanned and bagged the contents of Steve-O's second load.

The total came to twelve hundred dollars and change.

Rather sarcastically, the owner said, "Do you have coupons?"

Tara said nothing. Staring the bitter lady down, she took out her debit card and slammed it into the chip reader. She went through the motions then stared at a newspaper rack and waited for approval of her purchase.

The three newspapers commanding the prime real estate at the top of the rack were the *USA TODAY, Santa Fe New Mexican*, and *Albuquerque Journal*.

Likely a weekend edition, the *USA TODAY's* headline read **Romero Partially Contained.**

Tara shook her head. Hopeful, but not at all true.

Below the *Santa Fe New Mexican's* masthead, the main headline read **Is There A Romero Cure On The Horizon?**

A war is on the horizon, she thought glumly.

The *Albuquerque Journal's* headline was much gloomier than the others. **No End In Sight As Unstoppable Virus Continues Westward March** prefaced a story asking where the President was and what he planned to do with the "ambulatory infected."

Tara marveled at how the newspapers all seemed to be glossing over the real news that dead people were coming back to life. As if putting it in print would erase any chance people back East and down South were just seeing things. Or, perhaps, the reports were just a bunch of copycats making it all up.

Or that all the YouTube posts documenting unprovoked attacks were really being produced by pranksters who would soon be caught.

Ha ha, jokes on you, America.

Only Tara knew better. War of the Worlds, this was not.

"Take your card," said the lady. "Need help out?"

Snapped from her train of thought, Tara declined the offer.

The nearby doors opened and a crush of people entered. Ten at first. Then another half-dozen pushed through the automatic doors just as they were closing.

It looked to Tara like one of those videos of Black Friday shoppers just being let into a Best Buy. Only there was no organization to this. No focused rush for the television aisle.

Some of the people stopped and stood rooted just inside the doors. Heads on a swivel, it was clear they didn't have any idea where to start.

A woman shouted, "Damn it, Dennis, grab us a cart!"

As the man with her lunged for a cart, another man with the same idea grabbed hold of the cart's handle and shouldered him aside.

Fisticuffs were averted by the boisterous woman running a second cart into the offender's thigh.

She said, "Take this one, asshole," then pointed her man, Dennis, in the opposite direction.

Clearly, tensions were high.

Wondering what the matter was, Tara told Steve-O to take a cart and head for the truck. As soon as she saw Steve-O manage to push his way past the incoming stream of humanity, she got the domineering woman's attention.

"What's up?" she asked.

"The President just declared Martial Law. It's because of the Romero thing. And I bet it's way worse than they're telling us. Even though the President sounded like he was in control, his body language said different. He looked like a broken man. Like Meek, that dickless prince on Game of Thrones."

Tara thought, *Sounds like your man, lady.*

But out loud, she said, "Was he broadcasting from the White House?"

She nodded. "Supposedly he was addressing America from the situation room. But I call bullshit on that. I've seen pictures and video of Washington D.C. It looks like Detroit did five years ago. Looting and shooting the norm, I hear. Buildings burning. Museums boarded up. Artifacts being moved to secure locations. If all that's going on, no way the President is staying behind. Call me a naysayer if you want. But the Secret Service would never go for that."

The sliding doors vibrated in their tracks as a body slammed into them. Then the mechanism inside squealed as the man responsible clawed his way inside.

Pushing one cart and pulling the second, Tara bellowed, "Make a hole!"

Repeatedly chastising and cursing the throng pushing against her, Tara made it outside the doors. The Shelby was a few yards to her right.

As she set out in its direction, a woman took hold of the front of the lead cart and tugged it from her grasp.

At the truck, with the tonneau hinged up, Riker was helping Steve-O transfer the groceries from the cart to the load bed.

Simultaneously raining blows with her clenched fist on the woman's locked fingers and keeping her at bay with a splayed hand planted on one shoulder, Tara yelled for help.

Hearing his name, Riker turned and saw Tara literally beating a woman off of her cart. Drawing a bead on the forty-something with the Sig Legion, he hollered, "Do your own shopping, *lady*."

When that didn't work, he set off toward the melee. It took only three long strides to get there. Along the way he had raised the pistol over his head. Upon arrival, he brought it down grip first on the woman's wrist.

It was a short chopping motion with not much force behind it. A love tap compared to what he was truly capable of.

Still, it did the trick.

The woman cried out and released her hold on the cart. No other choice. Two of her fingers were split down the sides.

Blood was already striking the gray cement. Little crimson dots at first. Then a constellation of them as the woman bent over and screamed at the ground.

Riker said to Steve-O, "Get in and buckle up." Turning back to Tara, he said, "Grab a cart."

Spitting a stream of curse words at Tara, the would-be cart-jacker slunk off for the entry, holding her wrist, face screwed up in pain, and staring murder at Riker.

Keeping the Sig out for all to see, Riker dragged the nearest cart to the Shelby.

Saving the thanks for later, Tara arrived with her cart and immediately started throwing the bagged groceries into the backseat alongside Steve-O.

Finished emptying the final cart, Riker closed the tailgate and locked the tonneau. Walking around to the rig's left side, he let his eyes roam the lot and street separating the two gas stations.

What he was seeing now—cars speeding down the rows in the nearly full lot—was in direct opposition to what he had experienced during his walk to the Shell station.

As if a dial had been turned, in the span of forty minutes, the attitudes on display where the citizens of Santa Fe were concerned had gone from calm and courteous to full-blown crazy.

A pair of Santa Fe PD cruisers, lights and sirens engaged, squealed off of Saint Michaels Drive and roared onto the Smith's lot.

Riker had just holstered the Sig and taken the wheel when the pair of Ford Explorers rolled by the Shelby and came to a full stop before the store's sliding doors.

Likely drawing inspiration from the chaotic scene playing out all around them, Steve-O launched into song, the first lyrics of Eastbound and Down filling the cab as the Shelby's motor thrummed to life.

Without making eye contact with the officers exiting their SUVs, Riker selected Reverse and slowly backed out of the parking spot—a smooth J turn that left the Shelby pointed toward Saint Michaels Drive. Staring straight ahead, hands at the proper spots on the steering wheel, he drove away, slow and steady, as if

Tara was a DMV tester and securing his first-ever license to drive was on the line.

Chapter 63

As Riker steered the Shelby off of the Smith's lot, a rusty pickup and a two-tone Suburban collided head-on at slow speed right in front of him.

Jinking the wheel to avoid the tangled vehicles, Riker saw the drivers exit their rides. There was nothing *slow speed* about their dismounts.

And fisticuffs *were not* avoided.

The SUV driver landed a wild haymaker that sent the pickup driver crashing limply to the turn lane.

"Do you know the song Eye of the Tiger, Steve-O?"

Winding up his performance after the prescient lyric in Jerry Reed's song having to do with being *eastbound and down, loaded up and truckin'* Steve-O said, "No I don't, why?"

Riker said, "'Cause it looked like that guy just got knocked the hell out by Rocky Balboa, that's why."

Steve-O said, "Do you know the lyrics?"

Picking up speed on Saint Michaels Drive, Riker slipped over into the far eastbound lane.

"I know *rising up, out of the streets* and that's about it."

"Good," Tara said. "Last thing I want to hear is you singing." Staring at the long line forming to turn into the Smith's, she asked, "What sparked all of this?"

Handing the iPhone back to Tara, Riker said, "This new Presidential alert is to blame. Apparently, the prospect of a nationwide curfew is unsettling to the folks of West Santa Fe."

"Not just that," she said, scrolling and reading the text of the message. "Mandatory evacuations were ordered for big cities in Texas and Oklahoma."

"I didn't read that far. The President had my full attention at *nationwide curfew*. That's some wishful thinking. People won't stand for it."

"It's really happening," she said, throwing her head back. "The *fucking* zombie apocalypse is really *fucking* happening." She pulled up something on her phone. Then she went to the Shelby's navigation screen and punched in an address.

"How far?"

"Thirteen miles." She zoomed the screen in. "Look for 285 North."

Slowing and craning, Riker found the ramp he needed. It curled around south by west then delivered them onto 285, which the navigation computer also called Saint Francis Drive.

Most of the traffic on the divided four-lane was moving south, toward the downtown core.

Seven miles of 285 later, and Riker had passed only two northbound vehicles.

Behind the Shelby, awash in the rays of the rising sun, the city's earth-tone structures looked warm and welcoming.

He sensed that was far from the truth. Riker had a bad feeling they were witnessing a city entering the first stages of its death throes.

Off to the right, the sun was beginning to slide behind a wide bank of low-hanging clouds. It seemed giant-sized as it shimmered and pulsed its way from view.

Ahead of them, glowing angry shades of red and orange, were low foothills that ranged off north by west to an eventual meeting with the southern end of the Rocky Mountain Range.

Tara pointed over the dash. "Somewhere out there is Casa de Riker."

"We can't call it that," Riker said. "Too pretentious."

"What do you suggest?"

Steve-O said, "Let's wait until we see it."

"Always a voice of reason," Tara said. She tapped the navigation screen. "One mile and you get off at Exit 168 and look for Tesuque Village Road. After that you'll see a big elevation gain through about seven miles of twisty turns."

"What are you basing that on?"

"I've seen pictures of the view from our new place."

Slowing to take the exit, he said, "Don't always believe everything you see on the internet."

"That's what you said about the mansion. Sure changed your tune when we got there. Can we agree that pictures on the internet sometimes don't do the real thing justice?"

Seeing the sign for Tesuque Village Road, Riker grumbled something about women always thinking they're right, and then signaled to get over.

Tesuque Village Road cut north by east through gently sloping desert dotted with low-scrub and gnarled and wind-bent trees. After three miles of mostly straight stretches connected by a handful of shallow curves, the two-lane had a drastic change in personality.

Tara had been correct about the twisty turns. She'd also accurately predicted the elevation gain. It was substantial and caused ears to pop.

What she couldn't see on the navigation screen was that once Tesuque Village Road became Paseo Encantado Southwest, the two-lane narrowed considerably and was potholed and frost-heaved on the shoulders.

The Shelby shrugged off the imperfections as it took them past a number of drives bearing addresses of homes not visible from the road.

Shortly after the road narrowed, more elevation was gained. As Paseo Encantado Southwest climbed, the ponderosa pine and juniper became more plentiful, going from sparse copses to thick groves in less than half a mile.

During the final half-mile to the end of their route, trees began to crowd the road as it climbed sharply north by west to a wide, treed shelf backstopped by a pair of knife-edged ridges of red rock. The ridges came together above the shelf to form an inverted V.

Somewhere back there is our new abode, Riker thought.

Though he and Tara were both listed on the deed, it was the first static dwelling he had ever owned. And he was damn proud. Who cared if both of their names were on the title. It was theirs and they had their mom and dad to thank for being such great parents.

Blinking away the forming tears, Riker spotted a *Dead End* sign.

As the Shelby came even with the sign, the road exited the trees and the navigation system's robotic-sounding female voice alerted them that they were at their destination. A half-beat later, the road spilled them onto an enormous cul-de-sac fronting a steel gate bearing the same address currently displayed on the navigation screen.

Slowing the Shelby to a walking speed, Riker said, "We're here."

There was a metallic click and Steve-O was free of his seatbelt. Throwing both arms over the seatbacks, he said, "About time. My butt hurts."

Stopping a truck-length short of the gate, adjacent to a panel on a post containing a covered keypad, Riker regarded Tara.

"71645, right?"

"Yep."

He hesitated.

She said, "What are you waiting for? Key in the code."

He had something he needed to tell her but didn't know how to frame it.

So to buy himself more time to think, he said, "Tell me about this mythical place I cannot see."

"It's called Trinity House. The man who designed it worked for the government on the Manhattan Project over at Los Alamos. You'll be pleased to know that Trinity checks most of your boxes, and all of mine."

Though Riker liked the name and history, he said nothing.

Tara continued, "We're more than ten miles from any kind of population. The house is a little over six-thousand square feet. You've got four bedrooms, six bathrooms, a spa, workout room, two kitchens, a library, and lots of storage. All of that is spread out over one-level that feels like it's two separate living areas. Imagine two half-circles joined end to end. They curve outward … facing south by east. Left of center, a four-car garage juts south from the joined living area. If you don't want to use the garage, right of center is the main entry. In the middle of it all is a domed great room surrounded by a beautiful courtyard."

"What about me?" asked Steve-O. "Whose side do I stay on?"

She said, "There's a fifteen-hundred-square-foot guesthouse beyond the great room. It'll be all yours."

Fingers steepled, a broad smile forming on his face, Steve-O asked, "Is there a pool?"

She nodded, "And a hot tub. Workout room, too."

Riker asked about security.

"It's got it all. At least everything on your list. It commands the highest vantage of the half-dozen properties up here. And the entire compound is ringed by twelve-foot-high walls and is not visible from the road unless you know exactly what you're looking for. And this gate we're *still* staring at? It's made from solid steel and hydraulically operated."

Riker said, "Solar *and* geothermal?"

Tara nodded. "And I bought the furnishings for a steal."

"You nailed it, Sis."

"Let's go, then."

Riker took a deep breath. He said, "I have something I need to tell you."

Thinking, *This can't be good,* Tara folded her arms across her chest and shot him a questioning look.

"I invited Benny."

Shaking her head, Tara said, "You did what? That was *not* part of the plan, Lee."

Fearing a fierce backhand might be Tara's next response, Riker leaned away from her.

Having somewhat composed herself, she said, "Is he on the way?"

Riker said, "He's already here."

"And you know this, how? You left your phone at the mansion."

"I have his number memorized. So I called him on your phone. When you and Steve-O were inside the Smith's."

"And?"

"My Amazon orders made it. He brought them all inside."

"Amazon orders?"

"What do you think I was doing on the computer every night at the mansion? Looking at porn?"

She said nothing.

"I've never had money. Now that I do, I want to spend some. Steve-O told me about Amazon Prime. I signed up and it was off to the races for Mr. New Money."

A conspiratorial tone to his voice, Steve-O said, "Did you get *my* stuff?"

Riker nodded.

Tara said, "Of all people, why Benny?"

"He's my only friend from back in the day who I still keep in touch with. Plus," Riker added, shifting in his seat to face her, "Benny loaned me the money to buy my old Ford F-150. Which meant I could use my money to buy all the tools I had to have to get back to working."

"So you owe him. I get it. Should have just paid him back. Maybe even stepped up and bought him a *brand-new* Ford F-150. Anything but bringing him *here*, Lee."

"I'm sure he no longer has a crush on you, Tara."

This got Steve-O's attention. He said, "If he bothers you, Pretty Lady, you send him my way. I'll set him straight."

She said, "That's sweet. But I can handle my own business, thank you very much."

Riker said, "That's not all. Benny brought along his newest girlfriend."

Steve-O nodded approvingly.

"I always hated his girlfriends more than I hated his constant pestering."

"That's not all," Riker admitted. "She told a friend."

Steve-O was again all ears. He said, "Go on. I'm listening."

Eyes bugged, veins in her neck bulging, Tara bellowed, "This place isn't big enough for two women, let alone three. Not with the world going to shit."

Riker said, "And her friend brought a friend."

"Male or female?"

"Male," said Riker. "The friend's friend is an off-again, on-again long-term boyfriend. Reason he's on again is that he just got out of prison. Which wasn't supposed to be the case. He got early release, or something. So I can't really be mad at Benny's girl. However, I am pretty pissed at Benny. Because he didn't guard the address. Left it out for his girl to see. She copied it and passed it on to her friend. Benny and his girl arrived yesterday. Apparently, the other couple rolled in a few hours ago."

After saying nothing for a long ten-count, Tara hissed, "Well, open the gate and let's see who good ol' Benny has stuck us with."

Chapter 64

Under Steve-O's watchful eye, Riker punched in the code.
There was a soft click of locks disengaging, then the gate rolled away to the right under power.
"That's real quiet," Riker said. "Motor must be underground."
After Riker drove the Shelby onto the property, the gate automatically closed behind them.
The first they saw of Trinity House was the curved drive. Red and gray pavers laid down in a herringbone pattern swept away from them, left to right, past the front entry, ending in front of a one-level garage sporting four oversized doors.
At first glance, Riker figured the garage could hold four to six cars.
Confirmation came when Tara said, "Realtor lady insisted we could fit six vehicles and some extra toys in there."
Steve-O said, "Wave Runners are *toys*."
"Finding a lake may be a problem," said Riker. "But we'll look into it. I am a man of my word."
He stopped the Shelby just inside the gate on the drive and shut her down.
To the right of the overhead garage doors, where the garage met the tan-stucco house, was a smaller entry door inset with a rectangular window.
The main front entry was off to their right. It was maybe fifteen feet wide and twenty tall, with a turret of sorts rising from it. The doorway was arched at the top, as were the turret's multiple alcoves.

The east wing curved gently away from the entry. Based on Tara's description of the place, Riker presumed the west wing arced away from the garage in the same manner.

Low-to-the-ground light fixtures lined the brick path snaking from the drive to the main entry. It was a couple of yards wide, maybe thirty feet long, and split the front yard into two like-sized parcels. Blue spruce, small juniper, and some kind of high-altitude pines were scattered about the two parcels. The trees cut up the home's south-facing elevation, yet still let through an abundance of natural light.

Though Riker could only see a portion of the front door, it looked to be an oversized oak item reinforced with steel bands. And though he didn't know much about design, it was clear to him the architect of Trinity House drew inspiration from Pueblo dwellings.

Tara said, "Where's Benny?"

"It's early," Riker said. "Remember? No matter what Mom was cooking, he was always last up after a sleepover."

Tara nodded. "I remember."

Riker padded off to the garage. Cupped his hands by his face and peered through the window.

Tara said, "What do you see?"

Though Riker was staring at two things inside the garage, he said nothing.

In the center of the nearest stall, almost touching the ceiling, were dozens of cardboard boxes. They ranged in size from smaller than a shoebox to large enough to contain a washer or dryer. Some of the biggest boxes were reinforced with what looked to be white ash one-by-fours and wrapped with plastic film for all-around stability.

Most of the boxes showed signs of damage likely incurred during transit. He saw crushed corners, gouges in cardboard, and shipping peanuts spilling from some previously opened packages.

The one constant among the dozens of boxes was the black shipping tape used to secure them, and a curved blue logo Riker interpreted to be a smile.

In the middle distance, partially obscured by Mt. Amazon, was an American muscle car. It was long and sat low to the ground on wide tires.

Causing Riker's momentary loss of words was the car's color. It was a particular shade of green that seemed to glow, even in the garage's gloomy environs.

He tried the knob.

Locked.

Having seen enough to kick-start the dull throb behind his eyes, Riker backed away from the door, only turning to face Tara and Steve-O *after* he had drawn the Sig and disengaged its safety.

Steve-O asked, "Are there Sickos in there?"

Wearing a blank expression, Riker shook his head.

Face a mask of concern, Tara said, "What's in there that's got you spooked?"

A familiar voice carried across the drive. "Sorry, Lee. Curiosity got this cat. I only opened a couple of your packages."

Riker looked past Tara and Steve-O. Saw his lifelong friend emerging from the end of the brick walkway. He wore broken-in Levi jeans and nothing else. Though also pushing forty, the man was solidly built, with a visible six-pack and well-muscled arms.

Bare feet slapping the pavers, the man yawned and stretched his arms out at his sides.

Both figuratively and literally, the mere sight of his friend was disarming to Riker. He holstered the Sig and, momentarily relegating the Dodge Challenger in the garage to the back recesses of his mind, mirrored Benny's greeting.

The two men embraced and slapped backs.

Benny was grinning wide when they separated.

Riker said, "Jesus, Benny, what's with the long hair and beard?"

Unable to resist the opening, Tara said, "You going to walk on water with those big ass feet?"

"I may look the part," said Benny. "But I'm nowhere near as pious as the Son of God. Plus, my eyes are brown."

Tara couldn't help but laugh. The passage of time had a way of taking the edge off of old resentments.

She said, "Where's everyone else?"

Riker raised a hand, effectively warding off the question.

He said, "The car in the garage, is it yours?"

Benny shook his head.

"Nope. My van is parked on the other side of the garage. The Dodge belongs to Crystal and her boyfriend, Raul."

"It's got Oklahoma dealer plates. Did one of them just buy it?"

"He said they traded in Crystal's Nissan. That barely covered the down, so they financed the rest at high interest."

Steve-O set off for the garage to see what a muscle car looked like.

Seeing Steve-O walk away, Riker pulled Benny in close. He quickly told him about the murderous rampage at Clines Corners and then touched over what Clay had said about the pursuit through town and its grisly results.

Eyes going wide, Benny said, "You think?"

"That car in the garage matches the description Clay gave."

Tara waited until Steve-O was out of earshot. Seeing him mimicking Riker's pose at the door—hands cupped on cheeks, face pressing the glass—she said, "How were they acting when they rolled in? Nervous at all?"

"We were asleep when Crystal called to say they were here. I let them in the gate, opened the garage, then showed them the guesthouse. I didn't feel the need to get pissed at Crystal for bringing Raul here. I certainly didn't feel right about turning them away in the middle of the night. Figured one look at you, those two would mosey off to find alternate accommodations."

Riker said, "So they're still asleep?"

"Crystal told Rose that her and Raul got behind the retreating National Guard soldiers early yesterday and then drove all day and night to get here. Rose made them sandwiches. Not my circus, not my monkeys. So *I* went back to bed."

Riker said, "You don't find it strange that the dealership just happened to be open to working a deal considering the Romero thing and everything else going on?"

Benny said, "Seems fishy to me now that you mention it."

Rose called out to Benny from the end of the brick path, then padded wordlessly to the center of the drive. If Benny was Shaggy in the Scooby Doo cartoons, Rose was his Velma. She stood a couple of inches over five foot. She wasn't slim, nor was she heavyset. She fell somewhere in between.

Strands of auburn hair fell on her shoulders, while bleached bangs framed a cherubic face. And perched on her button nose was a pair of wire rimmed glasses.

Benny made introductions, then nodded in Steve-O's direction.

He asked, "Who's your friend in the Stetson?"

No sooner had Benny asked the question than they all watched a fireplug of a man with a polished bald head and drooping handlebar mustache barge through the garage door. In his hand was a chrome revolver. He wore jeans and a white tee shirt. No belt, no shoes. A mess of black tattoos, most of questionable quality, dotted his arms and neck.

In the wrong place at the wrong time, Steve-O was smacked by the door's edge and sent back on his heels, one arm windmilling, the other securing the Stetson on his head.

At the same time, Riker was inching his hand toward the holstered Sig.

Simultaneous to those two actions, Tara slipped from behind Benny and her brother, the former beginning to shake, the latter suddenly gone rigid, his every muscle humming like a cable under maximum tension. Lips pressed into a thin line, she formed up by her brother's right elbow, a murderous glare directed at Raul.

"I was wondering the same thing," said the man Riker assumed was Raul. "I was torn between retarded Garth Brooks or retarded Waylon Jennings. Maybe retarded Garth Jennings could be his stage name. That is if he can sing a lick." Waving the chrome revolver in Steve-O's direction, he asked, "Well, Retard, can you or can't you?"

Recovering from the sudden impact of the door opening in his face, Steve-O flipped the man the bird. "I'm not retarded," he shot back. "I just have an extra chromosome. And you should really watch where you're going, *Baldy*."

Raul bristled at that. Said, "Better put that finger away, boy. You don't ... I'm gonna break it off and shove it where the sun don't shine."

Steve-O held his ground.

Benny said, "Relax, Raul. These are good friends of mine."

"Couple of darkies and a retard. For the record: Crystal is against all this. I don't know what she sees in you, Rose. But you can stay. You *are* pretty easy on the eyes. Benny and the Jets, though—"

Riker cut him off. "Why did you have to kill all those people at Clines Corners?"

"Crystal's card got declined. We needed gas. What's a poor boy to do? Let's just say that negotiations broke off real quick." He waved the revolver in a tight little circle. "That old bitch forced me to bring out the *closer*."

Tara said, "You have to go, dude."

Raul said, "You're mistaken, bitch. It's you who has got to go. This place isn't big enough for all of us. I just got done doing three-to-five in an eight-by-ten. No way I'm going to settle with a guesthouse while you all get the mansion." He shook his head and moved the revolver's muzzle from Benny to Riker. "What say you, John Henry?"

"My sister is right," Riker said. "Best you and your lady get your stuff, get in your new car, and go find someplace where the company and accommodations are more to your liking."

"Why don't you just fuck right off. I'm the one holding the gun. I think *you* and the gang are going to need to readjust your expectations. Lower the bar, so to speak." He stood on his toes and looked over everyone's heads. "And I'll be repossessing that snazzy pickup of yours. Lord knows I've had my share snatched out from under me."

Free hand palm up, Raul wiggled his fingers.

Riker saw it for what it was: universal semaphore for *Relinquish the keys.*

Showing Raul his left hand, Riker said, "I'm going to pull the fob from my pocket. Real slow. No monkey business."

"I see what you did there," Raul said. "Monkey business." Chuckling, he kept the revolver trained on Riker. Straight for center of mass. Twenty-five feet or so. Considering the short barrel on what looked to be a .357, odds were tilted toward the miss column. A miss for Riker, however, didn't equate to a win. Because he was flanked by two people he loved. One was family. And one so close he might as well be.

Two or so feet of loved one on each side of him.

Not good odds.

He needed a diversion.

So he thumbed a certain button on the fob as he dragged it into the light.

Everything seemed to slow as the command was relayed from the fob to the Shelby via unseen radio frequency.

Back to back to back. In the span of a second, maybe two, there was a mechanical click and whine, then a low rumble of gas combusting, followed at once by the throaty growl of exhaust escaping through tuned pipes.

With the remotely started Shelby vying for Raul's attention, Riker tossed the fob in his direction.

Likely under the influence of some kind of hard drug, meth was Riker's assumption, Raul had a hard time deciding what commanded his attention more: Should he catch the fob? Or keep the revolver trained on the big man?

Seeing the split-second's worth of indecision flash across the interloper's face, Riker made his move.

As the Sig cleared the holster, he was doing two things at once.

Acting upon the mantra cycling through his head, he thumbed off the safety and stuffed his finger into the trigger guard. While his right arm was in transit from bent and vertical to straight and horizontal, he was stepping to his right. His every intention, should it come down to it: Taking a *miss* that might be headed for Tara.

Already halfway to a completed draw, all Raul needed to do was extend and squeeze the trigger. When it came to revolvers, however, *squeeze* had two meanings, each varying in time from start to finish.

Seeing as how Raul hadn't placed any kind of urgency on cocking the hammer beforehand, the first action the pull on the trigger was reserved for was drawing the hammer back. By the time the second component of Raul's action commenced, Riker was fully shielding his only living kin and had superimposed the red reticle on the man and done some trigger pressing of his own.

As he was wont to do at the range, anticipating the recoil, he dragged his first shot down and to the left. Instead of the 9mm round striking where he wanted, an inch or so above the shorter man's breastbone, a blossom of crimson erupted on his white tee shirt, just under the right breast pocket, where all kinds of vital organs were packed in tight.

Detecting the hiss-crackle of a bullet passing close by his face, Riker witnessed his second round strike a couple of inches to the right of the first.

Good recovery.

A second star-shaped red blotch instantly became one with the first. The added kinetic energy accelerated Raul's trip to the ground that the first bullet strike had begun.

The hollow thud and whip-like crack of Raul's bald head hitting the pavers proved to be a cringe-inducing sound Riker knew would be all but impossible for him to unhear.

As the first report from the Sig was crashing across the courtyard, Steve-O's bird had dropped, and the put-on bravado was usurped by a look of shocked surprise.

Before the back-to-back booms of Raul's return fire had even registered, Steve-O and Benny were both in the middle of falling to their knees.

While the initial hollow-point slug leaving Raul's Colt Python at fourteen-hundred-feet per second cleaved the air between Riker's left cheek and Benny's right ear, the second carved a chunk of flesh from Benny's right bicep and kept on going.

Screaming as his knees hit the ground, Benny pitched forward, landing on the already damaged arm.

Body beginning to shake from the surge of adrenaline, Riker steadied his gun hand and shot Raul once more, in the head, for good measure.

There's no getting up from that. Riker turned his attention from the unmoving corpse to Benny, who was now in a fetal position atop a rapidly spreading pool of his own blood.

"Tell me where you're hit," Riker cried as he rolled Benny to his back and worked at prying the man's blood-slickened arms away from his heaving torso. "Let me see. Let me see. Where are you hit, Benny? Stay with me. Where are you hit?"

Hissing through clenched teeth, Benny said, "My arm. It's numb. Can't feel a thing."

Behind Riker, Tara had also gone to her knees. Only she wasn't injured physically. She was stunned and, likely on the verge of going into shock, emptying everything from her stomach onto the sun-dappled pavers.

Rose's screams had reached a crescendo when a sleepy-looking Crystal filled up the doorway Raul had just exited.

As the bleached blonde fell to her knees, weeping into her hands, a stout, gun-metal gray Pitbull terrier barged past her.

Addressing Crystal, Riker said, "Keep your hands up." Sig trained on the woman, he told Tara to bring him her phone. "Unlocked," he added as his sister rose on wobbly legs.

Taking the phone, Riker leaned in and said, "Take off my belt and fashion a tourniquet for Benny."

She worked the belt loose and stared at Riker. Clearly shock was setting in.

Motioning Steve-O over, Riker whispered in his ear, saying, "I need you to get the multi-tool from Dolly and take the

New Mexico plates off her. Take them outside the wall and bury them deep."

Working the belt over Benny's damaged arm, Tara said, "What are *you* going to do, Lee?"

Tapping on the iPhone screen, he said, "Only thing I can do ... turn myself in."

Tara shook her head. "No. You can't. You want to be trapped in a cell when society falls?"

Steve-O said, "Baldy shot first."

Riker said nothing until the connection was made. After listening to the dispatcher, he said who he was and from where he was calling. Then he began to recount what had just taken place at Trinity House.

Finished, Riker thumbed off the phone. As he was bombarded by questions, he fixed a hard stare on the wanna-be Mallory. "Why did you go along with it?"

Her mouth moved but no words came.

Riker said, "Save it for the sheriff, then. Probably for the best, anyway."

Epilogue

Trinity House

Four Days Later

Riker woke up on the couch in the great room. It had been his *bed* for the last two nights while Tara tested out the beds in the master suites located at each end of their rural mansion.

For now, Benny and Rose were staying in one of the smaller bedrooms, albeit *smaller* being a little bit of a misnomer.

Sitting up, Riker slipped into a pair of black 5.11 chinos and dragged a sweatshirt over his head. Next, he took his bionic off the hewn-timber coffee table and snugged it on. Finished cinching the laces to both Salomons, he planted his hands on the wood-plank floor, extended his legs, and began knocking out his daily twenty-five, the first twenty-two for veterans lost daily to suicide, then finishing the set in memorium to his trio of fallen buddies.

As Riker was knocking out the pushups, he smelled on the air the heady aromas of bacon, coffee, and something cooking in oil.

Stomach grumbling, he rose and plucked his holstered Sig and pair of spare magazines from underneath the couch cushions.

Compared to the solitary existence he'd been used to living, Trinity House was like a frat house and sorority all rolled into one. Par for the course, the gourmet kitchen was a beehive of activity this morning.

Seated at the massive live-edge walnut table, Rose was shoveling fry bread and bacon onto two plates. Sliding one to Benny, she looked up and greeted Riker with a wave.

Beaming, Benny said, "Saved plenty for you, brother."

"I only need coffee," Riker said, "But you better have saved some scraps for Dozer. He gets cranky if all he finds in his bowl is Purina dog chow."

Tara was bellied up to the stove. With an economy of movement, she transferred a trio of pancake-looking things from a skillet of bubbling oil to a plate piled high with more of the same.

She said, "Steve-O fed Dozer his scraps."

"Steve-O never has scraps," said Riker, incredulous. "That boy always hoovers his plate clean."

Tara said, "Eat. Drink. Then use my phone to call the District Attorney."

"Won't they call me if the grand jury isn't going to convene?"

"Squeaky wheel gets the grease, Bro."

"Alright, alright," said Riker, taking a seat across from Benny and his girl.

Favoring his bandaged right arm, Benny slid the phone to Riker left-handed.

"How's your wing?"

"Hurts like a bitch. Itches, too."

Chewing a bite of fry bread, Rose said, "That's what the pain killers are for."

"Better be careful with those," Riker warned.

Benny said, "Speaking from experience?"

Riker nodded as he punched in the phone number listed on the D.A.'s card.

He drank coffee and listened until the call went to the recorded message. He didn't leave a message of his own. For shits and giggles, he hung up, then punched in 911 and put the phone on speaker.

Nothing. There was no stock recording telling him *circuits are busy, try again.*

Dead silence.

Thumbing the end button, Riker slid the phone back to Benny.

Tara said, "Nothing scheduled?"

Riker said, "Apparently not today."

Dozer moseyed in from the east wing. Tara greeted him with a strip of bacon, which he wolfed down greedily.

"Speaking of the man who wears the country music Mount Rushmore on his shoulder, where is he?"

No sooner had the question left Riker's lips than the older man burst from the hall, futuristic-looking aerial drone in hand and babbling about Sickos.

Standing, Riker said, "How many? Bolts or Slogs?" He was already heading toward the garage when the answer came.

"Three Sickos," said Steve-O. "I don't know what kind because they didn't see me."

"But they'll still follow the drone here, Steve-O. You have to remember that."

"I wanted to spare you the long walk," replied Steve-O.

"Let's go," said Riker, grabbing a coat and gloves from a table in the hallway.

Moving through the mostly empty garage, Riker pulled on the black buckskin gloves and snatched his long rifle and go-bag from near the door.

Exiting the garage, the first thing he saw were the twin bloodstains on the herringbone pavers. The one where Raul had died was nearly black and man-sized. The other was about as big around as a beach ball. A constellation of blood spatters ringed the smaller of the two.

Though Tara and Rose had turned a hose on the blood as it was drying, the pavers were porous and had soaked it up.

Riker asked, "How far out are the dead?"

"In the southeast clearing. Near the bottom of the draw."

Coming up from Santa Fe, thought Riker. Good thing they were in the draw, because the lack of homes beyond meant he could shoot safely in that direction.

The morning sun was weak and watery and trying its best to burn through the hanging fog.

Coming out of the thicket of spruce and pines standing between Trinity House and where the land opened up, the view down the draw was impeded by only stunted scrub and some juvenile juniper.

Straight away Riker smelled smoke on the air. Another dozen paces into the clearing and he detected the sickly-sweet odor of death mingling with the particulates hanging in the air.

Looking south by east, over top of the trees edging the draw's far side, he saw smoke plumes lifting into the air.

Turning to Steve-O, he said, "Santa Fe is burning."

"I saw helicopters fly over just after dawn broke."

Riker said, "I heard them from inside. What kind, Steve-O? Sleek and fast? Or big and slow?"

Steve-O's face screwed up. After a moment of thought, he said, "In between the two. They had rockets and a gun underneath where the pilot sits."

"I'm guessing they were either Apaches or Cobras," Riker said. "Good eye."

Steve-O pointed downhill. "There they are. Three adult Sickos. I think the lady is slow. The men, I couldn't tell."

Riker said, "We better put them down before we find out the hard way." He chose a flat spot of ground next to a tree trunk and sat cross-legged. Once Steve-O was behind him, he rested his elbows on his knees and aimed the rifle downhill.

Chambering a .308 Win round into the Era 3 Klepto bolt gun, he peered through the high-power Leupold scope.

The female zombie was ranging right of the male zombies. It looked to Riker that he had a couple of minutes until she would reach the opposite side of the clearing. The males had gotten themselves into a pickle. They were stuck between a pair of trees that had been blown down and come to rest across each other. The pocket the zombies were trapped in was maybe two hundred yards downhill and resembled an inverted V from Riker's vantage.

Overlaying the crosshairs on one bobbing head, Riker threw the safety and drew in a deep breath.

Exhaling, Riker pressed the Jewell trigger. The report crashed across the clearing.

Nothing happened to the targeted zombie.

Miss.

Back to the drawing board.

But the female was angling their way, and Steve-O was letting Riker hear about it.

"Relax," said Riker. "I have my pistol to fall back on if she gets too close. I should have targeted her first anyway."

It took two rounds to put down the female zombie, which just so happened to be a Slog, youthful appearance notwithstanding.

Taking his time, Riker expended only three bullets in dropping the two males.

Steve-O asked, "Are we going to check them out?"

"No, buddy. I shot them. Think I'll let Benny police them up once he's able to."

"You don't want to try to find out where they're from?"

"I'm afraid to, Steve-O. And that's the honest truth. I guess that would fall under the heading of ignorance is bliss. However, there is one thing I need to do." He set the rifle aside, put his right foot up on a fallen snag, and fished the multi-tool from a pocket.

Pulling up his pant leg to expose the ankle monitor the judge in Santa Fe had ordered him fitted with, he went to work on removing the device.

The Gerber multi-tool made quick work of the reinforced strap.

Looking on, Steve-O said, "What are you doing, Lee?"

"What I should have done two days ago. I don't think court will be convening anytime soon. If ever again."

He chucked the relic of a falling world into the brush. Slinging the long gun, he put an arm around his new friend, and walked with him back to Trinity House.

The Riker siblings and Steve-O will be back in Book 3 of Riker's Apocalypse in early 2020.

Thanks for reading! Reviews help. Please consider leaving yours at the place of purchase. Please feel free to Friend Shawn Chesser on Facebook. To receive the latest information on upcoming releases first, please join my mailing list at ShawnChesser.com. Find all of my books on my Amazon Author Page.

RIKER'S APOCALYPSE (THE PROMISE)

Also by Shawn Chesser

Surviving the Zombie Apocalypse

TRUDGE

SOLDIER ON

IN HARM'S WAY

A POUND OF FLESH

ALLEGIANCE

MORTAL

WARPATH

GHOSTS

FRAYED

DRAWL: DUNCAN'S STORY

DISTRICT

ABYSS

RIKER'S APOCALYPSE: THE PROMISE

CUSTOMERS ALSO PURCHASED:

JOHN O'BRIEN
NEW WORLD
SERIES

JAMES N. COOK
SURVIVING THE DEAD
SERIES

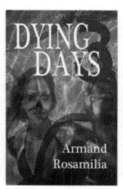

MARK TUFO
ZOMBIE FALLOUT
SERIES

ARMAND ROSAMILLIA
DYING DAYS
SERIES

HEATH STALLCUP
THE MONSTER
SQUAD

36624775R00227

Made in the USA
Lexington, KY
16 April 2019